September Moon

Alexa O'Brien Huntress Book 8

By Trina M. Lee

September Moon

Copyright © 2014 by Trina M. Lee

Editor
B. Leigh Hogan

Cover Artist
Michael Hart

Published by
Dark Mountain Books

Chapter One

There was a bite to the September night air. Summer faded fast in these parts. A layer of bright yellow and orange foliage coated the city of Edmonton. Fall moved in quickly with winter nipping at its heels. It would be nice if we could make it another six weeks without snow.

My hand crept to the dagger on my hip. The jade handle was cold and smooth, a reassuring comfort as I prowled the night.

"Feels good to be hunting again. I've been craving a good beat down." Jez spun her favorite dagger between her fingers before palming it like a pro. "Although I gotta say I'm a little concerned. It's not every night we hunt a demon hybrid."

I nodded. It had been some time since the two of us had stalked the night seeking a target. Too long. But jumping back into the thick of things by chasing down some kind of demon spawn wasn't quite how I'd envisioned this evening.

The residential street we walked was quiet. Darkness blanketed almost every house we passed. Everyone was asleep, as they should be. Everyone except us, the creatures of the night.

"I'm definitely overdue for a good scrap." I scanned the night for anything amiss. "Best way to let off steam. Other than sex."

"Ugh. Don't even talk to me about sex. I'll probably never have it again." Jez's red lips curved into a melodramatic pout. "Must be nice to have three men ready to please you at a moment's notice."

My jaw dropped, and I stopped walking to stare at her, aghast. "Care to rephrase that?"

"Did I say three? Oops. My bad. I meant two. Definitely just two." She whistled softly. "Didn't mean to hit so low below the belt there. I guess Kale's always going to be a touchy issue, huh?"

"Just a little. Where is he anyway?"

Kale Sinclair had done his damndest to avoid me since I'd come home from a trip to Las Vegas a couple weeks ago. Even though he was supposed to be here with us, watching our backs, he was MIA, which was becoming the usual for him.

Our personal relationship was to blame. Too much had gone on between us, both good and bad. Maybe we would never overcome it. But I still wouldn't have left him on a demon hunt without backup.

"No idea," Jez said with a shake of her head, her golden ponytail bouncing. "He barely returns my calls these days. It's his guilt, I'm sure. Keeping him locked in that room with endless women for days at a time. It's not healthy."

"I'm afraid for him." I spoke softly, finding it hard to give voice to my concern. "I wish there was something I could do."

Jez stopped dead in place, forcing me to do the same. Grabbing me by the shoulders, she gave me a shake that knocked my teeth together.

"You have enough shit to deal with right now without making Kale's problems yours. He's the one who can't control himself. He's the one losing his marbles. He's the one who tried to kill you. Don't you dare feel bad about that."

She gave me one more shake, then released me. I frowned, irritated but unable to argue. She was right. I cared deeply for Kale, but we all had our own battles to fight. I couldn't take his upon myself.

We resumed our pace, quiet and stealthy, toward the large brick schoolhouse two blocks ahead. There, we anticipated finding the thing we had been sent after.

Shya had insisted this was an easy hunt. So easy he could entrust the task to two mortals. A lesser demon had escaped a summoning and, after running amok, was now hiding out, fearing Shya's wrath. Of course, anything Shya said had to be taken with a grain of salt. Not only was he the most powerful demon laying claim to this city, but he was also someone who wanted to use me as a living sacrifice.

I had a duty to protect my city, something I had just begun to accept. Yet duty was the main reason I was lurking around the old schoolhouse in the middle of the night.

After the first few days back in town, the relaxation and calm of being home had grown tiresome. Boring. Much as I hated to admit it, I needed this kind of action on a regular basis. I was nothing without the hunt.

"Any news on the vamps in Vegas?" Jez asked, pausing to glance down a side street as we passed. She raised her nose to the wind, sniffing the air.

I caught the scent too. Sulfur. I reached to feel it mentally, sifting through the strange energy patterns marking the demon's path. It felt heavy and chaotic, creating a distorted mess of noise in my head.

"Other than Jenner's continued insistence that we go fuck ourselves? Not so much. I think he just needs to let off steam though." I turned in a slow circle, taking in our surroundings. "Do you feel that? This thing feels deadly."

Jez gave a nod; her lips curved into a small smile. "I do. Definitely a far cry from our usual vampire hunt. It's kind of exciting."

My skin crawled. An unsettling sensation followed.

My hand kept going to the hilt of the Dragon Claw where it sat securely in its sheath against my hip. A long leather jacket kept it hidden. The curved blade was longer than my forearm. It wasn't an easy weapon to conceal.

"Let's keep going. We've got this." I forced myself to put one foot in front of the other. Taking deep breaths helped to clear my head and combat the seed of fear that had sprouted. Too many things feed off fear. The only time fear was useful was if it aided one in staying alive. Most of the time it just got one killed.

The large red-brick building stood ahead in the distance looking a little like Hogwarts. The windows were dark. A fence surrounded the property, but it posed no real obstacle to anyone attempting to enter.

I grew uneasy as we went. Projecting an energy circle around the two of us took effort. The closer we drew to the old school, the stronger my certainty that we were sneaking up on something very evil. We reached the edge of the school property and stopped. Whatever it was, it was in there. Somewhere.

"Well, look on the bright side. At least it's a break from vampires, right? You could use a break." Jez didn't sound convinced.

"Can't argue there." We crossed the small soccer field separating us from the front door.

Jez followed close but far enough to watch my back while I checked out the door. The locks were old, and the security system, non-existent. Manipulating the lock was unnecessary; the door swung open with a loud, horror movie-style creak. *Fabulous.*

Right away the scent of blood slapped me. The smears inside the entryway were fresh. Very fresh.

Together we entered, slowly, wary of making our target aware of our presence. I did my best to cloak our energy, but it was never a guarantee. Still, I preferred to have the element of surprise on my side.

The ceiling was high, filled with shadows that even my wolf eyes couldn't completely penetrate. Paranoia gripped me. What if something was watching us from up there while we had no idea?

I had to give myself a shake to clear my head of such thoughts. Having little choice but to follow the trail of blood, I proceeded inside with Jez hot on my heels.

"You have to admit," she whispered, her voice breathy. "This is pretty damn exhilarating."

"I'll admit that when we walk out of here alive."

The trail led us down a long corridor, past classrooms, to a stairway. It smelled funny, kind of musty and dirty with the telltale scent of demon. More sulfur.

My hand automatically went to the cross around my neck. It was silver and very old, a birthday gift from Kale a few months ago. I didn't like to take it out of my house much, preferring to keep it safe. Still, I had started wearing it on occasion and especially when I knew I'd be seeing Shya. It really pissed him off, and I loved that. It lay beside the black onyx amulet I now wore all the time.

I mouthed the word 'demon' to Jez who nodded and twirled her dagger again. This time she fumbled, and it hit the floor with a loud clatter. I sucked in my breath and waited for the target to find us first.

"Shit," Jez hissed, her face scrunched up in mortification. The sound of the dagger slapping the hard floor had been loud. It had definitely announced our presence to anything that might have not yet been aware of us.

When nothing leaped out of the shadows, I continued on.

We followed the staircase to the second floor, suspicious that nothing had come at us. The thought did cross my mind that perhaps we should turn back. I was a big bad in the world of vamps and shifters, but as far as demons went, I was nothing. Something kept me moving. I'd like to think it was more than sheer morbid curiosity.

The second floor was also composed mostly of classrooms. The scent of blood grew stronger. For just a moment, the bloodlust threatened to rise. I fought it back, refusing to be made a slave when clearly somebody had just been killed here.

That's when the noise started. A scraping, like a chair across the floor. It came from the far end of the hall.

I drew the Dragon Claw slowly to avoid the lovely metallic sound of a fast draw. It hummed happily in my hand. The large, slightly curved blade shone despite the dim lighting. It was hungry for blood.

We moved a little faster, approaching the noise before I could change my mind. Turning into the last classroom, we came face to face with the creature. A full on shriek spilled from me, echoing in the silence. Jez gasped and gave a shout. Unable to blink or breathe, I stared at the demon, dumbstruck.

It had a humanoid appearance though that was where the similarities ended. The entire body was devoid of hair. Its feet had a cloven appearance, and its spine jutted out at a horribly unnatural angle. Its back was to us, and it busily slurped away at something I couldn't yet see and was pretty sure I didn't want to. The thing was either deaf or didn't give a shit since it had yet to acknowledge us.

"What the fuck?" Jez put a hand to her mouth as we caught sight of what the demon was doing.

It turned suddenly, a strip of flesh hanging from its mouth. Its face was grotesquely deformed, as if someone had stepped in the center of it. Horns protruded from its forehead. Its eyes were the most frightening, goat-like pupils in a milky white pool. They fixed on us, and the thing snarled.

A mouthful of razor sharp teeth got my pulse pounding faster. The remains of the person it was eating were unidentifiable. Chunks of flesh covered the floor and the demon's claw-like hands. The coffee and bagel I'd had earlier threatened to make an appearance as I watched it suck in that piece of dangling meat like a spaghetti noodle.

It lunged toward us, flailing like a newborn calf that didn't yet know how to use its limbs properly. In an uncharacteristic move, I took a step back.

Jez surged forward to bury her dagger in its chest. With a heavy arm, it smacked her, sending her crashing into a desk that overturned. She rolled and got to her feet, pulling another dagger from her boot.

I snapped into action and hit the thing with a psi ball as it lunged for Jez again. My attack threw it back, down beside the mutilated corpse. I swung the Dragon Claw, hoping like hell that Lilah had been telling the truth back when she told me it would kill demons with a physical form as well as vampires. This demon looked pretty damn physical to me.

The blow never landed. The demon threw one of the student desks at me with more strength than any such creature should ever have. It hit me dead on, taking my feet out from under me. The desk landed on my chest, crushing the breath from my lungs. Jez was there, throwing it aside and dragging me to my feet. I struggled to breathe, but I had no time to recover.

The demon clamped a heavy hand around Jez's ankle and jerked her off her feet. It pulled her close, like she weighed nothing. Smacking its lips, it wore a gruesome smile. She swung wildly with her dagger, plunging it into the demon's arm repeatedly. Murky black blood bubbled up from the wounds she inflicted, but the demon continued as if unaware.

I moved fast, swinging the Dragon Claw. I sliced a deep gash across its chest, and this time it did react. With a loud wail, it tossed Jez aside and came at me. Smoke rose from the wound. It stunk like death and sulfur. I waited for it to get closer, and then I plunged the dagger deep into its guts. The wailing grew louder and more shrill, hurting my ears.

Pulling the blade free, I lined up my swing and let fly. The blade sliced through its thick neck, and its head flew across the room to land with a sloppy slap on the teacher's desk. The demon's body fell at my feet, twitching and convulsing. Then it began to slowly dissolve until all that was left was a thick, black goo staining the floor.

"What the fuck was that?" Jez gasped, her eyes wide as she watched the goo bubble and pop. "Since when do demons do that?"

"That couldn't have been a pure demon. Not one that was ever an angel." I gazed down at the mess. Was Shya behind this? "Crap like this can't just walk free among the rest of us. Not without someone powerful to call it."

"Someone like Shya?"

"Or maybe someone like the FPA. Someone in their lockup. I don't know."

I couldn't imagine why either party would want to unleash something so twisted in the city. I had a bad feeling that I was going to find out.

Jez retrieved her dagger from the black sludge, used the edge of a desk to give it a wipe, and stuck it back into her boot. "I bet you're really missing the Vegas vampires now."

Chapter Two

"What the fuck was that, Shya? I don't appreciate being sent after shit like that without more warning. I'm not sure what you've been up to, but I don't want any part of it."

I disconnected the call with the press of a silent touchscreen button, missing the days when one could slam down the phone in anger. I doubted the demon would even hear that voicemail message, but it was the only way I could reach him without going to his house or summoning him through the demon mark on my arm. Since leaving the school, I had been a jumble of mixed emotions. Mostly, I was just mad.

"No answer, huh?" Jez nodded, twirling an unlit cigarette between her fingers. "Maybe it's better that way. Do you really want to know how that thing got here? Let's just be glad there's nothing left of it but goop."

She had a point. I probably didn't really want the answers I was going to demand, but that wasn't going to stop me from finding out. If I was going to protect this city, I needed to be in the know about this shit.

"Shya's really tripping red flags for me these days," I said, watching the activity on the other side of the room. "I want to know what he's up to."

The Wicked Kiss was almost finished undergoing renovations. The task was so much bigger than I'd anticipated. The nightclub was still open despite the many changes taking place. We were doing our best to work on one area at a time. It was difficult, but things were starting to come together.

The new flooring looked great. Non-slip luxury vinyl was a must. It was grey and designed to look like natural wood. The dance floor and bathrooms were done in the same material with a faux stone design. Deep red walls fit the bloodletting theme of the club without being bright or garish. Various types of fantasy artwork adorned the walls. From dragons to warriors and even vampires, the artists had finely crafted each piece.

I sat back against the new booth seat, enjoying the way it squished beneath me. The hard seats we used to have had been replaced with soft leather couches in a U shape. Not only was it more comfy, it made more use of the space, allowing for more people at one table.

As cozy as the new booth seats were, they were nothing compared to the sofa sets filling the space to the right of the bar, near the back hall entrance. Several L shaped black couches surrounded a large center table. It was early yet, but they were already occupied.

"I'd like to know what he was up to." Jez nodded toward the doorway where Kale had just emerged from the back. "Obviously it was more important than having our backs during a demon hunt."

My gaze narrowed as I watched him swagger through the club. Kale had done a great job of avoiding me recently. He paused to watch the guys working on the new stage. The last one had been destroyed while I was away. Kale wouldn't tell me how, though I could imagine.

"Guess he needed a fix." I should have shielded so as not to feel the saccharine energy Kale exuded. The truth was, I wanted to feel the flutter in the pit of my stomach, the intrigue, and even the hunger for him. Despite our twisted relationship, I enjoyed all of it.

He eyed the patrons hungrily, on the prowl again already even though he most likely had just left a victim in his bed. In black dress pants, a dark shirt, and leather duster, Kale wore sex and blood like a fragrance. Alluring and unbearably gorgeous, his presence demanded my attention.

Our eyes met across the distance. He paused, as if considering the best way to avoid me now. Screw that. I was mad, and he was going to hear about it. With a wicked glare plastered firmly on my face, I beckoned him over with a finger.

"I didn't expect you ladies back so early," he said, sliding in beside Jez across from me. His pupils were huge, and his energy hummed with a high frequency. He had definitely just been feeding.

"Where the fuck were you?" Jez snapped. "You were supposed to watch our back while that flesh-eating demon tossed us around like dolls. Oh wait, no, you were supposed to keep that from happening. Way to drop the fucking ball, Kale."

With a shrug, Kale leaned back in the booth, feigning casual. Only the tension in his energy betrayed him. "You both look just fine to me. I assume you killed that thing."

"What the hell was it?" I asked. "Tell me what you know. And God help you if you're keeping secrets for Shya."

"Are you kidding me?" he scoffed. He pinned me with brown and blue eyes, managing to appear both hurt and irritated. "I'm going to pretend you didn't say that. Shit, Alexa, I thought you knew me better than that." When I stared stonily at him, he continued. "Some kind of hybrid demon. A slave race or something."

"What was it doing here?" Jez jumped back in. Together we fixed Kale with our best no-nonsense glares.

Kale held his hands up. "Whoa, settle down. You're asking the wrong person. I don't ask Shya more than I need to."

I studied him, wondering how much he was keeping from me. Instinct told me it was more than what happened to the club when I was away. There was something else.

"Why did you bail on us, Kale? We used to hunt as a team all the time." My phone vibrated in my shoulder bag, but I ignored it.

"Yes we did," he agreed, glancing between Jez and me. "Things have changed. Neither one of you should trust me at your back now."

"But we do," Jez insisted, looking to me for support. When I dropped my gaze into my lap and remained silent, she snarled, "Ah, I see. This is more weird shit with you two. Well you know what? Get the fuck over it. You guys are ruining the group, and I really need you both right now."

Both Kale and I stared at Jez in surprise.

Her lower lip quivered ever so slightly. "I need a drink," she muttered, all but climbing over Kale to get out of the booth.

I waited until she was out of earshot to say, "She tries to hide it, but Zoey's death hit her hard. She's having a tough time getting over it."

Kale was visibly relieved to have a change of subject. "Makes sense. Zoey was the only woman Jez has been with who knew what she was and who understood it. Jez fell hard for her. Harder than she let on."

"I'm worried about her. She was a little fast and loose in Vegas. I don't think she's slowed down much since we got home."

It hadn't been all that long since Jez's girlfriend was killed by a demon queen targeting my wolves. I felt guilty about her death even though I knew Jez didn't blame me. She was drowning her sorrows these days, and I was starting to suspect it went further than booze. It was worrisome.

"Jez will be ok. We'll take care of her."

"Will we, though? Or will I?" I asked pointedly, fidgeting with a stray lock of long, blonde hair.

We stared at one another, awkward and tense. I couldn't resist the temptation to stroke him with a gentle push of power. He stiffened, sitting up straighter. Just like I wanted him to, he pushed back against me. The effect was a metaphysical connection that buzzed with an electrifying sensual heat.

"That is exactly why I've been avoiding you," he said with a groan. "You make me fucking crazy. And for the record, I would never abandon Jez in a time of need."

I dropped my hold on the power dancing between us, feeling burned by his words. He didn't pull back like I'd expected. Instead he brazenly shoved power into me, not with the intent to harm but to tempt my hunger for him. It worked, tickling me in unseen places.

Everything in me recognized him as mine. He resented me for that and understandably so. However, that was a two way street. We had both wronged the other in unforgiveable ways.

"Nothing is going to change what we've both done, Kale. It is what it is, and we have to move forward."

"It's not that simple."

"Why isn't it?"

His energy dropped away, and he shielded so tight against me that I could feel the effort he exuded. "You can't just pretend everything is ok. It's not."

"I know that." I stared at the bar where Jez sat with a cocktail in hand. "Maybe she's right; maybe we need to get the fuck over it."

Kale pressed his lips tightly together and shook his head. "One day you're going to realize why that will never happen. Until then, maybe we should keep our distance. I think it's for the best."

I gaped at him, dumbstruck and speechless. Was he for real? "What the fuck, Kale?" I managed to squeak out. "I thought we were friends."

He leaned across the table and captured my hand in his. It was warm, almost hot. His shields were useless at this proximity. I could feel the strength of his power and how it so easily aligned itself with mine, ready to bend to my will.

"We were friends," he said. "And then we were more. And now we need to be as close to nothing as possible. It's best for both of us. Think about it."

"No." I shook my head vigorously and jerked my hand away. It was too tempting to use the influence I held over him to manipulate the situation. "I don't want to think about it. Nothing you say can convince me that we should act like strangers."

"What about Arys? Or Shaz? Can they convince you? Because I'm willing to bet they would agree with me." He raised a dark brow in a silent challenge.

Fury slammed into me like a Mack truck. My face grew hot, and I had to think carefully so I didn't spit out the first obscenity to hit my tongue. "Did you seriously just try to use Arys against me? That is so shady. I get that you're having some issues of your own right now, but don't ever use Arys against me. That's bullshit."

Kale shrugged and stood. "We need a break, Alexa. I'm sorry you don't agree. If you can't accept that you need it, then accept that I do. I will love you until I cease to exist. But this—" He waved his hand between us. "This is wrong. And we both know it."

I slumped in my seat. Like a stubborn child, I crossed my arms and glared, refusing to agree when I knew damn well he was right.

We stared at each other, each of us seeing the path that we could have taken, the one he was willing to walk if only I would join him. The one I couldn't walk without turning my back on everything I shared with Arys. I had left Kale no choice.

"Whatever, Kale," I said flippantly, refusing to let the sharp pain show on my face. One thing I had learned in Vegas was a good poker face. It was handy now. "Do what you need to do."

The sudden onslaught of rage that burst from him was overwhelming. He pounded a fist on my new table before leaning in so close our noses almost touched. "You are the one who turned your back on me," he shouted. "You, Alexa, are the one who made me yours and then left me hanging, aching for you while you spend your days in another man's bed. You put me under your spell and walked away. Don't act so surprised that it's come to this."

His anger fueled my own, and I came up out of the booth with a blazing fury. "Don't you fucking dare say I walked away. I want you in ways I can't even begin to describe. The effort it takes for me to resist everything I want to do to you is fucking unbearable sometimes. Don't for a second think you're the only one who suffers. Even after what you did to me, I still fucking love you."

Kale froze. He was clearly at a loss for words. He backed away a few steps, and it took all of my strength not to reach for him. He ran a hand through his dark hair and hung his head. When he looked at me again there was sorrow shining in his beautiful, mismatched eyes.

"I'm sorry," he said so softly I barely heard him in the noisy din of the nightclub. "As long as this desire burns between us, there will always be pain. Maybe we can't put out the fire, but we can stop feeding the flames."

He turned his back on me and walked away before I could argue. It was just as well. I had nothing to say to that. I sat back down in the booth, shaky and emotional. I wasn't sure if I wanted to cry, scream, or throw things.

Kale went to the bar and joined Jez. She glanced over at me before turning back to him. She sat in Willow's usual spot, and I wondered where he was tonight.

My phone vibrated again, and I quickly dug it out of my bag. It was my sister. Our relationship was still on rocky ground, and though we were slowly reconnecting, it wasn't like her to call me repeatedly without a damn good reason.

"What's up, Juliet?"

I grabbed my bag and headed for the door in search of quiet. I swept through the lobby, squeezing through the small crowd waiting to get in. With a nod to Justin, my most trusted security guy, I escaped into the parking lot.

"I've got a bit of a situation I'd like you to take a look at. Would you mind coming by?"

She gave me the address of a familiar park on the north side of town. I glanced back at The Wicked Kiss, wondering if I should grab Jez. I opted to leave her with Kale. They needed some time together.

Borden Park was empty other than the small crew of FPA agents gathered around a body. The dead grass crunched under my feet as I crossed over to them. Apprehension gripped me as I anticipated what I was about to see.

Juliet stepped away from the others, greeting me with a quick hug. She smelled of wolf and perfume, but most importantly, she smelled like family. I savored those few precious seconds.

"Thanks for coming," she said with a smile that hardly covered her frown. "It's pretty rare that we see a public kill like this. It looks like a typical vampire kill. I wanted to see what you think. Maybe you'll have an idea why they would do this."

Tossing her dark curls, Juliet turned back to the crime scene. She didn't fit in with the other agents. They were all clad in dark suits while she stood out like a bad ass in jeans and a cropped leather jacket.

A light shone onto the body, illuminating it in a ghastly fluorescent glow. The first thing my brain processed was the colors: blonde, red, black. The dead woman was wearing security guard attire. She'd likely been jumped while on the job. Her wide eyes stared beyond us to something horrific that no longer existed in the here and now. Flecks of blood painted her short blonde hair in grisly shades of crimson.

A smear stained her lips. It was hard to tell if they'd been trying to turn her. If so, she might still rise. There was no specific time limit on that kind of thing. It could take hours or days. It was different for everyone.

The throat of the corpse was shredded; the clothing, torn from the struggle. Several puncture wounds marred her neck. It was a vampire kill all right. They'd made a real mess of it. Either a newbie or someone who just didn't give a damn. It wasn't unusual for a vampire to take joy in the kill. Getting carried away tended to happen. I knew. It had happened to me.

Every agent present watched me, waiting for my opinion. Closing my eyes, I tuned them all out and reached to feel the residual vampire energy humming around the body. Though I couldn't identify who had been here, I could tell who hadn't. I was relieved to find the scene absent of any trace of Kale.

"Yeah," I said, opening my eyes and turning away from the dead woman's stare. "It's a vampire kill. It could have been random. This doesn't happen often. Not like this."

Juliet grew quiet and thoughtful. I could see her wondering if my vampires were responsible.

"Don't ask me why they would pull a stunt like this," I added with a shrug. "The vampires in this city know they'll be hunted for public kills. It doesn't make any sense."

I began to get the sinking feeling that the FPA was pinning this on me, figuratively if not literally. Did my sister think I knew about this?

"Shit," Juliet muttered. Hands on her hips, wearing a scowl, she reminded me so much of our mother. "Go figure, this has to happen when Briggs is out of town. Several of our people were called to Toronto, so we're operating with fewer agents than usual."

"When does he get back?" I didn't want it to seem like I didn't trust her to handle her shit until then, but Thomas Briggs was an experienced Fed. Juliet was twenty-three and totally out of her league being left in charge.

"I don't know. Could be any day now, or it could be as long as a week or two. Business at the nation's head office can be unpredictable." She noticed for the first time that I was alone and raised a curious brow. "Where is your other half tonight?"

I considered withholding that information but decided it wasn't all that risky. If she thought Arys could have done this then it would be best for me to set her straight. "Arys is in Las Vegas. Just a two-day trip. He should be home tomorrow." Arys had been in constant touch with his Vegas family since we'd left Sin City. There would likely be many trips back there in the near future.

I would have gone with him if Shya hadn't grounded me to my own city. The remembrance of the binding sparked my anger, and I swallowed it back down with great difficulty. I couldn't leave town if I wanted to. Shya's insistence on keeping me close spoke volumes as to how close or how desperate he was.

"I can't determine if there was a specific reason they chose this woman, or if it was random." Juliet glanced back at the body her fellow agents were now bagging up. "Should we be afraid for public safety?" She peered at me with dark brown eyes, much like my own. Suspicion flickered in their depths. Beneath that I saw the keen wariness of her wolf.

"What exactly does that mean?" I returned her wary gaze with one of my own. "Is there something you're getting at, Juliet?"

Juliet bit her bottom lip and crossed her arms. She was trying to repress her emotions. It was an action she'd never grown out of. "I wish Thomas was here. He's better at handling this crime scene stuff than I am." She gave a self-deprecating laugh. "I'm not sure I'll ever get used to it."

"You and me both." I watched the agents go about their business, going through the motions as if it was just another day for them. It was so robotic and emotionless. Again I questioned who the real monsters were. "So what's up with you and Briggs anyway? When did you start sleeping with him?"

Her jaw dropped, and I grinned. "Alexa!" Her gaze darted fearfully to the nearby Feds. "Nobody knows about that. How did you know?"

"I picked up on it at the sports bar when we had that little meeting. So...is it serious?"

A part of me wanted her to say no. It was totally unfair, but I thought my baby sister could do better. Briggs seemed like a stand-up guy who believed he was doing the right thing. The problem was that he wasn't.

Capturing my arm, Juliet dragged me away to a nearby picnic table. Perching on the edge, she smiled so wide I thought her head might split in half.

"I think so. I mean, I hope so. It's still pretty new. We're just seeing where it goes."

Somehow I stifled a groan. "Are those his words or yours?" Her smile faltered, and I felt like a supreme asshole. Couldn't I just keep my mouth shut and let her be happy?

"It's mutual. Why? Do you think I'm making a mistake?"

My love life was so far from conventional that it put me in no position to give advice to anyone else. The wolf in me wanted one man while the vampire in me wanted another. And the fragile mortal heart in me wanted the one who knew my weakness because he'd lived it. I had no place to judge the choices of another, even Juliet.

"No, that's not what I said. I just don't want you to get hurt. You work together; he's your boss. And what about the age difference?"

Juliet laughed, a short snap of sound that echoed in the quiet park. "You're joking, right? You sleep with vampires who have lived hundreds of years. Not to mention the wolf that destroyed our family. You weren't even legal when you screwed that asshole."

"Whoa." I held up both hands in surrender. "We are so not going there again. I get it. I'm not exactly well equipped to judge your situation. If he makes you happy, then I'm happy." I punched her lightly on the shoulder and smiled. "But if he hurts you, I'll castrate him myself."

"I suppose that's fair." She tried to fight the smile that pulled at her lips and failed. Then it vanished as she prepared to interrogate me. "Speaking of those vampires you know so well, is there any chance any of them could have killed our victim?"

"Them? Or me? I'm assuming that you're including me in your suspect list." The defensive edge in my voice was sharp and impossible to hide. I didn't like what she was getting at.

"Come on, Lexi. Of course I know you didn't do it." She rolled her eyes, trying to be playful and lighten the mood. It failed. "But you're tapped into the vampire activity in this town. You can't blame me for asking."

"I don't. I blame you for what you're thinking but not saying. I know you, Juliet."

Juliet stared at me as if trying to choose her next words carefully. It's hard to be professional when accusing your sibling of shady activity. We knew. We'd been down this road before. "You're one of them, Alexa," she said, forgoing her nickname for me in her seriousness. "In fact, some might even say you're the most powerful one among them. I wouldn't be doing my job if I didn't ask."

Arguing with my sister was high on my list of least favorite things. So I swallowed my impatience and irritation. No reason we couldn't discuss this rationally. "You're right. I am. And I'll deal with it. Ok?"

"We'll be investigating as well. If there's a rogue vampire on the loose then we have to stop him."

"Does that mean you'll be sniffing around my club?" I allowed my displeasure to show. "There's no way in hell I'll let you raid the place again. Not without a damn good reason."

A muscle twitched in her jaw. Her eyes sparkled with annoyance, but she did a good job biting back the urge to snap at me. "I may end up stopping by. I'll try to keep the raiding to a minimum."

A black SUV with darkened windows pulled up. The agents began loading the body into the back. I wondered if they would give the murdered human a proper burial. They had refused to allow it for my dead wolf several weeks ago. Instead he had likely ended up in the creepy lab back at FPA HQ.

Bitterness choked me. I hated that my sister believed in her cause. It was something I would never accept.

"I'd better go," she said, giving my hand a pat. "Thanks for coming by. I appreciate it. Let's do coffee soon."

I watched her get into a black sedan with another agent and drive away. After waiting to ensure they didn't return, I ambled back over to where the body had lain. A trace of blood still stained the air, a bittersweet odor that brought with it many memories acquired in the past year. Very few of them were pleasant.

As I stood there, analyzing the tone of the residual energy, I got the keen sensation of being watched. I whirled around just in time for the air to ripple behind me. I drew the Dragon Claw with inhuman speed and swung.

The sound of metal on metal was loud in the still park. My dagger crashed against the sword Falon held ready for the blow. I felt the reverberation all the way down my arm to my shoulder.

With teeth clenched, I backed away, putting a few feet between us. "Are you stalking me, asshole?"

"Not at all, shit for brains," he quipped without missing a beat. "I'd rather have my liver eaten by vultures in hell for all eternity than willingly follow you around."

"Since when do you ever do anything willingly?" I fired back. "You're so far up Shya's ass, I can't tell where he ends and you begin."

The fallen angel glared in silence, and I felt victorious. The majestic spread of his silver wings and those fierce silver eyes didn't scare me anymore. Not even the glowing sword sparked fear within me, though it was intriguing. I saw Falon for what he was: a has-been riding the coattails of a good-for-nothing demon.

He recovered quickly. Sliding the sword back into the scabbard on his hip, he smirked. "If you'd like to know, I was here watching your sister."

My sense of victory fled immediately as dread settled in to take its place. "Is that right? Might that have anything to do with the body she just carted off?"

"It might." The smile adorning his unnaturally handsome face turned absolutely malevolent.

I met his gaze head on, refusing to be intimidated. "Care to elaborate?" I asked. "Or are you just wasting my time?"

"Just making sure the good people at the FPA are occupied with their vampire hunt. Can't have them sniffing around where they aren't wanted."

"Yeah, that really gets annoying, huh?"

He ignored my jibe and moved to examine the grass where the body had been. He bent to touch the dry, crispy park floor. Then he smiled to himself before throwing a dark glare my way.

I turned and headed toward my car without a word or a glance back. The dagger was still gripped firmly in my hand.

"Hey, Alexa," Falon called, the lilt of a laugh in his smooth tone. "When is your twin flame due home? I'd hate for him to miss what's coming."

My body stiffened, and each step felt like my feet were encased in lead. I stopped and turned back to look at him. "That was a really pathetic attempt at getting under my skin, Falon. You need to work on that. Better luck next time." I resumed walking, painfully aware of his gaze upon me as I went.

His chuckle was a low murmur on the night air. It made my skin prickle. It took great strength to keep moving without looking over my shoulder.

Chapter Three

I hightailed it away from Borden Park with a squeal of tires. Falon was one of the last people I wanted to be around. The most unnerving part was knowing he could lurk anywhere unseen in an incorporeal form. Even inside the car with me.

With a noise of disgust, I drummed a finger on the wheel in time with the radio. Slow, deep breaths helped to calm the rising storm threatening to wreak havoc on my mind.

What I wanted to do was go home for a bath and a drink. Instead I headed back to The Wicked Kiss to make sure the doors were closed after last call. Things had been rowdier than usual since I got home. I was convinced that had something to do with Kale and what went on there while I was away. People were pushing the boundaries there, him included.

The parking lot was almost empty. Good. I wouldn't have to kick too many people out then. Kale's old Camaro was still there, which was a bad sign he'd be banging and bleeding some lucky woman all day. Jez's Jeep was gone, and a pang of worry struck me.

Something was amiss. The metaphysical remnants of death lingered to touch me with cold, clammy hands. I was alert and ready as I made my way across the parking lot. With the doors closed, no light spilled out to cast a warm glow. That didn't prevent me from seeing the body sitting propped against the front entry.

It stank of blood and violence. It was a woman with multiple puncture wounds, heavy red lipstick, and long black hair. I turned to survey my surroundings before kneeling beside her. I didn't sense anyone else out there with me. Only the true immortals could hide their presence, the angels and demons. This kill wasn't one of theirs.

With a frustrated sigh, I reached to touch her. Cold, lifeless, and tainted with a honey sweet vibe I'd know anywhere. Kale. My first thought was that he'd dumped her here, but that didn't fit his MO. It was definitely suspicious. Even more so was the scrap of paper balled up in her hand. I tugged it out, careful not to tear it. In the pale lighting of the nearest streetlight, I was able to make out the words: *Long live the queen.*

"What the fuck?" I muttered. It was a threat, a shitty one at that. But the fact that it was on Kale's victim made me suspect that it wasn't only for me. I was curious to see what Kale had to say about this. Too bad for him if he didn't want to talk to me.

The body couldn't have been dropped long ago. The club hadn't been closed more than an hour. I shoved the door open and sent the first vampire I came across outside to get rid of it.

"Where's Kale?" I barked at anyone within earshot.

The place was relatively empty other than the staff and a few lingering regulars. After last call, the back rooms filled up quickly. Kale was back there already. Again. *Shit.*

My gaze passed over Willow's empty barstool. I briefly wondered where he'd been all night. More often than not he was parked at the bar drinking tequila.

"In the back," Justin said with a thumb jerk toward the rear. "I'm taking off now. Need anything before I go?"

I scrutinized the big man. "Do you know anything about the body outside? Looks like one of Kale's blood whores."

"Not a damn thing. Sorry." He rubbed a hand across his short, black hair. A frown creased his brow. "Do you want me to hang around a bit longer?"

I considered it. Justin was a big, intimidating guy. He had once scared the crap out of me. I did feel safer with him around. "No, thank you. Go do your own thing. It's all good."

"Call me if you need me, Alexa. I mean it."

It was nice to have people I could rely on. They were growing fewer in number. I flashed him an appreciative smile and waved as he left.

I stared around at the remaining patrons. Suspicions flooded my mind. I didn't trust a damn one of them. The city's underworld was talking. The vampire queen rumors were flying, and evidently they were being blown out of proportion.

I felt torn. I had questions for Kale, but I could hardly burst in on him while he was between the legs of another mortal conquest. That could end in many ways, none of them good. My other alternative was to go home and deal with it tomorrow night. It didn't feel right. Like I wouldn't be taking the situation seriously enough. I could spend the last few hours of the night seeking the one who dumped the body, or I could wait for a better time.

My gaze landed on the back hall entryway. I thought about Kale back there, bleeding some pretty thing. It taunted me. Would it be so bad to just knock on the door?

Yes. Yes it would.

Fuck it. He was part of this problem. He too had remarked on this vampire queen nonsense. In fact, he had said I was in denial about the whole thing. It wasn't denial; it was reluctance.

I marched back there to confront him. Even as I drew closer to Kale's room, I wished for a voice of reason to bring me to a halt. Letting myself be alone with him in the back was asking for trouble. But if he wanted to see a pissed off vampire queen, he would. Every damn vampire in this city would. They were going to drive me to it.

I let my fist fall heavy against Kale's door before I could reconsider. I was tired of feeling like the outcast, the one every vampire saw as a threat. Never had I purposely flexed my power among them. That was about to change.

"Kale, open the fucking door," I hissed through clenched teeth. "I'm not leaving until you tell me what you know about the dead woman outside. The one who came out of this room earlier tonight. Open up!"

There was silence inside the room. I could feel him in there. If he was hoping I'd go away, he was going to be disappointed when I kicked the door down. After a minute I heard rustling inside, moments before the door cracked open. Kale positioned himself in the opening, preventing me from seeing beyond him. His hair was a tousled mess, and his shirt was open, drawing my gaze to his bare chest.

"What part of keeping your distance do you not understand, Alexa?" he asked, wearing a bored expression.

Before I realized what I was doing, I hauled off and slapped him. My hand stung, but it was worth it to smack that smug look off his face.

"Hate me all you want to, Kale, but don't make the mistake of disrespecting me." I shoved the crumpled paper at him, taking advantage of our proximity to send an aggressive jolt of power through him. "I found this on the dead body of a woman you were with tonight. Wanna tell me what you know about it?"

He rubbed a hand over his cheek and grinned. The crazy vamp seemed to be enjoying my temper. He glanced at the paper and shrugged. "I don't know what this is about." Kale shook his head and started to close the door.

I kicked the door out of his grasp. It slammed against the wall and bounced back. A naked woman with mousy-brown hair huddled in Kale's bed beneath the blanket, staring fearfully at us.

"Don't screw with me. Something is going on around here, and you know what it is." I kept my feet planted firmly in the hall. If I crossed the threshold, there was no telling what would happen.

Kale regarded me as if I were a child throwing a temper tantrum. Crossing his arms, he stared down at me with intrigue and chuckled. "You get bored by yourself, don't you? Look, I'm sorry Arys isn't here to entertain you and Shaz is off...wherever...but I'm done with being your third choice. Whatever you're going on about can wait until tomorrow."

Stunned didn't quite cover it. I stood there in total shock, fighting hard to hide my reaction to the burn that his scorching words had delivered. It hurt to see how his resentment toward me had grown. But I understood why. What I was about to do next wasn't going to win me back any points in his books.

I was tired of being the one that didn't fit, the one who walked in several worlds and belonged to none. The wolves didn't want me. The vampires didn't respect me. I was done being threatened and misunderstood. This city was going to find out who I was. I just hoped we were all ready for that.

Looking into Kale's eyes, I saw a hardness there I wasn't used to. Worst of all, I saw a spark of hatred.

I hit him with my power, grabbed hold of his life force and brought him to his knees. My intent wasn't to kill but to hurt. His energy bent easily, responding to my manipulations. Kale made a pained noise but did an admirable job of keeping his composure.

"The only respect I seem to get from vampires these days comes when I have them on their knees," I said with a slow, angry smile. "Now why do you think that might be?"

The power rose fast, quickly overflowing into the atmosphere around us. I was aware of the vampire essence in the building. It was time to send my own damn message, even if I had to use Kale to do it.

Concentrating hard, I could feel every vampire in the city. Drawing on my bond with Arys, I mustered all the power I could and slammed it into every vampire I sensed, starting with the one right in front of me. I was sorry about those who didn't deserve it, like Justin. Still, it had to be done.

I had done this once before in a moment of extreme rage brought on by seeing Shaz with the vampiress he'd gotten involved with. The force flowed through me, crashing over each vampire in my mind's eyes like an ocean wave. I felt it hit each target in a massive ripple effect.

It would have been satisfying if it didn't hurt so damn much. Pain racked my brain as my mortal body acted as a channel to so much supernatural power. Every time I did this, it came easier than the last time, but it hurt a hell of a lot more too. It was breaking me down.

It was a swift assault, hard and fast, a warning rather than a true attack. The message was clear. If they wanted to challenge me, they would lose. I released my hold on the energy and stumbled. Shoving myself backwards, I hit the wall across from Kale's door and struggled to stay upright. Blood ran steadily from my nose to stain my shirt.

Kale lay on the floor in the doorway, spitting blood and glaring daggers at me. I wiped my nose with the back of my hand, smearing blood across my face. Wicked laughter bubbled up inside me.

"Sorry, sweet thing," I said between gasps for breath. "I'm done with secrets and assholes."

I shoved away from the wall and, swaying like a drunk, made my way toward the exit sign glowing at the end of the hall. The high of the power rush was dizzying, leaving me feeling disoriented. It wasn't usually this bad.

"The truth always comes out, Kale," I called over my shoulder. "You want me to stay away from you? Consider it done. But I *will* find out what it is you're not telling me."

Perhaps I would feel bad about this later. But hell, I owed him one.

Vampires and secrets. Story of my life.

I almost collapsed on the pavement outside. Once safely inside my car, I sat there with my head back, staring up through the sunroof.

'Want to tell me what that was?' Arys's melodic tone whispered through my mind. 'Is everything ok?'

Of course he had felt my little stunt. In an attempt to practice what I preached, I was honest. 'No. It's not. It's been a shitty night. Nothing I can't handle though. Don't feel like you have to rush home.'

'Then what was with the power play?' His skepticism came through just fine. I even knew the look he'd be giving me if he were here.

'I needed to send a message. Pretty sure I accomplished that. I'll tell you everything when you get home. Promise.' Truth be told, I missed Arys like crazy. And he'd only been gone two days. We were made to be together, and I felt it in the worst way with fourteen-hundred miles between us.

'I'll be there tomorrow night. It's killing me to be away from you.' His admittance was colored with annoyance. 'I'm not coming back to Vegas again until you can come with me.'

I shared his irritation. Shya grounding me to the city was not something I'd anticipated. 'How's everything there?' I needed to know things were under control there. Our visit to Sin City hadn't gone without incident.

His amusement came through strong and clear. 'All is calm for now. I don't expect that to last long, but for now everyone is trying to keep a low profile. Until I leave again anyway.' After a few sappy exchanges and declarations of love, Arys slipped away to resume whatever he'd been doing. It likely involved blood.

I started the car, taking a moment to enjoy the sound of the Hemi engine. When my vision ceased to swim, I pulled out of the parking lot and headed for home. The short stretch of highway between Edmonton and Stony Plain was a blur. By the time I reached the limits of my small hometown, I realized I'd been driving on autopilot.

That little stunt had taken more out of me than I'd expected. I felt weakened and needed a pick me up. Days had passed since I'd taken blood, and I suddenly craved it with a burning hot intensity. When I turned into my driveway to find Shaz's blue Cobalt, the bloodlust went from serious to deadly.

Shaz had spent the evening bonding with Coby, a new wolf in town and my best friend's fiancé. The two had become fast friends, which pleased me greatly. Coby needed the guidance of an experienced wolf. I'd been the one to turn him, but I wasn't the right one to guide him. Shaz, a male wolf and former Alpha of the local pack, was better suited to that job.

An unholy urgency had me out of the car and into the house in seconds. The scent of wolf mingled with a vanilla candle, teasing my control. I tracked Shaz's scent upstairs to my bedroom where he had just emerged from the shower.

"Hot damn, my timing couldn't be better," I said, my voice a breathy whisper.

He took one look at the blood on my face, and his jaw dropped. "What happened to you?"

I was already tearing my clothes off. I needed him now. My dagger landed on the floor in a pile with my clothing and shoulder bag. "Just a little nosebleed," I said, distracted by the heady Were blood pumping through his veins. "I need a little nip. Do you mind?"

Shaz looked me over and desire sparked to life in his jade green eyes. "Not at all."

I tore his towel off and tossed it. There was no time to admire his fine physique. The bloodlust was in the driver's seat, and I was merely a passenger. With both hands on his chest, I shoved him down on the bed. I buried my face in his throat, breathing deeply of his scent.

It hit me like a punch in the stomach. The bloodlust twisted into something deeper and darker than what it already was. It wasn't just blood I wanted but the vibrant energy of his desire for me. Sex and fear produced the most potent, satisfying energy. It was an essential part of the feed.

I slid a hand down his body to his manhood, stroking him until he was hard and ready. It didn't take long. With the hunger driving me like this, the anticipation of warm, tangy blood on my tongue and a lover between my legs was all the foreplay I required.

Shaz was tense beneath me, awaiting the moment my fangs would slice through his flesh. His excitement grew rapidly, and I reminded myself that I needed to take care with him.

Not all that long ago, he'd been sleeping with vampires at The Wicked Kiss to get off on the rush. I shouldn't have been victimizing him at all, but since resuming our intimacy in Vegas, it was one of the ways we felt most comfortable together. Though as good as Shaz was at playing the submissive, he could dominate like a champ too.

I timed it perfectly so that my fangs pierced his skin as he slid inside me. It took me to a place where words and thought stopped. Shaz's wounded flesh was hot against my tongue. He gripped my hips tight with clawed fingertips. A growl accompanied the groans and sighs. I wasn't sure which one of us it was.

I moved fast atop him, delighting in the way he felt. I feasted on the erotic energy of our lovemaking. In no time I was high as a kite and feeling no pain or weakness. At last I collapsed beside him with great satisfaction. My lungs heaved, and my heart pounded. I laughed, a sound of whimsical intoxication. It was all about the bliss moment, and I wanted to savor every second.

"Start talking," Shaz said, rolling onto his side to face me. "Tell me what brought that on. Not that I'm complaining."

"You're not going to believe the thing Jez and I hunted tonight." I reached to slide a hand through his damp platinum hair before stroking it down the side of his face. "I'm going to hit the shower and tell you all about it."

I bounded off the bed with a spring in my step. Though I was still feeling some of the fatigue from earlier, the crushing burnout was gone. The worst of my hunger had been sated. I'd been careful not to take too much. It was dangerous for both of us.

From the shower in the en suite bathroom, I told Shaz about the nasty flesh-eating demon. Raising my voice over the sound of the water, I described it in great detail. I focused on that part of my night, leaving out any mention of Kale. It just wasn't necessary.

When I re-entered the bedroom, I found Shaz passed out, snoring into a pillow. So much for my storytelling skills.

The sun wouldn't be up for two more hours, but I was ready to fall into bed. I yawned and abandoned the idea of going downstairs for a snack. My white wolf was much more appealing. I turned off the lights and climbed into bed. Shaz turned toward me in his sleep, curling his naked body around mine. I snuggled in close against him and hoped for a deep, dreamless slumber.

I wasn't sure how much time passed before I sneezed myself awake. A noxious odor tickled my sinuses. Sulfur.

Alarm bells rang inside my head. I focused on remaining still though the change in my breathing surely revealed that I was awake. Fear sat like a heavy weight upon my chest. There was a demon in the room with us.

Chapter Four

I wasn't at all surprised to discover Shya. That, however, did nothing to eliminate my terror at finding him in my bedroom. Since my fear manifested best as anger, I sat up seething.

"What the fuck are you doing?" I snapped at the demon who stood close enough to touch. How unnerving.

"Ah, you're awake," he said pleasantly, as if he'd dropped by for coffee and was pleased to find me at home. "I apologize for the unannounced visit. I won't be long."

Shaz stirred beside me, and with a flick of his wrist, Shya stilled his movements. Shaz continued to snore, unaware of the demon's presence.

"What did you do?" I shook Shaz and panicked when he couldn't be roused.

Shya's red eyes seemed to glow in the darkened room. I was disoriented, unsure if it was just before sunrise or just after sunset. Shya couldn't take physical form during daylight hours. How long had I been asleep? My head felt foggy, so it couldn't have been long enough.

"I would prefer to do this without incident or interruption. Shall I render you unconscious as well?" Amusement laced his tone. He was constantly amused, until he was pissed. Then he was downright terrifying.

"Prefer to do what without incident?" I questioned, holding the blanket tight against me to hide my nudity. Roused from sleep in one's own bedroom was not a great way to be confronted.

I could see him well in the dark thanks to keen wolf vision. So I saw the dagger he withdrew from his jacket before the last of the moon's rays glinted off the dragon etched into the blade. My heart raced, and I struggled to swallow around the lump in my throat.

Shya chuckled, an evil sound that crept through my bones, leaving me feeling violated and scared. "Stay calm, Alexa. I'm not here to kill you."

When he reached for me, I was anything but calm. I lashed out to shove him away, knowing better than to grab for my power. Mine was child's play compared to what he was packing.

"Don't touch me," I cried when he came at me again.

"Be still, and I won't have to hurt you. Much. Of course, I can just do this."

His power hit me hard and fast, pasting me flat on my back in the bed. Frozen in place with the searing heat of his magic burning me from the inside out, I could only watch as he advanced on me with the dagger in hand.

It wasn't a large blade, six inches at best. But even the tiniest blade could do serious damage in the right hands. The worst part was that any blade made or carried by a demon was more powerful metaphysically than it ever could be as a mere physical weapon.

I struggled to break free of his hold, but it was useless. I couldn't move. The demon reached for me again, and I cringed. He grabbed hold of my hair and realization settled in.

"Are you stealing my hair? Goddamn you, Shya. What are you doing?"

"Nothing more than a lock. You'll hardly notice it."

When he used the blade to separate a chunk on the top I shrieked. "Cut from underneath at least, so I can hide it. What the hell are you thinking?"

Perhaps my biggest concern then shouldn't have been a missing chunk of hair. I wasn't really operating at full capacity. This all felt like an extremely bad dream. I knew the horrible things that could be done with a lock of hair. Hell even a strand of hair was enough to twist some very horrid spells. Whatever he wanted my hair for, it was bad.

"You women and your vanity," he tsked. "So ridiculous." To his credit, Shya went for a piece from underneath, slicing it off in one clean swipe of the blade. He stuffed the long chunk of ash blonde hair into a pouch that disappeared back into his jacket.

"What are you going to do with that?" I demanded. "I have a right to know."

"You and Jez did a good job with that minion. I didn't expect it to be so easy for you. I'm impressed." He changed the subject entirely. "And that message you sent to the vampires was long overdue. Good for you."

His praise was absolutely bizarre. I stared at him, trying to keep my true feelings from showing in my eyes. "What was that thing we killed? Why was it here?" I needed something better than a litany of questions; that was getting me nowhere.

Shya perched on the edge of the bed beside me and stroked a hand through my hair that was spread out on the pillow. "That, my dear, is what happens to humans when they sell their soul to my kind. They become a slave, serving in the underworld. Minions. Nothing more, nothing less. It was summoned here. A bit of an accident I'm afraid. Gabriel is still perfecting some of his skills."

I went cold inside at that revelation. Gabriel was barely an adult, just nineteen. He was also an incredibly powerful witch, one who had been lured in by Shya. If he continued on the path he was on now, he would become one of those disgusting flesh-eating monsters.

Shya grabbed my arm and laid it on the bed so my wrist was exposed. It was making me crazy to have to lie there and watch him.

"Please tell me what you're doing." I wasn't about to beg but was feeling pretty damn close.

"Just taking some blood, my dear. Nothing to worry about."

Oh hell no. I fought so hard to break free of his hold on me. As the dagger came closer to my skin, my panic surged.

"Shya, don't. Please. Can we just talk about this? I know you have plans. Maybe I can help you. It doesn't have to be this way. Whatever you want my blood for, I'm sure there's another way." Desperation oozed from me in the grossest way. I hated myself for begging a demon for mercy.

The dagger bit into my flesh, slicing a clean line across my wrist. Blood welled up immediately, and Shya had a chalice there to catch it. I watched in horror as my blood dripped into the metallic cup.

"Your desperation is understandable. We are enemies, you and I. Though we share some goals, like the protection of our own personal secrets, ultimately we are not allies." He massaged my wounded arm, encouraging the blood to keep flowing. "I too am desperate. One day, Alexa, you will learn the value of your empire, and you will fight to protect it as I do now for mine. Then you will understand why I do such things."

"What does that even mean? Don't play word games. Is it really so impossible for you to be straight up with me?"

"No, of course not." He smiled, a broad grin revealing toothpaste-commercial perfect teeth. Illusion. His appearance as a Japanese man was a lie. I had never seen Shya's true face, nor did I want to.

"Chalices of blood aren't used for tea parties, Shya. Give me some fucking answers. Something. Anything." My fear began to dissolve as my anger became genuine.

"You're dying, Alexa," he said, startling me into silence. "The power is killing you. I'm sure you can feel it every time you call it. The nosebleeds and headaches are getting worse, aren't they? It's only a matter of time until it kills you. Not much time I'm afraid."

His words reverberated with the truth. It wasn't news. Not really. This topic had come up before. But hearing him say it like that, so casual and matter of fact, it scared me.

"What's your point?" I met his gaze head on, holding steady despite how hard it was to stare into those red eyes.

"Only that we are both running out of time to find a way to get what we want."

I was starting to figure Shya out. If I up and died on him because I called too much power one time too many, he couldn't use my death the way he hoped.

"You have no idea what I want," I seethed. "Get the fuck out of my house."

Shya looked into the chalice and, satisfied with what he saw, released my wrist. "I know you don't want to go dark and lose the balance of your twin flame bond."

"You don't know shit. Get out." I had to keep repeating myself because if I let him talk he would say something sly and manipulative. Letting him inside my head was not an option.

"Does it frighten you? Everything you're about to become?" He went on, unfazed by my hateful demand.

His gaze landed on the amulet I wore, and he reached for it. The touch of his hand against my chest made my skin crawl. He turned the black onyx amulet over a few times before dropping it.

When I didn't utter a word, Shya continued. "You're smart, resourceful. I like that. You'll make a foe I can be proud of."

He could have taken the amulet and robbed me of my chance to save my wolf. When he didn't, I was both relieved and wary. The amulet would keep the wolf within me when I transitioned, but it wouldn't save my light from being consumed by Arys's darkness.

The pressure holding me frozen disappeared, and I was able to move again. Shya vanished along with it. He was gone so suddenly, I found myself wondering if he'd really been there at all.

I lay there staring at the window, watching the darkness fade as the sun rose. I didn't dare close my eyes again until I knew there was no way he could return.

* * * *

"I can't believe he was in here and I had no idea." Shaz rubbed a hand through his disheveled shock of white blond hair before dragging it over his face where the barest hint of a five o'clock shadow was starting. "Are you sure you're ok?" Gently he took my arm and traced a finger lightly over what remained of the cut from Shya's dagger. It was minor, little more than a scratch now.

"Yes, I'm fine. Physically. Mentally, I'm absolutely terrified. And more than a little pissed off." I sipped from a mug of hot coffee, seeking comfort in that simple, familiar action. "He hit you with something so you wouldn't wake up. It was probably for your own good."

Shaz had spent some time away, in the mountains, running as wolf and freeing himself from the restraints of home. He'd come back with an attitude I wasn't accustomed to, ready to take on anyone and anything. Shya had probably saved his life by keeping him unconscious.

I was reminded of the Vegas trip when Shaz had willingly gone into a cage fight and killed another wolf. His willingness to kill to protect us hadn't been what disturbed me. It was his lack of remorse.

Shaz reached for the sugar and added another spoonful to his cup. We sat at the small table in my kitchen, drinking coffee and watching the moon rise. My mind raced, going over everything Shya had said and done recently.

"Shya said he was desperate," I mused, enjoying the warmth of the mug in my hand. "I think he's trying everything in his power to find that scroll. Which means I need to be looking for it too."

Shaz nodded thoughtfully. "So where do we start?" My heart fluttered. His devotion would never cease to amaze me. Shaz was a true embodiment of the wolf's loyalty.

"I have no idea. Where would you hide an ancient artifact that could give a demon serious power?"

"A church," Shaz suggested. Then he frowned. "Or is that too obvious?"

I chewed my lip, lost in thought. Shya had said the scroll would enable him to claim Lilah's throne. Though I didn't know the gritty details of what that meant, I knew she was of higher rank in the demon world than Shya. He was evil enough without rising to greater power. And whatever he planned to do with that power, it would be good only for him.

"I need to talk to Willow. Maybe he can shed some light on a few things. There's a lock, a door, or a seal of some kind that Shya wants to break. I'm not quite clear on the details." I shook my head. My brain was cramping.

I knew just enough to know I needed more. The trip to Las Vegas had been my way of taking some time away from Edmonton and away from Shya. Now it was time to face what was coming.

"We need to reach out to the city wolves, Lex. They could be allies worth having." Shaz rose to refill his coffee, pausing to rumple my hair affectionately on his way by.

"They could also kill us the second we walk into their territory." I laughed, but it wasn't really funny. That was a very real possibility. "I don't have a lot of experience with the city wolves, but I hear they're a territorial bunch. Approaching them might be dangerous."

Shaz shrugged. "It might be. We don't have a choice though. There's only two of us. It's not like we're much of a threat. We don't have a pack."

"True enough. At least you got to leave willingly." I tried to make light of it, but I was still feeling the burn of being kicked out of my pack. They were justified in their decision. They believed I was a threat to their safety, and they weren't wrong.

"And I was happy to." Shaz returned to his seat at the table. He set his mug aside and took my hand, leaning in to rub his cheek along mine in a wolfish nuzzle. "I belong with you. Besides, I think we've both kind of outgrown the pack."

"Yeah, that didn't take all that long, did it?"

The small town pack was made up of soccer moms, lawyers, and other everyday people who sought a normal life in a place where they could safely be both human and wolf. Both Shaz and I had grown into adulthood in that pack. It was a safe place to get comfortable with my wolf. And now it was time to move on.

"You're right about the city wolves. I've known that was coming since Shya demanded I lead the wolves and vampires for him. I told him I would talk to them. I didn't say what about." Putting it off wouldn't do me any good. Connecting with the city wolves was vital. There was no guarantee they would help me, but there was only one way to find out.

"So we should probably go there first. We can head to The Wicked Kiss afterward to talk to Willow," Shaz said, his casual tone forced.

"You don't have to go in there. You know, if you'd rather not. I can talk to Willow anytime." I didn't want to make this awkward. Shaz's past junkie behavior had not started with The Wicked Kiss. Though that was where it had spiraled out of control.

"I'm fine, Lex. The Vegas club was intense, and I handled it. Don't make it something it's not. Please?"

The sincerity in his gaze silenced my protests. Giving him a hard time would be hypocritical. So I kept my mouth shut. It wasn't easy.

"Sure," I managed. "No problem. I'm going to go get ready. I should probably call Kylarai back. She's left like five voicemails about needing me to find a dress."

My best friend, Kylarai Kramer, was getting married in less than a week. It was a rush wedding, thrown together very quickly. Kylarai had her heart set on a September wedding so she was furiously planning her ass off while I did my best to keep up.

Shaz snickered. "I can't wait to see you in that dress. I hope it's some insanely ridiculous getup with ruffles and sequins."

"Hey," I protested. "What did I do to deserve that? Ouch."

We shared a laugh, and it felt so good. It had been so long it seemed.

"Ky is going to make a beautiful bride," Shaz said. "A werewolf wedding. This should be interesting."

"I'm a little nervous," I admitted. "I hope nothing goes wrong. Nothing involving me at least."

"Nah, it'll be a blast. We'll party. We'll run. It will be a good time. And you could sure use one."

He was right about that. I disappeared upstairs to get dressed, needing to escape the sudden awkwardness that had settled over the topic of discussion. I was excited to see one of my dearest friends get married, yet it created this tension between Shaz and I, this strained awareness that wedded bliss would never be our future.

A call to Kylarai perked me right up. As I did my favorite smoky eyeliner and grey eye shadow, she gushed all about the flowers she had selected, the rings they'd picked out, and her inability to decide how to do her hair.

"Coby must be loving this," I laughed. "I can't remember the last time I heard you so chipper. It's nice."

"It really is. I have never felt this connected to anyone. It's like we were made for each other. It's so funny how things work out." Joy practically poured out of the phone as she spoke.

It certainly was interesting how one event led to another. If I hadn't attacked Coby on the street in a fit of vampire hunger, he wouldn't be there with her now. I guess good can come of bad after all. It's all a matter of patience, watching to see how the pieces fall together.

While I slipped into jeans and a Motley Crüe t-shirt, Kylarai rambled on about the dress fittings.

"I need you and Jez to try on dresses. We need time if any alterations are to be made."

"We'll be there, Ky. I promise. In fact, I have to call Jez right away. I'll remind her."

When I did call Jez a few minutes later, there was no answer. She would never bother to check her voicemail, so instead I sent her a text telling her to meet me at The Wicked Kiss or to call me back.

I ran a brush quickly through my long hair, pausing to examine the piece Shya had cut. I frowned in the mirror at the short stubby chunk before tucking it under out of sight. Bastard.

After gathering my knee-length leather jacket and the Dragon Claw, I descended the stairs to meet Shaz who had made use of the main floor washroom. He was ready and waiting for me. Freshly shaved and casual in jeans and a t-shirt, his platinum hair was slightly disheveled but stylish.

I paused on the bottom stair and openly gawked. "I never tire of looking at you. Even when we were new wolves back at Raoul's, I would sneak glances at you, hoping you wouldn't notice."

A blush colored his cheeks. "I noticed. When I wasn't too caught up doing the same."

He swept me off the stairs and into a warm embrace. With a hand beneath my chin, he brought his lips to mine. It was both tender and firm, reminding me of simpler things in a simpler time.

I was overjoyed that our shared affection had survived the years and the hardship thrown at us. However, I was also saddened by all the things it would never be, the shattered picket-fence dream I hadn't known I'd harbored until recently.

The kiss ended, and our eyes locked. I opened my mouth as if I might spill everything racing through my mind. Nothing came out. Shaz nodded, needing no words. We left the house before the moment could be ruined. We had no time to waste on what could never be. My focus had to be on what was.

Chapter Five

Unease lurked within me when Shaz and I arrived at the werewolf hangout. It was a warehouse-style nightclub on the south side of town. A weathered sign hung above the front door, bearing the name: Doghead.

Finding the scroll was important. But making connections with the wolves in this city was vital. So here we were.

"How do you feel about this?" Shaz asked. His hand was on the door handle, ready to exit the safety of the car.

"I'm nervous. I hope they listen to what we have to say before they tear our throats out."

Against my better judgment, I took off the belt that held the Dragon Claw around my waist. Bringing a demon-forged weapon into a den of wolves would be suicide.

Leaving the car filled me with a fresh wave of uncertainty. I would not go in there stinking of fear. I took a deep breath and reminded myself that I was here as a friend not a foe. Maybe I no longer had a pack to lead, but I'd earned the Alpha title and would not act like anything less than that.

I'd hoped we would slip past the bouncer at the door and blend into the crowd inside. No such luck. We were stopped at the door and searched for weapons.

"We're here to speak with whoever's in charge," I declared when questioned. "We just want to talk. That's all."

The wolf manning the door scowled at us. He openly sniffed us, scenting for a lie which he would not find. Big and burly, he was intimidating for sure, but I'd dealt with worse.

"Follow me." A man of few words. I liked that.

We followed him through the bar, which was smaller on the inside than the exterior made it appear. Concrete floors and basic black tables gave the place a very colorless appearance.

There was not a single human in the place. Everyone we passed was a wolf. There had to be well over a hundred. Each of them bore a tattoo on the side of their neck, marking them as members of a pack. Judging by the different tattoos, I'd guess two or three different packs frequented the place. Envy left me with a sour taste in my mouth.

"Wait here."

The bouncer gestured to a table covered in empty beer bottles and a plate of chicken bones. With a grimace, I pushed the mess to one side and sat down. Shaz and I exchanged a look. He gave a small shrug and sat back to wait while I perused the vicinity.

The dance floor was littered with women dancing to a fast-paced country song. More than a few heads turned to catch a glimpse of the attractive newcomer, but Shaz was oblivious to them. Most of the men occupied pool tables. Those that didn't were gathered around a small stage where a pole dancer did her thing, inciting shouts and cheers.

My palms grew sweaty, and I wiped them on my jeans. The fact that I felt more at home in a bar full of vampires did not sit well with me. This should be the place I felt comfortable. This was where I should have belonged.

I was painfully aware of the approach of an Alpha couple. The dominant power oozed from them like a balloon with a slow leak. Subtle but constant. The Alpha male slid onto a seat across from us, glared at the mess on the table, and with a sweep of his hand, shoved the whole thing onto the floor. Bottles shattered and chicken bones flew. I squelched the urge to grimace.

"Somebody clean up this goddamn mess," he barked. "What the hell am I paying you for?"

He was older than I'd anticipated, in his fifties or sixties I'd guess. His short hair was more silver than brown. Hard blue eyes gleamed with the predatory spark of his beast. Average height with a bulky build, he carried himself with the confidence of one who has learned to fear nobody. It was impressive and intimidating as hell.

My gaze was drawn to the totem moon tattooed on the side of his neck. It was a crescent moon made up of tribal-style curls and twists with one thin line joining each point, making it a full moon as well. It was a perfect match to the one adorning several other wolves.

"Sorry about that," he said, his gaze lingering on us each in turn. "It's hard to find good help these days."

Several waitresses and a bus boy rushed over to clean up the mess. Another placed a fresh beer in front of the Alpha before asking if we'd like anything. I declined while Shaz asked for a beer.

The Alpha female slid onto her seat and immediately offered us her hand. "Please ignore the disruption. I'm Hanna, and this here is Dayne. We're the Alphas of the Doghead pack. The head pack of the three existing city packs."

"Alexa," I said, grateful for her show of hospitality. "Former Alpha of the Stony Plain pack." Shaz jumped in with his introduction. Hanna laughed and commented on the uniqueness of his name while I sat there awkwardly, unsure of what to say next.

Hanna was close to Dayne's age from what I could tell. Tall and thin, her athletic build was draped in expensive high-end clothes. Her smile shone in her hazel eyes, but I could see a ruthless glint beneath the surface. The deep auburn red of her hair seemed like it should have come from a bottle, but I was pretty sure it was natural. She too bore her pack tattoo on her neck beneath her left ear.

"We don't get outside wolves in here very often," Dayne said, his voice as gruff as his manner. A muscle twitched in his sharply chiseled, square jaw. "This is well protected territory."

"We're not here to infringe on your territory. We just want to talk." Shaz's demeanor was calm, subdued. Coming across as aggressive would be a big mistake.

"So talk."

Shaz looked to me, letting me take over. I didn't know where to begin.

"We were the Alphas of a small town pack. The Stony Plain pack," I began. "Now it's just the two of us. It seemed appropriate to reach out to your pack. I was hoping you would consider a friendly alliance."

Dayne's frozen stare bore into me. The wolf behind his eyes seemed to surface for a moment, regarding me with a haughty glare. "I know who you are, Alexa. Rumor has it, you're more vampire than wolf now. So tell me, why would I want to form an alliance with you?"

I could answer that many ways. Having him look at me like I was something he'd found on the bottom of his shoe made me want to tell him he was lucky I didn't force his hand with a power play. I knew wolves though, and that would only start a war I wasn't prepared to fight. I currently had bigger problems.

"I am still wolf. If you know that much about me then you must know that a demon has staked his claim on this city and every person of power within it. You included." I paused, giving them a moment to appreciate the severity of my words.

Dayne pulled a cigar from the inside pocket of his leather jacket. He took his time lighting and puffing on it, all the while never taking his eyes off me. "Is that so?" He finally said. "And what might this demon want from my pack?"

"Servitude. He wants me to lead the vampires and werewolves of the city, to work for his cause, as servants in his empire."

Dayne moved fast. He was on his feet, cigar in hand, in my face with a menacing sneer. "You think you can take over my pack, bitch? Just fucking try it."

Shaz was at my side, putting himself between me and the big wolf. "That's not what she said." He held his hands up in a sign of surrender. "Please, let her finish."

Hanna grabbed Dayne's arm and pulled, but the big man remained rooted to the spot. "Sit your foul-tempered ass down and listen, honey." To me she said, "Sorry, sweetheart. Men. You know how it is."

I nodded and faked a smile as an acceptance of her apology. My wolf was tense inside me, feeling out of place and ready to either flee or fight. I'd rather not do either. Somehow I managed to stay seated and calm. Tapping my power was tempting but throwing the Alpha wolf on his ass wasn't going to convince him that I wasn't more vampire than wolf.

Dayne glowered at me from his taller frame. His wolf looked out at me, issuing a silent but dangerous challenge. When I didn't react, his shoulders settled ever so slightly, and he returned to his seat.

"Keep talking," he growled, taking a large swig of beer.

I swallowed hard, seeking the right words to make him see the truth. Clearly the wolves here lived in their own tidy little world. Couldn't say I blamed them. I would too if everyone would just leave me the hell alone.

"Shya, the demon, he's got plans for all of us. We need to come together to resist him. The fact that I'm here telling you this should earn me some credit. If I planned to overthrow your pack, I wouldn't come for a visit first." I paused, and when Dayne indicated I should continue, I told him everything I knew about Shya.

Dayne's expression never changed, though Hanna openly gasped and commented as I spoke. She was much calmer of the two of them. I wasn't stupid enough to think that made her more reasonable. But one could hope.

"So what then?" Dayne asked in a gruff voice when I'd finished. "We either help you, or you make us your bitches for the demon?"

"No, of course not," I said, incredulous. He was not listening. "This is not a threat. It's an invitation. If you tell me to fuck off then that's what I'll do. I'm giving you an opportunity to form an alliance with one of the most powerful people in this city. Me. If you don't want to, it's not my loss."

Hanna and Dayne exchanged a look. With a hand on his arm, she stared at him, communicating without words.

"Isn't this why we have such a strong pack?" She asked him. "So when trouble comes, we're ready. This demon may not be our problem yet, but he wants to be. And I'd say that's trouble."

Dayne's silence was heavy and uncomfortable. He stared at his wife for a long time before turning back to us. "If you don't mind, I'd like to speak to Hanna alone about this. Just give us a few minutes."

The Alpha pair excused themselves, disappearing through a door marked: Staff Only.

Shaz finished his beer and stretched. "That didn't go so bad. I think they believe us."

"I'm starting to think this is more trouble than it's worth."

I used the time to try calling Jez again. Still no answer. This was unlike her. The uneasy feeling I'd been plagued with all night began to grow.

"I'm going to find the restroom," Shaz announced. "I won't be long."

He stood up and turned away right in time to collide with another wolf. The collision caused the other guy to spill his drink, most of which soaked his shirt and dripped down his pants.

"Oh, man, I'm so sorry," Shaz said, grabbing frantically for the napkin dispenser on the next table over. "Please, let me buy you another drink."

The wolf exploded without warning. He smashed his glass on the floor at Shaz's feet before slapping the napkins out of his hand.

"You fucking clumsy idiot," the wolf growled, his eyes flashing with the beast within. "You ruined my goddamn shirt. Do you know how much this cost me?"

"Look, I'm sorry. I'll pay for it. But it was an accident." Shaz spoke calmly though a muscle twitched in his jaw. "Let's just take it easy here."

The angry wolf's nostrils flared as he took in our scent. His gaze dropped to Shaz's neck, seeking a tattoo that would mark him as a brother but finding none.

"How did you get in here?" He snarled. "You're not pack. You're trespassing on our territory. Guess what we do to trespassers here."

"We came to see Dayne and Hanna," I butted in when I probably shouldn't have. But the two male wolves were staring at one another with a vicious need for violence. I had to do something. "They know we're here."

The feisty wolf looked me over, his wolf eyes lingering a little too long for comfort. He was a big guy, built like a football player and clearly eager to fight.

"Well, aren't you a sweet little thing," he drawled, ogling me like I was a piece of candy he wanted to taste. His gaze returned to Shaz, and he said snidely, "Let me take your girl home tonight, and we'll forget it ever happened."

Shaz's calm, even tempered approach shattered with those words. He threw a punch I never saw coming. It seemed to surprise the aggressive wolf as well. Shaz's fist connected with his jaw in a smack loud enough to be heard over the music. But Shaz didn't stop there. He followed it up with another.

I was knocked aside in the flurry of fists. Snarls and growls drew the attention of everyone in the vicinity. We all looked on in interest as the fight went on. I stood there unable to believe what I was seeing. Getting involved wasn't an option. The two males were fiercely going at it, throwing and taking punches that would have killed a human man. Jumping into that would mean taking a hit. Using power was also out of the question. I'd come here to proclaim I was still wolf. I intended to stick to that plan.

Nobody made an attempt to jump in or separate them. In fact, only a few people continued to watch after first glance. This kind of thing must happen a lot at Doghead.

The scent of blood only caused the fight to escalate. The two men crashed into a table, knocking it over, sending glassware and other items scattering across the floor. I shouted at Shaz to stop, but my command went unheeded.

Power rose up like a breath of wind inside me. I squelched the urge to use it. The scent of heady Were blood was tempting. Thankfully I'd recently fed that ugly hunger.

Shaz managed to get his hands around the other guy's throat. He slammed the guy into our table, squeezing until his face turned purple.

"Shaz, stop this shit right now," I shouted.

Grabbing a hold of his forearm, I tugged hard, but he wouldn't be budged. Instead, he flung me off like I was little more than an annoying insect. With one hand, he gave me a shove, barely looking at me as I flew backwards. I landed hard in the mess of broken glass and table debris.

Glass shards sliced into my palms as I pushed to my feet. Shock and fear threatened to undo my composure. I could feel sad about Shaz's reaction later. Now, I had to stop him from killing a Doghead pack member.

Dayne arrived on the scene with an angry shout that had people moving as far away from us as possible. I had to act fast, before he got his hands on Shaz.

Knowing I might regret it later, I grabbed Shaz's arm again, this time letting the force brewing inside me flow. I didn't take it easy on him. With a slam of power, I forced him away from the other wolf and into the closest chair that was still standing.

"You're lucky I respect you so much, or I'd have you on your knees," I hissed between my four fangs. I maintained my hold despite the pained sounds it forced from him.

Turning to Dayne with apologies already spilling out, I found him unleashing fists on the wolf Shaz had nearly killed. The wolf dropped to the floor, submitting entirely to his Alpha.

Most of those watching did their best to pretend they weren't. A few wore obvious expressions of glee at seeing the troublemaker cowed before their leader. After a few more angry words from Dayne, the wolf slunk off to lick his wounds somewhere in private.

"It seems our boys can't play too well together," Dayne said. His eyes were pure wolf, and his fangs gave his already hard face an additional sense of menace. "I apologize. I don't doubt that my wolf started that brawl."

"I'm sorry too." I winced as I plucked a piece of glass from my palm. "I never intended for anything like that to happen."

"I believe you." Dayne regarded me thoughtfully. His wolf seemed to scrutinize me, searching for signs of weakness. "You should probably leave."

He was kicking us out? Son of a bitch.

"And our alliance?" I asked, refusing to go without an answer.

"We don't have one. I'm not convinced that's in our best interest right now." Dayne tilted his head to the side, watching me expectantly like the curious animal he was.

I searched the bar for Hanna. She had been my best chance of having Dayne take me seriously. But she was nowhere to be seen. I had no choice but to take her absence as her answer.

I wanted to argue, to beg him to take me seriously. Instead, I spun on my heel and headed for the door, fully expecting Shaz to follow. He did. So did Dayne who came to the door to ensure we left.

A rage unlike any I'd known in some time threatened my control. The wolf was pushing against my insides, seeking release. Being around so many wolves had really stirred up my beast. I wanted nothing more than to be furry on four legs, chasing Shaz through the night.

Ignoring Shaz when he called my name, I stalked across the parking lot, seething. He caught up to me, grabbing my arm and spinning me around to face him.

"Get off me." I jerked my arm away and took a few steps back.

"Lex, I'm sorry. I don't know what happened. I just lost it." Shaz ran a hand through his platinum hair a few times before reaching for me again.

I stepped away to avoid him and threw up a hand to ward him off. "Don't. Just fucking don't. I don't know what's gotten into you recently, but I don't like it. You blew it in there, Shaz."

His gorgeous green eyes were all wolf. The wolf didn't give a damn about the fight, but I could see Shaz struggling to show remorse. It would have worked if he'd been feeling it. He wasn't sorry.

"I know. There's nothing I can say. I get that. But I am sorry."

Too furious to speak, I got in the car with a loud slam of the door. My fingers shook with rage as I tried to slip the key into the ignition. Blood made my fingers slippery, and I had to fish some fast food napkins out of the glove box to wipe my hands.

Shaz got into the car looking both mad and guilty, a difficult feat I was sure. "Are you ok? I'm sorry I pushed you."

"Fine," I said, short and clipped. "It's already healing."

We sat there in silence while I struggled to take deep, calming breaths. It was too late for regrets, though I wished I'd come alone.

"I'll fix this. We can come back, talk to Dayne after this blows over. It will work out." Shaz didn't sound convinced.

I wanted to slap him. Somehow I kept my hands to myself. "What you did in there, that's something Arys would do. You used to be the calm, cool one. Remember? What happened to that?"

Shaz shrugged and slumped in his seat. "I don't know, Lex. People change. I changed."

"I feel like I don't know you anymore." The words just slipped out, a breathy whisper that might as well have been a scream. He turned sharply to look at me, but I kept staring straight ahead at the Doghead sign. Once my hands steadied, I put the car in gear.

"Welcome to my world," he muttered, turning away to stare out the window.

When I hit the brakes at the edge of the lot, I slid a glance his way. A sinking sensation settled in my gut. I'd done such a good job of convincing myself that Shaz and I were back on track. The truth was, I wasn't sure we ever could be.

As much as I wanted to believe we were all good, I knew that things had changed too much. They were still changing. Our private encounters were comprised of my need to feed and the desperate act of two people going through the motions, seeking but never finding the intimacy we'd once had. Maybe I was so desperate to hold onto the past that I was unwilling to accept that we had no future.

Shaz looked at me with a raised brow. Feeling like my thoughts must be written all over my face, I averted my gaze and eased the car into traffic.

* * * *

When we pulled into The Wicked Kiss parking lot, I tried to beat back the nervousness that gripped me. It had been some time since Shaz had been there. The first thing I noted was that Kale's old Camaro was absent. That was a relief. It was early though, barely midnight. Despite the early hour, Willow sat at his usual place at the bar. More relief.

"Damn am I glad to see you," I said, clapping him on the back before sliding onto the stool next to him.

Willow nodded and raised a tequila shot in greeting to Shaz who sat on his other side. Then he peered at me with a serious stare, reading me in a way that I still wasn't used to. Perception was one of Willow's talents. He could see right through the projected walls I tried to hide behind.

"Bad night already?" he inquired. "Do tell."

"Our visit to Doghead didn't go so well. Unfortunately. Anyway, I need to talk to you." I wished I could be alone with him so I could vent about Shaz. "Shya was in my bedroom. He took my hair and my blood. I can't put this off anymore. I need to know more about this scroll he's looking for."

"I'll tell you anything I know. As long as you're sure that you're ready to hear it." Willow's smile was warm and friendly. He had a way of making me feel like I could tell him anything. And I had. Many times.

I gazed into his gold-flecked green eyes and saw the answers I sought within them. Everything had gone down so fast since I learned that Shya needed me as a sacrifice. Soon after, I'd taken off to Vegas. I

49

hadn't been able to bring myself to question Willow because deep inside I knew there was more to his sudden appearance in my life than he let on.

"You know, don't you?" I asked. "What Shya wants, why he needs me. You know all of it."

Willow smiled and his shoulders sagged as if a weight was lifted from him. "You'd better have a drink, Alexa. There are some things I need to tell you."

Raising his hand to get the bartender's attention, Willow had extra shooter glasses and a fresh bottle of tequila perched in front of us in no time. I wrinkled my nose at the shot he put in front of me.

After sliding one to Shaz, Willow raised his shot and said, "To the creatures of light who walk in dark places."

At his insistent look, I raised my glass. There was no bracing for what was coming. Liquor was my only human vice, for now. But tequila, that was an ass kicker of a drink that would put me on my face if I wasn't careful. I clinked my glass against each of theirs before downing the contents in one swift gulp. I slammed the shot glass down and reached for a slice of lime. "Oh God, that burns."

Willow watched with amusement glittering in his eyes as I coughed. "Ready? Or do you want another?"

"As ready as I'm gonna get." I motioned for him to start talking. "But pour me another one. Just in case I can't handle whatever it is you're going to tell me."

The tequila burned in my stomach, but I gripped the shooter as if it was a security blanket. Willow tossed back another shot. Then he took my free hand in his.

"Before I fell, I was sent to look for the scroll. The same scroll that Shya's seeking. I was also instructed to protect the Hound of God he was after. You." Willow paused, letting that sink in. "I grew to care very much for you. Unfortunately, I failed you when I fell." Willow stopped. He seemed to be searching for the right words. He opened his mouth to continue then shook his head and reached for the tequila bottle.

I looked down at our joined hands. The way I felt with Willow, safe and loved, it made sense now. "I think part of me knew that you were here for me," I said. "I felt it."

"I fell in love with Christina. It was wrong but it happened, and I have no excuses. Shya found me with her. After I fell, he wanted me to join him. When I refused, he threatened to kill you both. He made me decide between the two of you." Willow's voice grew husky. He stared at the liquor bottle, remembering. "So I did what I had to. I chose the one who was born to stop him. I chose you."

My jaw dropped. A small cry slipped out. "Shya killed Christina?"

"It was his way of punishing me for refusing to join him."

Tears pricked the back of my eyes. I hadn't thought it was possible to loathe Shya more than I already did. Willow was the kindest soul I knew. Of all of us, he was the last person who deserved to suffer.

"I'm so sorry," I choked out, blinking back blood tears that blurred my vision. "Why didn't you tell me this before?"

"It wasn't the right time."

Shaz cleared his throat, drawing both of our gazes his way. "Sorry to interrupt, but did you just say Alexa was born to stop Shya?"

"I did." Willow nodded and gestured to the drink clutched between my fingers. "You might need that now."

Without hesitation I slammed the shot. It went down a tad easier than the first had. "I don't suppose you know exactly how I'm supposed to stop him."

"I don't. Those details are not known by many. Others have a role to play in the outcome though. We need to be ready."

"Shya said he was desperate, last night, in my bedroom." I recounted the details of Shya's visit, careful not to leave anything out, even the parts I'd rather forget. "He said the power is killing me. It's too much. I think he's afraid I'll die before he gets his chance to use me."

Shaz scowled and poured himself another drink. He never said a word, but he didn't have to. The look on his face was just another reminder that he didn't belong here, plotting against demons in a vampire bar. Fighting with other wolves at Doghead, that's where Shaz belonged.

"Shya's running on limited time," Willow said. "It doesn't surprise me that he's getting desperate. There's no telling what he might do now. If you die before he can use you as a sacrifice, he's screwed."

Since I'd come close to death more than once recently, I could see why Shya was feeling limited. All I had to do was call more power than I could handle, and it was all over for me. "Are you sure about that? Every time I think I know what role either I or the scroll plays, the story changes just enough to make me second guess what I already know. I'm starting to get the feeling what I know so far isn't entirely accurate. Does Shya really know what the hell the scroll is for and what to do with it? Does anyone?" My shrill tone gave away my desperate panic.

"Honestly, I don't even know if what I know is the truth. It's a demon relic. Demons aren't exactly known for the truth. But here's the kicker. If what I know is true, then this can only be done with you. Because of your twin flame connection."

"Are you saying this is because Lilah is part of a twin flame union too?" I stared in surprise at Willow, my mind reeling. It made sense since Shya needed this scroll to take over Lilah's throne and the unholy power that went with it.

"It's got to have something to do with the twin flame connection. Someone knows what that is. But it isn't me. I wasn't told how the scroll came to be, just that I had to find it. Too much information can be a bad thing. Since Shya's limited by time, he's going to greater lengths to find it. I know he's been summoning other demons for help. I don't think it's working out so well for him yet." Willow appeared thoughtful. Then he said something I didn't want to hear. "He's gotten Kale involved in the search. You should talk to him about that."

"Kale?" I scoffed. That name left a sour taste in my mouth. Or maybe that was the tequila. "He's helping Shya? I can't believe him!"

Willow held up a hand to silence my rant before I could really get rolling. "No, it isn't like that. Shya's got him running around, checking out places of worship that the demons can't get into, in case the church is holding it. He's not doing it for Shya. He's doing it for you."

My gaze met Shaz's. He tried to keep a neutral expression. It didn't work. Kale was a sensitive subject. "Why would a demon relic be hidden in a church?" I carefully tried to avoid the topic by focusing on the details.

"To keep the demons from reclaiming it," Willow answered with a shrug, like it should be self-explanatory. "I don't know who hid it or if it even is in a church. But Shya seems to think so. Like I said, talk to Kale."

"Kale and I aren't on the best of terms right now," I said, unable to hide my bitterness.

Willow shoved the liquor bottle back my way. "Might I suggest you get over it? He's your second, Alexa. You need him."

"My second?"

"Talk to him, Alexa."

One more shot, and I was ready to claw my own tongue. "You said Shya's been searching churches. I suppose that's as good a place as any to start."

"I'm coming with you. I can help identify the places demons can't enter." Willow drank back a large swallow straight out of the bottle. He shoved the almost empty bottle aside and rose. "I was your guardian once. I'll be by your side through this."

I was at a loss for words. With a strangled sob, I threw my arms around his neck and hugged him close. "I'm so sorry Shya took her from you," I whispered, blinking furiously. "I promise I will make him pay for that. Somehow."

Willow's embrace was tight and affectionate, a friendly squeeze that allowed me a glimpse into the lonely creature that he was. He was a victim of love and circumstance. He didn't deserve to suffer like this.

Shya wouldn't get away with what he'd done to Willow. I didn't know how I'd make good on that promise, but I would find a way.

Chapter Six

"Son of a bitch." I swore softly while scrolling through a web page listing every church in the city. "It's going to take days to check them all out. Maybe weeks. We don't have that kind of time."

The three of us sat in my car, mapping out a game plan. With so many possibilities, it was a tad discouraging.

"It won't be so bad," Willow answered, leaning across from the passenger seat to get a look at the list on my phone. "What we want to find are the churches that I can't enter. Those will be our best bet. Start with the catholic churches."

"Right. There's only fifty listed right here. That's not even all of them." I wanted to get this first search over with before Arys got home.

Willow pointed to an address on the map. "Let's start there."

I found myself staring at him again in solemn silence. The urge to fuss over him was strong. I wished there was something I could do to ease his pain. Insulting him with pity was not my intent so I bit back the sympathetic tirade and started the car.

"We need more manpower," Shaz suggested. He sat in the back seat, hands folded behind his head. "If we had more people we could split up, cover more ground."

Jez and Kale immediately came to mind. I didn't have a lot of people I could trust with this. Unfortunately, my sister and the FPA were not among the few. Too bad. They definitely had manpower.

"We have to be careful. If Shya finds out we're doing this, he's going to be pissed." I called Jez again and once again got her voicemail. After leaving yet another message, I hung up and turned to the guys. "I guess it's just us for tonight."

Neither of them questioned me about Kale, and I was thankful for that. My impending death and predicament with Shya had to be my priority. My scorned lover would have to be patient. He would get his turn to put me through the ringer.

We started with the address Willow had suggested. I didn't know what I was looking for, didn't have a clue where to start. When the fallen angel was able to cross the threshold, he declared it to be a dud.

"So what's with that anyway?" Shaz asked when we were back in the car on our way to the next address. "Why are you able to walk into some churches and not others?"

Willow turned in his seat to face Shaz. "The churches I can't enter are those with an angel standing guard. The pure divine presence of the angel guardian prevents the fallen from entering."

I nodded in understanding. That made sense. "Am I correct in assuming that a church in need of a guardian must have something worth protecting?"

"You certainly are. It could be anything. A person, a holy object, Lilah's scroll. Where there is an angelic guard there is something in need of guarding." Willow took on a wistful tone. It made my heart hurt for him.

"Shya's got to be doing the same thing," Shaz mused. "Or maybe he already has. Would he be using humans to access the places his demons can't go?"

"It's possible," Willow said, inclining his head in a half nod. "Demons are manipulative liars. They're very good at what they do. It wouldn't take much to convince the weak of faith to do his bidding."

As I drove, I listened to the two of them discuss the situation. It was overwhelming, to say the least. Shya could have any number of people out there hunting for this thing. I had very few. I really did need to touch base with Kale, at least to find out where he'd already looked.

The next few places also proved to be a waste of time. Then, we pulled up in front of a building I recognized. I had been here not so long ago. The church was massive. Huge white pillars bordered the entrance. We ascended the white stairs leading up to the double doors and an uneasy sensation took hold in my gut.

Willow reached for the door and froze mid-action. "I can't go inside. Which means you have to."

"The priest here has the same dragon as me," I whispered, suddenly afraid. "He said Shya was trying to force him to help find the scroll."

Shaz raised a brow in curiosity.

A light filled Willow's eyes, and he seemed almost relieved. "Then I'd say we're on the right track by being here." He gave me a gentle shove toward the door. "Go on. I'll wait right here."

Exchanging a look of uncertainty with Shaz, I reached for the door and pushed it open. I was surprised to find it unlocked after dark.

It blew my mind to think that there was an angel here with us, unseen yet very much present. Somehow, it was also reassuring, despite my unease, which grew with every step.

I paused in the entryway, letting my gaze sweep over the impressive ceiling. It was like a giant dome, covered with paintings. Candles burned on the altar at the front. I saw no one, but I felt the human presence within.

"Hello?" I called out. My voice echoed in the silence. "Father Andrew?"

A moment later he emerged from a back room. He wore an expression of disbelief. "Welcome," he said, spreading his hands in an open gesture that matched his greeting. "It's wonderful to see you again, Alexa. What can I do for you?"

"Honestly, Father, I don't have a clue." I made my way down the aisle between the pews with Shaz at my side. "I'm looking for the scroll. The one Shya seeks. I need to find it first."

With his grey hair brushed neatly into place and brown eyes shining with an inner joy I couldn't fathom, Father Andrew reached to shake each of our hands in turn. I couldn't help but look for the dragon he bore despite it being hidden by the long sleeves of his shirt.

"You certainly do, my dear," he agreed. "I wish I could point you in the right direction. I do not know where the scroll is nor do I wish to. But I will help you in any way I can."

Shaz gazed around the vast interior, and I could almost see what he was thinking. If the scroll wasn't here, then what was the church's angel protecting?

"Shya's running out of time to find it," I explained. "He's resorted to desperate attempts. I'm afraid of what he might do."

"It's been several months since he's paid me a visit. Not that I mind of course. I long for the day his reign of terror is over." Father Andrew began to put out the candles using an elaborately decorated candlesnuffer. "I can make some calls, reach out to my fellow brethren, those I know are still trustworthy."

The scent of candles tickled my nose. I held back a sneeze. "That means a lot to me. Thank you."

"I wish there was more I could do." Father Andrew paused, then added as if it were an afterthought, "Your vampire friend came by not so long ago. He said he was the one you took the demon mark for. I can't imagine what would make a Hound of God willing to pay the price for a vampire, but whatever it is, it must be special."

Awkward. I suddenly couldn't bring myself to meet Shaz's gaze. I cleared my throat and managed to squeak out, "Nobody deserves to be marked by Shya."

Before I could change the subject, there was a loud bang, as if something had hit the front door. Hard. The sound of angry muffled voices was audible.

I was off and running through the church to throw open the door. Willow was on the front step, and he wasn't alone. Brook stood there smirking, his black wings flared wide. So one of Shya's demons had found us already. Fantastic.

Brook's black gaze landed on me and a devilish smile crossed his face. He watched me emerge from the church with open satisfaction.

"Well isn't this interesting?" He taunted. "Shya is going to be thrilled to hear I found you here."

"So you were looking for me?" I challenged, striding right up to face him head on.

The demon stared down at me, trying to intimidate me with his size and wings. It didn't work. Nobody could be more intimidating than Shya. At least, nobody I had met so far.

"Aren't there other places you should be?" Brook sneered. "Like your bordello of blood, for instance."

"I'm pretty sure it's my God given right to attend church any time I damn well please," I hissed, emphasizing God so that the demon flinched. "Care to join me?" I waited for a snide remark but received only a deathly glare. "Where's Falon? He's much more entertaining while being a major pain in my ass."

"It would be wise of you to remember that we can watch you unseen, wolf. Even if you get your hands on the scroll, we'll be watching. Be warned." Brook followed his threat with a flap of wings and a burst of power that threw me off my feet.

The impact of my ass against the ground rattled my teeth, but I was otherwise unhurt. Still, it didn't stop Willow from launching himself at the demon. There was a boom of sound, like thunder, and the two of them tumbled down the steps to the sidewalk below.

This wasn't the first time Willow had gotten violent with Brook. I wasn't sure if they had personal history or if the demon was just an easy target for Willow's inner pain and rage. Shaz pulled me up, and we watched the two immortals trade blows. They didn't hold back, unleashing assaults on one another that would have destroyed any one of us mortals.

I cringed, feeling like a helpless spectator. They could beat each other bloody repeatedly, and it wouldn't accomplish a damn thing. Shouting their names seemed only to encourage them.

Father Andrew appeared outside, his face twisted in an expression of utter disbelief. "What's going on?"

Brook immediately forgot Willow. His attention turned to the priest, and he aimed his attack precisely. Without thought, I threw myself at Father Andrew, knocking him down and taking the demon's blast myself.

It tore a cry from me. I was on the ground, curled into the fetal position, whimpering and wailing. It felt like fire washed over me, through me, and all around. The burning sensation was beyond agonizing. Tears streamed from my eyes, scarlet fountains that exposed the darkness inside me. I gasped for breath, finding each lungful took great effort.

Shaz sprang into action. He shoved the priest back inside the church, shouting at him to stay within the consecrated walls. Then he placed himself between Brook and me, but it was unnecessary. Brook had backed off the moment he saw me take the hit meant for the priest.

All at once the pain subsided. I lay there trembling and gasping.

"Did Shya's instructions include wounding his sacrificial wolf?" Willow shouted.

Brook lifted his chin defiantly. "What are you going to do about it?"

The two of them glared into one another once again. I shook my head and stood up slowly, waving off Shaz's offered hand. I couldn't afford to look weak in any way in front of Brook.

"No more of this," I said, raising my voice to be heard.

Before I could spit out the nasty threat brewing on the tip of my tongue, Falon appeared and ruined it. He stepped between the two immortals and shoved them apart. Spreading his silver wings wide, he used them to keep Brook and Willow at a safe distance.

"Father Andrew," Falon gushed at the priest lingering in the doorway as if they were old friends. "How nice to see you again. I apologize for the disturbance."

Father Andrew said nothing. He merely stared in stony silence at the asshole angel. There was definitely some history there. Couldn't say I blamed the priest for his reaction, or lack thereof.

Falon turned his attention to Brook. "Shya would like a word with you. Better hurry. He's not in a good mood." To Willow he said, "Settle down, guardian. Nobody is going to harm your precious Hound. Yet."

"Why am I starting to feel like I can't go anywhere or do anything without having one of you foul things tailing me?" I asked, leaning on Shaz while I regained my bearings.

"Because you can't," Falon said with a twitch of his lips that looked more like a grimace than a smile.

Brook disappeared in a cloud of sulfur. One down. One to go. It wasn't looking promising.

"Are you going to follow me everywhere all night?" I was exasperated with Shya and his lackeys. Part of me was ready for this to all go down and be over with.

"Of course not. How pathetically boring would that be?" Falon made a face of disgust. "You know there are others you could be stuck with other than me or Brook."

I sighed and said with a sarcastic drawl, "Oh, Falon, don't get my hopes up like that."

After uttering an apology to Father Andrew, I marched back to the car. We left Falon standing there, glaring after us. When I glanced back, he was gone.

I burned with a raging hot fury. Shya thought he could have his demons stalk me as I searched for the scroll too. Screw that. Having Shya put an end to my hunt for the scroll as soon as it began was not an option.

* * * *

I was reluctant to bring my search to an end. But a sudden surge of strength and a shiver down my spine told me that my dark vampire was almost home. When Arys touched my mind to tell me he had just landed at the airport, I was relieved and unsurprised. He wanted to meet at The Wicked Kiss. The search would have to wait.

It had only been a few days, but I couldn't wait to lay eyes on Arys. During the drive back to the club, the familiar flutter of butterfly wings beat a steady rhythm in my stomach. I felt like a lovesick teenager. How ridiculous.

In the parking lot of The Wicked Kiss, I fussed with my makeup before heading inside. Shaz followed Willow in, leaving me alone with my thoughts.

Pulling my fingers through my hair, I stared at my reflection in the visor mirror. I thought about Doghead. It was important to form an alliance with Dayne and his wolves though I couldn't blame him for wanting nothing to do with me or the vampires tied to me. Maybe it was better for the wolves to stay in their own little world.

I glanced at the front door of the club where a queue of people waited to get in. Shaz didn't belong in there with the vampires. He belonged at Doghead. He just didn't know it yet.

I headed inside, breathing a sigh of relief at the absence of Kale's Camaro. Avoiding me was probably best for both of us right now. Willow was right. Kale and I did need to talk, but it would have to wait until we could be rational. That could be a long time.

I bypassed the line and strode inside. Arys wasn't there yet. That gave me a few minutes to consider my next plan of action. Shya had been searching for the scroll for years. I had a lot of catching up to do.

Willow and Shaz were at the bar. I joined them, slipping behind the bar with Josh, the bartender, to help myself to a glass of whiskey. Every time I sipped the deep gold nectar, I was reminded that my time to enjoy my favorite human vice was running out. My enjoyment of the drink was marred by thoughts of Falon who had happily pointed out my impending doom.

"What do you think, Alexa?" Shaz asked, startling me out of my thoughts.

"Sorry, what?" I flashed him an apologetic smile. "I'm just a little distracted. What were you saying?"

"Tomorrow before sundown. We should get an early start on the rest of the churches on our list."

I nodded. "We might have to split up so we can cover more ground. We'll need more people too."

Willow eyed me thoughtfully. "If Shya tracks anyone, it'll be you, through his mark. You need to find a way to use that against him. Lead him away from where you're really searching. Send someone else to those places."

"Good call," I said, savoring the whiskey burn as it slid down my throat. "What would I do without you, Willow?"

He nodded and squeezed out a tight smile. "One can only imagine."

The two of them chattered on about the scroll, discussing possible locations. Shaz was certain we had to think bigger, outside the obvious. A cramp in my brain made it hard to follow. There was just so much to consider.

I scanned the club, admiring the recent renovations and changes. One of the few local bands that were brave enough to play here rocked the new stage. People clustered around the stage and spilled over onto the dance floor. Humans partied their asses off while vampires moved among them.

The activity at The Wicked Kiss had always been excessive, but these days it was especially wild. Patrons were pushing the boundaries, breaking the rules. As I watched a couple dry humping on the dance floor, I shook my head and sighed. I still didn't know what went on there while I'd been away in Vegas, but I was pretty sure Kale had hosted one hell of a party.

Before I could ponder ways to find out, a cool breeze flowed through me, and Arys walked in. In jeans and a t-shirt with that sexy black mess of hair, he made the world stop for just a second as all I saw was him. My heart stuttered, and my breath caught. Then I flew into action and dodged people as I tried to get to him.

Arys grabbed me in a hug that lifted me off my feet. A spark of light lit up the space around us as our power collided. Being in his arms, I felt safe and strong. How had I missed him so badly in just a few days?

When my feet touched the floor again, Arys tipped me back and planted one hell of a kiss on me. His lips moved on mine, commanding and passionate. Several sets of eyes were upon us, but I didn't care. Damn I had missed him. I melted into his kiss. It was the perfect greeting, ruined only by the sarcastic observation that drew me out of the moment.

"And you say that I'm too dramatic for my own good," said a familiar voice. "Really, Arys, you live for drama."

I looked up to find Jenner standing there, watching us with absolute disdain. Average height and build, arms covered in tattoos, Jenner was a looker for sure. He was also one of my biggest haters and Arys's brother through a shared sire. I hadn't anticipated seeing him so soon after what had gone down between us in Vegas.

"What the hell are you doing here?" I blurted. "Don't you have a city to protect?"

Jenner had taken over Las Vegas after the death of his sire, the previous ruler of the city. Arys had gone there with every intention of taking over, and to some extent we had. Leaving Jenner in charge in our absence had been our only choice. He hadn't been too happy with the rules we'd made for him.

"I came to help. But hey, if I'm not welcome, I'll happily grab a flight home." Jenner's ice-blue eyes flashed with annoyance. He pinned Arys with a fierce glare. "I told you she wouldn't want me here."

"Help?" I gaped at Jenner, then Arys. "Are you kidding me?"

"Alexa, you can't afford to be picky. Jenner has power and the willingness to show loyalty to his bloodline. I'm sure you can find a way to make him feel welcome." Arys's deep-blue gaze sparkled with unspoken amusement. He seemed to be enjoying my surprise.

"How do we know we can trust him?" I cast a glance back at the bar where Willow and Shaz watched us with thinly veiled interest.

"You don't," Jenner said, moving in closer so he could really peer into my eyes. "You may not know it yet, but you need me. So I'll pretend you didn't greet me with such contempt and give you the chance to try again."

Crossing my arms over my chest, I plastered a blank expression on my face. My tone was dull, forced, and as fake as my words. "Oh, Jenner, thank you for coming all this way to help out little old me. I can't imagine what I would do without your giving nature to help me through this difficult time."

"That's more like it." Jenner shoved past me, knocking me aside with his shoulder.

Power flared between us as the link we'd formed surfaced. It brought a scowl and a scoff from Jenner who quickly vacated my personal space. He walked through the room, scrutinizing everything before finally pausing at the bar to speak to Shaz. I watched him with growing suspicion.

"So what did you promise Jenner to get him to come?" I asked, flashing Arys a warning look. "And more importantly, why exactly do you feel it's necessary for him to be here?"

"I promised him we would owe him a favor. We need him, Alexa. When everything goes down with Shya, a guy like Jenner can be vital. He's our blood. He will strengthen us." He pulled me close for another kiss. Knowing how to get a reaction out of me, he nibbled my lower lip. "Just try to play nice with Jenner until this all blows over. Well...not too nice, of course."

I sighed, enjoying his teasing kisses. Then I gently pushed him back so I could search his intense gaze. "Arys, this isn't going to blow over. Not until I'm dead."

"Don't talk like that."

"It's true. You saw it yourself. Don't get all soft on me now. I don't think you need Jenner's help to kill me." Putting up a tough front was the only way I could discuss it with him. Sometimes I thought I was ready to just get it all over with. Other times just the thought was enough to send me into a panic attack.

Arys winced as if I'd sliced him with the Dragon Claw rather than just words. "Don't talk like that," he hissed with a viciousness that scared me. "You're not the only one living in fear of that moment. We are in this together. Trust me when I say we need Jenner here right now." He paused to scan the room. "This isn't the right place to talk about it."

I stared stonily at him, feeling successfully rebuked. It wasn't fair of me to take my worries out on him. "I'm sorry. I know this isn't going to be easy on you either."

All the talk of Shya and the scroll in recent weeks had resulted in either strained silence, violent arguments, or wild sex. Anything to keep from acknowledging the inevitable: my death was coming. No matter what role Shya played in that, Arys would be the one to kill me. He had seen it in a vision shown to him by a witch. But I had felt it deep within me long before I knew that. What made it hardest was that Arys wanted it. He desired my death. And he would have it.

He kissed me again, on the lips and then the forehead. He lingered, breathing in my scent. I held tight to him, allowing myself a brief moment of helpless clinging.

"I missed you," he murmured, stroking a hand through my hair.

"I missed you more." I smiled, reveling in the comfort I found in his presence. "But do me a favor? Get Jenner out of my club."

Arys followed my gaze to where Jenner stood by the bar, eyeing up the women on the dance floor. "Why? I thought he could stay here in Harley's old room."

"No way," I said before I could stop myself. "I don't want him lurking around here making everyone uncomfortable."

"Or you don't want him here where Sinclair will run into him." Arys nodded knowingly, a frown creasing his brow.

"Yeah, or that." Might as well be honest. "Kale's not exactly the most mentally stable person I know. Anything could set him off. If he finds out about Jenner..." I trailed off, unable to finish that thought.

Arys's jaw clenched, and he spoke through gritted teeth. "You don't belong to Kale."

"No, but he belongs to me in the same twisted way that Jenner does. I have enough shit to deal with now, Arys."

"Nobody belongs to you like Sinclair does," Arys repeated, a claim I'd heard before and still hated, his tone harsh and angry. "He's dangerous, and you need to stay away from him. I love you, sweet wolf, but it's getting harder and harder to keep myself from getting rid of him altogether."

My temper went from simmer to boiling in two seconds flat. "Don't you fucking dare. You got to call the shots in Vegas. Your city. Your business. This is my city, Arys, and Kale is mine. Back off."

I loved Arys in ways I couldn't begin to describe. And at times, I loathed him just as much. It was the clash of light and dark, the constant conflict we would always face. Unless our bond was destroyed. Upon my death the darkness would claim me; the balance would shift. I didn't really know what that meant for us. I was scared to find out.

I held up my hand. "I don't want to fight with you." I touched his face, needing to absolve the tension between us. "Let's talk later. It's ruining the reunion bliss."

"Can we talk after we screw?" Arys's wicked laughter sent a rush of heat to my loins. He pressed a kiss into my palm before teasingly dragging a fang across my sensitive skin.

"Whatever you want, baby." I laughed. "But seriously, can you get Jenner out of here? I don't want any vampire drama."

Me and my big mouth. To accompany my words, Kale walked through the door. Right on cue. *Shit.*

Chapter Seven

"You've got to be kidding me," I muttered beneath my breath. There was no disguising the sudden increase in my heart rate.

Kale didn't pause or hesitate. He strode right over to me, ignoring Arys like he wasn't even there.

"Have you talked to Jez recently?" Kale asked though his gaze was quickly drawn to the newcomer among us.

He stared at Jenner, analyzing him with a look. When Jenner suddenly looked our way, I knew Kale had felt him out. I held my breath, wondering if Kale could sense Jenner's tie to me. God, I hoped not.

"I've been calling Jez all night. She's not answering. Why? What's up?" Did I sound nervous? I must have reeked of fear, but having Kale and Arys in such close proximity was nerve wracking.

"She was supposed to meet me over an hour ago. She's not answering for me either." Kale managed to drag his gaze back to me. He nodded toward Jenner. "Who's your friend?"

"He's not my friend. He's one of Harley's vampires. From Vegas." I cleared my throat and did my best to maintain eye contact. "Anyway, it's not like Jez to bail. Do you think something is wrong?"

"I was hoping you could tell me. I've been calling your phone."

I dug through my shoulder bag to find my phone buried in the bottom. There were several missed calls from Kale but still no return call or text from Jez. That wasn't like her.

"Sorry. I didn't hear it. We should probably look for her."

"We?" Arys interrupted, unable to stay quiet any longer. "You're not going off with him."

I stared at him in disbelief. "Really? Jez could be in trouble, and you want to start round two already? Give me a break, Arys."

The two vampires exchanged a dark look. I had to give them some credit. They had done a good job of avoiding a confrontation since their last one. I had no desire to witness another.

"Kale can look for Jez without you," Arys insisted. "You and I need to talk. We should head home."

"You take Jenner home. I'll meet you later. Jez has been on a reckless streak, and I'm afraid it's catching up to her." I was prepared to stand my ground. Jez needed me.

Arys shook his head. He had a determined set to his jaw. "I'm not letting you go anywhere alone with him."

"What are you so afraid of, Arys?" Kale asked, a challenge in his words. "I'm not the one destined to kill her. She's safer with me than she is with you."

Arys didn't hold back. He threw a punch that knocked Kale back a few steps. I gasped and covered my mouth in shock, expecting the worst.

Kale merely chuckled and rubbed his jaw. The bastard was definitely crazy. I didn't trust him, not for a moment. But we both loved Jez, and we had to find her.

"Arys, keep your hands to yourself," I said, stepping between them. "Kale, you shut up. All that matters right now is that Jez is ok. Until I know that, I don't give a damn about anything else."

Almost as if he knew it was the last thing I needed, Jenner chose that moment to saunter over. I did my best to shoot him down with a dirty look. He looked right through me.

His frozen gaze slid from Arys to Kale, then to me. There was a sliminess to his actions that struck me as snake-like. What was this bastard up to?

"Is there a problem?" Jenner asked. "Anything I can help with? I am here to serve my queen after all."

The sarcastic venom that dripped from his words brought forth a dark part of me. I was immediately pissed. Before I could tell him off, he grabbed my hand so the power flashed between us.

My power recognized him instantly as mine. It linked us, burning with the heady rush of our bloodline. I turned quickly to look at him, finding a devilish smirk plastered on his face.

The shock and disgust on Kale's face said it all. Jenner, ever the showman, was putting on this little display for Kale's benefit. Evidently Arys had been sharing some of our personal business while he was away.

I jerked my hand away, and with a snap of my fingers, I flung Jenner across the room. He landed on one of my new tables and rolled onto the floor. Kale spun on a heel and headed for the door.

"Get Jenner out of my club," I snarled at Arys. "I don't know what kind of crap the two of you are trying to pull, but I don't need it. Tell Shaz to catch a ride home with you. I'm going to look for Jez."

Arys caught my arm, stopping me from following Kale. "I didn't know he was going to do that. I'm sorry."

"You told him about Kale. That's none of his damn business. Is Jenner just here to make my final days miserable?"

"No, I promise you, he's not. We need him."

I pulled away, and this time Arys let me go. I cast an angry glare Jenner's way. "I don't need him. I have more than enough haters in this city already. Until he can prove useful, I don't want to see him."

"I'll be at your place when you get home. We need to talk," Arys called after me as I sprinted for the exit.

I ran through the parking lot, making a beeline for Kale's car. The honk of a horn startled me as a car screeched to a stop to avoid hitting me. I waved in apology and continued on.

"Kale, wait," I shouted. "I'm coming with you."

He paused at his car and pulled keys from a pocket. "Don't bother. I can find her on my own."

"She's our friend and our partner. I'm coming with you," I insisted, stepping in front of the door before he could slide the key in.

Kale stepped back to avoid touching me. I took the opportunity to swipe the keys from his hand.

"Alexa, cut it out. Go back inside."

"It's not how Jenner made it look. He's not quite my biggest fan. Please, let me explain."

"So you've enslaved another vampire. What's to explain?" He grabbed for the keys, but I deftly avoided his grab.

"It isn't like that. Jenner made a lot of trouble for us in Las Vegas. Binding him to me was Arys's way of punishing him for that. He's only here to help. Then he goes back." I unlocked the car door and slid across the driver's seat to the passenger side. "Get in. Jez needs us."

Kale stood there looking conflicted. Finally he uttered a curse and got into the car. I handed over the keys, which he took carefully so our hands wouldn't touch.

It had been quite some time since I'd been in Kale's car. It smelled like him. Leather and subtle cologne brought forth a flood of memories. I took a deep breath and stifled a sigh.

"You're taking a big risk by being so close, you know," he said. After starting the engine, Kale eased out of his parking spot. If he was hoping I would change my mind and jump out, he was going to be disappointed.

"Well, you're not the one who's going to kill me, remember? So what's the problem? Afraid you'll regret what you said last night?"

Kale slid a sidelong glance my way. His blue and brown eyes glittered with a mischievous light, one I recognized from every tense encounter we'd ever had. "I meant every word. It's better for both of us if we keep our distance. You can't argue that, and you know it." He maneuvered the Camaro into traffic, heading south toward Jez's side of the city.

His attention was on the road, allowing me a moment to enjoy looking at him. Kale held himself with the self-assurance of one who had survived many centuries. He was poised, regal in a way, and undeniably handsome.

"I miss you, Kale," I said before I could decide not to. "I miss what we used to have. Our friendship. We made a great team."

When he didn't respond right away, I dug my phone out and tried Jez again. No use. My next call was to Juliet who I begged to help me out with a trace on Jez's phone. She promised to do what she could and call me back if she found anything.

We left the downtown core bound for Jez's trendy neighborhood. Her behavior had been wild lately. Grief was a bitch.

"I miss you, too." Kale's admittance was uttered with bitterness. "More than you'll ever really know."

I wanted to insist we could get our friendship back. I didn't though, because it would be a lie. Even as I tried to deny it, I was painfully aware of the dangers of our proximity.

"Ok, so what's the plan?" I asked, redirecting the conversation. If I could get him talking about something other than us, maybe we would both relax.

"I guess we start at Jez's apartment. Hopefully your sister can trace her phone. It's not like Jez to skip out on a hunt. Whatever she's up to, it can't be good."

I nodded, already fearing the worst. "She's on a mission to dull the pain. That never ends well for anyone. It doesn't work."

Kale laughed, a scornful sound. "No, but it sure feels good to try."

"Yeah, I know." So much for keeping the topic off of us.

We fell quiet, but it was awkward and strained. The uneasy conversation had been less obvious.

"So tell me about Jenner," Kale said, regarding me with a sly smile. "What could he have done to warrant such a punishment?"

It bothered me to hear him refer to being bound to me as a punishment even though I'd said it myself. It had been punishment for Jenner as well as a way of keeping him loyal to his bloodline. But that had never been my intention when I made Kale mine.

"Really? You want to talk about this?" With a raised brow I gave him a critical once over. He motioned for me to continue. "Ok, fine. Jenner is the star of his own show. He screws and bleeds victims on stage in front of an audience. When Arys lost the poker game they played, Jenner made us take the stage. He wanted to watch us together. So we turned the tables on him and made him part of the act."

Kale's hands tightened visibly on the steering wheel. His expression never changed. His attention was on the road. Yet the telltale vibe of jealous anger seeping from him spoke loud and clear.

I swallowed hard and added, "Nothing happened with Jenner. I manipulated him into taking my blood. We didn't...it wasn't physical."

The quiet that fell was nerve wracking. I wished that he would say something, anything. His eerie silence was freaking me out.

"So you mind-fucked him," he said at last. "And now he's yours. He's going to crave you like a drug that never leaves his system, and he'll never find relief. Definitely a hell of a good way to torture a guy."

I knew what he was doing. Still, it wasn't in my nature to keep my mouth shut when being judged. "He had it coming, and I'm not sorry," I spat the words with more force than necessary. "But you, Kale, I will never stop being sorry for what I did to you."

We stopped at a red light, and our eyes met. I willed him to see the truth. Hurting him had never been my intent. The hardness in him felt foreign. The walls he had formed between us were built from pain, betrayal, and love. A deadly combination.

The rest of the drive to Jez's was spent with only the sound of the radio to fill the void. I stared out the window, watching the city streets fly by. As we passed restaurants and bars filled with humans going about their lives in blissful ignorance, I felt a longing I hadn't known in a very long time.

The commercial area gave way to residential. We pulled up in front of Jez's building to find the windows of her second floor apartment dark. Because of the underground parking, we couldn't know for sure if she was there.

"It doesn't look like she's home," I commented, refusing to go about this night in strained silence. "You said she was supposed to meet you? Could she have run into some kind of trouble on the way?"

"We were supposed to hunt a new vampire with a taste for kids. She was eager to tag him. I can't imagine what would keep her from doing that."

We got out of the car and entered the lobby. After pressing the buzzer and receiving no response, I manipulated the door lock with little effort, and we were inside.

"You've gotten so good at those little things. I bet you can pull off some pretty impressive shit now." Kale's observation was accompanied by a smirk.

"Let's hope so," I quipped. "I have a feeling I might have to in the not so distant future."

I paused to allow him to ascend the stairs first. I knew better than to allow Kale at my back. He swept by me with a knowing look and a snicker.

Jez wasn't home. Standing outside her apartment door, I could feel the absence of her lively Were essence.

"What now?" I asked. My phone rang as Juliet came through for me. She read an address to me that sounded familiar, but I couldn't quite place it. "Thank you, Juliet. I appreciate your help. Don't tell Briggs, or he'll think I owe you guys another favor."

"Little sister isn't so bad after all," Kale said after I'd hung up. "Good to know."

I typed the address into the map on my phone. It was The Spirit Room, a rock bar I'd been to a time or two. It wasn't a place I knew Jez to go. What could be going on there that would keep her from meeting Kale or answering her phone?

"I know this place," I said, showing Kale the map. "I went there with Brogan to find Gabriel the night Falon swiped him and took him to Shya. Can't imagine why Jez would be there."

"Well, let's go get her."

The drive to The Spirit Room wasn't nearly as awkward. Now we had a purpose, a goal that united us once again as a team regardless of our personal issues.

My mind raced, concocting a series of possible scenarios we might encounter. None of them were good. I feared that Jez's heartbreak was driving her into a place that might not be so easy to come back from.

"Is this the place?" Kale slowed the car down as we approached the rock bar.

A group of black leather-clad guys and girls stood outside, smoking cigarettes and marijuana. Loud music poured out the front entry onto the street. Jez's golden locks were not visible in the small crowd.

"Yeah, this is it."

We parked across the street and surveyed the building for a few minutes. I didn't see Jez's Jeep anywhere.

"Alright, let's go find our leopard." Kale reached for the door handle, and I stopped him with a hand on his arm.

"Remember, this place is primarily human. We have to blend in. No vamping out."

My warning was met with an eye roll. Kale shoved the car door open and got out. "Don't make the mistake of thinking I'm the only one with control issues."

He slammed the door before I could snark back at him. I followed, pausing to ensure my dagger was hidden by my jacket. Then we crossed the street and slipped inside the busy nightclub. Kale's comment ate at me. I had lost control in The Spirit Room the last time I'd come here. Maybe I was the weaker link here.

The club was dimly lit and smelled mostly like the fog from a fog machine. Waitresses hurried about with trays piled with drinks while a live band rocked the stage. The place was packed.

I scanned the busy bar for Jez. "Do you see her?" I shouted over the music.

Kale shook his head, his gaze on a group of women clustered around a table. I recognized them as the ladies from Crimson Sin, the werewolf led band that regularly played The Wicked Kiss.

"Let's ask the werewolf. She's the only Were I see, other than you." Kale leaned in close to be heard. His sudden nearness sent a small adrenaline shot through me.

"You go ahead," I said. "I'm going to check the ladies room and take a look around."

I didn't wait for a reply. Putting distance between us before he picked up on my nerves was essential. I couldn't help but be jumpy around him. After all, he had tried to kill me.

Kale approached the Crimson Sin girls while I ducked into the ladies room. As I'd suspected, there was no sign of Jez.

When I emerged, I almost collided with Gabriel. The tall, lanky Goth kid held his hands up to avoid touching me. His eyes were wide with surprise, but the expression quickly faded, replaced with one of wary scrutiny.

"Geez, Gabriel, why don't you just wear gloves? Wouldn't that make your life easier?"

"What are you doing here, Alexa?" He was uneasy, holding himself as if he were about to run.

"Settle down." I took a moment to enjoy his discomfort. "I'm not here for you. I'm looking for my friend, Jez. The leopard. Have you seen her?"

Gabriel was the enemy. He couldn't be trusted. I had tried to make him see that Shya had nobody's best interests in mind but his own. Gabriel had chosen to ignore my warning and aligned himself with the demon. Since he was a witch with a shitload of power, that concerned me.

He was also a precognitive clairvoyant. With just a touch he could see things nobody should be able to see. After touching my hand once when doing a spell, he had seen me as a vampire. It was something he refused to talk about.

"No, sorry. I wish I could help." He was lying. For a guy with so much power, he was forgetting the werewolf rules.

I moved fast, slamming him against the wall before he could work some spell on me. With my hand on his throat, I squeezed.

"Don't fucking lie to me, Gabriel. I can smell the stink of it all over you. Tell me where Jez is, or I'll send you back to Shya with pieces missing." The horror that spread across his face seemed to be from my touch more than my threat. Good. Whatever he was seeing about me, I hoped it scared the shit out of him.

He grunted and struggled to speak. His garbled noise was impossible to decipher. I eased off but tapped my power in case I needed to blast him. "Upstairs. Staff door near the fire exit," he choked out.

Kale appeared wearing an amused grin. "Careful now, Alexa. Shya won't be too happy if you kill his witch." Knowing Shya, he had probably marked his prodigy. He would know if I hurt Gabriel.

"If I kill him?" I questioned. "Or if *we* kill him?" I'd like to think I was joking, but a vicious smile tugged at my lips. Gabriel had been someone I wanted to help. Then he joined the dark side and became my enemy. Bad choice.

"Seriously?" Kale asked, perking up in interest. "I do love tag teaming with you."

"You can't do shit to me," Gabriel sneered. "It would break Arys's deal with Shya. Do you really want to bring hell on your dark half?"

The kid had balls. Unfortunately, he was also right. Arys had made a deal with Shya to save my life. In exchange, Arys had promised to turn Gabriel. Shya wanted his black magic prodigy to be a vampire from our bloodline. I would do everything I could to keep that from happening. But killing Gabriel wasn't the way.

"I don't know, Gabriel," I said, tapping clawed fingertips on the wall beside his head. "You tell me. You're the one who can see shit that hasn't happened yet. How bad can it be?"

"That's right. I see many things. For a woman who has such little time left with a heartbeat, you seem to be wasting a lot of it on me." Gabriel's fear had faded. Now he was ready to fight.

I released him and stepped back, watching as he shoved past Kale and disappeared into the throng. There was no sense letting him get to me. Easier said than done.

Kale spied my crestfallen face. "Hey, don't listen to the kid. He's on puppet strings held by a demon. You can't trust anything he says."

Having Kale feel bad for me didn't help. If anything, it made it worse. I shrugged. "Forget it. Let's go get Jez."

Finding the fire exit at the back of the building was easy enough. Right beside it was a staff door that opened into a staircase. We followed the stairs up to a small second floor that was pretty much just an attic. It appeared to be a backstage area for the musicians. Guitars and amps lined the wall. A drum set sat in the corner. A large sectional couch took up another corner. It was occupied by two guys rolling a joint on the coffee table.

They both looked up at our approach. One of them went right back to busting up his weed, ignoring us completely. The second, a young guy with a bleached blond Mohawk watched us with curiosity in his bloodshot eyes.

"We're looking for a friend," I said. "Her name is Jez. She's tall, feisty, long golden hair. Have you seen her?"

I barely finished speaking when I sensed her. Kale was already striding across the room to a closed door on the opposite side. Muffled voices could be heard from inside along with the sound of an acoustic guitar.

Kale burst through the door with me hot on his heels. The people inside barely looked up. They were too immersed in the party going on. This second room was smaller with a large mirror on one side and vanity space for rockers to get ready before a show. About a dozen people were crammed onto the one small couch and two easy chairs in the center. Others sat on the floor, passing a joint.

Jez was squeezed in on the couch. With a rolled up twenty in hand, she leaned over a tray of powder cut into thin white lines.

My jaw dropped. I blinked a few times, unable to believe what I was seeing. Kale didn't share my hesitation. He surged forward, shoving through anyone in the way. He grabbed her arm, almost upsetting the tray, which was saved by the person next to her. Kale literally dragged her off the couch.

She was a mess. Her hair was unkempt, and makeup smears lined her red-rimmed eyes. She looked at me as if she couldn't decide if I was real or not. Then her gaze traveled over Kale, and she swore.

"What the hell are you guys doing here?" She stumbled along beside Kale, trying to pull away but too fucked up to succeed.

"What does it look like? Dragging your drugged-up ass out of here." I was fuming, but I was also scared. Never had I seen Jez in such rough shape.

"I'm not ready to leave." She slapped at Kale, but it was a futile attempt. "Just go home and leave me alone. Please."

"We're not leaving without you." Kale's tone was hard, but his eyes gleamed with a softness I only saw when he looked at Jez. He was worried too.

Jez struggled with Kale as he dragged her from the room. Just the one person who was not entirely human bothered to get involved.

"What's going on here?" The guy sauntered over to me with a cocky sneer. He smelled human, but something about his energy convinced me there was more to him. It was vague though, hard to place. Definitely something I'd never encountered before. Whatever it was, it felt dark.

"Save it," I snapped. "I don't know who you are; I don't really care. Jez is my friend, and she's leaving here with me. Don't get involved."

"Or what?" He challenged. "I'm Arrow, by the way. Jez is a friend of mine too. If she doesn't want to go with you, she doesn't have to."

"A friend?" I scoffed. "Really? What's her last name?"

Arrow smiled and shook his head. There was something serpentine in his dark-hazel eyes. Chains hung from his tight black leather pants. He wore a t-shirt with an upside down pentagram and a knit hat with a Dead Kennedys patch. He had about as much eyeliner smeared around his eyes as Jez did, but I think his was on purpose. With long ebony hair that fell almost to his shoulders, Arrow was sexy in a slimy rocker guy kind of way.

He got up in my face, boldly pressing in close. He spoke low, so he wouldn't be overheard. "You're not welcome here, vampire bitch. So why don't you take off and stop crashing our party?"

A few of the others present watched us with mild interest while the rest continued to snort coke and God only knows what else. I glanced at Kale who stood in the doorway with Jez tightly in his grasp. Kale looked at Arrow, then me and nodded.

I grinned into Arrow's smug face. "I don't know what you are, but I know you've got a heartbeat, and I'm guessing you bleed too. We are leaving. With Jez. Come at me again, and I'll tear your fucking throat open."

Exposing myself to everyone as something other than human wasn't my intent. So instead of a grand display of power, I opted for something more subtle. A push of force strong enough to crush the air from Arrow's lungs and double him over without laying him out flat. Then I shoved him aside and followed my friends out.

Arrow gasped and coughed, clutching his chest. But he didn't make the mistake of trying anything else. When I looked back he was watching us go, smiling through the pain. He was definitely more than human.

Jez was unsteady on her feet. Slurring her words, she mumbled a series of nonsensical phrases. Kale kept her up and moving until we reached the bottom of the stairs where she collapsed.

"Oh my God," I cried as panic seized me. "Is she going to be ok?"

We couldn't take her to a hospital. Human doctors simply could not have access to a shifter. My thoughts strayed briefly to Fox, a wolf with medical knowledge who made himself accessible to the Stony pack. I didn't want to call him unless it was life or death. It was safer for him if he wasn't involved with us at all.

Kale gathered Jez's limp form into his arms. "Stay calm, Alexa. Her heartbeat is fast but steady. I think she'll be ok. Her blood reeks of drugs and alcohol. We need to get her awake and talking. Let's get her out of here."

Kale carried Jez through the club and back to the front door. I followed, trying to force myself to breathe. Terror wrapped its cold hands around me and squeezed.

Chapter Eight

"Are you sure this is a good idea?" I asked, skeptical when we pulled into Kale's driveway with a screech of tires.

"Of course. She'll be safe here."

Together Kale and I managed to wrangle Jez out of the backseat where she'd been lying in a haphazard heap. Kale tossed me his keys before scooping Jez up and nudging the car shut with a foot. I ran ahead to unlock the front door. I wasn't convinced that either Jez or I were safe alone there with Kale. Stepping inside his house felt weird, like walking into a lion's den of my own free will.

After Kale got Jez inside, I swung the door shut and ran around trying to be useful. A quick search in the cupboards produced coffee and sugar. While the coffee brewed, I grabbed a glass of water and a towel.

Kale was around the corner from the kitchen, in the living room. Jez was sprawled on the couch, and he lightly slapped her face, trying to elicit a response.

"I'm surprised you have coffee," I commented, gazing about the room. It looked like something out of a magazine with matching couches and a coffee table set with mass-produced artwork on the walls. His house didn't look or feel lived in.

I knelt beside the couch, dampened the towel, and pressed it to Jez's face. Her breathing was haggard, and her skin was pale.

"I keep it around for the cleaning ladies that come in once a month along with a few other things. It's a piss poor attempt at maintaining a human appearance, but it works."

Kale leaned in close as we both peered at Jez in worried silence. His proximity forced me to breathe his scent of leather and cologne. A flood of memories accompanied that aroma. No good.

"I'm worried about her," I whispered, gazing down at Jez's makeup-smeared face. "I knew she was upset about losing Zoey, but I didn't think it was this bad."

"She's good at hiding her emotions. She can't hide anymore. We'll help her get through this." Kale sounded so calm, so sure. He almost made me believe it.

I smoothed Jez's hair back from her face before giving her a shake. Waking her up became more crucial with each moment she was unconscious. I needed her to talk, to ease my fears. I said a silent prayer. If Jez partied her way into an early grave, I would never forgive myself. It was because of me that Zoey had died. Lilah had been targeting my wolves. Zoey had been mine to protect after an unspoken promise I'd made her father.

"This is all my fault," I said.

"Don't start that," Kale warned. "You didn't kill Zoey, and you didn't do anything to convince Jez to snort that shit up her nose."

I pulled back one of Jez's eyelids to find her eye rolled back; her pupil, dilated and unresponsive. Slapping her face and applying a cool compress was not helping. "This isn't working. We need to do something." My voice was high with panic; my pulse pounded with adrenaline. I couldn't just sit there and watch her fade away.

Kale studied Jez, likely listening to the strange pace of her heart. I could hear it too. "Why don't you try that little healing trick you and Arys seem to be able to do?" Kale suggested. He was stone cold serious. "It might help her body regain normal function while she works that shit out of her system."

"Healing really isn't my strong suit." It sounded like a lame excuse, which we didn't have time for. He was right. "I'll try it. Are you sure you want to be here for this? It might get kind of intense." There was no nice way to skate around the subject. Healing would require calling on the power I shared with Arys. The power would draw Kale like a moth to a flame.

"I'm fine, Alexa. Really. Besides, if anything happens, you'll have more than enough juice to take me out." He shrugged like it was no big deal.

"You'd like that, wouldn't you?" I shook my head and held up a hand before he could fire back at me. "Forget I said that. You have to give me some space. Maybe go pour Jez some coffee. If you don't mind."

Kale didn't argue. He allowed me to banish him into the kitchen. I knew he wouldn't stay there long.

It was hard to get into the zone. Knowing Kale was so close made it difficult to let go of my fear and embrace the power. Jez was relying on me. I had to put the risks aside and deal with them as they came.

Placing a hand on her forehead and another on her side, I closed my eyes and focused on Jez's scattered energy. It felt rough, lacking the strong, smooth flow it should have. I aligned my energy with hers, blanketing her brokenness with my wholeness. Then I called forth the power coiled in my core. It rose up like a soft breeze, ruffling my hair. Concentrating hard on my intent, I targeted her weakness and, with a gentle push, breathed positive healing energy into her.

I couldn't do anything about the drugs in her bloodstream, but I was able to strengthen her body's response to them. Shifters process drugs and alcohol faster than humans. For her to be this screwed up, she must have really partied hard.

Healing was still new to me. I didn't use my power this way near as often as I used it to harm or defend. In that moment, joined to Jez by something bigger than us both, I could feel the power of the light. It felt right.

Being aligned with her aura the way I was, I could feel the spark of darkness burning like a hot coal, hidden beneath the raw power of her leopard. Jez's demon paternity was likely part of this emotional rollercoaster she was on. She didn't talk about it much, but the one time it had come up, she'd admitted to wondering how much of her father lay within her.

I had no answer to that. The dark entity inside her rested, quiet, almost as if it was dormant. Waiting. The prowling wildcat within Jez seemed unaware of it.

I opened my eyes to find Kale staring at me. He stood in the doorway between the rooms with a steaming mug of coffee in hand and an unmistakable hunger burning in his predatory gaze. He moved with a slow, even gait. He set the coffee on the table, careful to keep his distance.

"Sorry to interrupt."

"No worries." I broke contact with Jez, satisfied when her energy hummed with a strong vibe. Unwilling to take my gaze off Kale, I stood up to face him. "Are you ok?"

"No," he admitted, looking conflicted. "But I've got it under control."

I knew that look. There were many ways to sate that kind of longing. None of them were without an element of danger. It took so very little for self-control to slip when the power guided the craving. Guilt slithered through me. It was joined by shame.

"Willow said we should talk. Apparently, there is something you need to tell me." Venturing into a potentially volatile subject was risky, but it was best to keep him talking.

"Did he say that? How nice of him." Kale tried to hide a smile. He and Willow had formed their own odd relationship while I was away. It definitely piqued my curiosity.

"He said that you're my second. And that Shya's been sending you to look for the scroll. Willow thinks we need to talk about that, and as much as I'd like to avoid it, I have to agree with him. So…start talking."

An amused grin spread across Kale's handsome face. Mischief shone in his eyes. It was a good indicator that he was slipping into that strange place where vampires go to hunt and kill, an inevitable side effect of being around the power I'd called. I really hoped we could just talk without me having to knock him out.

Kale seemed to be weighing his words, considering where to start or how much to tell me. Finally he said, "I stopped an assassination attempt on Arys while you were both out of town. A rebel group formed. They were plotting to kill him upon your return home. I made sure they never had a chance to try it."

He stopped, allowing me a chance to process this information. It wasn't easy to take in. I sat heavily on the end of the couch near Jez's feet and stared at him, stunned. "Why?" I asked, taking a deep, calming breath. "Why would you want to help Arys?"

"Shya instructed me to do it," he confessed, hanging his head as if ashamed. "But I didn't do it for him. I did it for you."

I swallowed hard, "Is this why I found one of your victims propped up by the front door?"

"Shya said I should make it clear to the city that I'm your second in command. The most powerful next only to you and Arys. It felt wrong when he said it. Once I started killing the rebel group, that changed. I guess not everyone is happy with that. I do want to back you, Alexa. Which is why I've been helping Shya find the scroll. You need to find it first." The smile faded from Kale's face, and he gazed at me with thinly veiled adoration. "It's not just him though. The vampires, the rebels, they're unpredictable. That incident at the Kiss when you got up close and personal with a stake…that's not over. Now that Lilah's gone, they're feeling liberated and anarchistic."

I was bombarded by thoughts and feelings. It was disconcerting to hear about the rebel group. I'd seen it before though, when a vampire had violently tried to plunge a stake in my heart while vowing to never be my slave. "I'm not Lilah. I don't want to rule over them. I just want to maintain a sense of order. It would be nice to have just one week where someone didn't want to kill me." I was overwhelmed by everything he'd just said. He could have let the rebel group take their shot at Arys. I wouldn't blame him for wanting that. "Shya must know that he can't trust you. Be careful, Kale."

"That's just another reason why we need to keep our distance. He's watching us."

"I know. He proved that earlier tonight when he sent Brook to Father Andrew's church. He's going to make it tough to hunt this thing down." I chewed my lower lip, lost in thought. There had to be a way to escape Shya's watchful eye. "He thinks I'm going to die before he has a chance to use me as a sacrifice. Is it wrong that I kind of want it to happen?"

Kale frowned. "You don't mean that. Giving in isn't like you. Don't you dare go down without a fight."

I laughed softly. "If it wouldn't drive you crazy, I would hug you right now. Thank you for caring in spite of everything."

"Don't thank me." He waved away my gratitude. "I'm not a good guy. I wanted to let them try for Arys. Believe me, it was hard not to join in on that action."

"I know," I said, nodding in understanding. "But you didn't. So you are a good guy. Still."

Kale smiled then, a wistful action that reminded me of the sweet-natured guy he used to be. "Let's not kid ourselves. I haven't been a good guy in over five hundred years."

Before I could tell him how wrong he was, Jez sat up suddenly with a loud gasp. She groped about in a disoriented stupor. "I think I'm gonna be sick," she groaned, falling off the couch with a thud.

Kale and I both sprang into action. We got her up and moving toward the bathroom. Her balance was off, and she leaned heavily on me.

"It's ok. I've got this," I said, waving Kale away. "I'll take care of the hair holding. Do you have something she can wear after I throw her in the shower?"

"Yeah, no problem. I'll put some clean sheets on the bed too."

No sooner had I gotten Jez into the bathroom and closed the door than she proceeded to vomit. I stood close enough to hold her hair back while she clutched the toilet.

Jez struggled to catch her breath. "Oh my God. Am I dead? Is this hell?"

"Not even close. It's Kale's bathroom."

Another round of vomiting had me cringing. It was amazing the things people would do to themselves in the search for escape. I was no exception. I'd done my fair share of stupid shit.

"I feel like death. I'm such a fucking idiot." She clutched the porcelain in a white-knuckled grip. Her body trembled, and she moaned, "Just put me out of my misery, Lex. Please. I'm begging you."

"You're starting to sound like Kale." I winced when my voice echoed in the acoustics of the bathroom. "Sorry, Jez. You're going to have to suffer before you'll feel like yourself again. Come on. Let's get you into the shower."

The sounds of agony and distress never stopped. Every move she made had Jez groaning and gasping with more than a little cursing thrown in the mix. I dug around in the cupboard under the sink and managed to find some mouthwash and a comb. Kale was definitely lacking in the way of female-friendly vanity items.

After getting Jez dressed in some sweatpants and a t-shirt provided by Kale, I dragged the comb through her hair while she sat on the closed toilet lid. "Are you feeling any better?" I asked, carefully picking my way through her golden tangles.

"I feel like I've been turned inside out. It's unbearable." Her voice was soft, lacking her usual feisty enthusiasm.

"You know, eventually I'm going to grill you about tonight. But I'll give you time to sleep it off and recover first. Then I'll expect some honest answers."

"I suppose that's fair." Jez was quiet for a moment. "Thanks, Lex. For taking care of me tonight."

"That's what friends do. I love you, Jez. Which is why I'm so damn worried about what I saw tonight. You really scared us."

She was quiet for so long that I grew worried. I finished up with her hair and stood there, searching for the right words. Jez turned to face me, tears glistening in her glassy, green eyes.

"I don't know what's going on with me. I don't even know who I am lately." Jez looked so forlorn, so lost. "I'm scared."

I pulled her into a hug, clutching her trembling frame tight against me. My wolf was eager to soothe her. Our beasts shared a connection that required no words. I would have given just about anything to ease her pain.

"I'm here for you," I promised. "So is Kale. We'll walk with you through this."

"I was just starting to let myself get used to the idea of having someone who understood me. Someone who I didn't have to play human for. We had this connection. It was better than I could have hoped. And then it was gone." Tears spilled down Jez's cheeks, and she clung to me like a lost child.

It took all my strength to blink back the tears of empathy that welled up. I wanted to fall apart with her. "I'm sorry," I whispered, stroking her wet hair. "I'm so sorry."

The night was fading fast by the time I got her into bed in the guest room on the main floor. I knew that Kale had a downstairs bedroom, but judging by the heavily covered window, it appeared as if he'd been spending some time there.

Jez was still pretty out of it, mumbling things that made sense to nobody but her. Being in Kale's bedroom was awkward. Even more so when Jez begged me to lay with her.

I glanced at Kale who stood silent in the doorway. He wore a pained expression as he gazed at Jez. "You should stay with her a while. I'll wait in the living room." He disappeared, leaving me staring after his shadow as it retreated down the hall.

Shrugging out of my jacket, I laid it and the Dragon Claw on a chair near the door. Then I crawled in beside Jez and pulled her close. She settled in against me, her fingers curling in my hair.

It shook me to the bone to see her this way. She was one of the strongest people I knew. Nobody was safe from the repercussions of love. Cheesy romance movies paint a picture of a big love moment followed by a happily ever after. That simply isn't reality. Love comes at a price, and it is never without challenge.

Lying there in Kale's bed with the feel of him all around me, I thought about the many trials and complications of love. If only it were as cut and dried as the whole boy meets girl crap.

Jez mumbled, a soft murmur into the pillow. "Don't leave me alone with him. It's not safe. He's a killer."

"Jezzy, your blood reeks like a cocktail of poisons. There's nothing enticing about it. Besides, it's Kale. Of course you're safe with him. I promise."

"He's like Jekyll and Hyde. I never know which one I'm dealing with." Her eyes were closed, and she began to breathe deeply as slumber dragged her under.

I said nothing, knowing that Kale could hear us. In no time Jez began to snore softly. I stayed until I was sure she wouldn't wake up, then carefully disengaged myself from her grasp. Trying to be quiet, I moved with silent footsteps to gather my jacket and dagger. With a look back at Jez, I hoped I was doing the right thing by leaving her with Kale. He loved her like a sister, and though he'd hurt her once, I trusted his devotion to her was strong enough to keep that from happening again.

I hoped that when I was vampire I would still see her as family, as pack. Though we were very different beasts, we shared so much. I never wanted to lose that.

Kale was in the living room, staring out the window at the fading night. "Do you need a ride?" He didn't look at me when he spoke. There was a hard set to his shoulders. He was stiff and uncomfortable.

"No, I'll call a cab. You should stay with Jez." I hesitated, watching him closely. "You know she didn't mean that, Kale. She's not really afraid of you."

When he continued to avoid my gaze, I knew for certain that's what had him so tightly coiled. "She should be. I've given her good reason to fear me."

"It's just the drugs talking."

"Is it?" He did look at me then. His mismatched eyes were haunted.

"Who was that guy back at The Spirit Room?" I asked, hoping to redirect his focus. "Or more importantly, *what* was he? Is there something going on there that we should be paying more attention to?"

Kale shook his head. "Don't worry about The Spirit Room. Things will take care of themselves there. Keep your attention on what matters. Shya and the rebel vampires. The guy getting high with Jez is a nephilim. The offspring of an angel or demon and a human. Nothing to worry about for the most part."

I frowned and pursed my lips in thought. I wasn't sure I agreed with that. Kale was right though; it wasn't my problem. Not right now anyway. I had enough to deal with.

"We have to keep Jez away from there," I said. "I felt something inside her during the healing. The dark part of her that is demon. It's in there, and it's waiting for something. Taunting death with guys like that can't be good for her."

Kale's interest piqued. His eyes widened, and he nodded. "If he goes near Jez again, I'll kill him myself. I don't give a shit who his daddy is."

"Good." I was satisfied with that, though I couldn't help but hope it didn't come to that.

"I'll call my cleaning lady and have her bring some groceries over. Jez will be safe here." Determination shone in his eyes. Again it was a tiny but reassuring glimpse of Kale's sane side.

"I know."

"I hate that she fears me."

A question burned on the tip of my tongue, one that I could not bite back. "And what about me? What about when I fear you?" I think I was hoping for more reassurance, seeking the Kale I longed for.

His expression changed in an instant. Gone was the friendly concern for Jez. Replacing it was a mask of malevolence. "I love it," he said with a deadly, stone cold seriousness.

"You said you want to back me," I challenged, trying to understand the many faces of Kale. "How can you do that when you're on this nutjob mission to destroy yourself? Does being my second affect your promise?"

Kale's promise to force me to end him hung over my head, a constant shadow that hovered in the back of my mind. I kept expecting it to blow over. It never did. Always we somehow came back to it.

"No. It stands." There was a dramatic pause as we stared at one another. "I'm yours, Alexa. And I'm here for you. But once it's all over, you have to set me free."

That was my cue to leave. I wasn't ready to have this argument. Besides, I didn't trust myself around Kale. The urge to smack him was as strong as the urge to kiss him. Would just a little taste of that honey-sweet energy be so bad?

The answer was a resounding yes. So I lurched into motion, careful to avoid Kale's personal space as I headed for the door.

"Take care of Jez. I'll call you later." I was relieved when he didn't follow me.

Once outside I called a taxi and paced the length of Kale's block, waiting.

Chapter Nine

It was almost dawn when I got home. No sooner had I stepped foot onto my property than I knew with absolute certainty that there were two vampires and a werewolf inside my house.

With a groan, I shoved the door open. I kicked off my shoes, closed and locked the door, then made my way down the long front hall to the kitchen and living room at the back of the house. There I found Arys, Jenner, and Shaz gathered around the island in an intense discussion. They looked up at my approach, each falling silent in turn.

"Did you find Jez?" Shaz asked with a slight sniff in my direction. "You smell like her. Is she ok?"

"You stink like Sinclair too," Arys added, his expression grim. The forced calm and the glint in his eyes conveyed his irritation loud and clear. He was spoiling for a fight, and I'd just arrived. He must have been stewing a while.

"We found her. And she'll be fine. Thank you for asking, Arys." I said his name with annoyance. "She was partying at The Spirit Room with a bunch of humans and a nephilim. We found her snorting coke. She's at Kale's now sleeping it off."

Shaz swore softly. "Damn. I'm sorry to hear that."

"That one is a loose cannon," Jenner said. "I saw it the moment I met her."

"I hardly think you're in a position to make that kind of judgment call. Jez is suffering from the loss of a lover. It's normal for her to act out. She needs help, and she'll get it." I glared at Jenner. "Why are you here anyway?"

Arys jumped in before I could really lay into Jenner. "I thought it best for us all to stay together. You shouldn't be alone right now. It's not safe."

There were many ways I could respond to that. Right off the bat I wanted to beat him over the head with my shoulder bag. Instead, I dropped the bag on the island and shrugged out of my jacket before going to the fridge.

"That's hilarious, Arys. Really. You're cracking me up." My sarcasm dripped as I grabbed a bottle of water and turned back to face him. "Seriously though, what the hell is Jenner doing in my house?"

"Hey," Jenner protested with hands up in mock outrage. "I welcomed you into my nightclub. It's practically a home to me."

"You also forced me to get on stage in that same nightclub for your enjoyment." I flipped him my middle finger before taking a large drink of water. I was dehydrated and suddenly starving. Healing took a lot out of me. I would need to replenish the energy I'd expended metaphysically as well.

"Yes, and we know how that turned out, don't we? I'm pretty sure you got the better deal that night." The calm but intense hatred that spread across Jenner's face was deadly.

"It's not a joke, Alexa," Arys broke in. He shot a warning glare Jenner's way before refocusing on me. "Things are in motion. Shya's going to drastic lengths to get that scroll, and we can't be sure how far he'll take it. We can't afford to underestimate anyone right now."

I moved about the kitchen, pulling a pan from beneath the stove and fetching eggs from the fridge. If I didn't feed the mortal hunger, it would worsen the metaphysical hunger, something I didn't want to deal with in a house filled with supernatural males.

"So you think that the three of you can offer me some kind of protection against Shya himself?" I asked, slicing up a tomato. I briefly entertained the idea of flinging the knife at Jenner but decided against it. "Come on, Arys. You know better than that."

I could feel his heavy gaze upon me as I prepared my sandwich. Like usual, there was something Arys wasn't saying. I knew him so well.

"I know that we can't afford to be careless. We're not taking any chances with your safety." Arys spoke as if his word was law. The usual. He had to know I was going to rip him a new one later when we didn't have an audience.

"What are you going to do, Arys? Follow me everywhere in case Shya pops in? And then what? You can't fight off that demon." It wasn't my intent to insult his manhood or his good intentions. Still, he wasn't being realistic.

He sat there scowling at me with a storm raging in his midnight eyes. I was dreadfully aware of the other two men watching our exchange. That's when it hit me.

"Arys," I began, speaking softly, like I would to a skittish animal. "Is it really Shya you're trying to protect me from by having them here? Or is it you?"

"Alexa," he spoke my name like a warning. He offered me nothing else. No denial or confirmation, and that was confirmation enough for me.

Jenner sat there smirking, enjoying the awkward moment of pending conflict. I wanted to hit him.

Shaz was quiet, watching us without missing a thing. He knew how quickly the conflict between Arys and I could boil over, although he'd never seen the worst of it.

"Look, Lex," Shaz jumped in. "It's just temporary. Until we know more about the scroll's whereabouts. Maybe we can't keep you safe from Shya. But we can damn sure try."

It was obvious to me that Shaz was trying to get me to back off Arys. I'd hit a nerve that Shaz seemed to be aware of.

"Fine, I get it." I relented, letting it go until I got Arys alone. "You want to keep me safe, and I can appreciate that. But you guys can't hover over me all the time. I need my space, or I'll go crazy."

"You can't go off alone," Arys insisted. His brow was set in a hard frown. The darkness filled his eyes, a warning of the wrath to come.

Time was running out. My death was fast approaching. I couldn't waste precious minutes arguing with him. "I know you want to find a way to stop Shya, but no matter what happens with him, I am still facing death. Gabriel saw it. Again, tonight. So instead of finding a way to avoid it, you need to find a way to accept it. I have."

My proclamation hung in the kitchen, an open challenge issued to my other half. Arys's struggle was understandable. For over a hundred years, he'd known I would die at his hand. Though he tried to downplay it, I knew he craved my death as much as he feared it. If the tables were turned, I'd be losing my mind.

I dropped the knife on the counter and went to him. He was tense when I pressed in close, slipping my arms around his neck. "Please, don't fight what's meant to happen."

"Is it though?" he questioned. "How can your death be something I simply accept as what is meant to be? I just can't wrap my mind around it being a good thing."

"You don't have to. I don't get it either. But I'm starting to figure out that the more I question things, the more questions it creates. The answers reveal themselves in time." I kissed him, a soft press of my lips to his. The power humming within him teased my senses.

Jenner snorted. "Well, isn't that downright disgustingly poetic?"

I pulled away from Arys, anger driving me. I grabbed Jenner's hand and forced my fingers between his. My power might have been weakened, but it wasn't dead inside me. It took very little effort to connect with his energy.

"I have more than enough assholes in my life right now, Jenner," I hissed, jerking hard on his aura. "If I have an opening in the future for another, you'll be the first to know. Until then, keep your snarky comments to yourself, or I'll be forced to do bad things to you. Got it?"

He gave a vigorous nod and tried to pull away. I held tight, willing to break his fingers if I had to. Finding his heady energy to be just what I needed, I drew it into me, sighing as it filled the depleted source inside me.

A strangled groan escaped Jenner. He stopped resisting and actually leaned into me. A cool breeze picked up, cloaking us in a blanket of power.

Jenner tugged on my hand in an attempt to bring my wrist to his mouth. With fangs bared, he went for the throbbing pulse. I hit him with a slap of power before he could pierce my flesh. It knocked him off the island stool, and both he and the stool hit the floor with a clatter.

I wasn't done with him yet though. Running on instinct, I stood over him, preventing him from getting up. "Now," I said, crouching down to meet his pale-blue gaze. "Why are you really here?"

Jenner blinked at me in confusion, then he spoke as if in a trance. "To help Arys. He's my brother, and I do love him, despite our differences over the years."

"You do realize he's the one who insisted I enthrall you, don't you?"

"Yes."

"Then stop acting like you have some vendetta to settle with me. You got off easy compared to some people."

Staring into Jenner's wide eyes, I felt empowered. Glamouring him hadn't been my intent, but it was a nice side effect. As long as he was talking, I needed to make the most of it.

"Has Sloane come back yet?" I continued, pushing for whatever I could get from Jenner. "Do you know where she is?"

"No," he said almost robotically. "She's kept on the move because Arys has been around."

"If she comes back, I want you to kill her."

"Alexa, that's enough." Arys moved so fast his stool bounced from leg to leg but didn't fall. He caught my arm and dragged me away from Jenner. "You can manipulate him because he's yours. You have no right to abuse that."

With both hands I gave Arys a shove. Rage exploded forth without the warning of a slow boil. "Don't you dare talk to me about abusing power," I shouted, my voice echoing in the otherwise quiet house. "You're the most manipulative vampire I've ever known. You don't get to make the rules and break them. It's one or the other."

Arys threw both hands up and backed away. "Calm down, Alexa. It's late. You're tired. We need to be united right now, not divided in conflict."

"Why not? It's the story of our entire destiny, isn't it? The light and the dark, unable to exist without the other and yet doomed to eternal conflict and destruction. It's got to make it easier for you to finally kill me."

Arys clenched his jaw and swore. He continued to back away into the living room, as if afraid he would lose control.

I was as stressed out as he was. It was going to devour us. The best thing for me to do was leave. We both needed to calm down before things escalated. I removed the belt holding the dagger around my waist and tossed the Dragon Claw onto the couch. Then I headed for the sliding glass patio door before Arys could stop me.

"Don't go," he said, watching me with a pained expression. "Please."

The wolf surged forward, beating back the essence of vampire clouding my thoughts and emotions. The beast demanded to be freed, and I longed to answer.

The sun had risen high enough to trap the vampires in the house. Only Shaz could come after me.

"Don't follow me," I pleaded, begging Shaz to heed my request. "I need to run. Alone."

Abandoning the food on the counter, I stepped out onto the patio, drinking in the sunlight even though it burned my eyes. Blood tears welled up, but I blinked them away.

"Fuck that," I muttered to myself, feeling betrayed by my emotions. I was trying so hard to downplay the severity of what lay ahead for me. It wasn't working. Standing there in the sun, terror shook me. I couldn't bear the thought of never again feeling its warmth.

As I walked through the backyard, I tugged off my clothing and let it fall to the ground. Then I unleashed the wolf, finding freedom when my four paws touched the yellowing grass.

Leaving Arys trapped inside the house was just another way of testing his limits. It would make him crazy.

This was what I needed right now. Vampires and demons couldn't touch me in the forest while the sun reigned in the sky. Nature called my name, and I answered.

My destination was the small but active pond, teeming with tiny creatures living in and around it. It was my happy place. The only place I could go to find solace that didn't involve making someone bleed. I ran at full speed to the forest behind my house. Weaving through trees, bounding over fallen logs, and listening to the constant chatter of birds overhead, I was home.

I kept expecting Arys to touch my mind, to beckon me back to the house. He didn't. My heart pained at our constant fighting. We needed to maintain a united front. Somehow. It wasn't going to be easy, but when was it ever? If we allowed ourselves to be torn apart before facing our greatest challenge, we would never be able to conquer it.

Being wolf was necessary for my sanity. It wouldn't be long before the vampire within me was fully manifested. As much as I'd like to pretend I was ready for that, I knew I never would be.

I found a nice patch of shade beneath some trees and curled up beside the pond. For a long time I lay there, wishing the human thoughts away, watching the birds hop around beside the water.

Shaz did a good job of staying downwind. He lurked far enough away that I couldn't smell him. I could feel him though.

I wasn't mad. If anything, I was reassured. The sun was high in the sky when at last slumber tugged at my eyelids. I gave in to the pull, happy to be among nature. Without the wolf to keep me balanced, I would have gone off the deep end long ago.

So much was yet to come. And despite the power I possessed and the reputation I had earned, I was afraid.

* * * *

It was mid-afternoon when I padded up to the house. I felt better. Calm and ready to go forward.

Shaz was on the couch with a blanket, as if he'd been there all day when in fact I knew better. He couldn't have been there more than fifteen minutes. Already he breathed deep, his chest rising and falling in the steady rhythm of sleep. Couldn't say I blamed him. I was tired too.

I clutched my clothing to my chest and with silent steps, made my way upstairs. My chances of running into Jenner were slim. The sunlight, which bathed the stairwell through an upper hall window, prevented that. I could sense him at the end of the hall, in the guest room. He'd be trapped there until sundown.

Arys looked up expectantly when I entered the bedroom. Leaning against the headboard, he held a sketchpad in one hand and a pencil in the other. He was nude from the waist up. The blanket pooled in his lap, hiding what lay beneath.

"Feel any better?" he asked. There was no sign of the tightly wound vampire he'd been earlier. He too seemed to be calmer though his was a solemn calm.

"A little. I needed to clear my head after a long night. The run helped." I tossed my clothes into the laundry basket in the corner and hit the shower.

I rushed through shampooing and conditioning my long blonde locks. It was easier said than done. Sleeping in the forest had been nice, but it wasn't the deep slumber I needed. First, Arys and I needed to talk. I emerged feeling both refreshed and exhausted. After towel drying my hair, I slid onto the bed facing Arys.

With his sketchpad forgotten, his gaze traveled over my body. He lingered on my thighs, my breasts, and the pulse beating in my neck. Then he dragged his gaze to mine. Our eyes locked, and my breath caught. Every damn time. Arys had only to look at me with that fire smoldering in the depths of his dark blues, and I came undone.

I took the sketchpad from him and set it aside. A detailed sketch of the fountain at the Bellagio Hotel in Las Vegas graced the page. It made me do a double take. I was continuously impressed by Arys's artistic side.

I slipped beneath the blanket and straddled him. Grabbing both of his hands, I leaned in for a kiss. It was tender and warm despite the slight chill to his skin. I wondered when he'd last fed.

A spark became a flame as our light and dark powers danced together. I wanted so badly to lose myself in him right then and there. With great difficulty, I broke off the kiss and leaned back so I could peer into his eyes.

"I'm sorry about what went on downstairs earlier." I stroked a hand down his face. "I was taking my frustrations out on you and Jenner. I shouldn't have."

"Don't apologize. We both deserve a good ass kicking anyway." Arys chuckled, a low, sexy sound that sent a rush of heat to my groin. "I just wish I could keep you safe. But I know that's not possible. None of us are ever safe."

He pulled me against him in a tight hug. I breathed in his scent of cologne and hair products, finding it comforting and more than a little enticing. Our bodies touched in all the right places. His skin was smooth beneath my fingers as I explored his body. My senses were ablaze.

"Why can't it be like this all the time?" I sighed. I could feel him inside me as well as beneath me. The supernatural force that flowed through us was intense but subtle, like a low burning flame. "It seems like the only time we're not fighting each other is when we're fighting someone else or making love."

"It's always been like that. Besides, how boring would it be if we were one of those long walks on the beach, holding hands in the moonlight kind of couples?" Arys pressed his face to the side of my neck, breathing deeply of my scent. He bit me, a pinch of fangs that stung but didn't break skin. "I love that look you get in your eyes when you're fuming mad. It gives me a raging—"

"Arys," I admonished with a blush. "Cut it out. Be serious."

"I am serious."

It wasn't the first time Arys had admitted to getting a hard on at the rush of my anger. To be fair, I'd responded with the same desire to his violent emotional outbursts. From sorrow to frenzied bloodlust and everything in between, we thrived on all of it.

"You know we have to see this through." The words almost stuck in my throat. I feared starting another fight, but we had to talk about this before it was too late. "You will have to kill me. There has to be a reason for it."

"Aww, Alexa, don't go there. Please."

I clasped his face in my hands and forced him to see how serious I was. "Arys, I need to know I can trust you to do what has to be done."

"How can that be something that has to be done? I just can't wrap my mind around it." He shook his head and dropped his gaze to avoid meeting my eyes.

"That's because you want it, and you're ashamed of that. It scares me too." With a hand under his chin, I forced his head up. "But I can honestly say that I would rather die in your arms than however Shya plans to do it."

Arys groaned. "Fuck."

"It's going to be ok. I'm sure of it." Saying it didn't convince me. My words were false, lacking conviction.

"Liar."

He kissed me again, and I gave myself over to it. Fear was debilitating and useless. I would not be ruled by it.

I adjusted myself atop him, excited by the way he felt between my legs. "Let's not live in that moment. I want to enjoy this one."

The sensation of Arys's hands on my body swept the worries from my mind. He touched me with a hunger that elicited a small quiver from me. The man oozed sensuality. I longed to get drunk on that potent elixir.

I clung to him, simply reveling in the way he felt. It was hard to keep my thoughts from straying to what was to come. I did believe deep down that our purpose had yet to be realized. However, the old witch Arys had spoken with had told him that the day he killed me, we would destroy one another. I could only assume it meant that the yin yang balance between us would be ruined. The darkness would consume me, and the light would fade. Unless someone sacrificed themselves for me, willingly taking my darkness. It was something I could never ask another to do.

I had only recently learned that was even a possibility. It was best kept quiet. Nobody needed to know. It was ultimately irrelevant.

Misery threatened to overwhelm me, so I kissed Arys with an undying passion to beat it back. The bedside lamp flickered in response. I reached down between our bodies to find him ready for me.

As I guided him to the inviting entrance between my thighs, I stared intently into him. I wanted to watch his face as I took him inside me. His expression changed from one of pensive anticipation to sheer pleasure. Having Arys deep within me was as tormenting as it was satisfying. How much longer would we have this? Would things change when I no longer belonged to the light?

"Stop thinking," Arys whispered, sliding a hand up into my hair. "Just be here with me."

I nodded, speechless, though words were not necessary. I set the pace, taking him into me again and again. His fingers tightened in my pale tresses, and his gaze dropped to where our bodies joined.

Known for his impatience, Arys rolled us over so that I lay beneath him. He nudged my legs farther apart and thrust deep. We moved together, a smooth rhythm that we perfected a little more every time we did this dance.

The sound of our moans and cries filled the room. The lamp flickered again and went out. The power expanded, filling the room with a warm breeze. It caressed my naked flesh even as it flowed through me. It seemed to be everywhere. I was empowered, feeling like I could take on the world with such a supernatural force thrumming through me. Riding the high like I was, victory felt possible. Hell, it felt inevitable. Tapped into Arys and all that we shared, I felt in my core that Shya didn't know who he was dealing with. Perhaps neither did I.

"I love you, Alexa." Arys's mouth was warm on my skin. "If I could trade places with you in all of this, I would."

He sought out that sensitive place beneath my ear, the one that made me purr like a kitten. A tickle raced down my spine at the touch of his tongue. There was a desperation to his touch that startled me. I knew what he wanted though he was reluctant to feed that hunger.

"I know you would," I murmured. I clasped a handful of his hair and turned my head to offer him my neck. "Don't hold back with me, Arys. I trust you."

He shook his head and made a strangled sound that was both a moan and a curse. "You can't. I don't even trust myself."

His actions grew frenzied. The pace of his thrusts quickened. He exuded anguish, which mingled with his total adoration to create a dizzying blend of emotion. Arys was at war with himself.

The vampires in my life were very intent in their insistence that they couldn't be trusted. The shitty part was that they were right. Vampires in general were unpredictable and dangerous. It didn't change the way I felt though.

"I am yours. Claim me."

The fight went out of him, and he gave in to the unholy need to spill my blood. His fangs pierced my flesh with vicious aggression, forcing a small cry from me. Arys caught the crimson flow on his tongue. I fell headlong into the dizzying wave of power that crashed through us.

Being there with him feasting upon my body, I couldn't shake the tiny voice warning me that he could not be trusted. It felt both right and wrong. We were made to exist together in a state of perpetual give and take. But when would that all come crashing to a halt?

Arys licked and sucked at my punctured vein. A low, sexy groan in my ear sent a tickle down my back, and I laughed softly. He raised his head to look at me with my blood smeared on his lips and fire in his eyes.

He searched my eyes, seeking something, condemnation perhaps. "Will you promise me one thing? After it's all said and done, when you're vampire, promise you'll forgive me."

"Arys," I said, touching his face. "That's not necessary."

"I'm serious. I need you to do this for me. Just say the words. Even if you don't mean them."

There was a hardness in his gaze that struck a nerve within me. He was projecting a tough shell, trying to keep me from seeing how vulnerable this was making him. He could hide his true emotion from anyone else but never from me. I felt his fear as if it were my own.

I nodded and pressed my lips to his. "Ok. I promise. And I mean that."

Satisfied with my answer, Arys rolled over to lie beside me, burying his face in the nook of my neck so he could catch the last few drops to slip from the wounds. His arm was tight across my middle.

I cuddled in close, stroking a hand through his disheveled hair. There was so much he wasn't saying, but he didn't have to. I recognized his worry, his trepidation at what was to come.

His worry was mine too.

Chapter Ten

"Don't let her out of your sight tonight, please," I pleaded with Kale, glad we were on the phone so I didn't have to look into those beautiful eyes. "I know she says she's fine, but she isn't."

Kale sighed, a heavy dramatic sound just for my benefit. "Fine. But she's going to be pissed."

"I would take over for you, but I'm going with Willow to look for the scroll. Or maybe we're just going on a wild goose chase. Hell if I know." I clutched the phone tight so I could hear Kale over the noisy din of The Wicked Kiss.

I sat at the bar alone waiting for Willow and sneaking glances toward the back hall where I waited for Arys and Jenner to emerge. Grudgingly I'd agreed to allow Jenner to feed from the willing victims at the club. I didn't have much of a choice. I couldn't very well have him killing in my city. The FPA didn't need more shit to pin on me.

Shaz had got an early start on searching for the scroll, insisting that he'd be able to cover more ground alone. His argument had been that he wouldn't be as closely monitored by the demons as Arys and I. I had agreed though I suspected that avoiding vampires and The Wicked Kiss had been his true intent.

"We should join you," Kale volunteered. "It'll give Jez a reason to go out. She's been lying on the couch staring at the television since we got to her place."

"You don't have to do that. Take her to a movie or something. And make her eat something healthy." It was a poor attempt at keeping them busy, but I didn't want to risk either of them over this.

"Why don't I let her decide?" There was a pause as Kale relayed my plans to Jez. I could hear her voice muffled in the background. Then Kale spoke again. "She wants to help you. Where should we start?"

I eyed the liquor bottles stacked behind the bar and licked my lips. Not tonight. I needed to be alert and fully functional.

"We're all splitting up. Why don't you two take the south side since you're there already? Check in with me in a couple of hours, unless you find something. Not that we even really know what the hell we're looking for." Frustrated, I twisted a lock of hair around a finger, shooting glances toward the back. What was taking them so long back there? And did they really need to go together?

"I had my suspicions about this too," Kale said, sounding so much like the calm, cool Kale I used to know. It was uncanny. It was also an illusion. "Still, Shya didn't start to really look for this thing until Lilah was bound and almost out of the picture. It's got to be worth finding."

"Yeah, I know. I just think there's got to be a better way. Someone has to know something."

"Well yeah, Lilah did. And now she's gone." Kale turned away to speak to Jez who was whining about needing a drink. "I have to go wrestle a wine bottle away from this wild cat. Talk to you in a bit."

An icy cold sensation stabbed through me, sharp and sudden, giving way to the familiar pang of bloodlust. The rise of vampire hunger hit me fast and hard, without warning. "Right. Talk to you later." I ended the call before Kale could detect the breathlessness in my voice. It felt like I'd been punched in the stomach.

I stuffed the phone into my pocket and spun on the barstool to face the crowd. Eyeing the human patrons like they were helpless gazelle grazing unawares, I scanned them each in turn with predatory intrigue.

The need to devour someone was strong. Before I could slip from the stool and melt into the throng of lively prey, a vision flashed behind my eyes. Blood, blue eyes, Jenner. Arys's voice whispered through my mind, calling me to him.

The hunger was getting stronger every time it hit me. My conscious control was growing fragile, along with what remained of my mortal strength. Shya was right. The power was harming me. It was running rampant through me, consuming the last part of me that was remotely human.

It should have been a sad or terrifying realization. As I glided down the back hall with an undead grace that was not yet my own, I felt only eager anticipation. My dark vampire called me, and I responded.

Arys and Jenner were in Harley's old room at the far end of the hall. The room had been given a makeover, but that didn't stop me from hesitating outside the door. It was impossible to go into that room without remembering everything that had taken place inside.

What was I doing? I came back to myself long enough to question how I'd so quickly gone from the club to the back rooms. It was a blur.

I backed away from the door, unwilling to discover what was going on inside. I knew Arys well enough to know walking away was safer than opening the door. Somehow I found the strength to retreat.

The sound of the door opening stopped me in my tracks. With building apprehension, I turned to find Arys in the threshold. He beckoned to me with a finger and a wicked grin.

Another step back. If I could just keep moving.

"Um, any chance you're almost done in there?" My words were hollow, lacking conviction. Even as I inched away, my lungs filled with the cloying human scents of blood, fear, and lust. It was as nauseating as it was enticing.

"Come inside." Arys stared at me, perplexed, as if he couldn't decide if I were prey or predator.

"I don't want to. Not with Jenner." Fear rose up to suffocate me, choking off my reply. Anxiety crushed me as I faced my future. It terrified me. "Try not to spend the whole night in there."

Arys's eyes were a deep, drowning black due to his dilated pupils. He was walking on clouds, and I was quaking, torn between bloodlust and the struggle for control. Without moving from his place in the doorway, he reached out to me with a metaphysical touch, draping me in the midnight velvet that was his thrall.

"Don't," I whispered, eyes wide as I fought the urge to go to him. He was luring me in, seducing me without a touch. It was mesmerizing and held the promise of pleasure and satisfaction.

Shame slapped me like an unseen hand. This was what Kale felt in my presence. I wanted to feel bad. I knew that I should. Instead, I felt empowered. And then guilty.

It took everything I had to break free from Arys's thrall. It was very much like fighting against myself. When my feet began to move, I turned to rush back the way I'd come. And ran straight into Arys.

I hadn't seen him move. He was just there in front of me, blocking my path. He reached to steady me, but I stepped out of his grasp. Slowly, Arys advanced on me, driving me back toward the room.

His gaze dropped to my neck where only the faintest pink mark remained from his bite. He was riding the high, seeking the thrill anywhere he could find it. It was a powerful feeling that knew nothing of rationale. It was all about the gratification of getting off on power and blood.

"Why are you fighting so hard?" Arys drew closer; his steps, slow and calculated. "This is a bad time to have a change of heart."

"I'm scared."

"I know. The smell of it is absolutely divine."

"I'm not ready," I all but shouted. There was a sudden ringing in my ears as white noise drowned out my gasps for calming breaths. "I'm not ready to be what you are." Clapping a hand to my mouth, I stared at Arys in bewildered horror. I hadn't meant for that to slip out.

He moved fast, closing the space I'd put between us. Pulling me close, he forced me to meet his gaze.

"It's too late for that. It's already inside you. Fighting it will only drive you mad." He kissed me then, slipping his tongue into my mouth. The taste of blood was tangy, silencing my unspoken protest.

I almost caved. The temptation was nearly more than I could stand. Digging deep, I found the will to resist. My fear was stronger than the hunger. This time.

I shoved away from Arys, holding up a hand to ward him off when he reached for me again. A blue and gold psi ball hovered in my palm.

"I'm going to wait for Willow outside. Don't kill anyone. That's a demand not a request." I turned my back on him, ready to slam him with the psi ball if he tried to stop me. He didn't.

Arys watched me go in silence. This was going to come up later. I was sure of it.

Forcing me to do something I wasn't ready for wasn't his intent. I knew that. Hell, I'd done it before. More times than I'd like to admit. It was the clock counting down the minutes left in my mortal life that had put the fear in me. It was harsh, unnerving, and entirely unwelcome.

My stomach clenched and rolled. I returned to the club to find Willow seated at the bar. I shook my head and gestured to the door. I couldn't stay inside a moment longer, or somebody would die.

He slammed back the three tequila shots in front of him before following me out. I didn't stop until I reached my car and sat safely inside. It was blessedly free of human scents, and I took a few deep breaths to steady myself.

"Is everything ok?" Willow asked as he slid into the passenger seat. "You look pretty shaken up."

"I was just reminded of how dangerous it is to be in the same building as two Vegas vampires while they're on the prowl." I dug my keys out and started the car. If I didn't focus on the real goal, I'd end up in a room with two vampires and a shitload of bad choices.

Willow studied me, the light in the parking lot shining through his dirty-blond hair. He looked so human in jeans and a t-shirt; his silver wings, absent from sight.

"You know, Alexa, it's ok to be afraid. You're facing something huge. It would be more worrisome if you weren't."

His presence was an immediate comfort. I nodded, grateful to have such a voice of wisdom in my life. "I keep thinking I'm ready. The bloodlust and the power, it's been part of me for so long now. I keep expecting it to get easier, but it never does. I'm afraid of how much it will change me when there is no light left to balance out the dark." It was what I feared most, what I would not say to Arys. When I turned, the yin yang balance of light and dark would shift, becoming unbalanced.

"So you were never really meant to be a vampire. That doesn't mean you can't still be you. Fear focuses on what has yet to come. You need to be at home in the present. It's all you've ever really got. It ain't over til it's over." Willow's hand was warm on my arm as he gave it an encouraging squeeze.

A voice in the back of my mind enticed me to go back inside. So I put the car in gear and drove away. "You never cease to amaze me, Willow. What I wouldn't give to have the wisdom and insight you have."

"It's available to all. Seek and you shall find." He beamed a bright smile at me and reached to mess with the radio. "So, you and I will take downtown tonight?"

I nodded, finding strength in his positive outlook. Willow had every reason to exist in a state of sorrow and rage, yet he didn't. I couldn't blame him for spending a hell of a lot of time drinking himself numb after what he'd suffered. Still, he continued to serve his purpose. I had to do the same.

Willow kept me talking as I drove. From Shya to Jez, I vented out my thoughts and fears while he nodded and encouraged me to continue. I knew what he was doing, but the therapeutic moment was cleansing, and I needed that.

When we pulled up in front of a small but quaint church, I was in a better mood, ready to tackle the task set before me. I got out of the car with a spring to my step. I didn't know what the hell I was looking for, but I was going to do my best.

I fell into step beside Willow, eagerly approaching the little church. "I can't help but feel this is all some kind of ruse," he said. "Having us all run around the city without a real goal seems like a good way to keep us all busy."

"Agreed." I nodded. "I've had a similar thought myself."

I strode up the front step and waited for Willow to open the door from inside. He disappeared, a moment later tugging the door open. When I saw how easy it had been for him to access the place, I assumed there was nothing there to find. Of course, maybe that's what someone wanted us to think.

I went to cross the threshold, and the demon mark on my forearm burst into flames. A heavy force jerked me from my feet, throwing me clear off the church's front step. I hit the ground hard and rolled with a shriek. The flames went out, leaving my arm raw and aching. I took a deep breath and shook the hair out of my eyes. *What the fuck?*

"Are you hurt?" Willow helped me up, grabbing hold of me so he could scrutinize the black dragon. "Your arm seems fine."

"I don't think I'm hurt. Much. What the hell was that?" I stared at the church door, which slowly swung shut with an ominous thump before examining the scraped flesh on my elbow. I'd left my leather jacket in the car. Hitting the concrete walkway that hard, wearing just jeans and a tank top, friggin' hurt.

Willow shook his head and swore. "That was what Shya took your hair and blood for. A curse. He really doesn't want you finding this thing first."

"That motherfucker," I seethed. "I'm fed up with that bastard demon dictating where I can and cannot go. Who the fuck does he think he is? I can't take this shit anymore. I'm done with it." While I ranted and raved, Willow stood quietly by, waiting for me to get it out of my system. His silence seemed to fire me up even more. "You know what? I've got to do something. He can't get away with this." I stormed back to the car spewing obscenities. My mind raced, concocting a hasty plan. I was done with Shya pulling my strings.

"It's just a run of the mill demon curse, Alexa. It's not permanent. Don't let it get you so worked up. It's a waste of energy." Like always, Willow was the voice of reason.

"I can't let him get away with this anymore. It's got to stop. I'm going to go see him."

"No." Willow was just suddenly in front of me, shutting the car door as I pulled it open. "Running straight to him in a rage could be exactly what he wants. There is not a damn thing you can do until the scroll makes an appearance. Until then, it's best if you stay away from Shya."

"But, I—" My protests died as he shook his head. The need for vengeance was all consuming, demanding to be answered. Yet I knew Willow was right.

"He will come for you eventually. There is no need to rush that moment. Everything happens in its own time. Trust me."

I fell quiet, accepting his wisdom as sound despite the anger boiling over inside me. Willow knew what he was talking about. Demons were still new to me, and I didn't think I'd ever truly understand them.

I focused on taking several slow, deep breaths. The fall air was cool and crisp. After a minute I felt better, calm and even refreshed.

"Ok," I said with a nod. "I trust your judgment. I'm just at the end of my rope with this."

"I get that. Really, I do." Willow stepped away from the car. A mischievous smile graced his lips. "But since we can't do anything here, why don't we go for a drink? It looks like you could use one. Or five."

"A drink? Are you kidding me?"

I got into the car, pausing to check my phone for messages. Nothing. Arys and Jenner were probably still at the Kiss getting drunk on blood, and other things. I couldn't search anything on holy ground, apparently, so I was now back to square one.

"Let's go to Woody's and shoot some pool. You can let off some steam, then we'll track down the others and come up with a new plan."

I couldn't come up with a better idea. And a drink sounded pretty damn good to me. "You win."

Woody's Pub was a little hole in the wall that gave the illusion of an abandoned building from the outside. Willow had taken me there the first night we met. It was strange to think that he'd known me before that night. A warmth spread through me as we walked inside. I was grateful to have a friend like him.

The small sports pub was relatively busy. Most of the patrons were middle aged and up. The scent of beer, chicken wings, and Old Spice hung on the air. The TVs mounted in the corners held everyone's attention. Whether it was hockey, football, or whatever they watched, it meant nothing to me.

"Willow, hi," the bartender greeted him. "Haven't seen you in a while. Can I get you the usual?"

"The usual would be great. Double it." Willow slapped some cash on the bar and led me to a free table near a pool table at the back.

I groaned, watching him gather pool balls in preparation. "Willow, I can't drink tequila with you. That shit is toxic."

"No more toxic than that whiskey you're always hugging." He tossed me a pool cue and gestured for me to go first.

"I beg to differ."

The bartender brought over a tray of tequila shots with a saltshaker and a bowl of limes. I grimaced as Willow handed me a drink. Holding his own, he clinked our glasses together. Forgoing the salt, he tossed it back, unfazed.

I stared into the small drink, disgusted. If I never drank that shit again, it would be too soon. No sooner had that thought crossed my mind than I realized this very well could be the last time I'd ever get the chance to drink with Willow.

With that ugly thought haunting me, I drank back the shot with a noise of disgust, banged the glass on the table, and reached for a lime. Holding the slice of fruit in my teeth, I lined up my shot and slammed the cue ball. The balls broke apart, scattering across the table. I sunk two solids. Not bad.

We shot a few games of pool as we made our way through the tray of drinks. It didn't take long for me to lose track of how many I'd had. The familiar numbness set in, reminding me why so many chose to get lost this way. Before long I would exchange it solely for blood. That should've bothered me, but the tipsy haze prevented a genuine reaction.

"That's three games for me. None for you," Willow bragged, tossing the chalk at me and laughing when it bounced off my head.

"Ow, you ass." I rubbed the spot it had hit, laughing far more than was necessary. My drunken giggle was fueled by the need to laugh. I didn't do it as much as I needed to these days. It's a wonder what a good, hard belly laugh can do for the soul.

The fun ended when the door opened, and two vampires walked in. They didn't hesitate or linger, heading straight for us instead.

I exchanged a look with Willow who tightened his grip on the pool cue. I did the same, knowing it was likely my only weapon. We were in a human bar. Tossing around psi balls would only lead to more trouble.

"At last, I get to meet the ill reputed Alexa O'Brien." The tall, blond one leading the duo strode right up to me, throwing a punch that knocked me back into the pool table.

I tasted blood. "Is that the best you've got?"

Licking a smear from my bottom lip, I smashed the wooden pool cue into the side of his head. The Dragon Claw hung on my hip, but I didn't want to kill them with witnesses.

"Let me guess, you've taken it upon yourself to do something about Arys's mortal queen," I said, swinging again. He caught it this time, and we both held tight, trying to overpower the other. "You assholes need to get it through your heads that I am not the enemy."

"Anyone with the power to rule two different breeds of monster is the enemy. Especially when I'm one of them." He tried to jerk the cue from my hand, but my grip was solid.

Willow had the other vampire pressed against the wall, holding him with an arm crushing his throat. Fools. If they hadn't known what he was, they were about to find out.

"I'm not interested in ruling anyone. My interests lie in protecting this city and the secrets we all keep, which you are right now threatening to expose."

"You kill our kind," the vampire hissed, baring fangs.

"I kill those who deserve it. That isn't going to stop. If you had any sense you'd realize I can be a valuable ally." I could feel eyes upon us. We were being watched by humans. No good.

"Yes, but at what cost?"

It was hard to keep from baring my own fangs at him in return. I focused on maintaining my human appearance. "Stop with the fang display, or I'll have my friend hold you down while I yank them out of your head."

Without waiting for a response, I kicked him square in the crotch and jerked the cue from his hand. He grunted and doubled over.

His recovery was fast. He forgot about the pool cue and with an angry grunt, tossed me over the pool table where I crashed to the floor, taking a few pool balls with me.

The bartender shouted at us to take it outside. A few shouts and jeers rang out from those watching. This idiot vampire was going to expose us all.

"Should I take him outside?" Willow asked, nodding to the one he held pinned.

We didn't have much of a choice. I gave him a slight nod before lashing out at the blond one with the power I'd told myself I wouldn't use in a human place. Lucky for me, they couldn't see the swirl of blue and gold though they could feel it, much the way one can feel static electricity.

"Get moving," I said, feeling his heart in my mind, knowing I could crush it to dust with only a thought.

I dropped the pool cue and ushered him out. Unable or unwilling to take his eyes off me, he walked backwards while I advanced on him. Willow called an apology to the bartender who rolled his eyes as if a good fight was part of a normal night for Willow.

Once on the street, all bets were off. I slammed a fist into the vampire's smug face, letting him take the anger I'd swallowed back at the church. He tried to fend me off, but I was too pissed. His face was a bloody mess when Willow called me off.

He still held the other vampire though now he had the guy on his knees with his arms behind his back. "Do you want to kill them?"

I did. But that would only prove to them and the other so called rebels that I was a dictator willing to wipe out anyone who displeased me. I was better than that. Wasn't I?

"No," I said, clearly surprising the blond one. "I want to talk to them." I stared at each vampire in turn, forcing them to look into my eyes. "Let's get something straight. I am not Lilah. I don't want to be worshipped or served or whatever the hell else you guys think. I want only to be respected."

I paused, letting that sink in. When neither of them spoke, I continued. "There's no reason we can't all just go about our business without shit like this going down. Arys and I can protect this city. That includes you guys. It's your choice. We can all play nicely in the sandbox. If you don't want to, then I will be forced to defend myself."

"Sounds fair to me," Willow quipped, wearing a grin. He was enjoying this.

"How do we know you're telling the truth?" The dark haired one on his knees gazed up at me in defiance.

"You don't. But there's only one way to find out. Does my reputation have me painted as a liar?" I challenged. I was many things. A liar was not one of them.

The blond scoffed but said nothing. His buddy continued to glare at me, but his determination seemed to die.

"We aren't human," he finally said, finding his courage again. "You can't police us. We're beyond that shit."

"A sense of order has to be maintained. It's the only way for us to continue our existence without the human government hunting us down. The FPA is watching us. All of us. Is that what you'd rather have?" My hand fell to the black jade handle of the dagger on my hip. It was a comforting habit. "I'm the one who's been dealing with them. If you'd all prefer that I stop and let them come for you, that's fine with me."

The two vampires exchanged a look. This was news to them.

"I suppose it makes sense that it's best for us all to keep a low profile," the blond grudgingly admitted.

"It sure does. We're going to let you go now. Tell your rebel buddies what I said. It's common sense really. The next vampire to jump me or my friends dies a horrible, slow death. I promise."

Willow stepped back, releasing the vampire he held. The two of them hesitated, probably considering another attack. They proved they had a sense of self-preservation when instead they slunk off into the night.

I sighed, relieved that I'd been able to send a message. I wasn't about to hold my breath, but I hoped it helped them see that they had it all wrong.

"Those assholes don't deserve to have an ally like you, Alexa," Willow said.

"Yeah," I nodded, feeling overwhelmed with the entire evening so far. The tequila haze had burned off, leaving me light headed and in need of coffee. "I know."

Chapter Eleven

Less than an hour later, I was standing outside a dance club, staring at a corpse. This night just kept getting better.

Willow and Juliet stood on each side of me. The FPA agents Juliet had brought were busy keeping the occasional curious passerby from getting a good look. Receiving the call from my sister stating that there had been another public vampire kill had really been the shitty icing on an already craptacular cake.

It had been painfully tempting to ignore her call. I knew my sister though, and ignoring her would only have her showing up at my club unannounced. I wanted to avoid that at all costs.

"Do you have any idea why they're doing this?" Juliet inquired, studying me with an uncharacteristic hardness to her brown eyes. "I mean, why now? Is there something going on that we should know about?"

"There's never anything you should know about," I snapped, harsher than intended. "I swear half the problems in this city are because of the FPA constantly digging around where they aren't needed."

Juliet glared at me, biting her lip as if to keep from telling me off. She might as well. Everyone else seemed to enjoy doing it. "I don't know where your attitude is coming from, but you can drop it anytime. I have a problem to solve here. If you don't want to help, then leave. But that will force me to take matters to the next level." With her hands on her hips and her dark curls blowing slightly in the soft breeze, Juliet looked ready to kick some ass.

I could out glare Juliet any day. Of course, there was little satisfaction in that kind of win. I glanced down at the body. A college-aged guy lay sprawled at my feet, his blood staining the concrete. A series of twin punctures marred his neck. After the discussion I just had with the two rebel idiots, I was especially ticked off that this had happened again. Either this was someone's lame act of rebellion, or we had a rabid newbie on our hands.

"Don't get all authoritative with me, Juliet. You won't win that battle." Despite my words, I spoke with a softer tone. Fighting with her was the last thing I needed.

Willow nudged me and gave me a look. When I just shrugged, he said, "Alexa, maybe you should tell Juliet what's going on. She's your sister. Surely she's trustworthy enough to know."

Juliet's eyebrows rose. She looked back and forth between us. "Tell me what? What's going on?"

I frowned at Willow who wore a neutral mask. Meddlesome angel.

Sharing sensitive information with Juliet wasn't something I felt comfortable doing. She was government, and I didn't trust them. Still, she was also my sister. Didn't she have a right to know I was going to die my human death?

"Anything I say to you is off the record. You have to promise to keep this to yourself." I shot a look over my shoulder to the other agents, ensuring they weren't close enough to catch this conversation.

"If you say something that affects my job, then I can't keep it to myself." Juliet tried to maintain her tough image, but it faltered, allowing me to see the worry she was fighting.

"Dammit, Juliet. Don't make this so difficult." It took great effort to keep from shouting at her. "There's a small vampire rebellion trying to make my life hell. It's because they think I'm going to die and become some hard ass vampire queen. And I am. Going to die, I mean. Soon."

She stared at me as if I'd spoken another language. Confusion creased her brow. "I don't understand. How can you know something like that?"

"It's been foretold by several people with the ability to see what's to come. Shya needs me and a scroll to take over Lilah's throne and the power that comes with it." There. I said it. And I did not feel good about it. I suddenly wished I could snatch back the truth. My gut told me I had just betrayed myself.

"But how? Why? This doesn't make any sense."

I nodded. "Trust me, I know. I'm still trying to wrap my mind around it. There's a lot of details I still don't have."

The color drained from Juliet's face. She shook her head, trying to process what I'd said. "Are you supposed to be some kind of sacrifice? Is that why he's kept you so close all these years? Son of a bitch."

"Something like that," I admitted as warning bells went off in my head. "Look, Juliet, you've got to understand that there's a lot we still don't know. I just want to find that scroll before he does. I know you guys are looking for it too. But please, take this seriously. It's dangerous. Too dangerous for a human-run organization."

She was quiet for a long time. Too long. My nerves grew increasingly frazzled.

Finally, she sucked in a deep breath and took a step closer. Leaning in so I could smell her perfume, she said, "You were never going to tell me this, were you?"

"I didn't think you needed to know. When I die, I'll become a vampire. I just assumed you'd find out when it happened."

From the incredulous look on her face, it was abundantly clear that she felt betrayed. Her eyes flashed with irritation, and her wolf looked out at me. I wondered briefly what she looked like as wolf. I had yet to see it.

"That is so fucking selfish of you, Lexi. All I am to you is government now, aren't I? You don't see me as family at all."

Keeping this mature and professional was vital. Unfortunately, this was my sister, and the antagonistic tone she used triggered my defenses. It got a rise out of me the way only a sibling can. "You're one to talk. You tried to arrest me! You let them hurt my friend." My wolf responded to hers. A growl rumbled in my throat. "Better not throw stones unless you're willing to take a few too."

Willow stepped between us, gently pushing each of us back a few steps. "Excuse me, ladies, but I must point out that it's nothing short of a miracle that you're both standing here today. In times as dark as these, there are very few you can trust. You knew each other before all of this. Is this world you both live in now so much stronger than the one you came from? Have you forgotten each other already?"

The wolf in me retreated, backing down in awareness of the truth he spoke. Juliet's gaze dropped to the pavement. Neither of us dared to be the first to respond.

Juliet turned away and barked, "Boys, get this body out of my sight. Make it fast." To me, she said, "Alexa, we'll talk later. I've got to get back to HQ."

Without a glance in my direction she kept walking, leaving the agents to scramble to do her bidding. Most of them were twice her age. I wondered how she suddenly had so much clout. I guess screwing one of the bosses came with a promotion.

That thought was accompanied by guilt. Some might say I screwed my way to greater power too.

"Have a good night, Juliet," I muttered to her retreating form. Taking Willow by the arm, I led him away. Once out of earshot of the agents, I groaned. "Telling her was a mistake. I can feel it in my bones."

"It might feel that way, but fear is deceptive. Trusting her again will be difficult. But it might be a risk worth taking. Give her a chance." Willow slung an arm around my shoulders and pulled me close in a half hug.

My phone rang as I approached the car. Digging it out of my pocket, I groaned when the call display showed me Justin's number.

"What's going on?" I answered, knowing he only called when something was up. Could this night just chill out already? God I needed a spa day.

"There's a wolf here that insists he needs to talk to you. Big guy. Older. Says his name is Dayne." Justin paused to shout at someone in the background to get off the bar. "Should I toss him out?"

"No, get him a booth and anything he wants to drink, on the house. I'm on my way." After I hung up, I turned to Willow. "That's weird. The Doghead Alpha is waiting for me at The Wicked Kiss."

We got in the car and headed for downtown. My mind raced as I tried to imagine what Dayne could possibly want. The real question was did I really want to know?

"This might be a good thing," Willow mused. "You wanted an alliance with his wolves. Maybe that's what he wants to discuss."

The effects of the tequila had faded quickly once the drinking had stopped. It was a handy perk of being a werewolf. Intoxicants didn't affect us the way it did humans. It took a hell of a lot of booze to put down a shifter. However, it had left me feeling tired. Or maybe that was the stress. I hoped Dayne didn't mind the delay, but I was hitting a Starbucks drive-thru on my way.

The Wicked Kiss was at its peak when we arrived. A line of people waited to get inside. That had once concerned me. Now it was a relief. As long as the humans were lining up to be victimized, it would keep the public kill numbers down. At least, that was the plan.

Arys's old and rarely driven Firebird was gone. I breathed a sigh of relief. I'd been afraid he would spend all night in the back with Jenner, reliving their glory days. I wondered if Shya had cursed him as well, though I knew nothing of the demon swiping any DNA from Arys.

"I'll hang out at the bar," Willow said as we crossed the parking lot to the front entry. "Let me know if you need anything."

"You don't have to hang around here if there's something else you'd rather be doing. Trust me, I would understand."

"No, it's cool. I have nowhere else to be."

It wasn't hard to figure this one out. He wasn't just tagging along to keep me company. He was protecting me. "Willow, is there a reason you're sticking to me like glue tonight?"

"Someone has to," he grinned. "It's my job. And I'm happy to do it."

I frowned, feeling insecure and a little worried. Willow had suffered enough. I didn't want him becoming a target for Shya. He'd already been down that road.

"Don't take any crazy risks for me, ok?"

"What's that? I can't hear you." He shouted over the noise as we bypassed the line and crossed through the lobby. "Go deal with your visitor. I'll catch up with you after."

I couldn't help but laugh. He had definitely heard me. It was easy to see why Christina had fallen in love with him. He was so caring and easily the most selfless person I knew. Why did those types always get the shit end of the stick? It was so unfair.

Justin pointed me in Dayne's direction. I found him sitting alone in a back corner booth, his meaty hand clasped around a beer bottle. A single empty sat in the middle of the table.

He looked up at my approach. His expression never changed. It was neutral, almost forced. Wearing a leather vest over a t-shirt and worn jeans, he still had that menacing air I'd found intimidating. Ice-cold blue eyes looked me over as I slid into the booth across from him. It wasn't the way a man appraises a woman but the way one wolf appraises another. It was unsettling.

"Sorry about the wait. I was across town when I got the call that you were here." I extended a hand in greeting, anxious when he waited a few long, awkward seconds before taking it. His hand was warm and big, making my hand look child-like in comparison. Dayne gave my fingers a squeeze before releasing me.

"Your hand is cold," he said, low and gruff. "Unusual for a werewolf."

I felt uncomfortable with his spoken observance. Hiding my hands in my lap, I said, "Well, I'm not your usual werewolf. Anyway, what brings you by?"

Instead of speaking right away, Dayne leaned back against the booth and took a long swig of beer. His gaze remained on me the whole time. The guy sure knew how to intimidate people. He hadn't really done anything, and yet I was on pins and needles.

"I've been thinking about that alliance you offered," he began. "I'd like to take you up on that. I just have one question. Would you be willing to do me a favor in return? Consider it a way to prove that I can trust you."

Conversations that started like this never ended well. I was uneasy. "What kind of favor?"

"I want you to kill someone."

That revelation wasn't as dramatic as it could have been, mostly because I'd been expecting it. I had known an alliance with his pack would come at a price. It wasn't surprising that he'd use it as a way to get me to do his dirty work for him.

"Who? And why?" I met his gaze with one equal in intensity.

"One of my wolves. It doesn't matter why."

"It matters to me. I don't kill without good reason."

We stared across the table at one another as our wolves held a silent battle of wills. Finally Dayne laughed, a rough, unpleasant sound.

"Right. Sure you don't." He finished off the beer and slammed the bottle down with a belch. "Look, one of my guys has turned rat. He's been talking with those FPA pricks. I can't trust him anymore. Normally I'd use my pack enforcer for this kind of thing. But I thought it'd be a great way to find out how good your word is."

"And that's enough to earn him a death sentence?" With eyebrows raised, I studied Dayne. "I don't know how you run your pack, but that sounds pretty harsh."

"Does it?" Dayne said with a lazy grin that was downright scary. "Are you telling me you don't deliver your own kind of justice when these vamps step out of line? I know you've killed wolves before. Don't pretend you're too good for this."

I swallowed hard and cleared my throat. "So what did he do? If you're this pissed, he must've given the FPA something you didn't want them to have."

"Oh, he did. He gave them evidence from our last pack hunt. A few times every summer we grab a guy from the sexual offender list, drop him out in the middle of that corn maze outside of town, and hunt him for sport." With a wolfish chuckle, Dayne pulled a cigar from his vest and twirled it between his fingers. "That's the kind of thing I'd rather not have Agent Briggs and his superhero task force banging on my door about."

I nodded when he held up the cigar, asking permission to light it. There was no smoking allowed in my nightclub, but I could make an exception this time.

Perhaps I should have been surprised by Dayne's pack activity. Instead I found it to be kind of genius. Nobody was going to put effort into finding a missing sexual predator. And it seemed like a good way to keep the wolves from unleashing their aggression on innocents.

"Your wolf was involved in this hunt?" I regarded him with neutral expression, careful not to let him see a reaction just yet.

"He sure was. I guess Briggs offered him a deal that he thought was worth selling out his family." Dayne's wide shoulders heaved in a slow shrug. "I won't stand for any of my wolves associating with the Feds. I'll never trust them."

I couldn't help but smile. It seemed that Dayne and I had a very common enemy in the FPA.

"You're speaking my language, Dayne. The FPA are bad news for all of us. They're up to no good. I've seen it."

"Yeah?" His eyes glinted with intrigue. "Like what?"

I debated on how much to tell him. Once I started talking about the things I'd seen in the basement of the FPA headquarters, it all came back to me. Dayne hung on my every word as I described the little girl that could summon demons and the insane man who spent all of his time locked up there drawing pictures of potential future events. I didn't leave out the labs or the morgue. The things we had found there had haunted several of my dreams since.

"Well, I'll be a son of a bitch," Dayne swore, puffing on his cigar. "I knew they were dirty, but that's a whole lot worse than I anticipated. Thanks to Stuart, the Feds have been sniffing around my pack. We have a few kids to protect, couple of young'uns that were accidentally turned and one that was born. I don't want them coming to any harm. See why Stuart needs to go?"

I had fully expected an alliance with Doghead to come at a price. Hunting down one of their wolves was beyond my expectations. Still, if the guy was feeding info to the Feds, it was bad news for all wolves. My loyalties had to lie with my beast. I was wolf first and always would be.

"Yeah, I understand where you're coming from. You definitely want to keep the kids away from them. They grabbed my sister when we were kids. Now she works for them." I'm not sure why I told him that. I didn't trust Dayne, not really. I knew better.

He let out a low whistle and shook his head. "Those fuckers ain't tearing my family apart. I'll wage war first."

He would not win that war, but I didn't bother to say as much. There was no telling what kind of resources the FPA had at their disposal.

"So, how many packs are you leading? You said three, right?" Changing the subject and acquiring more information seemed like a safe tactic. I didn't need him getting all fired up about the FPA.

"Yeah, three," he grunted. "Doghead is my pack. It's the biggest pack in town. There are two other packs, smaller. Your regular everyday people types. They each have their own Alpha pair, but both packs answer to me and Hanna. We keep them safe, and they do the occasional odd job for us."

"What kind of job?"

Dayne grinned. "Let's just say not all of the pack's income is exactly legal. Having cops and lawyers in the group makes life a whole lot easier. At least it did before Stuart ratted us out. The FPA is one sector of authority we just can't seem to get rid of."

I tapped my nails on the tabletop as I pondered this. "You know that killing Stuart will only encourage the FPA, don't you?"

"Fuck 'em. If they know I'm willing to kill a rat maybe they'll back off my pack." With a raised brow, Dayne puffed on that stinky ass cigar and chuckled. "Make it good and bloody, will you?"

"I never said that I would do it."

"Ok, so will you?"

I was torn. It was vital to keep the wolves and vampires from working with the FPA. They already had a handful in their arsenal. The kids sealed the deal for me. Both Juliet and I had been taken advantage of as young, naïve werewolves. And look how we turned out.

"I'll do it. But I have just one question."

"Shoot."

"What does it take to get into your pack?" My heart pounded in my ears as the question passed my lips. Why was I suddenly so nervous?

"Sorry, babe. No hybrids allowed."

I flushed, feeling it all the way to my toes. Nothing like being constantly reminded that I didn't belong to just one species of monster anymore.

"I'm not asking for me," I snapped. "I'm asking for the wolf I brought to Doghead the other night. He has no pack. He's loyal and the most fierce wolf I know. He deserves a pack to call his own."

"Is that right?" Dayne stroked a hand thoughtfully over the stubble lining his jaw. The beautiful moon tattoo on the side of his neck drew my gaze. I couldn't picture Shaz with one. Although I'd never envisioned Arys or myself with a demon mark either. "Let's see how it goes with Stuart. Then I'll consider it."

"Fair enough," I muttered, slumping back in my seat.

Dayne rose to leave, pausing to toss a business card down in front of me. "Drop me a line when you're ready. I'll have an address for you."

"Will do. Thanks for coming by." Feeling wooden and stiff, I made myself get up and accompany him to the door.

Several vampires stopped prowling the room for a conquest to watch us. I could almost see the assumptions forming. Well, what did they expect? There was more to me than what I shared with them. I shared something with Dayne too, and I was determined to make the most of it.

Dayne gave me a fist bump and a nod before disappearing into the parking lot. I lingered in the lobby, wondering if I'd just made a terrible decision.

What choice did I have? I needed this alliance.

Chapter Twelve

"Did you get your alliance?" Willow asked when I joined him at the bar.

"Yeah, for a price. He wants me to kill one of his wolves who's gone rat. He's been talking to the FPA." I ran a hand through my long hair and sighed. This was turning out to be a very long night.

"What did you tell him?"

"I said I'd do it. I didn't know what else to say. I need those wolves to have my back. If not now, then in the not so distant future. I'm sure of it." I met Willow's gold-flecked gaze, seeking judgment and, as always, finding none. "Did I make a mistake?"

Willow spun an empty shot glass between his fingers. "That's a question only you can answer."

I groaned. "Shit. I was afraid you were going to say something like that."

Feeling frustrated, I scrutinized the patrons. Everything was operating like it normally did. The humans were drunk and easy; the vampires were hungry and eager. Several of them still looked my way, talking among themselves.

Before I had time to reconsider, I found myself marching across the room toward the stage. When the band finished their song, I climbed the steps at the back of the stage and interrupted before they could launch into the next tune.

"I'm sorry," I whispered to the purple-haired werewolf holding the mike, noticing for the first time the Doghead pack tattoo on her neck. "Can I use that for just a second? I need to say something."

She handed it over and backed away to allow me to take center stage. The music died, and everyone present turned to gawk at me. Public speaking was not my forte. However, I forged ahead, needing to do this.

"Sorry to interrupt," I said, cringing inwardly as my voice boomed through the club. "I just wanted to say something to the vampires here. I'm aware that many of you are questioning my intentions. Please know that rumors of a dictatorship in this city are completely unfounded. Neither Arys nor I have any interest in such a thing."

I paused, scanning the crowd, meeting several sets of vampire eyes. Good. They were listening. But did they believe me?

Taking a deep breath, I continued, "My interests lie in protecting this city and protecting the secret we all keep. Anyone who seeks to rebel against that is rebelling against themselves. I will not hesitate to take out anyone who tries to harm me or those close to me. You can all decide for yourselves what kind of a city you want to dwell in. The rebels offer you mayhem and anarchy, which will only bring down the wrath of the FPA. I offer you what you see here, a safe place to be what you are without repercussion. Make your choice."

I handed the mike back to the wolf, gave her a shaky smile, and exited the stage. My legs felt like jelly. I had just issued a challenge to the vampires of the city. I hoped they made the right decision.

"That was ballsy," Willow commented when I reached him. He nodded approvingly. "Simple but to the point. I liked it."

"It felt necessary. I'm done with vampire bullshit, and I want them to know."

Willow's lips quirked in a silly, tequila-fueled grin. "Yes, but do *your* vampires know that?"

I leaned against the bar with arms crossed. Thinking about both Arys and Kale as *my* vampires felt weird. And I kind of liked it. "Good question. I sure hope you're not including Jenner in that."

"I wouldn't dream of it."

I rolled my eyes at the liquored up angel and checked my phone. There were text messages from Shaz letting me know he was having no luck and from Jez whining about me appointing Kale as her babysitter.

While Willow drank and the vampires prowled, I stood there lost in thought. Racking my brain for answers, I dug deep, knowing there must be something we were all missing.

The scroll was tied to Lilah's abandoned throne. She couldn't be the only one who knew its whereabouts. Or did she even know at all?

Something struck me then. A memory of the night I found her searching Veryl's office. I'd been cleaning out my office, done with the building we had used to hold meetings, discuss hunts with Veryl, and take private kill clients. Lilah had come in and asked me if I'd taken anything from Veryl's office.

"Willow." I grabbed his arm, startling him and causing him to spill. "I think I know where to look. Or maybe I don't, but we have to try. Come on."

I didn't wait for him to finish his drinks before making a beeline for the door. This was probably just another misleading step in this wild goose chase, but it was a lead worth following.

For the first time since my last face off with Lilah, I was starting to feel like I might have a chance. It had been quite some time since I'd visited the old office building Veryl had leased. Once the lease ran out, we wouldn't have access to it. I had to do this now.

As we drove through the city, I chattered nonstop to Willow, telling him about the night I saw Lilah there. "I asked her if something was missing. She said that it wasn't missing but hidden. I'm starting to think that Veryl knew something about the scroll, maybe he even had it. What else would she be looking for?"

"This thing had better be worth finding. Considering how many people are looking for it. Maybe the joke is on all of us, and there's nothing to find at all." Willow stared out the window, watching the street fly by.

"No way." I shook my head vehemently. "I've dealt with too much crap to have it be some elusive unholy grail. It's out there, and we are finding it first."

The building was dark when we arrived. I wondered when anyone had last been there. The door swung open with an ominous groan. I flicked on a light, not because I needed it but because it gave me a sense of false comfort. Everything looked as we'd left it.

The kitchen was missing the aroma of fresh coffee and Chinese takeout. I half expected to find Lena in there making a cup of tea. A pang of guilt and regret stabbed me, and my breath caught.

"This was where you worked with Kale and Jez? The residual energy here is strong. It's very complex. Joyful but violent too. Even a bit melancholy." Willow surveyed the kitchen before returning to the foyer.

"I killed Veryl here," I said, leading the way down the long hall of individual offices. "I also caught Lilah and Falon screwing here." *And almost did some screwing of my own,* I thought but didn't dare speak it.

"Sounds like there was never a boring moment."

I chuckled. "Have you seen my life?"

I walked down the hall, shoving office doors open. I paused in the doorway to the one that had been mine. My cheeks grew hot at the memory of Kale's bite. That had been a hell of a night. Only Jez's impeccable timing had kept us from doing something we could never undo. But that had happened anyway, in its own time.

We continued on to the end of the hall. The door to Veryl's office was closed. Anxiety twisted my stomach. Veryl's office was a place of many memories, most of them not so good. I grabbed the doorknob and pushed. It was stuck. The sound of splintering wood was loud in the stillness. Backing up a few steps, I braced myself and kicked the door, aiming for the spot beside the doorknob. The door flew open with a screech.

Even before I flicked the light on I saw the disarray inside. The overhead light illuminated the mess. I stared at what was left of his office, aghast. Someone had totally ransacked the place.

"Oh, fuck me," I murmured, taking in everything from the trashed remains of the old antique desk to the holes gouged out of the walls. Papers and computer parts littered the floor.

"Looks like someone beat us to it." Willow pushed past me and knelt to examine some of the paperwork strewn about. "Doesn't look like anything of great value here. Seems to be pretty basic case write-ups. Rogue vampire reports, that kind of thing. I assume he had something else worth finding judging by the looks of this place."

I took tentative steps, picking my way through the debris. I was too late. It had taken me this long to remember the clue Lilah had given me, and it didn't even matter. Someone else had gotten to it first.

"Fuck, fuck, fuck!" Picking up a board from a desk drawer, I hurled it at the wall in anger. And noticed something taped to the underside of it.

I rushed to retrieve it, finding a yellow sticky note with a carefully scrawled message that read: *Nice try, bitch. Did you think I would be that obvious?*

"Look." I handed the note to Willow. "I think Veryl wrote this. It must have been to Lilah. He knew she would come here looking." I swallowed hard, my mind racing. "I think he knew where the scroll was."

The sound of my heart pounded in my ears, and I wondered again if killing him had been a mistake. My own personal feelings toward the knowledgeable vampire had been manipulated. And I'd let it happen.

"If there was anything here worth finding, it's gone now." Willow rose from where he'd been sifting through spilled file folders. "Whoever did this must not have found much either. Or we would likely know by now."

"You think so?" I scanned the mess again, hoping something would jump out at me. Even the smallest clue might help.

"It seems likely. Of course, there's no way of saying for sure."

"So we've hit another dead end. I'm starting to think we should get used to that." I kicked the shattered computer mouse. A thought occurred to me, something I knew I shouldn't even give voice to. "Willow, is it possible to speak to the dead? A dead vampire, to be specific."

Alarm flashed across his face, and he shook his head vigorously. "Don't go there, Alexa. I won't let you. I can't. It's not safe."

"So it can be done."

"I didn't say that. You have no idea how dangerous what you're asking is. I'm sorry, but that is not the way to handle this. I can't let you try something that deadly."

His expression was pained, as if it hurt him to have to play the guardian card. If any of my men had told me no, I would have contested it immediately. It was in my nature. However, I knew Willow's protests came from a place of wisdom and experience that I could only imagine. Though that did little to change my mind.

"Look, Willow, I respect you more than I've ever respected anyone in my life. But we have to try anything and everything we can to beat Shya to this. If I could just contact Veryl, maybe he would tell me something we can use, maybe—"

"No!" Willow's voice echoed in the small room. It was commanding and startling, causing me to jump. "Don't you think Shya has probably already tried that? Talking to the dead is his territory, trust me. Not mine and certainly not yours. Just because you can do something doesn't mean you should."

"Ok, ok," I squeaked out, timid and uneasy with his outburst. "I get it. Talking to the dead is very bad."

"It's worse than that. It's a violation of natural laws. It comes at a price."

"What kind of price?" I just had to know, even if that made me annoying.

"It's different for everyone. It's personal. Promise me you won't try anything like that." When I didn't answer right away, Willow grabbed me by both arms and gave me a slight shake. "Promise me."

I gazed into his deep, green eyes and saw fury burning within them. But there was more. Fear. Anything that bothered Willow this much was worth taking seriously. I raised my hands in surrender. "I promise. Ok? Calm down, boozehound. You're freaking me out."

"Sorry." He released me and stepped back. "I didn't mean to scare you."

"If you want to talk to the dead, Alexa, I can help you with that." A familiar voice rang out from behind us.

I turned to face Falon with a scowl already plastered firmly in place. He leaned in the doorway, arms crossed, a smirk adorning his too perfect face.

"This time you had to have been following me. Unless Shya sent you. Either way, get lost. I don't have time for your crap." My greeting was met with a broad grin. Falon was going to frustrate me right to death one of these days.

"Is that so? Pity. And here I came to help you. But if you'd rather not, then that's fine with me. It's a waste of my time anyway." Falon feigned examining his fingernails before rubbing them on his long jacket.

I considered throwing a chunk of broken desk at him. "You never help me unless you've been ordered to. Thanks but I'd rather not have Shya's lackeys hanging around being a constant distraction. I'm not stupid or desperate enough to fall for that. Beat it."

Willow was quiet, watching the exchange with disinterest. Falon caught his eye and nodded, his expression veiled and hard to read. Was that a show of respect I just saw? Well, I'll be damned. I never would have dreamed Falon had it in him. It definitely made me more curious about Willow.

Falon's pale silver gaze landed on me again. He arched a brow and studied me with that piercing stare. It grated on my nerves.

"Do you really think it's a good idea for you to be separated from your twin right now, Alexa?" Falon taunted. He never budged from his place on the threshold though his words gave him a sudden air of menace.

My gaze narrowed, and I pursed my lips. Crossing my arms, I mirrored him down to the cocky expression. "I know what you're doing, Falon. Are you here to distract me? Or did you do this, and you're returning to the scene of the crime?"

Ignoring my accusation, he continued as if I hadn't spoken at all. "You're both at your most powerful when together. So why would either of you be stupid enough to run the risk of being caught without the other? Seems a tad careless to me."

That triggered my defenses. My beast came snarling up to peer out at him, making my eyes solid wolf. I bared fangs, fighting back the surge of panic that sent adrenaline slamming through my veins.

"What kind of fucking game are you playing here?" I demanded.

Willow stood stiffly, appearing unruffled. His outward calm was authentic, but he could snap in a heartbeat. I'd seen it.

"Settle down, Hound." Falon feigned a yawn of boredom. "You can't hurt me. And it would kill you to even really try."

"You really enjoy the sound of your own voice, don't you?" Willow asked with a snap of wings. His magnificent silver wings spanned most of the room. He was at my side, ready to fend off the asshole angel.

"Well, yes. I amuse myself. Take it easy, Willow."

I did hurl a chunk of broken desk at Falon then. My clawed fingernails dug into the wood as I snatched it up and let it fly. He raised a hand, and it exploded into millions of sawdust-size pieces.

"That was rude," he quipped. "And to think I came to tell you that Shya has your vampires. Would it really kill you to show a little gratitude?"

"What the hell are you talking about?" A sick feeling developed in the pit of my stomach.

Falon spun on a boot heel and walked away. He strode down the lengthy hall toward the door. "Shya wants Arys to turn Gabriel. Tonight. A deal is a deal after all, right?"

With a growl, I hurried after him. "Wait," I cried. "Why are you telling me this?" I almost plowed into Falon's back when he stopped abruptly. I jerked to a halt as he turned to me with a dark look.

"Because as little as I care about vampires, there are certain people walking this earth who should never be one. Gabriel is one of them."

Shya had forced Arys into a deal. The demon saved my life, and in exchange Arys had promised to turn Gabriel. Shya wanted to pair the power of Arys's bloodline with the dark magic already flowing through the kid, in essence, creating his own black magic monster.

"For the first and probably only time ever, I actually agree with you," I confessed, having mixed feelings about agreeing with Falon on anything. "But what am I supposed to do about it?"

"I don't know," Falon said with a shrug. "Be a hero. Show up. Save the day. That kind of crap. Isn't that supposed to be your thing? I'm sure you'll think of something."

Like so many times before this, I wanted to bitch slap the arrogant fallen angel. His snarky tone and derogatory stare really got my wolf riled up. "You could be trying to lure me there so Shya doesn't have to drag me kicking and screaming. This could just be a ploy to have me walk into a trap willingly." I searched him for a lie, but it was impossible to tell with him.

Rolling his eyes, Falon sighed dramatically. "What fun would that be? I'd much rather see you kicking and screaming."

I looked from one angel to the other. "Why tell me this and risk pissing off Shya?"

Falon reached out and gave me a pat on the head, like one would a small puppy. "There, there, little wolf. Don't strain yourself trying to figure me out. Save your energy. You're going to need it."

He turned away, and I grabbed for him with a desperation I hadn't known I possessed. I clutched nothing but air as he easily avoided my grasp.

"How did you find me?" I settled for the simplest question of the many storming through my head.

"I've been following you since you left your nightclub to come here. I wanted to see where you were headed before I revealed myself." A creepy chuckle accompanied his admission.

"Falon, you really suck, you know that? How do I know you're telling the truth?" I would never trust Falon. Everything he said and did was to serve a purpose, usually his own. Even his role as Shya's second was suspicious.

"They're at Shya's house. Go and see for yourself."

Before I could grill Falon further, he opened the door and swept out of the building with supernatural grace. He vanished from one step to the next.

Closing my eyes, I reached out to Arys, opening the mental door between us. My thoughts formed a question, and I waited impatiently for a response. There was resistance. Arys didn't want to let me in.

'It's not a good time, Alexa.' Uncertainty laced Arys's thoughts. 'Stay with Willow. I'll come to you as soon as I can.'

He shut me out before I could slam him with my protests. I'd done it to him as well, though that never made it any easier to have it done to me. It made me feel powerless and isolated.

I turned to Willow, feeling the color drain from my face. "I have to go to Shya's."

Willow nodded and gestured for me to exit first. "Let's go."

"How?" I shouted when we were in the car. I needed to vent out some of the built up emotion testing my limits. "How can he know that stuff? Do you think he's lying?"

There was a loud honk from the car behind me as I slid into his lane a little closer than intended. I didn't doubt that a middle finger had accompanied that horn. But I wasn't paying attention to stuff like that. I needed to get to Shya's. His house was outside the city, far enough that nobody could hear the inevitable screams. It was a sprawling modern manor with a backyard pool and way too much white décor. I hated it.

"You did say he was Lilah's lover," Willow pointed out, maintaining a sense of calm that I had long since abandoned. "Sure, he could be lying, though I'm not sure it's likely. Perhaps he's loyal to Lilah even now that she's in lock up. Maybe his goal is to thwart Shya's plans for greater power."

"Why though?" I shook my head, trying to figure out Falon's game plan. "That just doesn't make sense. When Lilah was holding my sister and Gabriel hostage, it was Falon who double-crossed her. He was still working with Shya."

"Was he though? Or would he have wanted it to appear that way?" Willow fiddled with the radio, stopping on the local country station. "That's the thing about the fallen. They're as unpredictable as demons. More so. At least with a demon you know where they stand."

The strains of a whiskey-swilling, ex-hating, truck-driving country song filled the car. I cast a quizzical glance at Willow. He had just spoken of fallen angels as if he was not one of them, which made me sad for him.

"Don't look at me like that," he said without ever meeting my eyes. "I can feel you pitying me. Believe me, that is the last emotion I want from you."

"Sorry." Eyes back on the road, I cringed and tightened my grip on the steering wheel. "I never meant to. I mean, you know I don't pity you, Willow. It just saddens me, you know, everything you've been through."

"Forget it. Really. It's nothing compared to what many face."

I wanted to argue, to tell him he was better than most. It wasn't fair that he got the shit end of the stick. I stayed silent, listening to the sappy country song and liking it against my will. When the song ended, I switched the station back to rock with an apologetic smile. I needed the crash of electric guitars to pump me up before I faced the demon that scared me to the tips of my toes. When Guns N' Roses came blaring out of the speakers, I sighed and tapped my fingers in time to the beat.

"Good call," Willow said. "This is better. Good ass kicking music. But please, try to stay calm. Getting too emotional will compromise your judgment. Shya will use that against you."

"It wouldn't be the first time. You'd think I'd know better by now."

The closer we got to Shya's the clammier my hands grew. This had to be a trap. Falon couldn't be trusted. Trying to figure him out was hurting my brain. He was right. It was a waste of energy to try.

"Don't let him kill me," I heard myself say as we turned into Shya's long driveway.

A cool breeze chilled me as I felt Arys. He was definitely here. He would feel me too. I didn't care that he pushed me away. I was done letting him make decisions for me.

"Are you sure about this?" Willow asked. "It's not too late to leave."

I stopped the car and killed the engine. Goosebumps broke out on my skin. "I'm never sure when it comes to Shya. But Falon's right. Gabriel has been corrupted enough by that demon. Making him a vampire would take that to a whole new level of scary."

I got out of the car and adjusted the dagger on my hip. A demon-forged blade wouldn't do me a lot of good here, but I kept it on me just the same.

The breeze ruffled my hair, and I smoothed it back. Deep breath. Before I could change my mind, I marched up the front step and banged on the door. It opened before I'd finished.

Shya peered out at me, his snake-like red eyes gleaming with sadistic glee. "How nice of you to join us, Alexa. I was hoping you'd show up."

Chapter Thirteen

I followed Shya into the house, feeling both safe and worried with Willow at my side. The demon spared an amused grin for the fallen angel. Their eyes met and something passed unspoken between them. It did not make me feel any better.

Hatred for Shya surged forth, driven by the angry wolf inside me. I had to rein in my temper so I wouldn't give in to the wolf's insistence that I rip his throat out. She didn't care that he'd survive it; she just wanted to make him hurt.

"I assume you both will be on your best behavior while you're guests in my home," Shya said, raising a brow as he cast a serious look at us each in turn.

"You can assume whatever the hell you want to. Where's Arys?" I stalked past the demon into the living room where I knew everyone would be.

Seated on Shya's pricey couch across from the fireplace was Gabriel, staring at his phone like a typical teenager. His long black hair hung to hide his face. He didn't even look up.

Jenner stood behind the couch, in the open space where the living room and kitchen joined. His tattooed arms were crossed, and he regarded Shya with open hostility. That earned him a few points toward my good graces.

I met Arys's disappointed gaze with one of my own. He sat back in an easy chair that matched the white couch. I didn't need him in my head to know what he was thinking. Guilt was written all over his face.

We shared a look of our own as I shook my head in solemn wonder. I knew Arys had made this deal and this was the only way to have his demon mark removed. Yet, I hadn't accepted that he would really do it. Taking Gabriel from what mortal life he had left was wrong. It wasn't Arys's place to make that call.

I'd expected to see Falon there. Despite his absence, the backyard patio was occupied by several demons. It stunned me, stopping me in my tracks. Upon catching sight of me through the floor to ceiling windows, half of them abruptly vanished.

"I don't suppose you're ready to have your mark removed as well?" Shya drew my gaze back to him with that grossly inappropriate inquiry.

"Does it look like I have fucking dreamwalker here for you?" I snapped. Shya knew I'd come to stop this madness. He was playing with me. By getting angry I was letting him win. I took a deep breath and focused on keeping myself centered and grounded.

Shya shrugged and smiled sweetly. "Well, soon perhaps. Anyway, we were just about to get started. Can I get you anything first? Coffee? Wine? A taste of Gabriel here?"

That got Gabriel's attention. He snapped upright, his phone forgotten. "What? No way. I don't want her touching me."

"The feeling is mutual," I muttered, pinning the kid with a fierce stare. "Do you really want to do this? You don't have to, you know."

Gabriel glared daggers at me. Shya had to be filling his head with nonsense about me. Every time I saw the kid lately, he acted as if I were the enemy. I hoped it was because of Shya and not because of what Gabriel saw when we touched.

"It's really none of your damn business, is it?" His snarky tone dripped venom. "Stop trying to save me, Alexa. I'm not your charity case. You have bigger problems anyway. You should be much more concerned with saving yourself."

The urge to slap the mouthy teen upside the head was strong. I tried to tell myself he was scared and merely acting out, but I knew that wasn't the case. Shya had offered him darkness. And he'd accepted.

I rounded on Arys, finding his expression hard and cold. "I'm not letting you do this. You know it's not right."

Hurst's words of warning echoed in my head. He had told me in Vegas that Arys must not turn Gabriel. I knew if Arys did this, we would all be made to regret it.

"I don't need your permission, Alexa. Gabriel has made his own decision, just like you did. You shouldn't have come here." Arys's dark-blue eyes flashed in irritation.

Shocked didn't begin to cover it. What the fuck was happening right now? I glanced at Willow who stood near Jenner, watching the confrontation begin. He shrugged and shook his head sadly.

I made an attempt to get inside Arys's head, needing to have his reassurance that this was all some kind of ploy to deceive Shya. When he blocked me out and continued to stare at me with that ice-cold intensity, my heart skipped a beat.

My cheeks burned with both humiliation and anger. I wasn't sure what he was pulling here, but doing it in front of Shya was low. What happened to the Arys who wrestled with himself nightly about my coming death in his arms?

'You're looking at him.' Arys's smooth as velvet tone echoed in my mind. He reached in as if he hadn't just slammed that door on me. 'Don't forget who I am, Alexa. Not now.'

'What does that even mean?' I pleaded, choking back the words that threatened to burst out in a torrent of emotion.

Instead of a telepathic reply, he spoke aloud. "I made a deal, Alexa. I have to see it through."

I was painfully aware of the watchful demons' gazes upon us from outside. Though they all wore a human guise, I felt as if the eyes of true monsters bore into my very soul. A shudder crept over me.

"Let's get started, shall we?" With a sly smile, Shya drew near. He gestured for Arys to take action.

Gabriel had dropped his phone on the coffee table. He stared at Arys with wide eyes, pupils large with sudden fear. The scent of it was tantalizing. I wasn't sure I could watch this.

Arys rose and motioned for Gabriel to do the same. Shya stood by, hands clasped in eager anticipation. I gathered the power coiled in my core. Who should I hit first?

"Don't even think it, Hound," Shya barked. "You interfere, and you won't be walking out of here tonight. I already have a guest room ready for a wolf. And the door locks from the outside. Don't test me."

His threat rang with promise. Would Arys let Shya lock me up in this house of horrors? Probably. If it meant not having to look at me while he decided how badly he still wanted to kill me.

Arys turned abruptly to me, as if he'd heard that last thought. Maybe it was just me, but I thought I saw him wince.

"Have it your way," I said, throwing my hands up in exasperation. "You're an idiot though, Shya. You should know that once Gabriel is a vampire, Arys and I will both have power over him. You're practically giving him to us."

Jenner scoffed but said nothing. I shot him a dirty look.

"Don't think I haven't considered that," Shya said. "I'm very good at planning ahead. Haven't you noticed?"

Sure Shya knew I had power over vampires, but did he know I could practically enslave them? He'd been a witness when I'd inadvertently done it to Kale. I wasn't sure if he knew I'd also done it to Jenner or that I could easily do it to Gabriel. Of course, that wasn't what I wanted. Having Gabriel enslaved to me instead of Shya was only the lesser of two evils.

"Please, Arys. Don't do this." I stood awkwardly, crossing my arms then uncrossing them. I didn't know what to do with myself.

"Ready?" Arys asked Gabriel who swallowed hard and nodded.

I lunged forward as Arys jerked Gabriel close. Raising a hand, he hit me with a shot of power that crushed the breath from me. It threw me back, slamming me against the island in the kitchen. I hit the floor with a painful thud.

Willow helped me up with soft words meant to calm. I was anything but that. If Arys wanted a fight, he would get one.

But Willow stopped me before I could lash out at my dark lover. He grabbed the hand I raised crackling with power and extinguished the roiling psi ball in my palm. The sensation of his angelic vibe was heavy and deep but also comforting and warm.

"You've got to choose your battles," Willow said, low and smooth. "This is not one of them."

"Listen to your guardian," Shya chimed in. "He knows what's best for you."

Relief passed over Arys's handsome features, piquing my curiosity. Before I could speak or act, he bared Gabriel's neck and bit deep into his throbbing jugular.

My breath caught, and I watched in silent fury as Arys bled the young witch. The scent of it mingled with Gabriel's fear. It called to me, a demand that would go unanswered. I held tight to Willow, praying he wouldn't let me go.

Jenner shifted from foot to foot beside us. As incubi and succubi respectively, he and I were both drawn more to sensual energy than fear alone. It didn't take long for Gabriel to respond to Arys as if he were a lover. A groan escaped Gabriel's lips, and he held tight to Arys until his strength began to fade. Caught up in Arys's thrall, Gabriel oozed desire. I closed my eyes, unwilling to look any longer. Every breath I took filled my lungs with blood and lust. It was suffocating.

I wondered what, if anything, Gabriel was seeing as he and Arys touched. The two of them stood there in the center of the living room with so many sets of eyes upon them. Arys was oblivious, lost in the euphoria of such a deep feed.

Holding my breath did little to help. All it did was force me to take a deeper breath as my lungs cried out for air. The heady aroma of Arys's desire mingled with that of his victim. The dark touch of the right vampire could bring any man or woman to their knees.

Gabriel slumped against Arys, his strength sapped save for what he used to cling to the vampire as if afraid to ever let go. His eyes rolled back in his head, and he mumbled something incoherent.

My fangs sprang forth, and I took an involuntary step forward. Willow's grip tightened until it was almost painful. I didn't care. I wanted what Arys was having. Why should I be made to watch and not take part?

Those were the thoughts of the bloodlust, the driving force that demanded my need be sated. It wasn't me even though it was. Conflicted and confused, I whimpered in frustration.

"Oh, please," Jenner grumbled beneath his breath. "You're going to make a terrible vampire."

Despite his cocky words, Jenner held himself rigid, gaze transfixed upon the scene before us. He wanted it just as bad as I did. Having centuries of experience was the only difference between us.

Unable to trust myself to speak, I gave him the finger, satisfied at the resulting glower. For just a moment I thought perhaps Arys would merely kill Gabriel and save us from having to deal with him as a newbie vamp. Part of me hoped for it, wanting it to happen.

'Do it,' I thought, hoping he would hear me. 'Kill him and end his misery before it can really begin.'

As if in response to my plea, Arys's head snapped up. Blood dripped from his mouth, and he gave Gabriel's face a light slap. Then he bit into his own wrist and offered the bleeding fount to his victim.

Shit.

The only thing keeping Gabriel upright was Arys. The kid groped clumsily for Arys's wrist, closing his mouth around the flowing crimson.

Arys's blood was too much. It brought a roar of power crashing through me. White noise screamed through my ears, and I broke free of Willow's hold. The true monster lying in wait inside me saw its chance and burst forth with a cry. I hurled myself at Arys, seeking to both stop this transformation and to end my own agonizing hunger. I hit him hard, nearly knocking us both to the ground. In his attempts to fend me off, Arys lost his grip on Gabriel who slumped to the floor, smacking the coffee table on his way down.

Blood stained Shya's white couch and area rug. The demon raised a hand to slap me with his demonic power, but Willow was there, throwing himself between us. Everything happened fast. Arys threw me off with a shout for Jenner to grab me. Willow and Shya faced off as only old enemies could. Enemies who were once brothers.

"You finish this, Arys," Shya hissed, though his red gaze saw only Willow.

Jenner dragged me off Arys before I could land the punch I'd been about to throw. Jenner was a good match for me. His physical strength was greater than mine, and our power came from the same place. But I had more of it. We grappled while Arys rushed back to Gabriel to feed him more of his dark blood.

I flung Jenner off with a push of power that tore a cry from him. He came back at me immediately. With a hand around my throat, he slammed me to the floor and straddled me. The breath was squeezed from my lungs. I gasped and choked, cursing my mortal limitations. For the first time perhaps ever, I longed to be free of them.

Staring up into Jenner's hate filled eyes, I lay perfectly still. I didn't try to speak or fight. I merely gazed into him with a single intention.

"Don't you fucking dare," he murmured with a fang-revealing snarl. "I will gladly knock you senseless."

The sensual succubus vibe seeped from me like smoke from a chimney. It poured out, reaching to envelope Jenner in its cloud of manipulative longing. He was mine. Surely he knew better.

"Arys, you'd better hurry," Jenner called, unable to take his eyes from me. "I can't hold her much longer."

"Jenner," I gasped out, directing the focus of my intent. "I know you want me, Jenner. Just one kiss. Maybe even a taste."

"Stop it." He shook his head as if that would break my hold on him. Leaning in close he said, "You better reconsider how much you want to show your enemies. We have an audience."

His grip on my throat relaxed and instead of sitting up, he buried his face in my hair and breathed in my scent. So much for Jenner's resistance. He was all mine.

"Just how you like it." A wicked laugh bubbled up. I sounded like somebody else, somebody without a shred of sanity left. It reminded me of Kale.

Having Jenner atop me on the floor of Shya's living room had not at all been part of the plan. Still, we were here now. I might as well enjoy it. Sliding a hand up between us, I gently caressed his face. Bringing my lips to his, I kissed him. I delved into his mouth, seeking his tongue with mine. He returned my kiss with an equal fervor. Feeding off his lusty energy, I took all he was giving until the power consumed me.

I threw him off me with the ease of a thought. Jenner hit the floor and rolled, narrowly missing the full-pane window. I was on my feet and whirling to let Arys have it, but I was too late.

Gabriel lay on the floor beside the couch, his lips pressed to Arys's wrist. Already his skin was pale, almost waxy. His breath came in shallow, uneven gasps. Death was already upon him.

"Son of a bitch," I swore, jabbing a finger in the air at Arys. "You really fucked up this time."

Arys pulled his wounded wrist away and lifted Gabriel's lifeless form onto the couch. He ignored me, turning to Shya instead. He stepped back and gestured to the bloodstained piece of furniture.

"There. I upheld my end of the deal. Now can you please remove this?" Arys peeled his shirt off to expose the big black dragon that covered his back.

Shya crossed his arms and stood stiffly in his finely pressed suit. Ebony wings framed him as he glided over to take a closer look at Gabriel.

"How long until he rises?" He eyed Arys with a haughty expression. For a moment I thought Shya was going to refuse to remove the mark.

"It's hard to say. Could be anywhere from a few hours to a few days." Arys's dark brows drew together, and he frowned, sharing my thought.

"And if he doesn't rise?"

"He will."

The vampire and demon stared hard into one another. The male bullshit in the room was thick. I was sick of it. Other than one oddly androgynous demon outside staring in at us, I was the only woman present. I would've loved to have Jez at my side.

"Fine." Shya nodded and gave a flippant wave. The dragon on Arys's back began to fade as if it were slowly being erased. In seconds it was gone completely. Shya flashed me a cryptic grin. "See how easy that was?"

The dragon on my armed burned. It had to be my imagination. There was no reason for me to stay another moment. Gabriel was dead. Before long he would rise. There was no telling what kind of vampire he'd be. With the black magic he possessed, I imagined it wouldn't be pretty.

"You can't protect him all the time." I nodded toward Gabriel. "Eventually I'll get him alone. He'll be mine, or he'll be destroyed."

Trying for a dramatic exit, I strode from the room without a look back. It would have been a lot more convincing if I didn't trip on the throw rug in the foyer. I recovered quickly, but the damage was done. Crap.

Willow followed me out. Shya couldn't possibly let us go without tossing one of his infamously menacing retorts after us. "The same goes for you, Alexa. Willow can't protect you all the time. Neither can your twin. Or he wouldn't be here. Tread carefully."

With one hand on the door and the other being tugged by Willow, I spun around to shout through the foyer. "Or what? You'll kill me? Bring it on. You need me, Shya. If you want to take me out and rob yourself of the sacrifice you need, then so be it. I'm ready."

My voice echoed in the high ceiling of the foyer. Shya regarded me with a calm but calculating stare. When he didn't respond, I allowed Willow to drag me out the door.

"You shouldn't have called him out like that," Willow admonished when we were in the car. "He's too unpredictable right now."

"I don't care. I'm so fucking done with this. I just need it to be over." My voice broke, and I choked back tears. I was mad goddammit; I had no reason to cry.

"This isn't about Shya, is it?" Willow stroked a hand through my hair and pulled me in for an awkward car hug. "It's about Arys."

The accuracy of that statement only made me feel worse. "Something is happening to us. I'm afraid of where we'll stand with each other when everything goes down. When he kills me."

"I can guarantee you that he's afraid too. I think you need to give him the benefit of the doubt. Don't assume anything. This has to be hard for him as well."

With a sniff and an angry swipe at the one tear that had escaped to run down my cheek, I started the car and peeled out of Shya's driveway. The back tires spun, kicking up a chunk of his lawn.

I drove away with the seed of sorrow taking root in my heart. Arys's cold refusal had hurt. I couldn't shake the sinking feeling that stopping Shya was the purpose we shared as twin flames. And I knew without a doubt that, just as the old lore foretold, it would destroy us.

Chapter Fourteen

The bright artificial light was hard on my sensitive eyes. The twenty-four hour Tim Horton's coffee shop was almost empty. I sat at a corner table with Willow, Jez, and Kale. Two cops sat on the other side of the building, eating a late night meal and chatting amongst themselves. I inhaled the bittersweet aroma of strong coffee before lifting the cup to my lips.

The four of us had gathered to discuss the events of the evening. I had called Shaz to fill him in while waiting for Kale and Jez to arrive. Rather than beckon him to join us, I sent him home with the suggestion that he should go for a run with Coby. He had resisted, wanting to come to me instead. But I couldn't allow it. Shaz was giving up too much to be with me. He was wolf, and he needed to act like it.

"I don't think there is anything to find at all," Jez griped, swiping a scoop of foam from her latte with a pinky finger. "If Veryl was the last one to know its whereabouts, it could be just about anywhere. But I doubt he'd be stupid enough to leave it in this city." Her hand shook as she licked the foam from her fingertip. She caught me staring, and I quickly averted my gaze.

"Forget the churches," I said. "We're done with that. Leave them for Shya's crew to pick through. They won't find anything. I think someone is trying to throw us off the right path. I'm not wasting any more time that way."

"So what now, then?" Kale leaned back in his chair, arms crossed over his chest. He stared across the table at me, his expression hard to read. "Where do we start? What do we do?"

I glanced at Willow who frowned as if he knew what was coming. "Well," I began. "I wanted to try contacting Veryl, but Willow insists it shouldn't be done. So unless any of you have any other ideas, I think there's no other choice but to wait it out. Either the scroll turns up or it doesn't."

"Contact Veryl?" Jez repeated. "Is that even possible?"

Every eye was on Willow. He ran a hand through his dirty-blond hair and sighed. "Yes. But like I told Alexa earlier, it's not an option. It's too dangerous."

Kale jumped in to back Willow up. "It's definitely a bad idea. Even you can't possibly be that reckless, Alexa."

"Can't I?" I demanded, my voice rising to draw the gazes of the cops to me. I dropped my tone to a hushed, loud whisper. "Everything is being taken from me. My sister is a government tool, my pack kicked me out, and my twin flame was with Shya tonight, turning Gabriel. What do I really have to lose?"

Jez looked back and forth between Kale and me. Her ruby red lips were pursed, and those green cat eyes sparkled with curiosity. "Is it really that dangerous? What's the worst that can happen?"

Willow gave an exasperated sigh and stared at the ceiling as if seeking guidance from an unseen force. "Nobody can simply talk to the dead. Ouija boards, séances, all that crap is just that. Crap. Anything that talks to you that way is not a deceased human. It's a bad spirit masquerading as whoever you want them to be. The only way to talk to the dead is to be dead. Got it?"

"What are you leaving out?" I searched Willow, sure he was leaving something out. The way he avoided my gaze confirmed it. I was starting to learn his tells.

He glared at me, a dark look that I'd seen him direct at Brook but never at me. It was a little scary. I was reminded that as good and dedicated as Willow was, he no longer belonged to the light.

"There is a ritual that can be used to access the dead and still come back. But it's not without serious risks. They aren't worth it. You can come back...changed. Inhuman." Willow paused, looking at each of us in turn. "It's not an option. I won't be part of it."

His adamant refusal struck a chord within me. I trusted Willow on many things. This shouldn't be any different.

"Ok," I said, patting his arm. "Let's drop it. I won't bring it up again."

Jez caught my eye and raised a finely arched brow. She wanted me to push the subject. I could see it in her eyes. However, she wasn't making the best decisions lately. I shook my head in answer to her silent question.

"Anyway," I continued, "I can't keep wasting time chasing after something that could be hidden on the other side of the planet for all we know. There are rebel vampires to deal with. I'm not letting them fuck shit up for me."

"And Arys?" Jez pulled a napkin from the dispenser and began to tear small pieces from it. "Sounds like he's fucking shit up too."

I didn't want to discuss that, not with Kale present. It was just too awkward. "I'll deal with Arys."

"Alrighty. Let me know if you need me to hunt down some rebel vamps." Jez barely looked up from the small mountain of napkin bits piling up in front of her. The girl was a jittery mess.

"What I need is for you to come try on bridesmaid dresses tomorrow afternoon. Kylarai will be expecting us."

"That's tomorrow?" With a crooked smile Jez pushed a golden lock out of her eyes. "No problem. I'll be ready. I can also stay at my own place alone until then too. If you guys can possibly let me out of your sight."

She laughed like it was a joke, but I could tell that she was upset. Too bad. I was not going to apologize for wanting to make sure she was safe after how we'd found her.

"We're done then?" Kale asked, pulling car keys from his pocket. "I'm going to take off. I'll drop Jez off at home."

"Going out to get your freak on before sunrise?" Jez snickered and elbowed him teasingly.

"Something like that." Kale rose with the sound of creaking leather. He seemed to be in a hurry to leave. Considering how strained things had been with us recently, I couldn't blame him. He paused to wait for Jez to gather her napkin mess. "Alexa, don't try anything crazy. Please."

A laugh burst out, and I almost spat coffee across the table. "Are *you* telling me not to do something crazy? Really, Kale. I don't think you're qualified to make that call."

I probably shouldn't have said it. Immediately I regretted it. Without another word Kale stormed from the coffee shop.

"Yikes," Jez giggled as she stuffed the napkin bits into her empty coffee cup. "Way to go, Lex. Now I get to sit in that car while he broods. Good job."

I felt like an ass. It was too late to take it back. "Be ready tomorrow afternoon at three. I'll pick you up. If you need help staying sober, call me. I mean it. Any time."

Jez's smile faded, and she gave a tight nod. "Thanks. I'll be ready." She leaned in for a quick hug before following Kale out. The click of her heels was loud in the quiet coffee shop.

I said to Willow, "I'm going to head home. If I'm not up and ready on time, Kylarai will have kittens." I gathered up the garbage left on the table and carried it to the trash container on our way out.

Willow and I stepped into the parking lot in time to see Kale's black Camaro vanish around the corner with a squeal of tires. I listened to the roar of the engine as it faded in the distance. He was pissed and rightfully so.

"I'm coming with you," Willow said, heading for my car. "I'll stay until sunrise. Don't tell me not to because I'm the guardian and you're the one that has to mind me. So get in the car."

His feisty attitude coaxed a smile from me. Though I didn't believe I was in any danger sitting at home, his concern was appreciated. Sunrise would steal him away.

"Arys isn't here yet." I breathed a sigh of relief when I pulled into the driveway. "He'll come." What I didn't say was that I planned on kicking Arys's ass off my property when he dared to show his face.

"Is that going to get nasty? From the look on your face, I presume that it is." Willow followed me inside, pausing to survey the large, dark yard. "It's really beautiful out here. You can actually see the stars."

With a brief glance skyward, I nodded. The stars called to my wolf, and I longed for the forest. I pushed the door open and began to flick on lights as I went through the house. It provided a false warmth that made the big house feel a little less empty.

"Yeah, I'm sure nasty is a pretty good word for what's going to go down." I dropped my keys on the island before shrugging out of my jacket and removing the dagger from my waist. "Our relationship is built around conflict. I know that's what they say happens to twin flames. But it doesn't make it any easier to accept."

Willow slid onto a stool at the island. His gentle gaze followed me as I fetched a snack from the fridge. He held up a hand in polite refusal when I offered him some apple pie. I devoured some leftover takeout, hoping it was still good. I was too tired to cook.

"Then don't accept it," he said. "You don't have to be a victim of circumstance, Alexa. Conflict may haunt twin flames, but that is only one side of your union. The other side is love. Don't forget that."

Something Lilah said rose up in my memory to haunt me with the truth. "Lilah once said the twin flame bond is a curse, not a gift. I wanted so badly to believe she was wrong. But some of the things she said, they're true."

"Don't say that," Willow warned. "Lilah is a demon. Nothing she speaks is the truth. She's a vile creature that sees and spreads only evil."

"No really, Willow. She talked about how the twins hate each other as much as they love each other. How there is no escape from one another. We are chosen, and we're meant to suffer." Suddenly I wasn't so hungry anymore. I shoved my plate away and poured a glass of water. "It's starting to feel like the truth. Like it is a curse. I mean, Arys and me, we can't even walk away from this. Too much time apart will drive us insane, just like it did Lilah."

"And Salem," Willow added. "You only know half of that story. It drove him mad too. The last time he caged Lilah, he rarely left her side. He couldn't bear to."

"But he still imprisoned her against her will. That's not love. Why would an angel and a demon even be twinned?" I scowled, disgusted with the harsh reality of the dark side of a twin flame bond. It wasn't all power trips and deeply personal lovemaking.

"For the same reason you and Arys are. A rare partnership with a shared purpose that can be achieved by no other. In anything so trying and difficult, there is always room for growth and revelation. Don't focus so intently on the hard parts that you miss the beauty of what you share."

I tried to take Willow's wise words to heart. Letting Lilah get inside my head was exactly what she'd want. I couldn't give her that victory. That was easier said than done, especially when I felt Arys's arrival. I groaned and shoved a hand through my hair. "He's here."

"I'll take off so you two can talk. Remember, you have everything you need to fulfill your purpose, but there will always be forces trying to stop you. That's where the conflict comes in. Pick your battles carefully." Willow slid off the stool and pulled me into a warm hug. Then with a ripple of the atmosphere around us, he was gone.

I turned toward the front door, waiting for the knob to turn. Willow had great advice. However, he could only see the situation from the outside. Being on the inside, having my twin turn on me, there was no letting that go. Emotion spilled through me. I was mad, hurt, and humiliated. The door opened, and it all came pouring out.

"You have a lot of fucking nerve to show up here after that crap you pulled at Shya's." I faced Arys with my hands on my hips and my body thrumming with electricity.

He stopped just inside the door with Jenner a few steps behind. The door swung shut with an ominous creak. Arys held both hands up, ready for my temper. The fact that he'd walked in expecting a tirade didn't make me feel any better.

"Alexa, let me explain." He approached as if expecting me to start hurling dishes down the hallway. "Can we just talk, please?"

"You want to try to explain what I saw you do tonight? Sure. Go ahead and tell me why you threw me across Shya's kitchen." I stared into Arys, letting him see the raw emotion in my eyes.

He kept coming down the long front hall toward me where I stood in the entry to the kitchen. Jenner crept over to the stairs and stealthily escaped to the top floor, leaving us the illusion of privacy.

"I'm sorry about that," Arys said, his gaze heavy upon me. "I had to turn Gabriel. Shya and I had a deal. If I didn't make good on that, he would never have removed that mark."

"You know, so far, you're off to a pretty shitty start. Try again."

He stopped about ten feet away. Close enough to face me like a man but too far away to slap. "I made that deal intending to keep it. I know that's not what you want to hear, but you know me. That can't possibly surprise you. As long as we bear Shya's mark, he owns us. I will not be owned by a demon."

"So you took the life of a young man barely into adulthood. You ignored Hurst's warning and we are going to pay for that." Accusation dripped from my tone. The image of Gabriel's body was burned into my memory. It shouldn't have happened. Not on my watch. I felt like I had failed him somehow.

"I upheld my end of the deal. Look how much control Shya has over you because of that mark. I had to get rid of mine. He can't have us both." Shoulders stiff, a frown creased his brow as Arys stared at me, pleading with those midnight eyes.

Guilt rose up to join the onslaught of feelings. Keeping Shya's mark was not by choice. The only way to get rid of it was to give him a dreamwalker. The FPA had one in lockup; I saw her. But I could never do that to her. She was safer where she was now.

"You know I'd get rid of this mark if I could." I sniffed as my temper flared. "The only way to do that is to hand an innocent person over to Shya. And I will not do that. Maybe it was easy for you, but I'm not quite that far gone yet."

I turned my back on Arys and went to clean up the dishes. He wasn't convincing me that killing Gabriel was necessary. He was just showing me how different we were.

I shoved things into the dishwasher with more force than required. The plates crashed against each other, somehow not breaking. I slammed the door shut and whirled around to find Arys right behind me.

"I understand why you haven't paid your debt to Shya," he said. "Can you try to understand why I had to pay mine?" He reached to take my hand. The heat of his skin reminded me of where that stolen warmth had come from, and I pulled away.

"Arys, you killed someone. In front of me while I begged you not to. Then you threw me across the room. No, I'm sorry, but I do not understand that, and I don't even want to." I was backed into a corner, up against the dishwasher. I needed some distance. "You should go home. I need some time alone."

"I'm not leaving you alone. We've already been over this."

"Give me a break."

"I'm not going."

We glared at one another until the power flowed between us with a scorching hot intensity. There were so many ways I wanted to react. Still, I thought of what Willow said, and I opted to take the high road by simply walking away.

"Fine. Stay then. You can bunk with Jenner or take the couch. I'm going to bed. Alone." I shoved by him, expecting resistance. He didn't stop me, but he didn't let me go either.

"We are not done talking about this, Alexa." Arys was hot on my heels as I climbed the stairs.

I rushed into the bedroom and swung the door shut. "You might not be, but I am."

The door bounced off Arys's foot as he kicked it open. My jaw dropped. He came closer, and I threw my hands up to ward him off. A burst of power went out from me, throwing him out of the room where he crashed against the stair railing. The wood creaked but didn't give.

Arys got up uttering obscenities. I was ready when he appeared in the doorway again. My fingers crackled with power.

"Go ahead. Do it," he taunted, holding his hands up in invitation. "I know you're pissed off, so get it all out of your system. Let me have it."

"Is that what you think?" I sputtered. "That I'm pissed off? I am so much more than that. You sold me out in front of Shya. You allowed us to be divided, and you humiliated me. I'm not just pissed; I'm hurt."

The truth hung between us. The atmosphere was thick with pent up energy seeking an outlet. I vibrated with the strength it took to keep from releasing the force I held.

Arys's face fell. "I had to. Don't think for a moment that it was easy to do that to you. I didn't want you to see any of that. When you showed up, I knew I had to make Shya believe we could be divided. The best way to do that was to make you think so."

I couldn't believe this. The way he had looked at me at Shya's, so stone cold, it hadn't felt like an act. "Well, call the fucking academy. That was an award winning performance. But you did divide us. I needed you to back me, and you didn't. So it wasn't just an act, Arys. It was a betrayal."

"No, it wasn't. I did it for us. Shya needs to underestimate us. If he thinks we're falling apart, he'll let his guard down." Arys approached quickly, backing me up against the dresser. With a hand beneath my chin, he tipped my gaze up to his. "It had to be real. So it was. You've got to understand."

I shook my head and pressed my lips together. It was the only way to keep myself from telling him to go to hell. I pushed him away, but he held tight to my arms, refusing to be budged.

"We went to Vegas with a united front," I ground out between gritted teeth. "We agreed to present that same united front to our city, to the vampires and the wolves. Then as soon as we need to show that to Shya, you abandon me. That's what I understand."

"It wasn't like that. You're not even trying to see this from my side." Arys's fingers tightened, digging into my skin, and his eyes flashed wolf for just a moment.

"Let go of me."

"Not until you calm down and discuss this reasonably."

"Don't tell me to calm down." My shout echoed in the room, hurting my ears. "Nothing you say is going to take back what happened tonight. You think that you played him, but you walked right into his trap. You turned on me while he watched. That was real." My wolf rose up to stare out at him, issuing a silent challenge. I wished he would leave so I could fall apart by myself.

Rage tinted the power flowing between us with a dark vibe. It hovered there, so close, almost palpable, our inevitable self-destruction. For the briefest of moments, I wanted it, if only for this agony to end.

"Alexa, don't." There was such bitterness in those two words. Arys trembled under the weight of the force thundering through us. "Don't push me away. I won't let you do that again."

"You won't let me?" The dark side of our bond was in control now. It whispered in my ear, a violent demand that I made sure he knew that no man controlled me. I was the dark queen here, and I would make him remember that. "You think that Shya controls me? What about you? I am done with your ego making decisions for me."

With a push of power, I reached out to drape him in my thrall. Oozing an intoxicating cocktail of seduction and malevolence, I attacked Arys by using his own greatest strength against him. Because our shared power was a double-edged sword, I could use it on him with ease. His eyes widened as he realized my intent.

"What's wrong, Arys?" I asked with the same stone cold stare he'd given me at Shya's. "You don't like it when I push back?"

He didn't fall as easily under my spell as Kale and Jenner, but he did fall. I saw it in his eyes. His pupils dilated, and his grip on me softened. A wicked smile stole over him. "Like it? Hell, I fucking love it," Arys murmured, leaning in to kiss me.

The sound of my hand slapping his face was loud in the sudden quiet. My palm stung, and I stared in shock, having surprised myself. Before I could overthink it, I shoved back with both my hands and my power.

Arys was ready for it, and he countered with a push of energy that hurt even as it taunted my desire. We were too evenly matched. Being a vampire gave him an advantage though. He could channel more than I could because of my mortal limits. That would change soon enough.

Frustration spurred me forward. I let loose with a flurry of hits that he did a great job of blocking. Except for the last one that landed with the smack of flesh hitting flesh.

His head snapped sideways, and I leaped back out of reach. A low chuckle came from him. Arys turned to face me, grinning as he wiped a drop of blood from his lip.

"You know how this ends just as well as I do," he said with a nod toward the bed. A sinful glint in his eyes revealed the monster within him. The darkness driving him was strong, called forth by our mutual wrath.

It was impossible to maintain a level of rationale with that force thrumming through me. Arys's cocky comment didn't help.

"Not this time," I snapped. "Not after what you did. It will be a cold day in hell before I pretend that didn't happen." I shook with rage. I was all fangs and claws, wanting so badly to take a swipe at him.

His twisted amusement faded, replaced by a deadly glare. "Get over it, Alexa. I did what I had to do. And I'm not sorry."

That did it. I snapped. I launched myself at Arys with an angry growl. Anticipating my temper, he braced for the attack. He caught me with a growl of his own and wrestled me to the floor. The echo of my beast shone in his eyes. Despite my struggles, he managed to pin my arms to my sides and bare my throat.

"What do you say, sweet wolf? Why don't I just take you now? We can end it here, and Shya never gets the chance to sacrifice you." Arys's voice was husky with the snarl of a wolf that could never manifest.

It usually frightened me to see the remnant of my beast lurking within him. Not this time though.

"Do it," I demanded. "Why put off the inevitable? You might as well destroy us now and save me the heartache of having an audience."

Something in my strangled cry gave him pause. "Is that what you want?"

A swell of emotion bubbled up to mock me, and I stifled a sudden sob. "I want the waiting to be over."

Arys gazed into my eyes, finding the anguish eating away at me. The storm in him settled, and he said in a ragged whisper, "So do I."

Again we were one. Just like that. Torn apart and thrust back together in a heartbeat. The curse of twin flames: endless conflict amid undying love. We lived with the hunger to consume the other even as we longed to be consumed. It was a hell of a thing.

I understood fully why Lilah and Salem had both suffered a loss of sanity. It was happening to us too. Knowing that, however, didn't make it easier to accept. The supernatural force commanding us seemed at times a conscious entity of its own. It hovered over us, swept through us, and lifted us up to a dangerous place full of false promises.

I didn't care. I was ready for it to be over.

"Do it," I begged.

Arys appeared torn, though the longing was evident in his eyes. He stared at my jugular, deciding how fast or slow to make my death. He would want to make it last, I knew that. I'd been inside his head. That's how he worked. Why rush the good stuff?

"Do it!" I repeated, using a slap of power to enforce my command.

He blinked a few times, and then the monster was back, staring down at me with a vicious hunger. I braced for the bite I knew was coming. He bared those razor sharp fangs and went for my neck.

A boom like a clap of thunder rattled the window of my bedroom. Jenner appeared in the doorway, hands raised, and power crackling about his fingertips. His shot hit Arys dead on, sending him pitching backwards to crash against the wall. A framed photo of a forest backdrop fell and shattered beside him.

Jenner dragged me to my feet and shook me until my teeth rattled. "You wanted to know why I was here," he snapped, slapping my face to break me out of the strange spell I'd fallen under. "This is why. To stop you two idiots from destroying yourselves."

I sucked in a few breaths, finding it hard to process what had just happened. I opened my mouth but nothing came out.

Arys lunged to his feet, and Jenner threw up an energy wall to keep him on that side of the room. It wouldn't hold Arys long, but it was strong enough to keep him busy for a few precious moments.

Jenner scanned my neck for a sign of injury, and I pulled away. I didn't need him falling under the same spell that had claimed Arys and me.

"You should have let him do it," I muttered.

"Do you think I came all this way to watch you guys fuck this up?" Jenner looked at us each in turn. His cold blue gaze stopped on Arys. "I'm doing what you asked me to do. If you want to keep her safe from you then you need to leave. Go home. I'll stay with her."

A protest formed on my lips, but it died quickly when I saw the shame on Arys's handsome face. What the hell had just happened here?

Several long moments passed before Arys finally said, "Thank you, Jenner. It's good to know I can still count on you. After everything."

"Save the sappy shit, ok? The past is the past. Now get the hell out of here before the sun rises." Jenner dropped his energy wall and pushed me behind him, watching Arys like a hawk as he strode from the room.

My heart squeezed painfully as I watched him go without a glance back. Only after I heard the front door slam downstairs was I able to breathe again. I slid down the wall at my back as great, heaving sobs erupted from me. Blood tears streamed down my face, betraying me in front of Jenner. There was no stopping it. The crimson river of tears fell to stain my hands, my clothes, and even the carpet.

I couldn't bring myself to look at Jenner. I was sure he'd be staring at me with judgment and disgust. So when he laid a hand awkwardly on my shoulder I was astonished.

"I'm not going to pretend to know what you're going through," he said. "But I hope you can find the strength to see this through to the end. I watched Arys suffer, tormented by dreams of a woman he thought he'd never know. I can't let him fail himself now, after all this time. Now that you're here and the two of you are together, please, don't give up on whatever it is you have to do. Or else all of this pain and suffering will have been for nothing."

He left me with that and returned to the guest room. I sat there on the floor of my bedroom with my knees pulled up to my chest while shuddery breaths shook me and silent tears streamed down my face.

Chapter Fifteen

No amount of makeup made me look any less tired and ragged. As I looked at my reflection in the full-length dressing room mirror, I sighed and tugged at the bags beneath my eyes.

"How does it look?" Kylarai called from outside the dressing room door. "Get out here and let me see."

The pale pink dress I wore was horribly ugly. Since it was impossible to lie to a werewolf, I'd have to do my best to grin and say nothing. There were sequins lining the bodice and puffy sleeves that made the dress appear like a reject from the 1980s. Kylarai had wanted the bridesmaids to wear pale pink, which wasn't a bad color in itself, but on this dress it was all wrong.

"Um, I don't know about this one, Ky." I emerged from the tiny changing room to a fit of giggles from Jez who stood there wearing a pink disaster far worse than my own.

"Oh dear." Kylarai frowned and sipped from a glass of water. She had declined the champagne that the store clerks had handed out to us. "That one looked a lot better on the rack. Ok, take it off. We'll try something else."

"What are you laughing at?" I asked Jez. "You look like a walking bottle of Pepto."

"Hey," she protested, flipping me off. "The 80s called. They want their sleeves back, Lex."

Poor Kylarai's frown deepened. She'd found it funny during the first few dresses we had tried on. Having a rushed September wedding was stressful, and I didn't envy the workload she had to deal with.

"What else have you got?" I asked Ky, retrieving my champagne glass from a small table off to the side of the change rooms. For the first time in my life, and likely the last, I would have rather had tequila. Willow was becoming a bad influence.

"Lucky for you both I've been saving my favorites for last. I knew you would hate those ones. I thought I'd have some fun with you." Before I could turn away Ky held up her cell phone and snapped a pic of me in the hideous pink number. "This is so going on the internet."

"What?" Jez and I both said simultaneously. My laughter was genuine then. It was greatly needed after the night I'd had. "Not cool, Ky. Not cool at all."

The sales lady returned with another tray of champagne. Jez happily grabbed one, and I watched her take a large gulp. She caught me staring and shrugged it off.

"Settle down, Lex. It's just champagne. Would you like me to pee in a cup for you?"

"And if I said yes?" I challenged with a smile, hoping I didn't hurt her feelings.

She groaned and adjusted the pink thing hanging from her slender frame. "Don't go there. You have no idea how hard it was to get Kale to leave me alone at my apartment. He was like an overprotective parent."

Good. Instead of saying that aloud, I said, "He cares about you. Is that a bad thing?"

Knowing she had no retort for that, Jez turned to Ky and held out a hand for the next dress. With her grey eyes sparkling, Kylarai pulled two more off a nearby rack and handed one to each of us.

"I hope you guys like these; they really are my favorites."

I retreated back into the dressing room and hastily struggled out of the nightmare I was wearing. "Here," I announced, tossing it over the top.

The newest dress was actually pretty. I was more of a pants and boots kind of girl so that was saying something. It was the palest of pinks, soft and warm, easy on the eyes. I slipped into it and adjusted the corset style bodice to fit my frame. Laces tied up on either side, giving it a feminine quality that I found appealing. The skirt was cut above my knees in the front but fell to my ankles in the back. A sheer layer of tulle underneath gave it just enough poof to make it flow behind me. The dress was so gorgeous it could have almost been a wedding dress itself. Even with the dark circles beneath my eyes and the loose, messy blonde locks clipped atop my head, I was awed by how lovely it looked.

"Kylarai, this dress is beautiful," Jez gushed from her dressing room. "It's way too gorgeous for a bridesmaid. I can't possibly wear this."

I exited my tiny room to find her emerging in a long one-shoulder number that fell to the floor. It was cinched at the waist with a silver decorative piece. The skirt flowed as she walked, cascading around her like a pale pink cloud.

We looked at each other and both squealed. "You look amazing," I gushed. To Ky, I said, "She's right. We can't look this good at your wedding. Isn't there some rule that bridesmaids are supposed to look like crap?"

"So you like it?" She asked, relief obvious in her face. "I want you both to be beautiful. What good are wedding photos if everyone looks like shit but the bride? I want everyone to be a knockout that day."

"When do we get to see your dress?"

"As soon as it's ready. It's being altered." Ky paused, and her face flushed. She pushed her shoulder length brown hair back and grinned. "Oh my God. I can't believe I'm getting married so soon. Are you sure it's ok that we have the wedding at your house? Your yard is just so perfect."

It did my aching heart good to see that smile on her face. On impulse I pulled her into a hug. She smelled especially wolfy, pine and musky fur. Breathing in her scent of wolf and perfume, I was reassured. Good things did happen to good people. "If anyone deserves a fairytale love story, Ky, it's you. If my yard is what you want then it is what you shall have."

When she pulled back unshed tears glittered in her eyes. Her smile couldn't possibly get any wider. It was adorable.

"Go take those things off so we can keep them perfect for the big day. If you need any alterations made, make a note of that, and I'll have it done right away." She dabbed her eyes and ushered me back into the changing room. I was disrobing when she called, "Are you going to tell us what's up with you? Or are you going to keep pretending everything is peachy?"

"What are you talking about? There is nothing up with me." I was glad she couldn't see my face. Hopefully she wasn't close enough to smell my lie.

"Arys almost killed her last night, and she doesn't want to tell you and ruin your excitement," Jez said loudly from her dressing room. "Sorry, Lex. But if you can't be honest with us girls, you'll keep it all inside and eventually spontaneously combust."

I glared at my reflection in the mirror as I pulled my jeans on and tugged my black Sons of Anarchy reaper V-neck into place. "Thanks, Jez. Nice to know you can keep things in confidence."

Kylarai was wearing that frown again when I emerged from the dressing room for the final time. "Alexa, are you all right? Please, don't hide things from me. It feels like we're drifting apart, and I hate that."

"I'm fine, really. We're not drifting. I'm just trying to put some distance between us so that you stay safe. Just until this is all over." I shot Jez a dirty look when she returned in her yoga pants and tank top. She brushed it off dismissively and drained her champagne.

"Until what is over exactly?" Ky's voice dropped when the sales lady returned.

"Everything with Arys and Shya. It's just best if you're not around me too much until it's all said and done."

She gave instructions to the sales lady regarding the dresses while I worked hard at stifling a yawn or two. The champagne had left a bitter taste in my mouth. I politely refused when offered another. Jez started to reach for another, looked at me, and changed her mind. We really needed to talk about the other night.

When we were alone again, Kylarai turned to me expectantly. "I understand. Really, I do. But please don't shut me out. I need to know what's going on with you. I care. Coby cares too. More than I think you realize."

"I know. That's why I need to protect you both by keeping you out of this. I'm already afraid that having me in your wedding will be a mistake."

"Do not say that. The wedding wouldn't be right without you. It's my special day, and I want you there. No worries. I mean it."

Kylarai held out a hand to each of us. "I'm so happy to have you ladies in my life. This would be a very lonely life without you. Now, let's go for dinner. I'm buying."

We went to a restaurant down the street that was known for its fabulous ribs. The three of us gathered around the table, chatting and laughing, enjoying the atmosphere. It was so carefree and human. For a short time I was able to put my worries aside.

Kylarai shattered my brief reprieve by getting serious on me again. "Lex, I don't mean to pry, but please tell me what's going on with you. What happened with Arys last night?"

Shutting her out wasn't fair. We were still pack, despite the technicality that said we weren't. She was my friend, my family. Stifling a groan, I took a deep breath and filled her in on everything I'd neglected to say.

When I finished she shook her head and sat back with a bewildered expression on her pretty face. "Your shared purpose is so close to coming to pass that it's driving you both batshit crazy. That hardly seems fair."

"Nothing is fair in this world though, is it?" I grimaced, stirring the ice in my strawberry daiquiri. "It is what it is. All I can do is hope the scroll turns up so we can get this over with. If it doesn't happen soon, Arys is going to kill me anyway. He's been expecting it so long that the wait is breaking him down."

Kylarai sipped from her virgin pina colada, looking thoughtful. "Not everything is unfair. You've got to try to see the silver linings, Lex. You're focused so hard on the storm clouds that you're missing the light show completely."

"Agreed," Jez jumped in with a knowing look. "Life is a journey, right? This is all leading you somewhere. Good things do happen to people like us. Eventually."

There was an awkward lull in the conversation. Kylarai broke the quiet with a cheerful, "So how's Kale? Good I hope. I wanted to invite him to the wedding, but then I thought that might just be incredibly awkward. What do you both think?"

I exchanged a look with Jez who laughed into her martini. I did my best not to discuss Kale with Ky. It was just too weird given their brief time as a couple.

"It's not like you were in love with him, right?" Jez pointed out. "Couldn't hurt to send the invite. Knowing Kale, he won't come. He's kind of a downer that way."

Ky was no idiot. She read between the lines with ease. "So what I'm hearing is that things are really strange between you two, and I shouldn't invite him."

"It's your big day, Ky. Whoever you want to be there should be there. Don't make those decisions based on me." I patted her hand, finding her aura warm and pulsing. It struck me as odd that it was so noticeably vibrant.

The waiter arrived with our order, giving me the perfect opportunity to change the subject. There just was no easy way to discuss having my best friend's ex tied to me like a prisoner of his own desire.

I dove into the cheeseburger and Caesar salad I'd ordered, finding it just perfect. Damn I was going to miss this. Eating a cheeseburger should not make one an emotional wreck, but suddenly I was fighting the urge to throw the damn thing in a fit of irrational anger. Why should everything be taken from me?

There was no one to blame but myself. And perhaps circumstance. Stuffing those feelings back down inside, I savored the burger, making note of each smell and flavor. I wanted to remember this later when the only food I craved would be human.

"So where did Shaz take Coby tonight? Are they having a real bachelor party? Strippers and all that fun stuff." I asked, thinking it seemed like a safe enough topic.

Kylarai had asked Shaz to take Coby out. Shaz had asked me repeatedly if I wanted him with me instead, but I had assured him that having a good time with Coby was the best thing he could do for me right now. His reluctance made him that much more adorable. Letting Shaz go was going to be one of the hardest things I'd ever have to do.

"I didn't even want to know," Ky said with a laugh. "I told Shaz not to tell me what he had planned. Just to bring back my fiancé in one piece."

"Well, what about you?" Jez said between mouthfuls of grilled chicken. "You deserve a final big bash too. We should party."

"The wedding is coming up so quickly. I don't have time to party."

Jez was aghast. "There is always time to party."

"Maybe a little too much time," I added, giving her a pointed look.

Jez frowned and pushed the chicken around on her plate with the fork, avoiding my gaze. "I know I fucked up, Lex. But we all suffer, and we all deal in our own way. You can't punish me for that."

The tone of our dinner went from fun and friendly to tense and awkward in a split second. It wasn't fair of me to act like judge and jury. I was just afraid.

"You scared the hell out of me, Jez. I've never seen you that far gone before, and I hope I never see it again. I'm sorry. I'll back off." Hoping for a smile, I offered her a fry from my plate. "Peace offering?"

She swiped the fry from my hand with the speedy reflexes of a cat. "I'm sorry, too. I shouldn't punish you for caring." Turning her emerald-green gaze on Ky, she said, "Ok, so about this bachelorette party. Where would you like to go? Bride's choice."

Kylarai was about to protest when she seemed to rethink it. "There is a band playing tonight I wouldn't mind seeing. They're local. Coby turned me on to them."

At the mention of a local band, my stomach flipped. *Please don't say it's at The Spirit Room*, I thought.

"They're playing at The Spirit Room," she continued, dashing my hopes with just those few words.

Jez raised her eyebrows, expecting my protest. I swallowed hard, finding the cheeseburger was now sitting heavily in my stomach. "Sure," I said with a forced smile. "We can do that."

"Do you want to go see the 'peelers' first? I don't mind. I can appreciate some nice man flesh. I just don't want it touching me," Jez quipped with a flip of her golden locks.

A giggle erupted from Ky. "As much as I appreciate the offer, no thank you. I have more than enough man flesh at home."

That was a relief. I wasn't sure I could stand to watch buff men tear their clothes off and gyrate for screaming women. While the human women would hunger for one thing, I'd be hungering for another.

"Someone may as well have some action at home. At the rate we're going we'll be old, sexless spinsters in no time," Jez said with a nod to me. When I frowned in response, she added, "Sorry, Lex. You have been pushing your men away though."

"Only Shaz. It's for his own good, you chatty thing. Don't think I'm enjoying it." I flung a fry at her, disappointed when she caught it.

"No more talk of depressing stuff. Aren't we supposed to be celebrating?" Ky brought our attention back to her, holding her glass up expectantly. Jez and I raised our glasses as well. Kylarai stared at us each in turn. Her cheeks were rosy, and she seemed to glow with an inner happiness. "To friends. And to overcoming the odds, no matter how bleak they may seem. To hope and the certainty that everything happens for a reason." Kylarai clinked her glass against ours and beamed like the sun itself threatened to burst from within her.

I studied her, seeking the source of her inner illumination. Sure marriage made a woman beam, but there was something else there. A gentle touch of her aura slapped me in the face with the answer. I struggled to maintain my composure. Was this for real?

Her aura was strong and solid, humming with a healthy vibrancy. Focusing intently on her energy, I was able to pick out another, weaker aura beneath hers. Unless I was very wrong, Kylarai was pregnant.

* * * *

We arrived at The Spirit Room after dark, early enough that we were able to find a table near the stage but not so early that the place was empty. Now that the sun had set, I was anxiously anticipating an appearance by my crazed vampire. *Which one?* A nasty voice in the back of my mind taunted.

Arys hadn't tried to contact me mentally or by phone. I wasn't sure if I should be worried or relieved by that. Leaving the house without Jenner had been simple enough thanks to the afternoon sun. Now that darkness had fallen, I expected one of my self-appointed protectors to show up.

The first band of the evening took the stage. They were hard rock with a lot of growling and screaming. Not quite my kind of rock, but it sure beat Top 40 crap.

"I just can't decide where we should go for our honeymoon," Kylarai was saying. "Coby wants to lie on the beach in Hawaii, but I'd much rather go somewhere romantic like Paris or Vienna."

"I vote Europe, for sure. Why not visit both Paris and Vienna? Walking through those cities would be a dream." I leaned forward, resting my face on my hands, and imagined strolling through the stone streets of Paris.

"I dated a chick who works for a travel agency. We parted on good terms. I'm sure I could get you guys a deal." Jez's offer was met with a gleeful squeal from Ky who clapped her hands together excitedly.

When the waitress came and Ky ordered another virgin drink, my suspicions were confirmed. She knew. So why hadn't she told us?

My phone vibrated, rattling against the tabletop. I grabbed for it quickly, hoping it was Dayne responding to the message I'd left him earlier. Before leaving the house I'd called him to say I was ready to do the job whenever he sent me the information I needed. Securing that alliance with Doghead was not an option. It had to be done.

It was Juliet. I ignored it, not wanting to disrupt this evening with FPA bullshit.

I sat there tapping my fingers on the side of my beer bottle, watching the people file in through the entrance. No hard booze for me tonight. Or maybe ever again. I needed to stay as alert as possible. Jez was doing a good job pacing herself. I pretended not to scrutinize her too hard, and she pretended not to notice I was doing it.

My phone alerted me to a voicemail, and I rolled my eyes. As much as I loved my sister, she still drove me as nuts as she ever did. I considered listening to it but was distracted when Arrow walked in.

Jez saw him too and held up a hand before I could spout obscenities. "Chill, Lex," she said. "We leave him alone, and he'll leave us alone. Trust me. It's best that way."

"Is that so?" I questioned. "Is that why he's headed over here?"

The tall, dark-haired nephilim was dead set on our table. Mischief lit up his hazel eyes. He wore a knit cap that hung off the back of his head, leaving some of his black hair falling free in the front. Dressed all in black, he moved through the room like a shadow. I made a mental note to learn all I could about nephilims. Surely Willow would have some valid information.

Arrow all but slithered up to our table, angling for Jez. My wolf rose up protectively, ready to rip his face off, and I had to force her back down.

"Hey, Jez. I called you last night. Did you get my message? I got my hands on some really primo shit." Arrow grinned and leaned in closer to whisper something the loud music prevented me from hearing. His gaze met mine, and he smirked.

I gripped the beer bottle so hard I heard the glass crack. Didn't he realize he was seconds away from taking it in the face? Deep calming breaths did little to convince my wolf to settle down.

"Oh yeah?" Jez replied, shooting me a warning glance. "Thanks but I'm not looking for anything."

"Are you sure? You know I'm good for free samples. Care to join me upstairs?" Arrow's delivery was smooth. The only thing working against him was the fact that he was male. Jez had to see right through him.

"No, thanks. I'm fine. Really." With a shake of her golden head, Jez waved him away as if aware I was about to snap all over him. "Have a good night, Arrow."

He studied Kylarai briefly before dismissing her. His gaze landed on me, and his eyes narrowed. "What about you? You look like you could use a pick me up."

"You don't say." The bottle was airborne, flying out of my hand across the table before I could decide to actually throw it. Oops.

Arrow reacted fast. Throwing a hand up, he stopped the bottle inches from hitting him. To make the feat even more remarkable, it hung there, suspended. After a few seconds that felt like a lot longer, the bottle felt straight to the floor where it rolled under the table.

I was out of my seat and rounding the table before anyone could speak. I grabbed Arrow by the throat and squeezed while reaching aggressively into him metaphysically, seeking out his heart in my mind. I'd never done it to a mortal.

"Feel that?" I growled, eyes flashing with the beast within. "That's me about to overload your fragile human heart."

Fearless and angry, Arrow glared viciously into my face. "You won't kill me."

"Oh no?" I held up my arm to show him the demon mark I bore. "Don't think for a second that your parlor tricks impress me. I know angels and demons. You don't come close to what they are."

"I am not part of your world, vampire bitch. Let's keep it that way."

"Call me that again, and you get my knee in the groin and a fist in the face. Now I'm going to say this just once. If you supply Jez with drugs again, I will know what it feels like to hold your heart in my hands."

He met the eyes of my wolf unflinching. His resolve was admirable. Good for him. He was also smart enough to know vacating the situation was safer than antagonizing me.

"Fine. No drugs for Jez. Got it. Now get your hands off me."

I let him go with a shove, ready to make him keep moving if he tried anything. He didn't. Arrow beat a hasty retreat across the room to disappear to the second floor. If I never dealt with the slimy, little wretch again, it would be too soon.

I turned to Jez, expecting her to be pissed. Instead I found her smiling.

"Wow, look at you defending my honor," she laughed. "I feel so loved."

I couldn't share her enthusiasm. "If you ever feel like you're slipping, if you're tempted to do something self-destructive, call me. Any time. I will drop everything and come to you. Promise me."

Jez's smile faded. "Geez, Lex. Way to really bring down the happy vibe here. What happened to it being a night of celebration?"

"Promise me," I repeated. In my mind I could still see her hanging limp in Kale's arms. Seeing the way Arrow had honed in on her weakness, attempting to exploit her, it made me desperate to protect her though I knew well that nobody could be protected from themselves.

"I promise," she said, her joyous mask replaced with one of sincere intent.

"Thank you." I did my best to appear apologetic. "Sorry about that, Ky."

I returned to my seat to find my phone vibrating on the table. With an eye roll and a groan, I went to hit the button to ignore the call.

Until I noticed that it was FPA Agent Briggs calling. There were many people I would ignore. He was not one of them.

Holding up a finger to show Jez and Ky I'd be back in a minute, I grabbed the phone and headed outside to take the call.

"Welcome home, Briggs," I answered. "I see you've made it back safe and sound. What do you want?"

He didn't waste time with fake small talk. Briggs was a man of few words, a likeable trait. "I'm sure your sister has called already. I felt it was only proper to call you myself. I respect you enough to give you fair warning."

"I haven't spoken with Juliet tonight. What's this about?" A prickle of unease traced a path up my spine.

"You haven't?" Briggs paused, causing my concern to grow. "Look, O'Brien, I'm going to level with you. Juliet told me that you're to be Shya's sacrifice. I'm sure you understand that from our perspective the most important thing is to keep Shya from completing his ritual. No matter what it takes."

I moved further away from the crowd gathered around the door, chattering and smoking. Barely aware of them, I peered into the darkened street in jaw dropped shock.

"And since you can't find the scroll the next best plan is to get rid of his sacrifice," I said what he did not. Betrayal settled in to make me nauseous. How could Juliet do this to me? "Are you coming to kill me, Briggs?"

"I'm sorry, O'Brien. There is logic in taking his sacrifice out of play. At least this way your death with be used to save many rather than to condemn them. It will be honorable."

My heart raced, and a loud ringing echoed in my ears. Perhaps this should not have come as such a shock, but it did. No way in hell was I going to lie down and let the FPA kill me.

"This isn't your fight, Briggs. I know you think it is, but it's not. Shya will be stopped. By me. Not like this. You know I will kill anyone you send after me."

"Shya could find the scroll at any moment. Is that what you want? To risk the lives of so many innocents?"

I shook my head even though he couldn't see me. My breath quickened, and a shock of adrenaline made me lightheaded. "Don't pretend to give a damn about anyone but yourself and your disgusting self-serving organization. You want me? Come get me, Briggs. But you better have the balls to face me yourself."

His voice was void of emotion when he said, "I'm on my way to do just that."

Chapter Sixteen

He hung up without giving me a chance to respond. It didn't matter. There was nothing I could say to that. I couldn't tell how much time I had until Briggs caught up with me. I assumed he would track my phone; he'd done it before. I could always ditch it somewhere, but that would only prolong this showdown. It was as cowardly as tracking it was. No, I'd keep it. Let them find me.

I listened to Juliet's message as I rushed back inside. In her frantic message, my sister pleaded for my forgiveness and warned me that Briggs was coming for me. She swore up and down that she hadn't expected him to react that way. *Too late for sorry now, little sister.*

"I have to get out of here," I blurted upon reaching the table where I'd left Ky and Jez. "The FPA know that I'm Shya's sacrifice. They're hunting me down."

"What?" Kylarai was aghast.

Jez nodded and said, "Those sons-a-bitches don't waste any time, do they?"

"You two should stay here. Watch the band and have a good time. They're tracking my phone so I have to take off. I'll lead them back to The Wicked Kiss. I want to do this on my terms."

I leaned in to give Kylarai a quick hug, but she stopped me by standing up and grabbing her purse. "Let's go then."

Jez was already up and waiting. I had never doubted she would want to have my back. But Kylarai could not be endangered.

"Ky, no. You can't come. Not in your...condition." It just popped out. When her jaw dropped, I rushed to add, "It's too dangerous."

"You know?" She squeaked out. "I just found out. I didn't want to say anything until more time had passed. Coby doesn't even know yet."

"I can feel it in your energy," I admitted. "It won't be long before others can scent it or hear the heartbeat. You should be lying low, Kylarai. This is incredible and rare. Don't take a stupid chance for me."

Her joyful smile was twisted into a mask of concern. "I can't just run off home and leave you to be hunted by the government, Lex. I may not be your beta anymore, but I'll always have your back."

"I can't let you do this. Go home."

"Don't give me orders. It's not your place anymore."

Kylarai was one of the nicest people I knew. She was also a passive aggressive werewolf who had killed her own abusive husband. If she didn't want to listen, I couldn't make her.

"Fine. Just remember, if anything happens to you, it will haunt me forever."

It didn't take long for me to hightail it across the river to the downtown core where my nightclub sat like a pulsing, living entity drawing in victims like moths to a flame. Jez and Kylarai had taken Ky's Escalade. It seemed safer to drive alone in my car in case of a ballsy street attack.

Both Arys's Firebird and Kale's Camaro sat in the parking lot when I turned in with a screech of tires. Already? The sun hadn't been down all that long. Kale had probably spent the day here fornicating and feeding. Arys was definitely waiting for me.

"Shit." I pulled into the closest available spot and jumped out of the car. After fetching the Dragon Claw from the trunk, I headed inside, slinging it around my waist as I went.

Justin looked up from where he stood checking I.D. to give me a nod. I skidded to a stop beside him. "The Feds are on their way. Don't let them in. Tell them to wait outside and let me know when they get here."

I waited for him to nod in understanding before slipping away, dodging between people as I went. Arys was at the bar with Willow and Jenner. Kale was nowhere to be seen, meaning he was in the back.

Having Arys within my sights brought on a surge of strength and confidence. The scattered thoughts and emotions that had plagued me on the way over were silenced. He turned to me with a dark brow raised expectantly, and against my will I swooned just a little.

"I was wondering when you'd show up," he said, that deep-blue gaze traveling over me.

"Look, Arys, I don't have time to get into what happened last night. Briggs is on his—"

He pulled me close and laid one hell of a kiss on me. Aggressive, needy, passionate, and even vulnerable, it set butterflies loose in my stomach. Swept up in the power of that sudden sensual act, I slid a hand into his hair and kissed him back with an urgency that rivaled his own.

When at last we pulled apart, I became embarrassingly aware of our small audience. Kylarai and Jez had just arrived to join Willow and Jenner as they waited for us to come back to our senses.

"I don't think this is the best time for some hot vampire action," Jez quipped. "Survive now. Screw later."

"What's going on?" Arys held tight to my hand as if afraid to let go.

"Briggs is on his way here to kill me," I heard myself say. I repeated the gist of my conversation with the FPA agent, which earned immediate protests from both Arys and Willow. While they made claims of making the FPA sorry for such an attempt, I was wondering if Kale was sane enough to keep Kylarai out of harm's way.

Deciding against that idea, I determined it would be best if Kale never emerged from his den of debauchery in the back. I wasn't sure he'd survive another confrontation with the FPA.

"Like I was saying back in Vegas," Jenner piped up. "You need to have the FPA working for you. If they won't do it willingly, you have to force them into it. Get some dirt on the right guy at the top, and they'll be all yours."

"That actually makes sense," I admitted. "Right now the only dirt I have is that Agent Briggs is doing my sister. I doubt that's good enough to make him see things my way."

"Then find something bigger."

Jenner was right. Blackmail might just be the only way to get through to a guy like Briggs. It was worth a try anyway. If I could just find the right tidbit of dirt.

Arys pulled me aside so we could speak privately. I noticed that both Willow and Jenner watched us closely.

"You told Willow about last night, didn't you?" I said, my gaze darting toward the door in anticipation.

"I had to. He needs to be aware of how close I came to losing it. That can't happen again. Not until the right time. I don't want to blow this, but I can't help but want it." Arys leaned his forehead against mine and sighed. "It's gotten so much harder than I thought it would be. I feel like I should hate myself, but I don't. I just want you."

A chill stole over me. Nothing quite like having my lover confess that he can't wait to kill me. "I know. It terrifies me, but I get it. At least, I think I do." I breathed in his cologne, finding the scent now triggered the memory of every time he had ever treated me as prey.

He reached to pull the clip from my hair. It tumbled down, a mess of long ash blonde which he plunged his hands into. "I knew this would be hard, but I never dreamed it would be this bad. I don't want to lose what we have."

"We won't. We will always be one. You know that." I leaned into his touch, finding comfort in the same hands that would kill me.

"It will be different though. All dark. I can handle it. I'm already there. But you belong to the light, my beautiful Hound. I don't want darkness for you." The emotion in his touch was an echo inside me. It brought too many things to the surface that we had no time to deal with right then.

I thought about the yin yang balance between us. There was a spark of my light in him. I had seen it there, small but significant. It kept him from being all monster. I would mourn the loss of that.

"I don't want it for you either," I said, stuffing an onslaught of worry and fear back down inside me. "You're not all dark either. Not yet."

"We can't be alone together. Not until this is over."

"I know."

I held tight to him, enjoying the way it felt to be in his arms. A lurking certainty haunted me, telling me that I'd better savor it while I still could because things were about to change.

The sound of raised voices drew my attention back to the bar. A couple of vampires were sniffing around Kylarai. From the looks of it, they weren't taking her brush off very well, even with Jez in their face threating to tear their eyes out.

Arys followed my gaze. "Kylarai shouldn't be in here. Not in her state."

"You knew right away, huh?" I nodded. "I guess that explains why every vampire in here is looking at her like she's a hot new item on the menu. We better go put a stop to that."

"You need to get her out of here. She's no use to you by being a liability." Arys took my hand and pulled me along beside him. He was repressing a lot of pent up shit, and his energy burned with it.

Jenner caught my eye as we approached. His unspoken question was met with a nod from me. He moved fast, a blur as he clotheslined the nearest vamp, laying him out flat on the floor. His fist smashed the face of the other, and a brawl broke out.

I pulled Kylarai aside, trying to shield her with my body. "Do you believe me now that you shouldn't have come here? I love you, and I know how deeply you care for me. But now you have someone else to put first."

I forced her to see how serious I was. This was not up for discussion. If I had to drag her stubborn ass out of there myself, I would.

Arys jumped into the melee and promptly killed one of the offending vampires. A shower of dust coated the floor. A moment later a barstool came careening over to us, smacking the back of my legs. I swore like a sailor but was thankful it hadn't hit Ky.

"You don't have to ask me again," she said. "I didn't realize I'd be making this much trouble for you. I just wanted to help. I'll head home, but you better call me the second this is over."

"Trust me, it's better that you go now. If you think the vampires are bad you should see the FPA. If they knew you were…" I faltered, unable to even consider what I was about to say. "They can never know about the baby, Kylarai. This has to stay as secretive as possible."

Worry filled her grey eyes, and she nodded quickly. Her lower lip began to quiver, and she bit it. I hugged her close before escorting her all the way to her Escalade. I only went back inside after seeing her safely leave the parking lot.

Returning to the scene of the action, I found not one but two piles of dust and ash. Jenner and Arys stood there proudly, and I wouldn't have been surprised if they'd high fived. Catching Arys's eye, I gave him a pointed look and shook my head. This was not the way to show the vampire population that we weren't dictators.

"Don't even say it," Arys said, proving how well he knew my thoughts. "Those two threatened a pregnant woman. No innocents. Ever. Remember? It had to be done."

I glanced around at the remaining vamps present. They were either blissfully unaware and caught up in their own hunt, or they were very obviously watching us.

"You're right. That kind of shit can't be allowed. I just wish it hadn't happened at such a delicate time."

"Should've just let me rip their eyes out," Jez insisted with a frown. "Some punishments can be worse than death. They leave a longer lasting impression as well."

"Next time, Jezzy. Their eyeballs are all yours." My promise was met with a ruby red smile.

"Thanks," I said to Jenner, hoping he noticed the lack of sarcasm. I was genuinely grateful for his willingness to defend a wolf he didn't even know merely because she meant something to me. Maybe he wasn't such a jackass after all.

There was no time to recover from that little disturbance before Justin called my name. Even amid the pounding music and loud chatter of patrons, I heard it. Because I'd been expecting it.

I turned to find him beckoning me over. "Showtime," I said to Arys.

The trepidation and anxiety that had plagued me since Briggs's call faded. Now that he was here, I was ready.

"So that eyeball thing?" Jez asked, staying close as we headed for the door. "Is that still cool? I mean, the FPA, they've got to have it coming."

"I'd like to settle this without bloodshed. Briggs needs to see things from my point of view. But if he draws first blood, then it's on."

Jenner and Willow accompanied us out to the parking lot. It felt damn good to have these people at my back. At least it did until I stepped out of the building and saw the small army Briggs had brought.

Two black vans full of agents sat in the parking lot, blocking my car in as if Briggs thought I was cowardly enough to flee. He hadn't seemed to grasp my personality yet.

Agent Thomas Briggs stood beside one of the vans looking like he'd just stepped out of a Hollywood CIA movie. It was his usual look. Dark skinned with short-cropped hair, in a black suit, he had his hands on his hips, one of which rested on the butt of his gun.

I didn't give him a chance to speak first. "You must have some seriously big balls to hunt down your lover's sister, Briggs."

His steely dark gaze remained unchanged, but the slight change in his energy gave him away. I had just revealed something his crew didn't know. Good. It was a tiny victory, but it counted.

The vans had emptied. Briggs was surrounded by agents, both men and women, but none of them were Juliet. I did recognize one of them however. Agent Hunter, the biggest asshole on their team, stood smirking at me as if I hadn't seen him almost cry the last time we'd met. He was a livewire, one to be watched, unpredictable and quick to break the rules.

"We're not here to discuss my personal life, O'Brien. Trust me, this is not something I'm going to enjoy." Briggs took in my companions with careful consideration. Willow was the biggest threat of us all, but I was willing to bet he didn't know that.

I held up a hand that crackled with power unseen by most human eyes but readily felt. "Oh, I am definitely going to enjoy this."

"There doesn't have to be any innocent bloodshed here," he spoke calmly, trying to appeal to my sensible side. Too bad for him. I didn't have one. "We are on the same side. Let's be rational about this."

I laughed, a devious sound that was more Arys than it was me. "Rational, huh? You clearly don't know the meaning of the word. I'm not going to lie down and die for you, Briggs. That's just not my style."

Briggs was quiet, regarding me with the silent contemplation of an intelligent man who thought he knew what he was doing. He probably did most of the time. But not this time.

"I thought you cared about this city. Over a million people call this area home. Would you really risk them just to prolong the inevitable?" He spread his hands in question before crossing his arms in an attempt to appear casual.

Briggs's gaze traveled over Arys, and he frowned ever so slightly. I was willing to bet that he'd thought Arys was still out of town. His plan had been to take me out while we were apart. Sneaky bastard.

"Well now, Agent Briggs, you appear a little surprised to see me," Arys said, picking up on what I'd just realized. "You weren't by chance thinking about killing my wolf while I was away, were you? That kind of behavior seems beneath you. Doesn't it?"

Briggs and Arys shared a moment. Whatever passed between them, it wasn't good.

"What are we waiting for?" Agent Hunter interjected with a rude sneer in my direction. "Let's take this bitch out."

"You never learn, do you, Hunter?" I tsked and shook my head at his pathetic attempt to be a tough guy. "I guess I'll have to break your other arm. But I doubt I'll stop there. I made you a promise, remember?"

During a scuffle with the FPA, Kale had broken the man's arm. It clearly hadn't taught him a damn thing about keeping his mouth shut or knowing when to back down. The last time I saw Hunter I had promised him that he would die at my hand, and he would love it.

"Is there something I should know about you two?" Briggs shot a dark glare at Hunter who pressed his lips together in a refusal to speak.

"What's to know?" I dared to saunter closer, stopping only when every agent had leveled their gun at me. "Hunter here threw me in with Kale after you guys drove him crazy. He almost got me killed. Oh, and he wants your job. But I'm guessing you already knew that. Better watch your back, Briggs. Your guys don't know how to be a team."

Briggs's gaze narrowed. He chose to ignore my remark, but I was sure he'd have a word with Hunter later, if they left here alive.

"Come with us, O'Brien. You leave peacefully, and we can avoid a showdown in the parking lot. I'll make sure you're treated in a humane, fair way."

I gaped at him as if he'd just spoken in tongues. "Are you fucking kidding me? A humane way? I'm not a dog going off to the pound, you self-righteous piece of shit. If you want me, you'll have to take me the hard way."

Hunter cocked his weapon. Several others followed suit. Briggs held up a hand, and they waited for his order.

"Stopping Shya has been our mission for a very long time. I can't let a chance like this pass me by. Stopping him should be your top priority too." His tone was smooth and steady, but there was a pleading glint in his eyes.

That should have been reassuring I suppose. Ultimately, I knew that Briggs didn't really want to kill me. In a city where many people did, it was refreshing, and even somewhat flattering.

"It is. You just refuse to see that. Things have to happen, Briggs. Someone will kill me, but it won't be you." I couldn't help the glance I shot Arys. I saw Briggs notice. Could his clever mind put it together?

For just a moment it appeared as if Briggs might give me the benefit of the doubt. His studious stare moved between Arys and me. Hunter shuffled his feet impatiently and received an unspoken rebuke from his superior. I smiled.

"I want to trust you on this. I do," Briggs said. "Unfortunately, I don't. You make your decisions based on what's best for your people, and I do the same. I ask you one last time, please come with us. I'd prefer to keep this from being a public event."

Damn. So he wanted to really do this. "You know I'm not going anywhere with you."

Briggs gave a slight nod. A shot went off. It didn't come from the agents before us though. It came from above. A sniper on the roof of the grocery store across the street took his shot. It never hit. Willow held the bullet in his hand before anyone realized he'd intercepted it. His great silver wings were flared wide behind him, and he hummed with power.

Before anyone could react, he threw the bullet with supernatural speed. It lodged in Agent Hunter's thigh, and he fell to the ground with a shout.

All hell broke loose. The Feds fired their weapons, launching both wooden and regular bullets at us. Arys grabbed my hand and threw an energy wall up in front of us. The bullets bounced off as if hitting a brick wall.

The sudden surge of power streaming through me was overwhelming. Arys drew on our bond to hold the wall against the onslaught. It nearly drove me to my knees. Instinctively I reached out metaphysically for Jenner. He was our blood and, being mine as he was, my power drew on him.

Willow rushed the agents. Bullets bounced off him as if he were stone. Some of them dropped their guns and actually fled. Those that remained found themselves staring into the angry gaze of a very pissed off fallen angel.

With a snap of his fingers, Willow jammed their weapons. A flick of his wrist and several of them dropped, holding their heads as an unseen force tore pained cries from them.

"Shall I keep going?" Willow approached Briggs slowly, like a cat sneaking up on a mouse.

Briggs had his gun drawn, but he didn't seem to know where to point it. He watched Willow with a growing horror as he realized his mistake in coming here.

"Call this off, O'Brien," he barked. "There is no need for innocent men and women to die. That's what we're trying to prevent here."

I laughed bitterly. "Your people are no innocents. Your definition of the word is clearly twisted. I've seen the things you all do. I've seen the basement."

"This isn't about the basement, goddammit."

"No, it's not," I agreed. "Not yet."

Despite the bullet in his leg, Agent Hunter lunged forward, flinging himself at Arys's barrier. He hit the invisible wall and fell back, dazed. *Idiot.*

I couldn't resist. He was just so close. I risked breaking the barrier to get to Hunter. I all but fell on him in my haste. The scent of his blood was overpowering, taunting a side of me that I was beginning to finally accept. Straddling the injured man, I began feeding him punches that snapped his head from side to side. Blood poured from his nose and mouth, but still I didn't stop. He squirmed beneath me, seeking to throw me off. I felt the Taser on his hip, very likely the same one he'd used to abuse me not so long ago. Pulling it free, I held it beside his face and grinned.

"Calm down, sweetheart. You're going to like this. I promise."

The intoxicating aroma of his fear tickled my senses. It was only the beginning though.

With their guns made useless, the Feds were left with stun guns and billy clubs, none of which would do them a damn bit of good here. Jez and Jenner jumped into the fray, happily bringing pain to any agent dumb enough to get in their way.

Arys stood close, preventing anyone from interfering with Hunter and me. When Briggs tried to go for his phone to call for backup, Arys plucked it from his hand with ease and crushed it beneath his heel.

The fight taking place all around me became background noise as I stared down into Hunter's frozen gaze. For the first time perhaps ever, I very much wanted to make a victim suffer.

"I bet you thought you'd come here and get off watching me take a bullet to the head," I said, stroking a hand down his bruised and bloodied cheek. Gripping his jaw tight, I forced him to meet my eyes. "I can't wait to taste your death."

I pushed a breath of heady sensual energy into him, encompassing him in my thrall completely. He ceased struggling and peered at me like I was the most wonderful thing he'd ever seen. I manipulated the force, seducing him with little effort. The desire rolled off him in waves that I greedily drank in.

In an act that was pure vampire, I rubbed my groin against his, just enough to feel the evidence of his growing lust. With one hand on his face and the other caressing the throbbing vein in his neck, I sucked in a deep breath and groaned from the strength it took to keep from ripping his throat out. He didn't deserve to go that fast.

I was vaguely aware of the dead agents piling up in the parking lot. Jenner and Jez had cut down almost half a dozen already. A few of them had acquired crossbows and stakes from the vans. Willow and

Arys were quickly parting them from their weapons. Briggs was shouting orders at a crew that was no longer listening. It was chaos.

"Do you want me, Hunter?" I purred. "Tell me how you want me."

He drew a shuddery breath and moaned. "Just kill me and get it over with."

"Now what fun would that be?" My fingernails lengthened into deadly claws and I knew if I scratched him I'd have to kill him. There was no way an asshole like Hunter would make a good wolf. "Tell me what you want."

He gave a strangled sound as he fought the command. Betrayed by his body and his will, he had no choice but to comply. "I want to fuck you. But it ain't real. I know it's not, you vampire whore."

I laughed, enjoying his tortured state of want and hate. "Oh, it's real all right. Your hard on feels pretty real to me."

Another push of power and Hunter was almost crying in his attempts to pull free of my manipulation. I wanted to take my time with him, but time wasn't something I had a lot of.

I looked up in time to see Arys and Briggs locked in battle. Briggs fought hard with several well placed hits. He was well trained, and it showed. When he slid a stake from inside his jacket and whirled around to plunge it into Arys's chest, I gasped.

Arys caught his arm before the blow could land. He gave it a twist, and Briggs twisted with it, trying to avoid a broken arm. The move put his back to Arys who slung an arm around his neck and jerked him close. Fangs bared, Arys was about to go for Briggs's artery.

The sound of a gun cocking was heard seconds before Juliet stepped out of the shadows. She pressed the barrel against Arys's temple.

"Let him go. Now."

Chapter Seventeen

"Think you're going to kill me with that toy, little wolf?" Arys snickered. "Damn you O'Brien women are feisty creatures."

Her response was to shove the gun barrel even harder against his temple. "Maybe it will kill you. Maybe it will just blow your brains all over the pavement and leave you with a gaping hole in your head. How bad do you want to find out?"

The commotion died down as everyone paused to watch this play out. Juliet was so much like me sometimes. What a pain in the ass.

"Do whatever you have to do," Arys said, seemingly unaffected by the weapon pressed to his skull. "Just know that by hurting me, you'll hurt Alexa. And haven't you already done enough of that?"

"Shut the fuck up," Juliet barked, but her wild wolf gaze landed on me. She took in the sight of me atop Hunter. "Alexa, get off of him. Slowly. Don't try anything."

Coming to the rescue of Briggs was one thing. He was her superior and her lover. I got it. But Hunter? Hell no. He was mine.

"Too bad," I said to Hunter. "And I wanted to play with you a little longer. I guess we'll have to finish this fast." To Juliet I said, "You're really showing what an amateur you are right now. The only reason any of this happened is because you can't keep your mouth shut."

"I'm loyal to the FPA, Alexa. It was my job to give up that information. I'm sorry. I never thought it would go down like this. There's no reason for anyone else to get hurt."

Every word out of her mouth pissed me off. She had betrayed me, proven that she was not someone I could ever trust again. It hurt. Like a knife in my back, the sting of her betrayal burned.

"If you pull that trigger, Juliet, I will make Briggs take Hunter's place here. And I will force you to watch while I make him beg like an animal." It was a vicious threat, a truly ugly thing to say. And I meant every damn word.

It was a standoff. Juliet held her gun steady on Arys while we all waited for her to react to my threat.

Disgust marred her pretty face. She stared at me as if seeing a stranger in my place. I knew the feeling.

Her attention was so focused on me that she never realized there was a vampire slipping through the shadows in the parking lot, coming ever closer to her. I was aware of Kale's sugary sweet energy as he blended into the dark that fell beyond the streetlight's glow. He must have come out the back exit behind the building.

He emerged directly behind her. A few agents shouted a warning, but he was too fast. In a blur of motion, Kale grabbed Juliet's gun arm and twisted it behind her back. The gun went off, firing a bullet into the ground beside them.

Briggs tried to take advantage of the moment to escape Arys's hold. It didn't work. He only succeeded in being forced to his knees. Arys didn't stop there. He forced Briggs all the way down, pressing his face into the gritty pavement.

Kale met my eyes with a grin. "Alexa, I believe you were in the middle of something."

Juliet struggled against him. He held her easily. She should have known better. Vampires love a struggle. She was only going to succeed in feeding his hunger.

"Yes, I was, wasn't I?" I smiled. Everyone's full attention was upon Hunter and me. He was afraid again. My seductive hold had slipped during Juliet's brief stunt. That was fine. Fear worked just as well, maybe even better in this case.

"Don't do it, Lexi," Juliet pleaded. "Please, don't. I know you're better than that."

"That's just the thing, Juliet," I replied, meeting her wolf eyes with my own. "You don't know me at all. And I don't know you. Maybe I never did."

Hunter stared up at me with eyes wide with terror. Arys and Kale both watched me with eager expectation. They wanted to watch this happen. Having them there, anticipating the moment when I would spill Hunter's blood, it drove me. Raising a clawed hand, I brought it down in one fell swoop. My claws tore through Hunter's throat, and blood spattered my face. The blood gushed forth to puddle beneath his head.

I brought a hand to my mouth and dragged my tongue over my bloody fingers. Juliet's hysterical cries were shrill, ear piercing. Her horror at witnessing my act of murder and retribution was understandable. She really didn't know who I was. I myself was just beginning to find out.

Arys watched me suck a scarlet-stained finger into my mouth with obvious intrigue. Poor Kale wasn't quite so restrained. The hunger in his enchanting eyes was palpable. I knew he wanted to join me. I could feel it. He and I made a deadly duo together.

"What do you want to do with them?" Arys nodded to Briggs at his feet and gestured to the remaining agents, most of which held their hands up in surrender.

I stood up slowly, licking the tip of a bloody claw. The rush of what I'd just done had me walking on air. I swayed as I stepped away from Hunter's corpse, but I was as steady as I'd ever been. Empowered by the circuit of power I shared with every vampire present, I glided over to where Arys had Briggs pinned on the ground. Juliet watched me with a hateful glare.

I gestured to the tense agents awaiting a decision. "Gather your dead. Leave your weapons. And get the hell off my property." To my vampires I added, "Hold these two until everyone else is in the vans. No more death tonight. Get Briggs on his feet."

Arys jerked Briggs up, forcing a pained sound from him. He held the agent's arms behind his back in a grip that I knew had to hurt more than Briggs let on.

"Don't think for a second that letting me live will keep you alive," Briggs spat. Rage filled his brown eyes. It was nice to see a real emotion on the usually strong and calm Fed.

I stood close enough to Briggs to smell his cologne along with his deliciously human scent. "I know you think you've got everything figured out, but you don't. I'm not just Shya's sacrifice. I'm not only a werewolf with vampire power. I am a Hound of God. A wolf called to battle evil. Do your research. Learn your shit. And stay the hell out of my way. Your misguided efforts are interfering with a greater plan. The death of your people is on you. Come for me again, and I will kill you, but not nearly as fast as I killed Hunter."

Fury poured from Briggs. It tickled my senses, taunting my bloodlust. I was starting to understand what Arys meant when he said my anger turned him on.

"Evil battling evil. I find that hard to believe," Briggs seethed. "You are a killer, O'Brien. Plain and simple. Warring with Shya doesn't change that."

I reached out but didn't quite touch him. Instead I touched his aura, running my fingers through it with intent. He responded as I'd hoped. A shudder racked him as he found pleasure in my metaphysical caress. It was just too easy.

"There isn't a person present here who doesn't have blood on their hands. Get off your high horse, Agent Briggs. You're a dirty Fed with an immoral agenda. I wouldn't doubt that your kill count is much higher than mine." I pulled on his energy before pushing it back with a hint of my influence, just enough to coax a groan from him. "I've seen the FPA basement. There are human beings suffering down there."

All at once I dropped the metaphysical contact and stepped back. My tone dripped venom when I said, "I never claimed to be perfect. You need to stop pretending you are. I'm not the enemy, and I will not be treated like one. The next time you get it into your head that I'm the problem, remember that I let you go. I won't do it again."

A low growl drew my attention to Juliet. She was all fangs and wolf eyes, snarling at me like a rabid beast. "You're a monster," she declared, like it was news.

"We're all fucking monsters, Agent O'Brien." I threw down the gauntlet with the use of her government title. There was nothing personal left between us. "Some of us have just accepted it. Unfortunately, those who deny their dark nature the most tend to be the worst offenders."

Neither she nor Briggs uttered another word. We released them, and they promptly climbed into the waiting vans. As I watched them drive away, I couldn't help but wonder when the FPA had become a bigger pain in the ass than Shya. This wasn't over. I knew it undoubtedly.

"That went well," I sighed.

"You know you're going to have to kill him someday," Arys said. "Briggs. He won't ever let up on you."

"Let's not go there tonight. I don't want to think about it." I joined Jez in picking up the abandoned FPA weaponry. It had to be safely stored somewhere, maybe in the storage closet beside the men's washroom.

A pounding bass beat preceded the slick black Dodge Challenger that pulled into the parking lot. It jerked to a stop beside me and a tall, burly werewolf stepped out. He was built like a rock. I wouldn't doubt he could bench press me with one arm. A bandana was tied around his head of short, dark hair. His short-sleeved shirt showed off a variety of tattoos. It was the pack's moon tattoo on his neck that told me all I needed to know.

His gaze took in each of my companions in turn before settling on me. Deep brown eyes took note of the blood on my hands and face. It got no reaction from him.

"You're Alexa?" He asked, continuing without waiting for an answer. "I'm Owen, Dayne's enforcer. He sent me to give you this." He handed me a small, sealed envelope. Inside was a Doghead business card with an address scribbled on the back. "He didn't want to send it via phone in case of FPA tracking."

"Smart," I remarked, making a mental note to pick up a burner phone or two. "They are very much on top of tech tracking. Is there a specific time he'd like this to happen?"

"The sooner the better. He wants me to shadow you. I'll keep my distance. You won't even see me."

I pursed my lips and studied him. I wasn't an idiot. Clearly Dayne had sent his enforcer to ensure I really did the job I said I'd do without screwing him over somehow.

"Fine," I agreed, handing an armful of guns to Willow. "We might as well get this over with. I don't have a lot of time to spare."

Arys broke in then, just as expected. I had to stifle a smile. "I'm coming with you," he said, a stubborn edge to his tone.

"I need you here," I said aloud but inside his head I said, 'You know we can't be alone together right now. It's not worth arguing about.'

A muscle twitched in Arys's jaw. His unease echoed through me. "I'll stay, but you have to take someone with you."

Jez and Willow both volunteered. Neither of them were right for this kill. Jez was still bouncing back from the other night, and Willow had no place helping me kill a werewolf who was unknown to him.

"Could you excuse me for just a moment?" I gave Owen a smile that I hoped was both secretive and friendly. Holding up my bloody hands, I turned toward the lively nightclub. "I just need to get washed up. I'd invite you in but werewolves tend to draw the wrong attention here."

"No worries. I'll wait out here." Owen headed back to his car and watched us go.

Discussing who was the safest choice to accompany me was not something I wanted to do in front of a stranger. The Doghead pack expected me to earn their trust. I expected the same from them.

Jez followed me to the ladies room where she hassled me while I washed up. The washroom was loud, filled with women doing everything from gossiping to makeup touch ups. A few of them were wary of my presence, but I wasn't the one feasting on them in a back hall bedroom. Yet. So for the most part, they ignored us.

"Come on, Lex. We make a great team. I need a good hunt to feel like myself again." She took the opportunity to reapply her bright red lipstick. Her watchful cat gaze kept darting to me in the mirror.

"If the situation were different I would take you in a heartbeat, Jez. But I think I need a vampire to back me on this one." I washed my face and hands, watching Agent Hunter's blood run down the drain. In a matter of seconds, the evidence of what I'd done was gone.

"A vampire?" She scoffed. "Not Kale I hope. You make each other crazy."

"Thanks for the update. I wasn't aware." With a wet paper towel, I cleaned up a smear of eyeliner. Then I balled up the paper towel and tossed it at Jez, who saw it coming in the mirror and deflected it expertly without ruining her lipstick.

"So what do you want me to do?" She asked, popping the lid back onto her lipstick. "Don't send me home. I can't sit there feeling useless. I could slip."

"No slipping." I gave her arm a warm squeeze. "You're going to beat this now before it has a chance to become something bigger than it already is. Stay here with Kale and Willow. I won't be long."

Jez pouted, turning those fabulous full lips on me as if she'd practiced the expression a thousand times. "If any vampires take a run at me, I'm plucking out eyeballs."

"You have my permission to pluck all the eyeballs your little heart desires." It was impossible to keep from laughing.

"I'd rather hunt a narc werewolf. You get to have all the fun."

When we returned from the washroom, Arys had made up his mind. "I don't like the idea of you killing for the wolves. However, I know that's your territory, and I have no right to argue that choice. But I want you to take Jenner with you."

Jenner didn't appear surprised. He had already heard this. I waited for his protest, but it never came.

"Really?" Disbelief colored the word. "All right. I suppose that makes sense." It did. Both Kale and Arys were too dangerous to be alone with in a situation that involved blood and death. Would it ever be like that with Jenner? God I hoped not. Once I turned, this kind of thing would stop. Wouldn't it?

"I'll stay here in case the FPA sends anyone back. Switch phones with me in case they try to track yours. My phone isn't under a real name. They shouldn't have it on their radar." Arys pressed his phone into my hand. Then he pulled me close for a kiss that was both longing and frustrated.

I shot a glance to where Kale fended off admirers across the room. "No getting into it with him. Promise me."

Arys rolled his eyes and kissed me again. "You ask a lot sometimes, you know."

"Don't worry, Lex. I'll keep an eye on them." Jez snickered when Arys playfully nudged her with an elbow.

Willow held out a hand. In the other was a tequila shot. "Address? If we don't hear from you in an hour I'm dropping in to check on you."

"Thanks, Willow. You're the best." I tucked the Doghead card with the address into his waiting palm after taking one more look at it. Then I turned to Jenner and shrugged. "Let's go kill a government informant."

* * * *

I wasn't sure what I'd been expecting when we pulled up to the address Dayne had given me. It was a warehouse, some kind of storage facility or shipping yard from the looks of it.

"I don't know why, but for some reason I was expecting his home address," I said, studying the surroundings.

Jenner and I sat in the Charger, watching and waiting for something amiss. The place was deserted, leading me to question whether or not it was abandoned. It seemed like a good private place to pull off something like this. It also seemed like a great way to mislead someone.

"That would be too easy," Jenner observed. "And too high risk. The last thing you need is a neighbor witnessing something they shouldn't. Unless you're willing to kill them too."

I most certainly was not interested in living out that scenario. The creepy warehouse would have to do.

"I'm going to go take a look around. Can I trust you to have my back?" I met his frozen gaze, seeking a spark of truth. Jenner might be Arys's brother, but he didn't like me, with good reason. I wasn't entirely convinced I could trust him.

"That's what I'm here for, isn't it?" A chuckle shook him. "I wouldn't trust me either if I were you, but I've already proven that I came to help out a brother. Give me a little credit."

"No, you proved that you wouldn't stand by while Arys killed me before it was time. That doesn't mean you won't take a shot at it yourself."

He held my gaze. It made me want to squirm, but I managed to sit still. The familiar energy he exuded was comforting, seeking to draw me in. I shielded hard against it.

"True," he admitted with a nod of his dark head. "I guess there's only one way to find out. And that's by trusting me."

"After the shit you pulled in Vegas, that's not likely to happen. Just don't fuck me over, or I'll have to kill you. And I really don't want to explain that to Arys. He didn't take it so well with Harley." Throwing Harley's death in Jenner's face was low. Still, he needed to be reminded of whom he was dealing with.

A glare made his face ugly and hostile. "Go. I'll have your back."

I wanted to say something to smooth over the mess I'd just made of the conversation. I opened my mouth but nothing came out. There was no friendly medium here.

Instead of trying to make friends with a vampire who hated me, I got out of the car and quietly closed the door. I reached out mentally to feel for anyone in the vicinity. Owen's wolf energy was distant but close enough to be felt. There was another wolf here too. Closer. It had to be my target.

For just a moment I reconsidered. Only the promise of a Doghead alliance kept my feet moving. Silent and stealthy, I crept around the perimeter of the large empty yard.

Coming to the conclusion that my target was inside, I made my way toward a back entry. Dayne must have sent him here. Could he possibly know why?

My senses were lively, taking in metaphysical information at a radical speed. I knew when Jenner had left the car and made his way along the path I'd walked. Owen was still distant, as he'd promised, though I was sure he'd come close enough to survey the place.

There was a squeal of metal as I inched open the back door. So much for approaching on the sly. No matter. He would smell me coming eventually.

The warehouse definitely was abandoned. It stunk to high heaven of mildew and something greasy, possibly rotten. It must have housed food products at some point. Gross.

I came through a small back room that led to the main area. It was wide open with a high ceiling and one dim light burning overhead. I came to an abrupt halt when the werewolf caught my scent and spun to face me from where he stood near the main door.

Shock registered on Stuart's face. I almost wished I didn't know his name. Too many personal details made this kind of thing a whole lot harder.

"He sent you? The hybrid?" The first words out of his mouth were followed by a few expletives. "I'm not even good enough for Owen? Ok, I see how it is."

"Let's not make this a discussion," I said, sliding the Dragon Claw from its sheath as I crossed the large room. "I'm here to earn an alliance, and you're here because you broke one."

"I didn't though. Really. The FPA thought they were getting some good shit from me, but I didn't give them anything they could use. I swear it." Stuart was frightened, a poor trait in any werewolf. He swiped a hand across his sweaty brow before pushing it through his thinning hair.

"Don't waste your energy talking. The bottom line is that you spoke to the FPA. That is an absolute no-no among our kind. It makes you a traitor. We all know what happens to traitors."

The wolf rose up behind his eyes. Perhaps he would fight after all. I wouldn't feel too great about killing him if he cried the whole time.

"I'm not a traitor," he insisted. The stink of a lie rolled off him. He knew damn well what he was. Good. That made this easier.

"You are, and we both know it. You've endangered children because of what you've done."

He didn't deny it. Shaking his head vigorously, he backed himself up against the front door as I approached. His fingernails lengthened into claws, and his eyes were solid wolf.

I rushed forward, hoping to land a killing blow before he could shift. I swung the Dragon Claw, aiming for a neck wound, but it sliced through air. Stuart dropped down in time to escape my assault. Seconds later he was a big brown wolf shaking free of tattered clothing. Fangs bared, he lunged at me with a snarl. I swung the dagger again, using it to keep him at bay. He snarled and snapped, unable to get close enough to attack.

With my free hand I hurled a slap of power at him, taking him down with a yelp. He struggled to his feet, but I was there with another blast. I held him pinned with a stream of energy heavy enough to take down a much larger animal.

Stuart struggled to break free. Twitching and flailing on the floor, he never ceased the growl that echoed in the vast, empty building.

I lifted the dagger, prepared to bring it down in one strong swoop. In his desperation Stuart twisted around and bit wildly at nothing.

Then he got lucky.

Fangs sunk into my ankle, and I shrieked. Before he could crush the bone, I kicked him hard in the face with my other foot. I followed up with the dagger, stabbing it downward, seeking any part of him I could hit. It pierced the flesh of his flank, and he released me.

The pain was excruciating. A werewolf bite was deadly, always meant to inflict as much damage as possible. Having no time to examine the wound, I swung again. This time the Dragon Claw founds its mark. It plunged deep into Stuart's chest. I jerked it free and prepared for another blow, but he fell face first into the hard concrete floor and didn't get up.

"That was impressive." Jenner's voice broke me out of the moment. He stood inside the main entry, watching with arms crossed. "Much faster than I'd expected."

"Ditto." I sat heavily on the floor and pulled up my pant leg. "Fucker bit me though."

"So? You heal fast."

"Not as fast as you. Not yet anyway. It friggin' hurts."

The bite was deep. All four fangs had punctured my ankle. Blood oozed from the wounds, staining my hands as I applied pressure to it.

Jenner made a noise, something between a gasp and a curse. I jerked my head up to find him watching me with blatant hunger. *Oh shit.* Bleeding in front of any vampire was dangerous, but bleeding in front of one who had tasted my blood and now belonged to me because of it, that was just downright careless.

"Jenner?" Uncertainty showed in my tone. I didn't know him well enough to know how he'd handle this.

"Why the hell did you have to let him do that?" Pushing away from the door, he moved toward me with a predatory gait. His pupils were huge, a deep, drowning black.

"Back off," I warned, a hand raised with a ready psi ball. "Don't make me take you down."

Jenner paused. His control was strong. It had to be. He was of our bloodline. At least, that's what I told myself as I struggled to get up.

The bite throbbed in time with my heartbeat. It would heal within a day or two naturally. Even faster if Arys healed it. I willed the bleeding to stop.

"I've dreamed of tasting you many times since you left Vegas." His sudden confession stunned me. "That's what happens when you enslave a vampire. They never stop craving you."

"Nobody is enslaved," I insisted, sliding the dagger back into its sheath. Killing Jenner was just not an option, even if he rushed me. "You're all so easily influenced by the power. It's an illusion."

His laughter echoed. "Illusion is it? Is it an illusion when you crave the touch of your forbidden lover? Certainly not. Is it illusion when a victim begs you for more? No. It is a very real, very undeniable desire." He continued to press closer, stopping only when he stood within arms' reach. "Our power is meant to enslave our victims. To make them ours in every way. Unfortunately, some of us are powerful enough to use that gift on each other. Lucky you."

"Yes, lucky me." I limped toward the door, keeping my distance as I passed him. "Come on; let's get out of here."

Jenner caught my arm before I saw him move. He brought my wrist to his mouth and boldly ran his tongue along the veins there.

"Don't even think about it," I murmured as apprehension flooded me.

"Too late. Would just a taste be so wrong? It would make being around you a hell of a lot easier." Despite his actions, he was still himself. Jenner's control was far better than Kale's, and for that I was grateful.

Instinct demanded that I slap him with a blast hard enough to toss him across the room. Experience had taught me remaining calm was safer.

"I knew I couldn't trust you. You should be helping me to the car not taking advantage of my injury." I focused on keeping my energy calm. Reacting to him was not an option, but hot damn was the touch of his tongue ever sensual.

"I won't do it without permission," Jenner spoke against my skin. "But I am asking."

Even as his words said one thing, his touch conveyed another. It was manipulative, enthralling, so much like what Arys and I commanded, only with a different flavor. I shuddered against the pull. This manipulative power was both my strength and my weakness. As they say, power doesn't come without a price.

"No," I managed to say though my voice wavered. "I'm telling you no. So stop the hypnotic incubus shit right now."

"Nice to know I haven't lost my touch," he said with a devious laugh. "If I can get under your skin, I must be doing something right."

To Jenner's credit, he did pull away from the pulse beating in my wrist. Though much like his brother, he was reluctant to so readily accept defeat. Catching me completely off guard, he sucked my bloody pinky finger into his mouth.

My breath caught, and I watched with wide-eyed wonder as he gently sucked the blood from my flesh. I trembled as the power swirled around us, capturing us in the eye of the growing tornado. I would never stop being amazed by what the vampires in our bloodline could do. It took great effort to pull my hand away.

"I apologize, my queen," he said emphasizing the word "queen" as if it were an inside joke we shared. "You ordered me to touch you once. I can't help but recall that night and feel cheated that I never got to fulfill that command."

"Yeah, well I'm not as much of a bed hopping vamp as you are. I prefer to sleep only with those I love. Besides, Arys would kick your ass." I shoved him away and limped for the exit.

Something stopped me in my tracks, and it wasn't Jenner this time. My senses burned. There were other vampires near.

"Not yet you aren't. Give it a few more decades," he quipped. "You're right though. Arys is not the forgiving type when it comes to you."

"Do you feel that?" I asked, slapping his arm to get his attention.

Jenner grew quiet, and I felt it when he reached out to appraise our environment. "I don't think we're alone here anymore."

"Vampires," I breathed. "A lot of them."

"These aren't friends of yours I take it?"

"Sneaking up on me while I'm conveniently trapped in a warehouse? Not likely." I didn't doubt this had something to do with the rebel vampires Kale had dealt with. This must be their answer to the open message I'd issued.

Jenner took the lead, hesitating for a moment at the door. "Let's try to get to the car. If we don't make it, we fight."

"Right." I nodded, but my stomach turned. A fair fight I could handle. A gang beating was nobody's friend. I'd only survived the last one because of Willow.

I followed Jenner outside, my hand ready on the hilt of the Dragon Claw. At first the warehouse yard appeared empty. Looks were deceiving. They were close. I could feel them.

One by one they emerged from the darkness. I stopped counting at twenty. At least a dozen stood between us and the car. And really, fleeing would only encourage their behavior. It would do nothing to enforce the role I claimed.

A shock of pain stabbed through my leg. They would smell the bite and know I was injured. We would definitely have to fight.

Jenner and I stood back to back, watching the circle of vampires form around us. We were surrounded.

Chapter Eighteen

None of the vampires were well known to me. I found some relief in that. It promptly died when I saw that they had Owen. He hung between two of them, having been beaten into submission.

Blood trickled from his nose and mouth. Still, he glared fiercely at the two holding him. Admirable. I couldn't help but worry that Dayne would blame me for this. I could not let Owen die here tonight.

I expected one of them to act as ringleader, maybe toss out some lame movie bad guy lines. Jenner didn't give them a chance. He immediately went on the offensive, hurling shot after shot at the ring surrounding us. His aim was true and deadly. Two of the vamps he hit exploded in a cloud of dust.

That was all it took. The fight was on. Those with power of any kind were quick to use it while others came forward ready to rip us limb from limb.

Having no other choice, I followed Jenner's lead. The nearest vamp baring fangs at me took a blast to the face. It maimed but did not kill.

"Focus your intent," Jenner hissed as he fended off three at a time. "Kill them in your mind. No mercy."

My concentration was scattered as I sought to watch all of them at once. It was impossible. They came too fast. I was overwhelmed. The pain shooting through my ankle didn't help.

The Dragon Claw felt good in my hand as I plunged it into the guts of one vampire who mistakenly lunged at the wrong time. A second one met the same ending. The victory was short-lived. Half a dozen descended on me using both fists and power. I went down beneath them, holding the dagger above me to protect my head.

'Arys,' I cried out in my thoughts, reaching for him in desperate need. Unable to form a coherent thought while fangs slashed at my arms and fists pummeled my head, I let him see and feel what I was experiencing.

'I'm on my way. Willow's coming now. Throw everything you have at them. No mercy.'

I would have found his words funny, as they echoed Jenner's perfectly, if I hadn't just taken a knee to the stomach. I rolled onto my side, clutching the Dragon Claw uselessly. The blows never stopped coming as both my back and my front received a flurry of hits.

Jenner was fighting hard, doing a far better job than I was. Still, he too fell victim to the sheer number of them. On his knees beside me, he groped for my hand.

The connection sent a surge of strength through me. I envisioned every vampire surrounding us flying backwards as if a bomb of power had gone off amid them, and then it happened. The power followed my intent, sending vampires sailing in several directions.

The simple act gave me a greater appreciation for Arys's bloodline. Together we rose. Pain shot through my ankle, and I whimpered.

"Give it everything you've got," Jenner ordered. "Don't hold back."

I struggled to fill my lungs with air. I ached in places I didn't know could ache. Our reprieve was brief. For every vampire we killed or beat down, three more took its place.

The air moved unnaturally, and Willow appeared beside us. I breathed a sigh of relief. His silver wings flared wide, and he drove back the opposing vampires. I thought it was over, that he had saved me again. I thought wrong.

No sooner had Willow appeared than the air rippled once again, and Brook stood there smirking with black wings spread like shadows behind him.

"Sorry, Willow," Brook said, his voice oily and his black eyes gleaming. "Can't let you interfere this time."

"That's not your call to make." Willow faced off with the demon. "Why concern yourself with the activity of vampires? What's it to you?"

The remaining vampires still outnumbered us. They all seemed a little too pleased to see Brook, like they'd been expecting him.

"A shared interest." Brook's hateful gaze flicked to me and back to Willow. "They seek to keep her from rising to greater power as I seek to keep Shya from the same. Therefore, a partnership."

Willow scoffed. "You're all idiots. The only one that can keep Shya from rising to greater power is Alexa. You all need her. You should be backing her, not trying to kill her."

Only one vampire dared to speak up. "We won't be ruled by a hybrid. She isn't worthy of being called one of us."

"That's because she's not," Willow snapped. "She's better than every one of you. That's why none of you will survive this night."

Slow, even breaths. I had to make a conscious effort to keep breathing. Every intake of air was agony. I suspected that more than one of my ribs was broken.

Brook wasn't interested in playful banter. He rushed Willow with a war cry. The impact as they collided produced an earth shattering boom.

It was all the vampires needed. Inspired by the demon's actions, they came at us again. With Willow preoccupied, Jenner and I were left to defend ourselves.

We stuck together. I was careful to keep Jenner at my back so he wouldn't accidentally come too close to the dagger. As I swung the deadly blade, I drew hard on the power I shared with Arys. It spilled into me like the breaking of a dam. Opening myself up to it, I felt that familiar rush and heard that white noise in my ears. It felt right, like it was me and I was it. I became one with the inhuman metaphysical entity as it thrummed through my mortal form.

The dagger fell from my grip as the force commanded me. With both hands outstretched before me, I unleashed a torrent of power. It cascaded over each vampire in turn, and like dominoes they all fell before me. Blood gushed from their eyes, nose, mouth, and ears. On their knees, some of them clawed desperately at the ground while others attempted to plead for forgiveness of their error. One by one they burst into ash and dust.

As great as my power was, it was only at half-mast without Arys. Drawing on him enabled me greater strength, but it was limited by my weakened mortal frame. Though most of the two dozen or so remaining vampires fell under my assault, not all of them were destroyed.

Jenner fought hard at my side. Many died at his hand, and as crazy as it seemed, he appeared to enjoy the fight. Brook and Willow were still engaged in a battle of wills, throwing one another around with ease. It was nothing more than a distraction meant to keep Willow from coming to my aid. It worked.

I saw Owen on the ground several yards away. He was bloodied and incoherent but alive. If I could get to him and make a circle, I could keep him safe.

That was easier said than done. I couldn't stop the flow of energy that was coursing through me. When I tried to, I realized with great concern that it was running wild on its own accord. It was beyond my control.

It didn't take long for my physical strength to fade. My body was not meant for a force this strong to last this long. With every vampire I took down I found it harder to focus, harder even to breathe. The wolf inside rebelled, seeking to break out. I fought back the beast, knowing I had no power in that form.

"Alexa, get up." Jenner's hand on my arm brought me back to myself. I hadn't been aware I was on the ground. "It's not over yet. I need you. Get up."

He jerked me to my feet where I swayed, fighting to regain a sense of balance. Blood ran from my nose and a blinding pain smashed my skull behind my eyes. This was it. The moment Shya had feared. The power was going to kill me, and he was going to miss it.

A laugh sounded especially loud in my ears. I was vaguely aware that it was me. Jenner's face swam into focus. He was bleeding from a gash on his forehead but otherwise looked pretty good.

A dizzy spell shook me and suddenly the ground was rushing up to meet me. Jenner kept me from hitting. Shaking me and shouting, he slapped my face. My eyes rolled back in my head, and I struggled to speak.

"Let go of me," I gasped. "I don't want to hurt you."

Before I could be sure he'd heard me, a vampire grabbed him from behind, and he was gone, fighting with an impressive command of both body and power. Never had I envied that until now, when my own mortal limitations threatened to kill me.

Arys's voice echoed in my head. It hurt to have him there, breaking into my already tortured thoughts. His concern was heavy, but I couldn't form a clear reply. It would take him a good thirty minutes to reach us. I would likely be dead by then.

The next few vampires that dared to come close enough to deliver a blow of any kind met a dusty end. The power went out from me, needing no direction. It was wild and erratic, targeting anyone who sought to harm me.

Unfortunately, for every vampire I destroyed, a piece of myself died too. As the power grew stronger, I grew weaker. The force needed me as a channel, and I was succumbing to the toll it was taking on me. My vision blurred, and my lungs burned. I collapsed heavily on the ground and prayed death would be swift. Anything to free me from this agony. The stabbing pain in my skull was too much.

Despite having kicked some serious ass, I wasn't going to win this battle. The rebel vampires in their misguided quest had the advantage by having numbers and bodies that were beyond human mortality. Though there were very few of them left, the damage had been done.

I saw him coming. A dark haired, bearded vampire made his way toward me. Picking up my dagger, he smiled. I could only watch as he raised it high above my head. Cringing, I waited for the blow to land, hoping it would be fast.

A dark shape flew past me, hitting the vampire solidly in the chest. He hit the ground hard. A black wolf sat atop him, fangs tearing viciously through skin and tissue.

Raoul? My exhausted and wounded brain was momentarily confused. It was Owen, tearing my attacker's throat out.

Using the last of my strength, I grabbed the dagger and swung, decapitating the vampire beneath Owen. He whirled to take on the next, but there was no one left standing. It had all happened so fast, and yet it felt like it had taken hours.

Owen came to me, his muzzle going crazy as he sniffed me, seeking out my various injuries. I clutched a handful of his thick, black fur and whimpered as my wolf sought to communicate with him.

We were unknown to one another and yet he had come to my aid. After having the vampires renounce me as an unworthy hybrid, this meant a lot. If I survived to cry in relief about it later, I would.

Owen himself was fine for the most part. I slumped against him, thankful that Dayne could not hold the death of his enforcer against me. That would have blown my entire alliance plan to hell and back.

"Alexa?" Jenner knelt beside me. He took hold of my battered face and forced me to meet his gaze. A shiner outlined his left eye now. "Are you still with me? You're not looking too hot, girl."

I tried to speak, but the barest whisper came out. It hurt. I pressed my face into Owen's fur and focused on his wolfish scent. He wasn't my wolf, but it was a comfort just the same.

My eyes closed, and I waited for death to come. I was ready now.

'Don't you dare give up now.' Arys's demand broke through the fog in my head. 'This isn't how it ends. Remember?'

I smiled, and my face ached. 'I remember.'

'I'm coming for you, my wolf. You are not dying tonight.'

I believed him. Though I was ready for the crushing pain to be over, I knew he was right.

Jenner pulled me into his arms. "Take whatever you need. Blood, energy. Anything."

Weakened as I was, just the mention of blood stirred my hunger. It wasn't Jenner I wanted. It was mortal blood. Owen. The scent of heady shifter blood brought forth the bloodlust with a vengeance. I was too deteriorated to act as my hunger demanded.

It didn't matter. The scent of sulfur brought with it Shya, standing over me in all of his unholy glory. I knew then that being dead was preferable to whatever he had planned for me.

"Enough," Shya barked at Willow and Brook. With barely a gesture he separated them, violently flinging them apart.

His red gaze landed on Brook. Without a visible motion, he suddenly stood in front of the demon. Brook cowered before him.

"Shya, I can explain. It isn't what it looks like." With his hands raised in surrender, Brook fell to his knees. Genuine fear shook him as he begged for mercy.

He should be afraid. I'd seen him be tortured because he'd pissed Shya off. Evidently demons didn't learn from that.

Shya uttered something that I guessed to be Latin. Brook's pleading grew to an irritating level. Pathetic. Shya pressed a hand to the other demon's forehead and repeated the Latin phrase. Smoke rose up between them and a shadow appeared. It moved as if it were a person though it took no shape. Creeping closer to Brook it pulsed with a heavy, dark essence.

Brook's wide eyes shone with terror. All of his shrieking and flailing did nothing to help him. Shya stepped back and watched as the shadow devoured Brook right in front of us. Wherever it took him, I knew I never wanted to see that place.

Both Brook and the shadow disappeared, and Shya turned his attention to me. *Great.*

"This is exactly what I'd hoped would not happen," he said, shaking his head as if scolding a child caught disobeying yet again. "Look at you, Alexa. At death's door, and I still have yet to find my scroll. I simply can't have you up and die on me."

"Sorry to disappoint you," I gasped out through the pain that shook me. "I guess you can't always get what you want. Life's not fair. All that crap."

Shya gazed down at me with anger burning in his crimson orbs. "Oh, you're not dying on me. I won't allow it."

Something in the way he said that struck a nerve. I looked to Willow for help, but he stood uncertainly aside. Being in between the way he was, neither angel nor demon, he didn't have the power Shya had.

Shya followed my gaze and chuckled, but it lacked his usual amusement. "Don't expect your guardian to step in now. He has no power here. Let's not turn this into something it doesn't have to be."

He extended a hand to help me up. Suspiciously, I glared at him. "Don't touch me."

Owen and Jenner stood on either side of me. They too seemed to know they were no match for the demon. I turned to them and whispered, "Go."

I couldn't blame Owen when he listened. Turning tail, he fled into the night. Good. Having him leave here alive was important.

Jenner stood his ground, and in that act I knew he really did love Arys since he certainly didn't love me. And yet, he stayed.

"Come now, Alexa. Don't make this difficult. I'd hate to have to torture your vampire in order to gain your compliance." A hateful smile tugged at Shya's lips. It was so typical of him to threaten harm against others in order to control me. The conniving monster knew what worked.

"Shya, stop. You reek of desperation. Have you really sunk so low as to torment lesser creatures to appease yourself?" Willow drew close, standing protectively over me. He faced the demon with a challenge on his face. It would have made me weep if I hadn't been so damn exhausted.

His interference was met with a slap of demon power so strong I almost threw up. Willow took the hit like a champ. Rolling along the hard ground, he got back to his feet and brushed himself off.

"You know this was cute at first," Shya said. "The fallen angel willing to risk it all for love while fighting to uphold his duties. Great story. Really. But we've already played this hand. And you lose, my friend."

"I won't let you do to Alexa what you did to Christina," Willow vowed, hatred giving him a hard edge I'd never seen before.

"You say that as if you have a choice. You couldn't save your whore, and you surely can't save your Hound." Shya advanced on Willow. The evil rolled off him like fog off the ocean, filling the atmosphere with a thick, stifling sensation. It burned, and I tried to shield against it but lacked the strength to do so.

"Don't touch him," I managed to say.

Shya ignored me, having eyes only for the one that defied him. My gaze landed on the Dragon Claw, and I used everything I had in me to reach for it. Jenner kicked it toward me, and my hand wrapped around the smooth black jade hilt. With a shaky hand I positioned the blade over the artery in my forearm. It wasn't supposed to end this way, but I couldn't allow Shya to take this any farther.

"Shya," I said, waiting for him to look my way. When he did, I flashed him a feeble smile. "Fuck you."

Sliding the blade through my flesh, I grimaced as it bit deep. It stung as the demon magic within the blade recognized me as the one it belonged to. Having been made with both demon magic and a piece of my hair, the dagger was bound to me. Tasting my blood made the dagger quiver, as if it sought to escape.

Willow was forgotten as Shya watched the blade he'd given me end my life. Wings spread wide, he uttered more Latin and promptly descended on me. He ripped the dagger out of my hand and threw it. With a hand on the bleeding gash, he spoke a series of words I didn't understand. I wanted to pull away, to fight him off, anything. Instead, I slumped against him and demanded that death take me. Oblivion was quick to claim me, and I welcomed it. I didn't care where it took me as long as it took me away from this place and away from this demon.

Chapter Nineteen

Everything ached. My body was stiff and sore but much better than the last time I'd been conscious.

Aches and pains meant that I was alive. Didn't it?

Cracking my eyes open I found myself in a room I'd never seen before. It smelled weird, like everything was brand new. Even the bed I was on creaked as if it had barely been used. Sitting up seemed to be more work than it was worth so I laid there staring at the ceiling. The room was dimly lit, casting shadows on the ceiling above me. The walls were painted a pale yellow. It was ugly.

When I could no longer stare at nothing, I turned my head to find a nightstand with a lamp and a bottle of water. A couch and television also occupied the room. A door on the far side opened into a bathroom. I knew where I was. Shya's house. As a prisoner.

"Son of a bitch," I swore. "I can't even succeed at dying."

"Nor should you hope to." The voice came from the couch. Falon sat there watching me.

"What are you doing here? Babysitting?" I did sit up then, finding that I wore nothing but one of Shya's soft kimono-style robes. That was alarming. Immediately I was pissed.

"Something like that," Falon said, sounding bored. "You really don't know when to stop antagonizing, do you?"

"Where's Shya?"

"He's busy with Gabriel."

"How long have I been here? Where's Arys?"

Falon leaned back, crossing one leg over the other. "You've been here since last night. You almost succeeded in your ridiculous suicide attempt. Lucky for you, Shya saved your ass. Again. Arys has been here to the house. Kale as well. Shya won't let anyone up here to see you."

"He plans to keep me here until he finds the scroll, doesn't he?" A bitterness coated the back of my tongue. I really needed to brush my teeth.

"He does." Falon nodded, regarding me with keen interest. It was suspicious.

"Let me guess. I'm under suicide watch."

"You are."

I was furious. The demon thought he could keep me a prisoner, like some pet tied up until he was ready to look at it. Fuck that.

Suicide wasn't an issue. It had been a desperate ploy to free myself of Shya, a rash decision in the heat of the moment. At the time it had felt like my only way out. I was still here, and that meant something to me. It confirmed the vision of my death in Arys's arms. It would happen as it was meant to.

A quick examination of my body revealed that I was healed, for the most part. Stiff muscles and a few aches and pains were the worst of it. I could breathe without pain. A vast improvement.

"Did you volunteer for this job, or did you just get stuck with me?" I asked, hoping it was some kind of punishment for him.

"A little of both I suppose."

Falon watched me intently as I got out of bed. It took a moment for my brain to catch up with my body. I sat there trying to will the room to stop spinning.

"Jenner and Willow? Tell me what happened to them." I shoved away from the bed and headed for the bathroom, clutching the robe tightly about me. "And where's my dagger?"

"Not a damn thing happened to them. Your dagger is back in its box in the trunk of your car. Which isn't here." Falon rose and followed me. "I'm waiting outside the door. Don't try anything."

I swallowed my rage. As much as I detested Falon, I loathed Shya. I had to save what little energy I had for him. This was so far from over.

"If you barge in on me, I'll castrate you with claws. Got it?" It wasn't the best threat I'd ever mustered, but it would have to do.

Falon smirked and nodded. "Whatever you say."

I was relieved to find some basic toiletries awaiting me. A toothbrush and toothpaste had never looked so good.

'Arys?' My silent plea was fearful, reluctant.

'What's he done to you, my wolf? I came for you. He threatened to harm your sister if I didn't leave.'

'He plans to keep me until he finds the scroll. So I can't up and die on him.' I let Arys feel the despair that racked me. 'I need you.'

He tried to keep me from sensing the depth of his concern but failed. 'Stay strong, Alexa. You have to.'

The simple connection to him empowered me in a wonderful way. I might be trapped in the dragon's lair, but I was still here. My purpose continued to exist and so would I.

After using the facilities and dragging myself through the shower, I stared at myself in the mirror. Dark circles beneath my eyes gave me a deathly appearance. A few faint bruises still marred my left side where my ribs had been broken. Otherwise, I looked relatively well, all things considered.

My hand went to the black teardrop onyx hanging from my neck. Shya had never seemed overly interested in the amulet, but I was thankful to see it just the same.

A bang on the door was my only warning before Falon burst in. I clutched a towel against my naked frame and scowled.

"Get out!"

"Oh please, it's not like I haven't seen it before," Falon said with a roll of his eyes. Leaning against the doorframe, his silver gaze slid over me.

A memory surfaced, a brief but poignant flash of the not so distant past. In front of a room full of witnesses including my own sister, Falon had stripped me naked. Lilah had then forced me to shift.

Falon's appraising stare wasn't sexual in nature. At least, it didn't feel that way. It felt like he was searching me for weakness, finding my flaws and enjoying each one of them.

"I said get out." To emphasize my demand, I grabbed the bottle of hand soap from the counter and hurled it at his head. It wasn't my finest moment, but I was seething. Falon was Shya's way of torturing me. I was sure of it.

He caught the soap bottle and erupted into laughter. "The great, fearsome vampire queen fights her battles with a bottle of hand soap. I wish they could all see you right now."

"I wish you would get out." I didn't have the energy to engage with Falon. My stomach growled, and a caffeine withdrawal headache lurked behind my eyes.

"I just came to make sure you were still breathing. And to tell you that some of your things are here. In the dresser."

"My things?"

I shoved by him, clutching the towel around me. Jerking the dresser drawers open, I was both happy and distraught at seeing some of my clothing and hygiene products. I pawed through the drawers, finding clean underwear, jeans, and a racer back tank top.

With a zebra print bra in hand, I turned to Falon with a raised brow. "Did you go into my bedroom and touch my underwear?"

"That doesn't sound like thank you."

"I hate you."

"And I love that you do."

We stood there staring at one another, me with loathing and Falon with grim amusement. It wasn't worth letting him get me all worked up. Taking a deep breath, I stormed back into the bathroom and slammed the door in his face.

The urge to cry tears of frustration gripped me as I dressed. Willing them away, I bit my lip until I tasted blood. If Shya brought me to tears so easily, I wouldn't be worthy of stopping him. I was a Hound of God. A little imprisonment couldn't shake me. Maybe it would even be beneficial.

When I emerged with restored confidence, I found Falon staring out the window. The delectable aroma of food snagged my attention. He waved a hand toward the coffee table in front of the couch. A tray of steak and pasta sat there, steaming.

"Eat something. Then do something with your face. Shya's hosting a party tonight to celebrate Gabriel's rising. Now that you're awake, he's expecting you to be there."

"What's wrong with my face?" I asked, incredulous. "You know what? Shut up. I don't want to hear the answer to that."

A stubborn part of me wanted to refuse the food, but I was starving. When I discovered the carafe of coffee, I wasted no time devouring all of it. I looked up between mouthfuls of steak to find Falon watching me. "Don't make me throw food at you. I don't want to waste any."

"He wants you to be comfortable here. Shya aims to keep you happy for as long as it takes to find the scroll. I'm sure he would be willing to meet your other needs as well."

My jaw dropped. "What the hell are you talking about?"

"I meant your blood hunger needs, you filthy animal. What did you think I meant?"

"You know what? Let's not talk anymore."

The familiar sound of a cell phone had me up off the couch, searching the dresser for the source of the noise.

"Oh, right," Falon said, still staring out the window. "That thing has been making noise. I assume your lovers are calling to console you with words of false comfort. How incredibly pointless."

I fumbled Arys's phone out of the drawer as it stopped ringing. The missed call was from Kylarai along with at least a dozen texts from both her and Jez. There was just one from Shaz begging me to be careful and reminding me to keep a lid on my temper so I would come home to him safely.

The many messages from my loved ones meant the world to me. But it was the message from Kale that tore my heart in two. It said only: *Crazy is easy. Sanity is hard. I have a promise to fulfill. Stay sane.*

As much as I hated to do it, I deleted the message. It wouldn't do to leave it on Arys's phone for him to find later.

"What does that mean?" Falon asked, having rudely read the message over my shoulder. "That vampire is head over heels for you, huh? He's either completely mad or unbearably stupid."

I whirled around, hiding the screen from his view. It unsettled me how he could approach like that. Being unable to sense angels and demons really sucked.

I was fumbling for a witty retort when a noise from outside drew me to the window. It was then that I realized my prison looked out onto the backyard. From the second floor I could see part of the patio with its couches and tables. The pool was also in view. It held my attention, and I stared with mouth agape.

The swimming pool was filled with naked people engaged in a full on orgy. Candles surrounded the pool along with wine bottles and elaborate trays of fine food. From my vantage point it was hard to tell where one body ended and the other began so entwined were the limbs of so many people.

From what I could see almost every one of the seven deadly sins was party activity. A huge table laid out with food and drink catered to the gluttonous needs of creatures who didn't need to eat to survive.

Wrath was in full swing as several demons engaged in some form of blood sport on the lawn. They were fighting one another, shedding blood and tearing limbs. It was all for the entertainment of the rest. How very demented.

"Demon only? Or human as well?" I asked, hoping unease did not show in my voice.

"Both. Gabriel's first feed is tonight. He rose at sundown so Shya is going all out." Falon too seemed to be controlling his tone so I wouldn't read into it. Somebody wasn't a fan of Shya's new little vampire prodigy.

I stared past the pool to the large expanse of yard beyond. A huge pentagram was burning there. The flames were low, a foot high or less, but steady and constant. In the center was a naked, bound, and blindfolded man.

"What if I don't want to attend this twisted party? I think I'd rather stay in and catch up on some TV."

Falon chuckled, a sound that filled me with hate. "Get ready. It's almost midnight. That's when Gabriel will make his first kill."

I turned away from the window, unable to wipe the images below from my mind. "Why do you work for him? Really. What do you get out of it?"

"I've never openly pledged myself to anybody. You just perceive it that way." Falon's expression was a mask of stone. His poker face was impressive.

I considered what he'd just said. He was right. I'd made my own assumptions based on his actions. But I'd learned that nothing ever was as it seemed with demons, and Falon was as dangerous as any demon I'd met so far.

As long as I was in the enemy's home, I might as well make the most of it. Perhaps I would learn something I could use against Shya later. The demon party below scared the hell out of me. However, despite the dark parts of me, I was a creature of light. I must tread in dark places to make that light shine.

That's what I told myself as I got ready to walk into the fire. When Falon led me from the room thirty minutes later, I prayed for the strength to face down the demon who dared to use me as a pawn in his vile game.

"I'm sure you're smart enough not to run," Falon said, gesturing to the dragon on my forearm. "You won't get far."

I followed him down the hall that overlooked the living room and descended the stairs. "Did you just call me smart? Hold on while I file that away. I want to remember it later."

Falon ignored me. Strutting along with his long trench coat flowing behind him, I could easily forget what he was. His human façade was so convincing at times. No wonder people were so easily misled by these creatures.

The living room was empty. Everyone was outside. As we crossed through to the patio door, my pulse raced. Many of the demons crowded onto the patio couches looked up as we stepped out of the house. They eyed me up with keen intrigue before commenting to one another on my appearance.

"She's smaller than I expected. Petite."

"I thought her eyes were blue."

"Do you think she colors her hair?"

"Only a fool would mess with a Hound of God."

That last comment was spoken in a furious whisper. A black-eyed demon leaned in close to another, proclaiming in hushed words that Shya would be made sorry for his sins.

I hid a smile. So not all the demons present supported Shya's decisions. Interesting.

Another interesting thing I noted was that they were all men. Falon ushered me away, guiding me around the pool to where Shya stood near the flaming pentagram.

"Why are they all male?" I asked Falon. Being on the ground level enabled me to feel the mix of human and demon energy. Every female present was undeniably human.

"Female demons are very few in number, as are female angels. Most of them are hybrids of a sort, nephilims and the like. Lilah and her kin are among the only true female demons."

"Why?"

"You're asking the wrong person."

Before I could question Falon further, he shoved me toward Shya and promptly turned away. Shya's red gaze landed on me, and his lips curled up into a sadistic grin.

"Alexa, I'm so pleased you could join us." He spoke as if I hadn't been forced into it. "I'm sure you understand why you're here. It's in everyone's best interest for now."

"You mean it's in your best interest. Being your hostage doesn't do me a damn bit of good. I have a wedding to attend. If you think I'm missing that, you can think again."

"Let me fetch you some wine. It will loosen you up." I gawked at him, finding the charming host act to be a true indicator of how mad Shya was. Was there such thing as a sane demon?

"Fuck your wine," I snapped. "Why am I here? I'd be perfectly happy to stay locked upstairs watching television."

Shya's gaze narrowed. "It's bad manners to be so ungracious to your host, Hound. Are you sure you want to piss me off?" The fake charm was gone, replaced with venom in the blink of an eye.

I swallowed hard. Incurring his wrath was not going to work in my favor. I knew that, and still it was so hard not to tell him to go fuck himself.

"Why am I here?" I repeated in a softer, more complacent tone. I'd play along for as long as I possibly could. It was going to be damn difficult. "I don't need to witness another of your...events."

"Of course you do. You'll be the guest of honor at one of them. Once I find that scroll."

The heat from the flames warmed my face. I stared at the man bound in the center of the fire. He was human, and he was giving off enough fear to make even the most well controlled vampire come apart.

I gave up. Talking to him was useless. So I reached out to Arys instead, letting him see what I was seeing.

'Just play along,' he told me. 'I'm not leaving you there.'

'Don't come here,' I pleaded. 'He could hurt you. Or take you prisoner too.'

'He can try.'

'Arys, don't.'

"Why so quiet?" Shya interrupted, giving me a knowing look. "Communicating with your vampire? He's coming for you. I wouldn't expect otherwise."

"No, he isn't," I lied. "Look, Shya, I can appreciate the dramatic imprisonment. But this is ridiculous. You already grounded me to the city. Let me go home."

Shya stared into the flames. There was an eagerness about him that disturbed me. "Help me find the scroll. As soon as we get this all over with you can have your life back."

Hooking his arm through mine, he pulled me along beside him. We walked the perimeter of the pentagram. I couldn't tear my gaze from the quivering man in the middle. I had a bad feeling I would watch him die tonight.

"Shya, please. My best friend is getting married. I'm supposed to be in the wedding." Trying to appeal to a compassionate side that didn't exist was an exercise in futility I knew. Still, I had to try.

He appeared thoughtful. "I understand that's important to you. Perhaps I'll make an allowance for that occasion. Falon can accompany you there. If things go well tonight that is."

"Wait, what?" I stopped walking, but he jerked me along, making me stumble. "What happens tonight?"

He put a finger to his lips and shook his head. "One thing at a time. I must see to Gabriel. He's eager to feed."

The thought of a blood-hungry, black-magic Gabriel scared me. Sure there were several humans present, but my werewolf blood would smell like premium compared to their regular.

Shya met my frown with a tight smile. His grip on my arm tightened painfully. I steeled myself, refusing to show weakness of any kind.

"I hope Arys arrives soon. It wouldn't be quite the same without him."

I knew better than to take the bait. Talking to Shya was getting me nowhere. Staying silent was my best option.

We circled the pentagram, coming back to the pool. It was impossible not to look. Several people had exited the pool to crawl all over each other on the grass. It was hard to view them as people. They were just bodies, writhing and squirming.

I hated myself for reacting to the lusty energy tainting the atmosphere. It was my succubus nature. The various powers possessed by vampires came from demons according to a wise, old vampire I'd met in Vegas. At times like this, I didn't doubt that for a moment.

How could it be that I was a Hound of God with vampire power rooted in demons? It was hard to wrap my mind around. I wished I could ask Willow. Hell, I wished I could be anywhere else in the world than here with Shya.

Shya dragged me over to the patio and forced a glass of red wine into my hand. "Humor me," he said when I tried to refuse. To a tall demon with long scraggly hair, he said, "Bring Gabriel out."

"So what's your plan? Are you just going to set him loose on the naked, sex-crazed humans?" I was leery of seeing Gabriel as a vampire. It wasn't going to be good.

"Yes, there will be some of that." Shya waved Falon over. To the fallen angel he said, "Keep Alexa close. Let her go only at the right time."

Then Shya was gone, moving through the crowd to await his vampire prodigy, pausing to make small talk with those who pulled him aside. Something big was about to happen, and I wanted to know what it was.

"What is he talking about?" I demanded, tugging on Falon's coat to make him look at me. "What's going on here, Falon?"

For a moment it seemed like he wasn't going to answer me. Then he grabbed my arm and dragged me away from the patio, off to the side where we could see the entire yard without being too close to anyone. I cursed when he caused me to spill half the wine in my glass.

"Brace yourself, wolf. Shya has plans for you."

"Please tell me he doesn't have the scroll." I closed my eyes and whispered a prayer beneath my breath.

Falon shook his head. "He doesn't. Yet."

"Then what's going on?"

"If I told you, it just wouldn't be any fun for me."

It was childish, and I regretted it the second I did it. I gave in to the need to lash out and kicked Falon in the shin. Since that wasn't enough, I followed up with a fist aimed for his face. It never landed. He caught my hand and twisted until I yelped.

He gave me a shove that was stronger than it looked. I landed on my ass on the yellowed grass. Wine soaked my jeans, and I threw the glass aside in a fit of anger.

"Stay put," he snapped. "It's not time for you yet."

I started to get up, but he shoved me back down, holding me there. A tirade was brewing on the tip of my tongue. It died when Gabriel emerged from the house. Shya must have kept him in the basement safely out of the sun's reach. Gabriel seemed to glow with the pale beauty of the undead. His shock of long, black hair shone, and his eyes shimmered with bloodlust. Nothing human remained within them.

Even from where I sat, I could feel the buzz of vampire power emanating from him. It was a sensation I knew well. Our bloodline was very strong in him. Shya had known exactly what he was doing by choosing Arys to be Gabriel's sire.

Shya stood at Gabriel's side. The demon waved a hand toward the pool and the bodies fornicating there. "For you, my friend," he said to Gabriel. "Consider it a gift."

It dawned on me then that the orgy wasn't merely for the benefit of the demons but to appeal to the incubus nature now commanding Gabriel. Shya had more or less provided him with an all you can eat and fuck buffet.

"You've got to be kidding me," I murmured, receiving a sharp nudge from Falon.

Gabriel didn't waste any time. He surged forward with inhuman speed, driven by a brand new hunger. And the blood began to spray.

Chapter Twenty

I didn't want to like it. Watching Gabriel tear through human after human while the demons looked on in glee sickened me. But not nearly as much as I wished it had. I couldn't deny the bloodlust that made me its bitch. I sunk claws into the ground, plunging them into the earth in a desperate attempt to remind myself who I was.

It was no use. The vampire side of me reigned. As long as Falon held me back, it would be ok. I couldn't hurt anybody that way.

As if he'd read my mind, Falon released me. I couldn't make sense of it. Why?

Shya caught my eye and winked. Then he held out a hand, indicating that I should join Gabriel in his slaughter. The demon was beyond mad. He was a sadistic son of a bitch that deserved the hell that awaited him.

I shook my head, a silent refusal. Still I trembled with the effort it took to hold back. Gabriel was a reckless newbie. He tore viciously into his victims, spilling blood while they screamed. It would take him a while to learn how to control himself, to manipulate the moment so that he could feast on their lust as well as their life.

Falon pulled me to my feet and pushed me forward. "Go on. Show him how it's done."

"Why?" It hurt so much to fight the bloodlust that I thought I might throw up and pass out.

"Look at him. He's a total mess."

"I'll kill him." I uttered the oath beneath my breath, but Falon heard. Once the idea took root in my mind, I wanted very badly to do it. That would teach Shya to fuck with Arys and me.

"Kill him, and Shya will never let you leave here. Do you want to spend centuries as his prisoner? Don't be an idiot."

Falon's warning faded away on the night. I knew what I had to do. Maybe Shya wouldn't let me kill Gabriel tonight, but there was something else I could do. I approached Gabriel, forcing myself to take small, calculated steps. Rushing into that mayhem would be the end of me. Falon shadowed me, a constant presence at my back.

Ignoring him, I stopped several yards from Gabriel and dragged a claw over the veins in my wrist. It was a shallow cut, just enough to produce a few drops. But it was enough.

Gabriel's head snapped up, and he looked at me with wild eyes. No longer could I see the naïve teenager in them. That person was long gone, eaten alive by a power too dark to be contained by him. He rushed me as I'd hoped he would. Holding up a hand, I grabbed hold of his vampy energy and brought him to a halt. By the time Shya realized what I was doing, I'd already pressed my bleeding wrist to Gabriel's lips.

With a push of power, I sought to twine our two energies together, to create the force that would make him mine as I had with Kale and Jenner. Shya would be sorry for messing with me when I had more control over his prodigy than he did.

Gabriel's tongue flicked over the wound. It wasn't the most moral way to deal with this situation, but since nobody else was playing the game with morals intact, they left me no choice.

The slap of burning hot demon magic broke the spell. I cried out and grabbed my head as Shya's power sought to find its way into me.

"Did you just try to do what I think you tried to do?" Shya was suddenly there, standing between us, holding Gabriel off even as he struggled to get to me.

The pressure in my head eased off, and I pulled myself to my full height to face him. "If you think I just attempted to bind him so he'll crave me and do anything I want, then yeah. I did. Thanks to you, it didn't work."

I never saw the backhand coming. Shya's slap was no mortal slap. My head snapped sideways, and I went down hard. I tasted blood, having cut my tongue on my fangs. There was no way in hell I was giving him the satisfaction of acting wounded. I glared up at him with vehemence blazing in my eyes.

"You're going to be sorry you tried that," Shya seethed. "I hadn't planned to torture you, but I just need you alive. I don't need you sane."

"Joke's on you," I laughed, risking another smack. "I haven't been entirely sane for a while now."

"Keep fighting, Alexa. I do love a challenge. I'd be lying if I said I haven't fantasized about breaking your rebellious spirit." Shya became aware of the demons' curious attention as they gathered. He couldn't lose face now. "I got my vampire from Arys. Now you'll give me a wolf."

I opened my mouth to tell him to shove it. Arys's cool wind swept through me, and I knew he was there. This was going to go from bad to worse. When he came around the side of the house, he was promptly swarmed by demons. Shya barked an order to restrain him, to make him watch.

Watch what? I wanted to ask but already knew the answer.

I met Arys's dark-blue gaze and shook my head, willing him to stay calm. He shouldn't have come.

'How could I not?' He asked inside my mind. 'I can't leave you here with him.'

Shya seemed reluctant to touch me. He told Falon to pin my arms behind my back and hold me steady. With my back to his chest, Falon held me so tight I thought my arms might pop out of the sockets.

"Gabriel, select one of these lovelies, whichever you prefer, and bleed them. Slowly. Make sure Alexa gets a good view."

Having sated the worst of his hunger, Gabriel managed to do as he was told. Dragging a blonde from the pool, he pulled her close, pressing her wet, naked body to his. He whispered something in her ear, and she fell under his spell. Crap. He was good for such a newbie. She stared up at him with a silly smile, oblivious to the bloody bodies littering the ground around her.

Gabriel had changed. The quiet, brooding teenager was gone. In his place stood a vampire with the confidence and command that only came with power rooted in darkness.

"Why are you doing this, Shya?" I dared to ask. "Like really, what's your goal here?"

Gabriel ran a hand down the woman's body, and she quivered at his touch. Her arousal was enticing. I was eager for her to bleed despite the many he'd drained already. The bloodlust rode me, and I was slipping.

"You claimed not so long ago to lead the vampires and werewolves against me rather than for me," Shya said. "Remember? I know you've taken steps to do that, aligning yourself with the Doghead wolves. So I've taken it upon myself to start my own army of wolves and vampires. Arys gave me Gabriel, and you will give me a wolf. Then I can create as many of each as I'd like. All of them descended from the two most powerful. Genius, isn't it?"

"Oh yeah, that's real fucking Einstein of you. I bet you're proud of yourself." My teeth banged together as Falon gave me a shake.

The horrible part was that it was smart. It could also never happen. Shya had to be stopped. If he continued on with this plan, it would spell disaster for the city whether he found the scroll or not. Torturing me with the bloodlust would work too. I would snap and go straight for that woman. And she would turn if I didn't kill her.

The blood hunger always began in the pit of my stomach. This twisted, dark need, it ached and gnawed, wearing me down.

In a shocking move, Gabriel slid a hand between the woman's legs. She melted at his touch, slumping against him and begging for more. As much as I told myself I didn't want to watch, I couldn't look away.

Falon's grip tightened, drawing my attention back to him. If I could just get him to let me go, perhaps I could prevent the attack I knew was coming. I couldn't hold off much longer.

Gathering the sensual energy flooding me, I focused on directing it at Falon. Immediately I felt him stiffen. Hating myself for doing it, I brazenly pressed my rear end against him. I was a woman, and I knew it didn't take much to incite a response from a man. Falon was no different. His body betrayed him, and he grew hard against me.

"You're making a very grave mistake, Hound," he murmured in my ear, low so that Shya wouldn't hear.

"Am I?" I asked coyly. "Let me go, and it stops."

"Do you think you're so powerful that even I will succumb to your wiles? Get over yourself."

"You already have. A few times now." My control was slipping. I watched Gabriel bite into his victim's wrist and groaned with the effort it took to keep my focus on the fallen angel holding me.

Getting Falon to release me was my goal, but dammit if I didn't enjoy his reaction. Knowing I could get to the fallen angel gave me an arrogant satisfaction. Too bad I didn't have the courage to try such a thing on Shya. He frightened me too much.

"You want me," I whispered, grinding against the bulge in Falon's pants. I was going to really hate myself for that later. "Let me go, and nobody has to know how bad you want to take me right here."

My movement was subtle, the barest of motions, but it was enough. Holding both of my wrists tightly in one hand, Falon grabbed a handful of my hair with the other and jerked my head back.

His breath was hot on my skin when he said, "I want what's between your legs because you're a manipulative bitch. That doesn't mean I want you. In fact, it only makes me hate you more. If that's even possible."

The weight of Arys's gaze was heavy upon me. He'd watched me manipulate others, like Jenner, and he had enjoyed it. He wasn't enjoying it now. I was willing to bet it had something to do with Falon's reaction to me when I'd taken his blood in Vegas. Arys had watched Falon kiss me in a moment of power-influenced passion. It wasn't real, but that hardly mattered. The action spoke for itself.

Falon did a good job containing himself. It wasn't good enough. Shya eyed us with anger burning in his red eyes. He intervened with a shot of power that threw Falon and I apart. I landed on my knees just a few feet from where Gabriel licked the blood from his victim's wrist.

"You may have power over vampires, but you do not have power over my demons," Shya hissed, giving me a shake as I tried to get my feet under me.

"Falon isn't a demon," I challenged, unable to just shut up. Shya brought out the worst in me. "If he can't resist me on his own, then he deserves to be manipulated."

Shya was furious. So much so that he grabbed the arm of Gabriel's victim and thrust her bleeding wrist in my face.

"Let's test your resistance, shall we?"

The woman practically oozed lust. Blood dripped from the wound, taunting me. I never stood a chance. With her bleeding arm inches away, the last of the fight went out of me. I simply wasn't strong enough to resist after what I'd recently been through. I needed it.

Ravenous and crazed, I snatched her arm from Shya and ran my tongue over the bleeding punctures before biting deep into her flesh. Regret would come later. In that moment I was lost to the bloodlust. It consumed me completely.

Blood coated my tongue, tangy and warm. I drew hard on her sex-charged energy. Right away I felt the rejuvenation begin. It flowed through me, strengthening where I was weak while sating the hunger. It wasn't enough. The vampire within me needed to take everything she had to give. I took her down beneath me, unmindful of those who watched. There was nothing but me and her.

I went for her throat while she clung to me in a mesmerized state of arousal and oblivion. The euphoria held me in its grasp, taking me to heights I never wanted to come down from.

Shya put a quick end to that. He grabbed my hair and violently flung me off the woman. To keep me from going at her again, he surrounded her with an energy circle.

Wiping blood from my chin, I glared daggers at him. I was still riding the high, and it was difficult to concentrate on reality after having been so brutally brought back to it.

At Shya's command, two demons from the pool orgy came forward to fetch the injured woman. They carried her off, into the house. I watched her go, feeling strangely detached.

"At least I got something out of you," Shya sneered. "As long as I've got you here, I'm going to take you for everything I can." He extended a hand, pointing at Arys across the yard. "Arys, please join your wolf and I at the fire."

Shya's wings flared with a loud snap that hurt my ears. The demons holding Arys released him. Many of them had ceased to pay attention to us. They were all engrossed in their sin of choice.

Arys swept me into his arms and buried his face in my hair. "I'm not leaving you again. I don't care how dangerous it is to be together. It's more dangerous to be apart."

Senses heightened from the feed, my emotions were on overdrive. I held onto Arys as if he were my lifeline, which in many ways he was. I concentrated on the way he felt pressed against me and the sound of his devotion as he murmured in my ear. Just in case we were parted, I needed to memorize these details.

"There will be time for the dramatic lovers' reunion later. If you don't somehow find a way to fuck up what happens next." Radiating condescension, Shya turned his back on us and stalked over to the fire, forcing us to follow or risk his wrath.

He stood outside the pentagram of fire. He motioned for us to stand beside him, which we did, albeit with great suspicion. A few demons gathered around the exterior of the large circle.

A glance back toward the pool revealed Falon preventing a hotheaded Gabriel from joining us. Good call. Whatever Shya had planned, there was no way a newbie vampire with power like Gabriel's could handle it.

"Don't enter the circle. And don't speak to the demon I'm about to summon, even if he speaks to you." Shya held out a hand and a dagger appeared, laid across his palm. It was the same blade he'd used to hack off a lock of my hair and bleed me while I lay paralyzed in my bed. I'd recognize the dragon etched into the blade anywhere.

Arys stood between Shya and me, keeping as safe a distance between us all as possible. I held tight to his hand, refusing to let him go. His presence was empowering, filling me with a sense of completeness I never knew I was missing until we were together.

My heart pounded when Shya began to chant. The language he used was unrecognizable. It sounded ancient, certainly not a language still in use. He tossed in a powdery substance, and the man tied in the center began to tremble. It soon became an uncontrollable shake.

Shya extended the dagger to me, hilt first. "If you don't mind, Alexa. Just a few drops to invoke the summons."

With eyebrows raised, I smiled nervously. "You've got to be kidding me. What's the catch?"

"No catch. Not this time. You're safe on this side of the circle. He's the sacrifice." Shya pointed at the bound man and continued to thrust the dagger at me. "I need mortal blood. Yours is guaranteed to get some attention. You have my word that you will be safe."

This didn't feel right. Everything in me resisted. I would not assist in sacrificing this man. "No," I said with stubborn refusal. "I'm not helping you hurt anyone."

"Don't say I didn't try to be nice about it," Shya snapped. He shoved by Arys and grabbed my hand. Holding it out over the flames, he slid the blade over my palm. "Whatever you're thinking, Arys, don't even try it."

Shya shook a few drops of my blood into the fire and released me. I jerked back, retreating from the pentagram, afraid to be too close. The scent of sulfur was immediate. I coughed as the thick odor irritated my lungs. Yellow smoke clouded the circle. It seemed to be contained, unable to seep beyond the border, but I still had to hold my breath against the sickening stench. When the smoke cleared, I almost dropped into a dead faint.

The demon standing inside the circle was easily one of the most horrific things I'd ever seen. It had a man's body, well built with thick muscles that bulged and rippled. Black wings like Shya's spread out from its back. However, it had the head of a goat atop that perfectly sculpted body. Blinking near black goat eyes at us, it looked us each over in turn. And then it spoke.

"Shya. I should have known. Only you would be fool enough to summon me." The demon's voice was low and gravelly. It sniffed in my direction and smiled. It was a strange looking thing.

"I need a favor, Saber," Shya said, fearless. After all, he was the master of this situation. The goat demon was trapped, unable to do more than scrutinize us. "I need help finding the key to Lilah's kingdom."

The goat burst into laughter. It sounded very human, but coming out of that animal face, it was both ridiculous and scary.

"Still chasing that dream, are you? She rejected you. Is that why you still want what was hers? For spite?"

"Because it is mine by right. I served her endlessly. She was my queen, my everything. And she abandoned me. I deserve what she would never give me. Even if I have to take it myself, it will be mine. Help me, and I will allow you to reign with me." There was genuine emotion in Shya's tone, something I rarely heard. Lilah had broken his evil little heart.

Saber stared at Shya, wearing a mocking grin. I blinked several times, still unable to believe I was seeing a grinning goat. I'd be seeing that face in my nightmares.

"I have no desire to reign in Lilah's kingdom whether she sits on the throne or not. Nor should you. Consider what will happen when she breaks free of the angels' cage. She will return and make you suffer."

Despite the scary face and creepy demon vibes, Saber was making sense. Shya was an idiot if he thought Lilah wouldn't return to her throne the first chance she got. Although I hoped for my own sake that the angels wouldn't make the same mistake twice.

"Then I suppose that is the risk I'm willing to take. Now, will you help me or not? You know of the scroll's whereabouts, don't you?" The calm Shya exuded seemed forced. He was desperate and trying hard to hide it.

"It's just eating away at you, isn't it? The need to have those who oppressed you grovel at your feet." Saber crossed his arms over his beefy chest. Eyeing Shya up like he was a worm, the goat headed demon snickered. "No, I do not know where the scroll is, though I do know something about it that may be of use to you."

"What is it? Tell me." Shya's snappy demand brought my gaze to him. So far this short interaction had been very enlightening. I was beginning to understand Shya's motivations. It went much deeper than the need for power. He was also seeking vengeance.

I had witnessed Lilah talk to him as if he were dirt. She had basically told him he was worthless. Apparently demons had feelings too. I wondered if just maybe Shya had even been in love with Lilah. In my experience it was love that spawned the greatest revenge stories.

"You must promise me something first," Saber said, and his creepy goat eyes landed on me. "I'll tell you what I know, and you let me take the Hound."

Those words echoed in my head, and for a moment I thought I might pee my pants in sheer terror.

Shya gaped at him with his mouth open in shock and anger. "I need her, and you damn well know it. She's not an option. There's your payment."

Saber glanced at the bound man and shrugged. "What makes him so special?"

"It's a life. A pitiful human life. You have no right to ask for more." The heat of Shya's growing ire caused the atmosphere to pulse and burn. It felt like the sun on the hottest day of summer. I considered jumping into the pool if only to rid myself of the wretched feeling. Arys held my hand, and his soothing energy helped.

"You're asking me for help. I have every right." Saber wasn't backing down. "Give me the Hound or let me leave."

"Alexa isn't property for you to bargain over," Arys spat, losing his temper. "There's a reason Lilah never wanted you, Shya. You're unworthy of acquiring anything on your own. Using other people as pawns, playing them against each other, you're nothing but a fucking puppet master with no real authority. We are going to end you."

Uh oh. I expected Shya to kill us both right then and there. Especially when Saber burst into laughter.

Instead, Shya merely smiled, the fakest, most plastic-looking of smiles. "Is that so? By all means, please do. Oh wait a minute, you can't. Not while Alexa is still mortal anyway."

"The vampire is right, Shya," Saber said when he managed to stop laughing. "There is a valid reason why Lilah didn't want you for anything more than a servant. You should just be glad that she's gone, for now."

"Tell me what you know about the scroll!" The screech Shya let out was astounding. It hurt my ears, and I cringed when the rising heat of his rage continued to grow.

The two demons glared at one another. I took a few steps back, pulling Arys with me. Unfortunately, no amount of distance would ever make me safe from Shya.

Finally Saber gave a short nod and said, "I will tell you. And you will never call on my name again. I want no affiliation with you, Shya." Pausing, Saber met my gaze, and I trembled. When he spoke again, it felt like his words were for me more than Shya. "The scroll is no longer a physical object. The ritual written upon it has been transformed, made incorporeal. There is one keeper of the key to Lilah's kingdom now. And all who know it are forbidden to speak that name. That is why you will never find it."

"Liar!" Shya hissed.

With a sweep of his hands, the flames rose until they stood high above us. Saber was enveloped in a cloud of sulfuric smoke. When it cleared he was gone, along with the man in the center of the pentagram.

I didn't know what to make of Saber's declaration. It could be a lie. But if it wasn't, then what?

I exchanged a look with Arys. I couldn't decide if this was good news, or very, very bad. I held so tight to Arys's hand I could feel bones grinding beneath my fingers. He was oblivious, watching Shya with veiled suspicion. The demon swore at the fire, and it promptly went out.

Turning on us, he clenched his hands into fists and flapped his massive wings a few times. "Don't enjoy this too much. The longer it takes me to find the keeper of that key, the longer I make your lives miserable." To a few demons lurking nearby, he shouted, "What are you looking at? I will be your king, and you will all bow down to me."

That sounded like crazy talk to me. Watching Shya meltdown was not on my to-do list. He was terrifying when calm. I imagined he would be a total mess during a tirade.

A vibration in my pocket indicated someone was trying to reach me. It didn't seem like the best time to check a text message, but I had to know. I slid the phone from my pocket to find a message from Jez that said: *Can't reach Kale. At TSR waiting for Arrow. I slipped. So sorry.*

Panic seized me as I thought of Jez waiting at The Spirit Room for a fix. Arrow would be all too happy to provide it. There was no way in hell I was staying at Shya's a moment longer.

"Shya, I need to leave, and you're going to let me," I said, daring to anger him further. "I have a friend in need. Since you're back to square one, you're going to let me walk out of here, and you'll have Falon return my things."

It took effort to keep my knees from knocking together. Those red snake eyes fell upon me, and I stared steadily into him.

"I'll do no such thing."

"You can't keep me here until I become old and grey just in case you find the fucking scroll," I shouted, losing my own temper now. "I am walking out of here, away from this filthy demon party and away from you. The only way you'll stop me is if you kill me. And I don't think you want to do that yet, do you?"

Shya's gaze never wavered. So intently was he transfixed on me that for a moment I thought he might actually kill me.

Arys added, "Just let us go, Shya. Have Falon follow us if you like, or anyone else for that matter. But we're leaving." There was no room for argument in Arys's tone. Like me, he'd had enough.

Shya stared at us in stony silence. I braced, expecting the worst. It took a lot to muster my best "don't fuck with me" expression. Shya was one of few people I truly feared.

"You know what? Go ahead. Leave." Each word brought Shya a step closer until he was standing directly in front of me. He didn't waste time with Arys. It was me he glowered at. "You just became a waste of resources anyway. But know this, if you willfully bring about your own death, I will make you suffer."

"If what Saber said is true, then I will die of natural causes long before you find what's left of the scroll." A smile pulled at my lips. I couldn't help but enjoy his failure.

Shya got unbearably close. Our noses were almost touching. One of his wings grazed my arm, and it was all I could do not to jerk away from the murky sensation that followed.

"Have you not been paying attention?" Shya murmured, low and sly. "Demons only tell their version of the truth. Don't be too quick to count me out, Alexa. You can't get rid of me that easily." He grabbed my arm with spindly fingers that bit into my flesh. The dragon there pulsed at his touch. "You owe me. I'm calling in the debt."

"You can't do that," I protested, keeping a straight face even though I wanted to shudder and grimace. His power slithered up my arm. I shielded hard against him, but still I felt it.

"I just did. You've had plenty of time to bring me a dreamwalker. I happen to know that the FPA has one in lockup. And I'm willing to bet that you know it too." The satisfaction in his glare was intimidating.

My mouth went dry, and I was at a loss for words. This had been inevitable, but it still felt sudden. I wasn't prepared to deal with my debt to Shya. I'd hoped I would find a way to get out of it. It was delusional.

It was a huge letdown to learn that he knew about the dreamwalker in FPA custody. He'd probably known before I did.

"Look, Shya, I know you're pissed, but come on. We don't have to do this now." I was eager to leave and even more eager to get his hand off me.

"We do though." His shifty gaze slid to Arys. "What do you say, Arys? Do you want to take her debt? I know you'll actually pay up."

"No," I snapped, yanking my arm from Shya's hand. "I'll pay my own debt. Leave Arys out of this. It doesn't concern him."

Shya's wicked chuckle made my skin crawl. "Suit yourself. You have one month to bring me the dreamwalker."

"Or what?" I shouldn't have asked. I didn't really want to know.

"I'm not going to tell you. Whatever you imagine won't even come close to what I'll do to you." Shya's sinister calm was more worrisome than his openly psychotic amusement.

Arys pulled me away, retreating fast as if he feared Shya would change his mind. The demon watched us go with thinly veiled contempt. I kept waiting for him to stop us, to shout, "Psych!" and laugh maniacally while he dragged me back upstairs.

I was careful to avoid eye contact with anyone. The demons were all too engrossed in their vile gratification to pay us any attention. Only Falon and Gabriel watched us disappear from the yard.

I didn't believe it until we were in Arys's Firebird speeding down the gravel road away from Shya's house. Even then I expected him to appear.

Chapter Twenty-One

In less than an hour, I had retrieved a very agitated Jez from The Spirit Room. Lucky for Arrow, he hadn't arrived yet. In between questions and shows of concern, Jez apologized several times on the way to The Wicked Kiss.

"You don't need to apologize to me, Jez. You're a grown woman who doesn't owe anyone an explanation. But if you know this isn't what you want, then it's time to deal with Zoey's death instead of numbing out on intoxicants."

I felt like the world's hugest hypocrite. My drug of choice differed, but I too sought out escape in false comforts. Still, street drugs were risky, and I didn't want to watch one of the strongest women I knew go down that treacherous road.

"I know," she mumbled, staring around the room, squinting against the dim lights that broke up the darkness.

We sat in a comfy corner booth. Arys had brought me there to pick up my car; he'd had it towed there. I hoped to hang around long enough to see Willow. Then I was headed home for the next two days. My plan was to lay low at home and spend as much time as wolf as I could before Ky's big day. I needed it.

While waiting for Willow to make an appearance, I checked the many messages left on my phone during my brief but serious absence. A voicemail from Dayne asked if we could meet. Another, from Juliet, I hit delete without listening to it.

I called Dayne back and told him to come by the club if he had time. It would be my last night in the city for a few days. I needed some down time.

My blood boiled as I thought of Kale locked in the back with another blood whore. He had abandoned Jez in a time of need after promising me he would take care of her. He had no excuse for that.

A waitress came by to refill our coffee. Jez didn't need booze to make her situation harder to handle, and I was nowhere near ready to swallow a poison of any kind. I felt good, great actually, after the incident at Shya's. Tired though. I was ready to sleep beside the pond in the shadow of the trees. My wolf was restless, needing release.

The coffee was bitter and strong. I stirred cream and two sugars into it, watching the back hall entry with a predatory scrutiny.

Arys had left Jez and me to speak in private, though he hadn't gone far. He lingered near the main door, speaking to Justin. I think he was afraid to let me out of his sight.

"I'm really looking forward to Ky's wedding," Jez said with a sigh. With a hand beneath her chin, she leaned heavily on her arm and stirred her coffee so that the spoon clinked loudly against the cup.

"Yeah, you look real enthused about celebrating love right now," I said with a smile. I patted her hand, stilling it with my own so the annoying noise would stop. "I think you should stay with me until the wedding. We'll get furry and unwind. I'm sure you need it as bad as I do."

"That sounds good, actually. I think you're right. I can't remember the last time I shifted." She was fidgety, twisting a sugar packet between her fingers until it exploded in a small shower of white powder.

Oh dear. White powder of any kind was likely a trigger for her. I swept it aside, pushing it into a small pile behind the napkin canister.

At her insistence, I spent most of the time talking, telling her about what went down at Shya's. She nodded as if she was listening, but her eyes began to droop. Fatigue was a withdrawal symptom. The poor girl probably needed some serious rest.

"When was the last time you slept?" I flicked her hand, and she sat up straighter, forcing her eyes open.

"Honestly? I'm not sure."

"As soon as I'm done here, we're going home. I'd offer you a bed, but I doubt you'd want to lay on anything in this building."

Jez made a face of disgust that was made absolutely hilarious by her inability to keep her eyes open. "Ew. Most definitely not. I'd rather sleep in the parking lot."

I sat there quietly, wondering how she could drift off with the loud music and voices thundering all around us. I guess a few days without sleep will do that to a person.

She didn't even stir when Willow appeared. He seemed to step out of nothing, becoming corporeal. Jez was slumped against the wall of the booth, drooling into the palm of her hand. I would have laughed if Willow hadn't pulled me out of the booth into a colossal hug.

"I'm so sorry. I couldn't stop him from taking you. I tried." Willow's words were muffled by my hair.

"None of this is your fault, Willow." I pulled back to find his eyes shadowed with regret. "I know you think it is because of the choices you've made, but I don't blame you for anything. Please, stop blaming yourself."

He smiled, but it didn't reach his eyes. "I'm trying."

"Try harder."

"Will do, boss."

I glanced from Willow to Jez, wondering why those I loved had descended into such self-loathing. It hurt me to see them suffer and to know I couldn't take away the pain.

I was wary of discussing demon business in a place where anyone could be listening. So I told him the gist of what Saber had said and left it at that.

"That doesn't surprise me at all. Shya must be having a fit over it though."

"He took it out on me. He demanded the dreamwalker that I owe him. I have one month."

Willow swore and shook his head of dirty-blond hair. "Why does that not surprise me? Try not to worry about it. We'll figure something out."

"I'm not sure there is a we in this case." My gaze dropped to Shya's dragon sigil. "This is very much a me scenario. I made the deal. I have to honor it."

"You're not going back into the FPA building. You can't, Alexa. That place is too dangerous."

"Save me the warnings and pep talks, ok?" I laughed, but it was forced and dry. "I have a wedding to get through without any mishaps or deaths. It's going to be harder than it sounds."

My name being shouted from across the room had me whirling to find Shaz dodging people as he made his way through the crowd. In his enthusiasm he lifted me off my feet and squeezed until I yelped.

"Don't ever do that again," he scolded, lowering me back to the floor. "You had me scared half to death. Arys wouldn't take me to Shya's no matter how much I threatened him."

"Good. You have to stay off Shya's radar. Trust me. You don't want to be on it." I hugged him close, reveling in the scent of wolf and aftershave.

"Thank God you're ok," he murmured before kissing me with raw emotion. That simple act was filled with love and affection. It made me wish so badly that I could be what he needed.

Willow excused himself, heading to the bar to avoid the kissfest.

"It's not over, Shaz. Shya isn't going anywhere. Not anytime soon, that's for sure."

"Kylarai is a wreck. She was planning to cancel the wedding if you didn't make it back in time."

"No way in hell is that happening," I vowed. "Somebody deserves to get their happy ending, and it's going to be Coby and Kylarai."

"Excuse me?" A gruff voice drew my gaze to Dayne who stood a few feet away, waiting for us to disentangle from one another. "I don't mean to interrupt. I just wanted to speak to you face to face."

Reluctantly, Shaz let me slip from his embrace. The sudden absence of his warmth made me reconsider. He extended a hand to Dayne.

"I must apologize for what happened at Doghead," Shaz said, remorse heavy in his jade eyes. "It was unacceptable and completely bad judgment on my part."

Dayne accepted both Shaz's hand and his apology. "Think nothing of it. My boys like to scrap. It doesn't take much for that shit to get out of control in a pack as big as ours."

"Would you like to sit down?" I glanced at the booth where Jez snored softly and led Dayne to an empty one a few booths away instead. "Anything you want is on the house, of course."

"Nothing for me tonight." Dayne sat heavily in the seat across from Shaz and me. His hard, rugged face made it difficult to gauge his mood. "I want to thank you for taking care of Stuart. Owen told me what happened with the vampires. He said you're a strong fighter and a true wolf despite your hybrid status. His opinion means a lot to me. If he thinks you're a worthy ally, then so do I."

He offered me a meaty paw of a hand, and I accepted it gratefully. My alliance! I was so excited I could have squealed. Amid so much chaos and uncertainty, it felt damn good to have something go my way.

"Thank you, Dayne. I'm sorry Owen had to be there for that. It was unexpected, and I'm glad he wasn't seriously hurt." *Or worse,* I thought.

"Owen has had his share of ass kickings. He can take a beating from a few vampires." Dayne laughed it off, making me think he didn't realize how bad it had been that night.

"He saved my ass. I owe him for that. And I won't forget it." I meant every word. Owen was very much a stranger to me, but he'd backed me when he could have run. That meant a great deal to me.

Dayne stuck a cigar between his lips but didn't light it. "I'd like to invite you both to run with us on the next full moon. It would be a good time to initiate Shaz into the pack."

Oh crap. I cringed, and my face flushed red hot.

"Wait, what?" Shaz was understandably confused, seeing as I hadn't mentioned it to him yet. He looked back and forth between Dayne and me, waiting for someone to explain.

"Um, I haven't exactly told Shaz about that yet," I said, feeling like a supreme ass. "I had wanted to clear it with you first."

Dayne nodded slowly, sensing the shift in the atmosphere. He stood up and pulled a Zippo lighter from his pocket. "I see you two have some talking to do. We'll be in touch. Have a good night."

I watched him go, counting the seconds until he disappeared through the exit. Then I turned to Shaz, ready to plead for understanding.

"Let me explain, ok?" I slipped my hand into his and squeezed. "You need a pack, Shaz. You're a strong wolf, but you've outgrown the Stony pack. Doghead is perfect for you. So I asked Dayne if he'd be willing to let you in."

Shaz didn't react for a minute. His hand was stiff within mine. My skin prickled at the sensation of his rising anger. "You set this up without even asking me if that's what I wanted? Why would you do that, Lex? You hate it when Arys pulls crap like this on you."

He had me there. Arys was famous for doing things he thought were in my best interest. I rarely felt the same way. "It was hypocritical. I know and I'm sorry. Is it really such a bad idea though?" If he could just recognize the opportunity for what it was, maybe he would see that I only wanted him to be happy.

He studied me intently, searching my eyes and leaving me to wonder what he was seeking. "What's going on with you? Are you trying to get rid of me?"

Dammit. Shaz could always see right through me. There was no fooling him. "Not the way you think." I held up a hand, pleading with him to hear me out when he swore and tried to stand up. "Shaz, please. Listen to me. I don't want you giving up your life for me. You deserve more than I can offer."

Running his hand through his hair, Shaz made a noise of disgust. "Are you kidding me? Haven't we been through this? I made my choice, Lex. I committed myself to you." He pulled away from me and leaned back in the booth as if he couldn't possibly get far enough away. "You need me."

"I do." I nodded. "You're my voice of reason, the one who keeps me from doing things I'll regret. But that can't be all you are, and you know it. Just think about it, about Doghead and how you can grow in a pack like that."

Suspicion furrowed his brow. He looked torn, like he couldn't decide if he should be mad or not. "I know why you're doing this, Lex. You're planning ahead, thinking about when you become a vampire. Do you think that's a deal breaker for me?"

"It should be. I will go all dark, Shaz. Once I lose my light, I won't be the same person. The blood bond will destroy the balance of light and dark between Arys and me. Everything will change for the worst."

A look of absolute horror marred his handsome face. "How can you say that? Are you just giving up? That won't change how I feel about you. I thought we agreed to take things one day at a time, to enjoy the time we have together without forcing it to be something it's not."

"We did. But what do you expect from me? Do you want me to watch you eventually grow old and die while refusing you the chance to live a full life?" My voice cracked, and I paused to gather myself. "I'm not sure you can do that with me. And I don't want to be the one who takes it from you."

Shaz's wolf stared out at me. He felt like I was giving him the brush off, but it just wasn't like that. At just twenty-four, Shaz had so much life left ahead of him. Letting him go was the last thing I wanted, but this wasn't about what I wanted. It was about what he needed.

"That's not your decision to make, Lex," he said, his voice calm but his tone heavy with restrained anger. "You don't get to tell me how to spend my life, and you sure as hell don't get to choose my pack."

"I'm sorry. It wasn't my intent to upset you or to make you think I'm trying to drive you away."

"Aren't you though?" He did stand up then, pulling away when I reached for him. His expression was one of hurt and dismay. "I pledged myself to you. My wolf belongs to yours. Nothing is going to change that. Not even your death. I just can't imagine why you would want it to."

Shaz didn't give me a chance to respond. He turned and walked out without a glance back. I sat there stunned, staring around the room but barely seeing it. What had just happened?

Slowly I let out the breath I'd been holding. "Fuck," I muttered. Matters of the heart were always the most complicated.

"Are you ok?"

I jumped when Willow's voice broke through my thoughts. I hadn't seen him approach. "Not really. Shaz is pissed off because I asked the Doghead pack to take him in as a member. He thinks I'm trying to get rid of him."

"Are you?" Willow asked, his calm and caring nature making it so easy to open up.

"Maybe. But it's not because I want to. I don't. It's because it's selfish of me to rely so heavily on him when I can never give him the picket fence life he longs for." Goddamn it was hard to say that.

Willow pondered this. He gazed at me with a thoughtful smile and patted my shoulder. "Alexa, millions of people have that picket fence life, and they are still not happy. Don't mislead yourself into thinking there is an ultimate happiness out there somewhere. You're only as happy as you let yourself be."

"There you go again being all positive and inspiring and junk," I joked, but I knew he was right. He was always right.

"If Shaz is happy with what you share right now, why take that from him? Why not just enjoy it while it lasts? Trust me. Those moments are fleeting. Don't rush the ending." Sadness stole over Willow, but he shoved it aside with one of the phoniest smiles I'd ever seen. The angel didn't lie well.

"I can't have them both," I said, my gaze straying to Arys. Feeling my stare, he turned to give me a look that smoldered.

Willow followed my gaze. "No. In the end there will only be one. Love is complicated. Hell, it's downright torment sometimes. Still, no need to rush the ending of a story that you're not writing. Play your part and let each day come as it may."

"Is that supposed to make me feel better?" I playfully punched Willow's arm.

"Doesn't it?" The sound of his chuckle filled me with warmth. I found encouragement in these talks with Willow.

"Yes and no," I admitted, dragging myself out of the booth.

Willow slung an arm around me and rested his head against mine. "If you spend all of your time worrying, you will rob yourself of the good stuff. Only the memories will last, and now is the time to make them."

"Roger that, wise all-knowing one." I gave him a sarcastic salute but took his words to heart. "Thanks, Willow. You make more sense than anyone else I know. I'm grateful to know you."

"Likewise, little Hound. Now go, take your friend home before some vampire gets it into his head to make a play for the unconscious leopard."

* * * *

235

The scent of autumn leaves tickled my sensitive nose. The yellow grass crunched beneath me as I rolled over and stretched. A chickadee sang its repetitive little song until I cracked one eye open and gave him a look. A frog hopped through the grass a few feet away, pausing to check me out before continuing to the pond. The sound of a snapping branch brought me fully awake with a start. I whirled around with fangs bared to find Jez sneaking up on me through the brush.

She pounced on me before I could lunge at her. Her powerful back legs were like a spring, launching her through the air. She landed on the now empty spot where I'd just been laying.

Tongue lolling, I gave her my best wolfy smile. She might be fast and superbly coordinated, but I was fast too.

Blood stained the fur of her face, and I wondered what poor creature had met his end in Jez's fierce paws. Coming home with me had been good for her. She'd been leopard since we arrived, and it seemed to be beneficial to her state of mind.

Jenner and Arys had taken up residence in my house. I had not heard from Shaz since he had walked out on me. He needed time to think things over. As for me, I needed to be wolf, like I always did when the vampire world became too much to handle.

Kylarai's wedding was the day after tomorrow. Despite my offer to help with last minute details, she had insisted that everything was under control. I suspected that she preferred to do it all herself in order to make sure it was done right. I could respect that. I knew the feeling.

She had had our dresses sent over. Arys had taken one look at it through the plastic covering and made an inappropriate remark about how hard it would be for me to keep it on.

I was excited for the wedding. It was one bright spot amidst all of this chaos. For one night it would be all about Kylarai. Not me or Shaz or even Shya. Just Ky. I couldn't wait to celebrate her.

Jez glided silently through the trees, stalking a little brown field mouse. Her tail twitched as she advanced on him. The gold and black of her svelte frame was truly beautiful. I found it impossible not to stare at her in awe. She was a magnificent creature.

The field mouse jerked, having caught her scent. He fled like a little maniac, zigzagging as he ran.

It was nice to spend time with her like this. Too often we were lurking in the darkened streets of the city, hunting vampires and other not so pleasant monsters. Unleashing the beast inside was more enjoyable with another. One could only wander the forests alone for so long before boredom became madness.

She loped off through the brush, and I followed along at a casual pace. I thought about Dayne's invitation to run with Doghead on the full moon. Would Shaz be willing to come along?

Eventually he would see that I just wanted the best for him. My intent wasn't to drive him away, merely to show him what could be. What I hadn't told him was that it terrified me to think of how I would be without the balance of light. I might be a stone cold bitch that saw him only as prey. If that were the case, he would be far better off without me.

Losing my light was something I tried not to think about. I shoved it out of my thoughts night after night, pretending it wasn't real, that maybe "one day" just wouldn't come. But it would. I knew that.

I bounded after Jez, hurrying to catch up when her longer legs carried her away. She disappeared into the trees, and I tracked her scent as I followed. Like so many times before, I was tempted to keep going, to continue on this path away from the house without ever intending to return. It was perhaps a shifter's greatest temptation, to remain as animal always and abandon the human world. I couldn't come out here anymore without considering it.

Arys would never let me go though. He would seek me out wherever my four legs took me. Knowing that was both reassuring and terrifying.

I broke through the trees into a small clearing and jerked to an abrupt halt. Jez was face to face with a whitetail deer fawn. It couldn't have been more than a couple of months old. White spots still dotted its back. It peered at Jez with big, dark eyes. Holding perfectly still, it waited. Jez sat back on her haunches, trying to appear less intimidating. I followed her lead and got down on my belly.

The mother lingered. I could smell her, but I couldn't see her. For the space of several heartbeats time stopped.

I knew Jez wouldn't hurt such a young, helpless creature. The fawn seemed to know it too. Ever so slowly it leaned forward inch by tiny inch until it's nose bumped against Jez's. Then it froze.

I held perfectly still, watching this special moment. A predator bumped noses with prey, and it was precious.

A crow shrieked at us from a tree overhead. The shrill caw sliced through the calm, ruining the moment. I felt like it had revealed our secret, announcing to the forest that we were frauds. That we were monsters.

The fawn turned tail and fled. I exchanged a look with Jez, finding joy in her eyes. I wanted to share it with her, but I stared at the crow instead. It stared back, accusation in its beady little eyes. The annoying bird knew we didn't belong.

It shattered my delusional belief that I could leave the world of humans and vampires to live out my days among nature. Being a wolf was very much a natural part of me that I truly loved. But it didn't mean that I belonged here with the forest dwellers.

Everyone saw me as a hybrid now. The vampires wanted to take me out. The wolves had given me a chance, but it had come at a price. And the humans had become prey. I walked in many worlds and belonged to none.

And it fucking hurt.

Chapter Twenty-Two

"Oh my God, oh my God, oh my God." Kylarai's squeal of delight echoed from the bathroom through my bedroom. "In less than two hours I will be Mrs. Coby Haines."

"Hold still," Jez admonished as she wrestled with Ky's hair. Over top of Ky's head, she flashed me an excited smile.

After spending two days at home, keeping to myself and running with Jez, I was feeling pretty damn good. This was going to be a great night. The wedding was scheduled to begin at dusk. The reception would follow. Arys would join us then. An invitation had been extended to Jenner though he had politely declined. Kylarai had also extended an invitation to Kale though I didn't expect to see him.

A few of the Stony pack wolves had spent all afternoon decorating the backyard. Several rows of chairs were lined up before a beautiful flower and vine draped archway. The guests would be facing the end of the yard where the forest could be seen beyond.

Buying property on the edge of town was one of the best decisions I'd made. After living at Kylarai's, I'd gotten spoiled and needed to have a forest-bordered property of my own. My closest neighbor was on the other side of the tree-lined graveyard that separated us. It was about as private as it could get. A great location for a werewolf wedding.

"I don't think I've ever seen you shine like this." I sat on the edge of the tub with a hand-held mirror doing my makeup while sneaking glances at Ky. She was beaming.

"I'm afraid I might pee myself when I get up there in front of everyone. Or pass out." A hand flew to her mouth, and she gasped. "What if I throw up?"

"Morning sickness?" Jez asked. She wielded a curling iron like a pro, creating perfect spiral curls in Ky's deep brown locks.

"No. Just nervous. I never let myself believe this would happen." She giggled, a high-pitched, anxious sound. "I also never thought I'd be thanking you for attacking a stranger on the street, Lex."

I couldn't help but chuckle. "It was my pleasure."

We could joke about it now, but what I'd done to Coby wasn't really funny. It made me think of the wolf Shya had forced me to make for him.

Screw that. I can have one damn day without that demon ruining my mood.

"Have you spoken with Shaz since the other night at the Kiss?" Ky couldn't see my face from her position, but she didn't have to look at me to give me that mother wolf tone.

"He told you about that, huh?" Carefully I applied eyeliner, creating a dramatic, 60s-style, cat-eye point. Now if I could just make the other eye a perfect match, it would be a miracle. "Shaz tells you everything these days, doesn't he?"

"He always has," Ky said softly. "He thinks you're afraid of how things will change between you two after you…you know, become a vampire. Whenever that happens to be."

"I am afraid because everything will change. Again. It never stops changing. And I can't be what he wants. You know that, Ky. Shaz and I will never have what you and Coby have." I saw the shadow of sadness pass through my eyes and had to look away from my reflection for a moment. Crying off my makeup would be a small disaster.

Ky tsked and shook her head, receiving a scolding from Jez. "You're out of your mind, lady. Seriously. What you and Shaz have has existed since he was a teenager. It still exists now despite all of the Arys stuff. Don't be so quick to write it off as doomed."

I suppressed a laugh when she said, "Arys stuff." Oh if only it could all be so easily summed up.

"How can it not be doomed? I can't give him the monogamous commitment he deserves. The last year has been nothing but conflict between Arys and Shaz regardless of the few times they actually get along. Besides, none of that even matters now. Once I turn, Shaz and I will be worlds apart."

Kylarai was swept up in the romance of her big day. She sounded like a lovesick teen when she said, "Everything happens for a reason, Lex. Trust that. It will all work itself out."

It sounded completely delusional to me, but I knew better than to say so. Instead I said nothing and focused on finishing my eyeliner.

"I still think you should enjoy it all while you can," Jez piped up. "Maybe if you got naked with Kale again, he'd stop banging everything that moves and find some peace." My jaw dropped, and I stared at her as if she'd just revealed the Caramilk secret. Kylarai squirmed uncomfortably in her chair and cleared her throat. Jez did a double take when she noticed my expression. "I'm sorry. Should I not have said that? I didn't think Kale was still a touchy subject for you two."

"He's not," Kylarai patted Jez's hand. "Not for me anyway. I think it's Alexa who finds Kale to be a touchy subject. No pun intended."

There was a moment of silence before the two of them burst into giggles. I groaned and hid behind the hand-held mirror, refusing to continue this conversation.

"He's a very intense guy," Jez mused. "I bet he's a passionate lover."

I stood up and set my makeup things on the counter. "In order to avoid this discussion, I'm going to the kitchen to get some champagne. Can I get you guys anything?"

"Oh, Alexa, when did you become such a prude?" Jez scoffed. "It's just a little harmless girl talk."

"So nothing for you then," I surmised, retying the belt of my robe before heading for the door.

"Bring me some champagne," she called after me, joined by Ky's request for some green tea.

Pausing in the hall outside my bedroom door, I took a deep breath and willed away thoughts of Kale. Whether she knew it or not,

Jez had set loose memories I tried desperately to keep caged. It rarely worked.

She wasn't wrong about Kale. He had made mad passionate love to me in the rain up against the wall of The Wicked Kiss. And I had every detail forged deep into the recesses of my brain.

Before I could remember the way he felt inside me, I rushed down the stairs to fulfill my mission. While waiting for the teakettle to whistle, I gazed outside at the elaborate wedding setup.

Two local wolves were setting up tables with overhead umbrellas for the dinner after the ceremony. The florist was busy at work, decorating each table with a gorgeous centerpiece made up of wildflowers.

The doorbell rang and I called, "Come in."

When I turned to find Shaz opening the door, I was struck speechless. How many times could I apologize? I'd sent him messages and called. He had ignored every one.

Our eyes met, and he froze. Holding the bag that contained his suit, he seemed to search for words. "I just thought I'd get ready here, if that's ok."

"Sure. The main floor bathroom is all yours. The girls have taken over upstairs."

"Thanks." Averting his gaze, he headed down the hall to the bathroom.

The teakettle whistled, and I rushed to silence it. After pouring a cup of tea for Kylarai and two glasses of champagne, I put it all on a tray and carefully made my way back upstairs.

I couldn't help but feel like I should have said more to him. Pushing the issue today of all days might not be the best choice, so I let it go and returned to my bedroom.

"Shaz is here," I said, passing out the drinks. "He does not seem happy to see me."

"Wait until he gets a look at you in that dress," Jez snickered. "He'll do anything you ask and forget that it ticks him off."

Jez's constant lighthearted jokes were her own way of hiding her inner pain. I knew that. So I laughed along with her even though we both knew that forgiving and forgetting were two very different things.

"Don't worry about it, Lex. He'll come around. He always does." Kylarai beamed and showed off her bouncy curls. Jez had swept them back from her face and pinned them so her veil could be attached atop her head. "How fabulous does my hair look?"

"Pretty damn fabulous." I touched Ky's silken tresses, admiring Jez's handiwork before she slapped my hand away.

We continued to get ready. A plethora of makeup and hair accessories littered the bathroom counter. When I had finished applying mascara and blush, Jez went to work on my hair. With a big barrel curling iron, she created large, loose curls that fell in waves down my back. Then she made a small braid on either side and joined them together in the back. It was subtle but classic in its simplicity.

"Thanks, Jez. Who would have thought you'd have such a handy hidden talent?"

"I have many talents, most of which you'll never know about." She grinned and sipped from her champagne.

As the clock ticked, Kylarai grew more restless. I was nervous too. This was a big deal for her, and I couldn't be happier.

I toyed with the black amulet around my neck. Brogan had instructed me to never take it off. Yet, I wasn't sure it was right for the dress I'd be wearing. So I tied it around my ankle instead. It hung on the outer edge of my leg, a small black teardrop against my pale flesh.

From my underwear drawer I retrieved the small box containing the old, silver cross pendant Kale had given me. It was a beautiful piece of jewelry. Lying against my chest at the base of my throat, it shone as if it was brand new rather than hundreds of years old.

"Good choice," Jez commented from where she stood at the counter applying her trademark red lipstick. Her hand shook slightly, the faintest tremor of withdrawal. "That pendant is gorgeous."

The sound of muffled voices downstairs could be heard from beyond the closed door. People were starting to arrive. Shaz must have let them in.

Kylarai reacted to the noise by clutching her chest in mock agony and letting out a little shriek. "Holy crap, ladies. I think I'm scared." Then she laughed so hard she began to tear up.

"None of that," Jez admonished. "You'll ruin your makeup. Save the tears for the big 'I do' moment."

The energy in the house buzzed with excitement. On impulse, I pulled Kylarai into a hug and squeezed. "I am so happy for you," I whispered, battling my own tears. "Now let's get you wrestled into that dress."

It took both Jez and I to get Ky into her wedding dress. It was a phenomenal strapless gown that hugged her tightly before flaring out below her waist. A simple pink ribbon tied around the middle was the only splash of color. The skirt was mostly made of tulle which made it fabulously huge. A train flowed from the back, trailing her like a white cloud.

Once Jez secured the veil into Ky's hair, the three of us stared in the mirror, each wearing similar expressions of awe and joy.

"You don't have to pee, do you?" Jez asked with a frown. "It's not going to be easy with a skirt like that."

"No," Ky laughed. "I'm fine. For now." She sobered quickly, and the joy faded. "Just so you both know, Coby and I, we're not telling anyone yet. About the baby. You know, just in case it doesn't work out."

It was incredibly rare for werewolves to reproduce naturally. Our biological makeup was of two natures, human and wolf. It just didn't make it likely. In most cases, conception simply never occurred.

"Hey, take a look at me." Jez held her arms out as if she were on display. "I was born, not bitten. It happens. Maybe not often but it does. Keep the faith, ok?"

Ky nodded, her grey eyes sparkled with renewed hope. "Thank you."

"Now," I said, clapping my hands together. "Let's go get you married."

When all three of us were dressed and ready, we headed downstairs. Jez got stuck fighting with Kylarai's skirt and train while I ran down ahead to make sure Coby was already in place outside.

I moved carefully in the pale-pink stiletto heels that added four inches to my short frame. No surprise, Jez had picked them out, but I'd had to admit that they were a perfect match to my soft pink dress.

The skirt flowed behind me as I moved, making me feel more feminine than usual. It was a nice change from bloodstained casual wear. I rounded the corner into the kitchen and living room area and almost collided with Shaz as he exited the main washroom.

"Whoa," he exclaimed, taking a step back as he looked me over from head to toe and back up. "You're beautiful, Lex."

A blush warmed my cheeks, but his words warmed the cold spot inside me where worry lived. "Thanks, babe. You're quite the looker yourself."

Hell yeah he was. In a black tux that perfectly hugged every angle of his body, Shaz was dressed to kill. His short, platinum hair was lightly gelled into place; his face, clean shaven. I'd seen him in a suit before but never quite this dressed up. It was a good look for him. Very sexy and suave. It was swoon worthy.

We stared awkwardly at one another until he began to babble about everybody being seated and in place. All we needed to begin was the bride.

"Right." I sprang into action. "I'll just tell Kylarai we're ready for her then."

Once Ky was positioned in the hallway, Jez took her place with Bryce, a local wolf acting as a groomsman. I loved that Coby was connecting with the pack. Even if I was just a little bitter still about being kicked out.

The wedding party was small. The entire event was cozy, consisting of less than a dozen guests. The Stony pack seemed to be shrinking.

When it came time to take Shaz's arm and follow Jez and Bryce out the patio doors, a sense of panic struck. One foot in front of the other, I managed to clutch my pink and white rose bouquet and descend the patio steps without falling on my face.

Shaz held tightly to me as if he knew I was afraid of embarrassing myself. Staring straight ahead at Coby made me forget my clumsy fears. He stood in front of the archway with the minister, waiting anxiously for his bride.

As we parted, Shaz gave my hand a squeeze. We lingered for just a second longer and then let go. I took my place next to Jez and turned along with everyone else to watch Kylarai's entrance.

The setting sun cast her in a pale orange glow. She walked alone, taking slow, even steps. Shaz had offered to give her away, but she had wanted to give herself to Coby. It was insanely romantic. The guests rose as she passed by. She joined Coby at the front and already her eyes shone with unshed tears. The energy jumped between them, creating a warm, loving atmosphere.

As the minister spoke, the rest of us looked on, each lost in our own thoughts. I could feel Shaz's gaze upon me. Our eyes met and so many things stormed against the dam I'd built inside that I was sure it would come crumbling down.

This would never be us. We would never bind ourselves together this way, declaring til death do we part. Though my spirit was elated with joy for my friends, it mourned the loss of something I had never had to begin with.

My sorrow shone in Shaz's eyes. It was an unspoken dream our wolves shared, to be mated always. The human within knew better though. In that moment, as we listened to our friends declare their undying love, we were forced to let go of a future that would never be ours.

My wolf didn't understand. She whined and scratched at my insides, demanding I go to Shaz and nuzzle him, to show him that our love lasted even if our time together didn't.

Breaking eye contact, I stared at my feet and willed myself not to cry. It was a ridiculous need brought on by the intensity of the moment. Maybe later I would mourn the picket fence life I never knew I wanted. Then again, maybe I never would.

Giving myself a mental shake, I concentrated on my two dear friends. Coby was as handsome as ever in his tux with his short, dark hair combed into place. His hazel eyes were all wolf. He was still new to our kind and easily overwhelmed. He held tight to Ky's hand.

They seemed to be oblivious to the rest of us. So caught up in their eternal vows, they had eyes only for each other. Again I felt reassured that good things can come of evil. Perhaps it was the greatest trick the light ever pulled on the dark.

"I now pronounce you husband and wife," the minister said, closing the Bible in his hands. "You may kiss the bride."

Coby pulled Kylarai into his arms, kissing her with a tender display of emotion. She touched his cheek with the soft caress of a woman who had found her soul mate.

I did cry then. It was impossible to stop the tears that escaped me. Touching a hand to my face, I was relieved to find them clear and pure. Blood tears at a wedding wouldn't go over well.

The guests applauded and cheered. A few whistled. Jez leaned in close and whispered, "I've never been so jealous in my life."

I nodded, choked up and unable to speak. She pulled a tissue from her cleavage and passed it to me, turning my tears into laughter.

It didn't take long for a dozen werewolves to go from serious ceremony to reception party. The guests took their turn lining up to congratulate the bride and groom before hitting the open bar where they helped themselves to drinks.

Kylarai had decided a buffet style was easiest. She was right. The caterers had set everything up and then left.

Speakers placed at varying points around the yard pumped out a lengthy playlist of tunes. Though she'd wanted a live band, it hadn't worked out due to the short time frame she had to plan.

I lingered near the table that passed as the bar. With a glass of whiskey in hand, I watched my best friend's face beam. She moved about the yard, making small talk with the same wolves who had demanded I be removed as their leader.

"Are you feeling sorry for yourself?" Jez sidled up with a raspberry vodka cooler in hand. "Because that shit isn't allowed at weddings."

My lips twitched as I hid a smile. "Me? No. Of course not."

"Good. I'd hate to have to slap it out of you."

The sun had set. Darkness stole into the backyard, broken up by a few strategically placed yard lights. People would start to shift soon. What would a werewolf wedding be without wolves?

"Do you want this, Jez?" I asked, watching Shaz across the yard speaking with Coby. "The whole happily ever after thing."

She took a long swig from the cooler before answering. "I didn't think so. I doubt I'm really marriage material. But yeah, I'd like the whole happily ever after. Who wouldn't?"

"You're not marriage material?" I laughed. "Well, that makes two of us then."

"Do you think you're robbing Shaz of this kind of life?" She followed my gaze to where he stood smiling and joking with Coby.

"No. I don't think it. I know it." In a very unladylike move, I slammed back the rest of my drink and promptly went for a refill. What the hell? It was a wedding after all.

Jez studied me, curiosity in her emerald stare. "I think you're wrong. Shaz knows what he's doing. Don't be so quick to take the blame for things that are out of your control." When I didn't respond right away, she nudged me with an elbow. "Come on, let's go dance."

A handful of people had claimed a free part of the yard as a dance space. They danced as couples and singles, spilling alcohol on the dying grass while their laughter echoed in the treetops.

I turned back to Jez. "I don't think I'm drunk enough for that yet."

"Well then bottoms up, lady."

She bumped my drink hard enough with hers to cause whiskey to splash over the side and hit my foot. I squealed and laughed, scolding her for almost spilling on my lovely dress. We were joking around, having a good laugh, which I desperately needed, when I felt that honey sweet energy wrap around me.

I spun around to find Kale standing at the edge of the yard.

Those gorgeous brown and blue eyes lingered on me as he drank in my appearance. Dressed in a black suit, he wore his leather duster and held a small gift-wrapped box in one hand.

I took an extra-large sip of booze before I crossed the lawn to where he stood. "I didn't expect you to come. But I'm glad you did."

"I'm not staying long. I just wanted to tell Kylarai how happy I am for her." Kale's gaze fell upon the cross lying against my chest. Boldly, he reached to touch it, touching my skin in the process, sending a slight shiver through me. "You wear it?"

"Sometimes. It means a lot to me." I covered his hand with mine and peered into him. "You mean a lot to me."

I wasn't sure why I said it. Perhaps it was the romance of the atmosphere. Perhaps it just had to be said.

I felt Arys before he stepped out of the house onto the patio. Immediately Kale and I each took a step back. Kale mumbled something and swept past me to find Kylarai. I touched the cross, feeling robbed of a special moment.

Arys wore a suit with no tie, his bedroom messy hair the same as always. I loved it though. It made me long to run my hands through his untamed tresses.

"Who invited Sinclair?" He sneered as he approached.

I swirled the whiskey in my glass and frowned. "Who do you think? Kylarai did. Got a problem with that?"

"Should I?"

"You're kidding right? We are not doing this tonight."

Arys shrugged and pulled me close. "Sorry. The first thing I saw when I came outside was you in this knockout dress and him drooling all over you. What can I say? I have a jealous streak when it comes to him."

"I've noticed. And he was not drooling."

Arys silenced me with a kiss. It was a dramatic display, purely for Kale's benefit I was sure. I broke it off before it could cross the line into inappropriate for public display.

"How was the ceremony?" Arys surveyed the backyard, making note of those present.

"Beautiful. Heart wrenching. I may have been more than a little envious." The liquor was breaking down my walls, encouraging me to speak candidly when otherwise I might have censored the depth of my emotions.

"I understand. It's hard at first, to watch those with mortal lives live out their days in ways that you never will. But it goes two ways. You will experience things they will never know."

I shot Arys a cynical look and scoffed. "Oh, please. You've actually been married. Don't make it sound like you didn't spend some of your vampire years playing human."

"I married her because I was pining after you, long before you were even born. Remember that. It was always about you." His expression was stone cold serious.

Taking my hand, he kissed the tips of my fingers. I sighed. His touch never failed to seduce me. The energy simmered between us, a low-level burn that held the promise of more.

"I think it may have been harder on Shaz," I admitted. "I suspect he's starting to accept that he won't ever have that with me. Honestly, I don't want to stand in the way of him having it with someone else."

"Don't you dare say that to him," Arys warned, running a finger along the back of my hand. "You'll crush him."

Guilt and regret surfaced to swim in the waves of emotion crashing through me. "I kind of already did. I encouraged him to join the city pack."

"Is that why he's dancing with that old lady instead of you?"

I followed Arys's gaze to find Shaz dancing with the oldest member of the Stony pack, a sixty-year-old grandmother who doted on her family and kept her wolf a well-hidden secret.

"That old lady would cut your head off with just her claws if she heard you say that," I laughed. When I spied Kale and Kylarai talking privately together, I tugged on Arys's arm. "Let's go congratulate Coby."

Making small talk with my former pack was one of the hardest parts of the night. I didn't do small talk very well, finding it awkward and unnecessary. I didn't for a minute buy their shows of feigned interest in my life any more than I expected them to think I cared about their day-to-day activities.

By the time I made it to Coby, I'd successfully managed to talk my way out of three different conversations and refill my drink three times. I would always respect these wolves. They'd been a huge part of my life for many years. But they weren't family anymore.

Coby's hug was extra special. It lasted longer than a standard polite embrace required, which warmed my heart because I knew that he had accepted me as family. It more than made up for the loss of the others. I wouldn't trade Coby's affection for all of theirs combined. A lot of wolves understandably despised the one who attacked them. Of all the people who might hate me, he was the one who deserved to most and yet didn't.

"Congratulations," I gushed. "Words can't possibly express how thrilled I am for you both."

Arys and Coby did the manly handshake thing while exchanging pleasantries. Then Coby flashed me a knowing grin, looked at Arys and said, "Do you mind if I dance with your girl?"

For a guy that hadn't known me that long, he knew when I was uncomfortable. But with the whiskey burning its way through my veins, I handed my empty glass to Arys and let Coby lead me away.

"Oh dear," I muttered as I tried to find the rhythm. Feeling a little drunk and very clumsy, I managed to keep up with him without tripping over his feet.

"Thank you, Alexa. For everything. And mostly, for not killing me." He chuckled, and the sound was so cheerful I couldn't help but laugh too.

"Don't thank me. It was Kale who pulled me off you." I nodded toward the tall, dark, and mysterious vampire engaged in discussion with Ky.

"I owe him a thank you, then." Coby slowed our pace when the song changed to one with a slower beat. "I just wanted to take you aside and talk for a minute. We don't really get the chance to do that much."

"No, we don't," I agreed. "I'm glad you're settling in here, in town with the rest of the pack."

Coby glanced around at the rest of the guests. "They've been great, for the most part. They're small town wolves though, and you're not. I know you have a lot to deal with, and I want you to know that I've got your back. Always."

"Coby, you're too sweet. Really. But you have Kylarai, and soon you'll both have someone else to take care of. I can't risk having anything happen to you because of your association with me."

The wolves were wasting no time pounding back the liquor. For a bunch of everyday types, they sure knew how to let loose when the situation allowed for it. A loud argument about sports was taking place near the patio while two ladies dancing nearby gyrated like the only thing missing was a pole.

"That's exactly why I want to be involved. I can't sit here in a small town pretending life is normal when fifteen minutes down the highway things are total bedlam in the city."

I shook my head and stumbled in a dip in the grass. The whiskey sure did a number on my equilibrium. I was ready for another.

"Coby—"

"Alexa, listen to me. I will do anything it takes to keep my family safe. I trust that you can handle most things, but don't hesitate to say the word if it becomes too much. You are my family too, and if you need anything, I'm here for you."

Though I would never willingly put Coby or Kylarai in danger, I knew that this declaration meant a lot to him. He was an Alpha wolf now, even if his pack was small and isolated compared to the city wolves. It was natural and necessary for Coby to grow as a wolf. He needed to make this pledge, and I needed to accept it.

"You're a good man, Coby. Don't ever let this crazy world change that."

As we danced he told me about his big honeymoon surprise for Kylarai. A trip to Hawaii followed by a visit to Italy that she didn't yet know about. They were leaving in the morning.

"Sorry," I said with a giggle after I tripped over his foot for the third time. "It's the whiskey, I swear."

Coby laughed along with me, but his chuckle was cut short when someone grabbed my hand and spun me away. The spin was a tad disorienting, especially when I found myself facing Falon.

"What the—"

"Pick up your paws, you clumsy wolf," Falon said, forcing me to follow his lead as he pulled me around to the music. "For such a stealthy creature you sure can't dance worth shit."

He was dressed for a wedding in a dark grey suit with a black shirt. His silver wings were absent from sight. The fallen angel was a good dancer, though that wasn't so surprising based on how long he'd existed for.

"Why are you here?" I struggled to match his rhythm, which made me realize how easy Coby had been taking it on me. I tried to stop, but Falon held tight to both of my hands, dragging me along.

"You actually clean up rather well, Hound. Who would have thought it possible?"

Falon danced as if it was completely normal for us to talk this way. Coby had backed off at the interruption, but he stood stiffly nearby, watching Falon with suspicion. I caught a glimpse of Arys. He didn't look happy.

"Did you just give me a compliment? Ok, now I'm scared. What's going on?"

"Don't get carried away. It's not much of a compliment. Even a pig would look better with some lipstick and a pretty dress."

I wasn't sure what to make of that, so I flashed him a mischievous grin and said, "You think my dress is pretty?"

"Of course I'd have to show up when you're drunk. You stink of whiskey. Are you even going to remember this tomorrow?"

The music changed to a slow song, and I groaned. "Trust me, I'm sure I won't forget even if I desperately want to. You have a lasting presence. And not in a good way."

Again I tried to stop dancing, finding that Aerosmith's *I Don't Want To Miss A Thing* made this situation a thousand times more awkward than it needed to be. Falon pulled me closer, slung my arms around his neck, and put his hands on my hips.

"Just dance. I need to talk to you, and I don't have a lot of time. Judging by the way your vampire is staring at me, he's going to come to your rescue soon."

I tried to put some space between us, but it was difficult. After what I'd done to Falon at Shya's, this was extremely uncomfortable.

"Talk fast then because I'm about due for another drink," I muttered, hoping I didn't do something to embarrass myself.

"You're lucky I even came tonight after what you did to me at Shya's, but this is bigger than how I feel about that." Falon slid a glance to each side of us, making sure nobody lingered too close. "Do not freak out about what I'm going to tell you."

He paused, waiting for me to agree. I was quickly running out of patience with Falon. "Stop dicking me around and spit it out. You're kind of crashing the party."

"I have the scroll."

Chapter Twenty-Three

I was dumbfounded. Then I was skeptical. "Are you fucking with me?"

"I wish. Saber was telling the truth. It's no longer corporeal. What he didn't say, because he doesn't know, is that I'm the one who has it."

I studied Falon, searching for a lie in his silver eyes. Thankfully we were only swaying to the music, or I would have certainly lost my footing. It was tough to wrap my mind around his claim.

"How is that even possible?"

For the first time since we met, I saw a glimmer of doubt in Falon. I wouldn't go so far as to say there was fear there, but it was pretty damn close.

"Is there somewhere we can go to talk?" he asked, dropping the pretense of dancing. "I have a feeling you're going to ask a lot of questions."

"Yeah, there's a place. I don't think Arys will wait here though." I put several feet between Falon and me, glad to be done with the dancing. Stopping by the makeshift bar, I poured myself a glass of whiskey before leading the way across the yard to the cemetery next door.

As I'd expected, Arys trailed along behind us. Coby and Shaz remained behind at his command, but neither of them appeared to be happy with that. They meant well, I knew that, but neither of them could do anything against Falon anyway. If he was here with ill will, I was pretty much screwed.

We crossed the large backyard and broke through the trees into the graveyard. The music and voices carried to us, but somehow didn't manage to ruin the peaceful effect of the place. The cemetery was comforting to me. The energy was calm and peaceful. Traces of sadness flavored the atmosphere from mourners who came to visit, though that wasn't very often. For the most part the energy of the graveyard felt simple and final. As if those whose remains occupied the ground were very far from this place. I liked that.

I perched on a headstone belonging to a William White and waited for Falon to continue. Rushing to believe anything he said would be stupid, and he was right, I definitely had a lot of questions already.

He leaned against a tall monument-like headstone across from me. "Listen up, Hound. I'm only going to say all of this once. If you're too drunk to remember this tomorrow, it's all on you."

"Yeah, yeah," I said, taking a large swallow of whiskey just to annoy him. "Start talking. Tell me why you have the key to Lilah's kingdom. If you do indeed have it, that is." Irritation furrowed his brow. I enjoyed picking at him if only because he loved doing it to me so much.

"Lilah secured her throne when she learned of Salem's intent to cage her. She made it impossible for another to claim her kingdom, unless they completed the ritual that was recorded on the scroll. The scroll was a physical object though the magic it invokes is pure demon magic. Veryl discovered it and hid it, using it as a way to control her. She found it after his death."

"I knew it," I interrupted with a self-satisfied whoop. So I had been on the right track after all by searching Veryl's office.

"Anyway," Falon continued with a glare. "She destroyed the physical scroll, containing the words upon it in nothing more than an unseen orb. A psi ball, if you will. She gave it to me before your sister sent her back to the angel's prison, and I want to give it to you."

"You've had it this whole time?" I scoffed. "Sounds like bullshit to me. Is that why you were banging her?"

He frowned and ignored the urge I'm sure he had to tell me off. "Demons don't half-ass anything. The power contained on that scroll is the only way to access Lilah's vacant throne. It was bound with twin flame power because she is a twin. Her kingdom is inaccessible to any other than her without the scroll. And only if all of the puzzle pieces are in play."

"And just what does that mean exactly?" I wasn't sure I liked the sound of this. The twin flame reference made my skin prickle.

Arys stepped through the trees, a silent shadow in the moonlight. He came to stand next to the headstone I sat on and motioned for Falon to answer my question.

"The twin flame power is the key. Created by twin flame blood, it can be destroyed the same way." Falon glanced from me to Arys and back, waiting for a reaction. "Of course, Lilah and Salem are immortals. Which is why it requires more than merely your weak mortal blood. Are you putting this together yet, Hound?"

"It requires my life." It hit me with a sudden earth shattering realization. It was Lilah and her damn twin flame that tied Arys and me to this. "Because I'm a twin flame Shya can use me to open it. That's his goal in keeping me alive while he looks for it, isn't it?"

"That's right. See you're not so stupid after all. And if you accept it from me, you can destroy it. It will die with you." Falon's silver gaze was intent upon me.

I swallowed hard, savoring the whiskey burn. Staring into the glass, I was suddenly certain that this was the last night I would ever drink it.

"And what happens to Lilah's throne then?" I dared to ask.

"It remains in limbo, indefinitely. At least until the bitch escapes again and blows it wide open. Of course this only works if you die before Shya takes the orb from you. He'll try. Once he knows you possess it, he'll stop at nothing to keep you alive until he can take it from you. And then he'll kill you and use it to claim all that nasty power for himself."

"Can't he just kill me anyway?"

"He needs the ritual, the words. First the scroll has to be manifested as physical once again, an easy enough task for a demon of his caliber. He'll tear it out of you and make you suffer every second until he sacrifices you."

"And I don't need to know the words to destroy it?" This was giving me a headache. It all sounded very complicated. Or perhaps I was overcomplicating it.

"You just have to die and take it with you." Falon was so flippant, like it was just that easy.

"How do you know it will work?"

"I don't. There's only one way to find out."

I stared at him, seeking a sign that he was misleading me. It just didn't make sense. What could Falon possibly have to gain from lying about having the damn thing?

"Why are you doing this? Aren't you on Team Shya?"

"I'm on Team Falon, nothing more, nothing less. Now are you going to accept this thing or not?"

"And if I don't?" I challenged, feeling backed into a corner. He wasn't leaving me much choice with that explanation.

"Then I give it to Shya and let him use you as a sacrifice and take my place at his right hand. You die either way. Don't let your foolish pride make this choice. I'm offering you the chance to prevent some seriously bad shit. Like hell on earth kind of shit."

Falon crossed his arms and regarded me with open hostility. His motives were questionable, but I didn't have the ability to detect a lie on an angel.

"Why does that matter to you? Seems like something you'd like." Arys spoke up for the first time. His expression was stone cold and hard to read.

"You have no idea what I like." Falon smirked, enjoying the mind fuck he was pulling on us. "I enjoy my share of chaos, but I don't share Shya's big apocalyptic dreams."

I sighed and gripped the headstone with one hand so I wouldn't drunkenly fall over the other side of it. "I really hate you right now."

"The feeling is mutual. Now, can we do this already?"

"Of all of the times for you to do this, you had to do it on the night of my best friend's wedding," I accused, detecting a slight slur to my words.

Falon regarded me with judgmental haughtiness. "I had to wait for the right time. It's not about you, really, so get over yourself. Shya has reached a point of power-crazed madness that made waiting any longer too risky. It's only a matter of time until he figures out that I have what he's looking for."

"How are we supposed to be able to trust you? This could all be a manipulation ordered by Shya, and we would never know," Arys said. He seemed much calmer than I felt, but he was shut down, making it difficult to know for sure.

"It could be." Falon shrugged and did his best to look bored with us.

"What about Gabriel?" I asked, trying to cover all bases. "How do you know he hasn't somehow seen this?"

"You really think I'd be stupid enough to let that kid touch me? Not a snowball's chance in hell. Which is what you'll have if Shya gets this damn scroll."

Falon was insulted by my question, but it was valid. "He's touched me, Falon. He saw things that he didn't even want to repeat. There's no way of knowing what he's seen or if he's told Shya."

"Fuck Gabriel," Falon hissed with enough vehemence to indicate how he really felt about Shya's prodigy. "That little shit is going to be a problem. Can't you control him somehow? Isn't that a vampire thing?"

Arys paced a few steps away and paused to read a headstone. He was thinking hard. I knew that without being inside his head.

"It is, depending," Arys said slowly. "He's of a strong bloodline with power of his own. That makes it unlikely that he can easily be manipulated. One like him never should have been made."

This wasn't the right time to shout an, "I told you so," so I bit my lip and kept my mouth shut. An owl hooted overhead, and I looked up to find wide, round eyes blinking at us from a nearby tree. It was so easy to forget that we were never really alone. The chances of something or someone lurking were always great.

"Better bring your witch friend then," Falon suggested. "You might need her to work some counter spells to block whatever he throws at you. Gabriel is dangerous, which is why Shya likes him so much."

"Do I detect some jealousy?" I taunted, snickering to myself.

I lost my balance and almost fell backwards. With my free hand I dug claws into the stone to hold on while I slammed back the rest of the whiskey. I definitely needed to be drunk to do this.

"You know, maybe I change my mind," Falon snapped. "Maybe I'll just give this damn thing to Shya."

Arys and I shared a look. I needed his input on this. So much passed between us. Words were not needed. He nodded, and my heart sunk. This was it, our purpose together. I felt it in every part of me. Even the whiskey couldn't drown that out. It was raw and real, demanding that I take Falon seriously.

It took great effort to say, "Tell me what I have to do."

Relief flooded Falon's sharp features. His shoulders slumped as if I'd just lifted a weight from him.

"I'll give it to you. And then tomorrow night you will go to the Charles Camsell Hospital property and destroy it."

"Why there? That's FPA headquarters."

"An unfortunate pain in the ass," Falon said with a nod. "It has to be destroyed where it was made. Though it's unseen, the door to Lilah's kingdom lies there."

That answered several questions. It definitely explained why the building pulsed with such evil that went far beyond that of the ghosts that dwelled within.

"We don't have to go inside the building?" Arys questioned, a dark brow raised in scrutiny.

"No. The building is just a man-made structure. The portal to Lilah's kingdom is in the earth itself." Shoving away from the statue he leaned on, Falon took slow steps toward me. "I must warn you. Shya will know the moment you step foot on the hospital property with the scroll inside you. He's gone to great lengths to monitor activity near Lilah's doorway. His response will be swift. Be prepared."

"What does that mean?" My head spun, and I hopped off the headstone, hoping the ground would feel sturdier. It didn't.

"It means he won't stand by while you destroy his chance. He will try to stop you. Bring backup and pray it's enough. Now," Falon held out both hands to me. "Shall we?"

I set the empty glass on the headstone and placed my hands in his. Trembling, I looked to Arys for support. He drew near, watching Falon intently.

"You better not be fucking us over," he warned the fallen angel.

Falon ignored him, staring at me instead. "Here comes the really shitty part. Are you aware that some demons seal deals with a kiss?"

My insides shriveled. "Can't we just shake hands?"

"Don't look so disgusted. You're the one who rubbed your ass all over my cock, remember?" Falon wore a mask of distaste, as if he felt ill. "I have to give it to you the way it was given to me. Just be grateful it's only a kiss. Demons have been known to seal a deal with much more."

"I'm not keen on your use of the word deal." Arys shifted to stand closer so that he was almost shoving between us.

Falon rolled his eyes in exasperation. "It is a deal. I'm giving and she's accepting. That's just the way things work. So either back off and let this happen, or I'll just be on my way."

I was petrified. The reality that I would die the following night hadn't quite settled in, yet I was shaking like a frightened child.

My hands grew sweaty in Falon's, and I tried to look apologetic. "Let's get this over with before I change my mind."

I don't think Falon wanted me to do that, despite his threat to leave. He never gave me another opportunity to back out.

Sliding his fingers between mine, he held tight. I gasped as the power flowed between us, a steady connection of his to mine. It was overwhelming and heavy, making it hard to breathe. I was ready for the kiss when he pressed his lips to mine but entirely unprepared for the jolt that came with it. Our hands pulsed where our palms touched. Dizzy from the sudden rush, I followed his lead as Falon deepened the kiss. His mouth was warm and inviting as he flicked his tongue against mine.

His technique was assertive without being aggressive. Gentle while also firm, Falon's kiss revealed to me a tenderness I never would have expected from him. It was a far cry from the hungry way he'd kissed me in Vegas, though that had been an entirely different scenario.

Power shifted between us as he pushed a dark, heavy energy into me. My sense of self-preservation screamed to break off the connection. Only the seething need to give Shya a little payback allowed me to accept it. For a moment I couldn't breathe as the force poured inside me. It was suffocating, making me lightheaded, though that could have been the booze. This really hadn't been the best decision to make under the influence.

The black-tainted energy took hold, winding itself around my essence, making itself a part of me. It was mine now, no longer contained by Falon. He swept my mouth once more with his tongue before breaking off the kiss. I opened my eyes to find him staring at me with a bizarre mix of intrigue and horror.

"If I didn't know better, Falon, I'd say you enjoyed that," Arys observed with a glare vicious enough to wilt flowers.

"Yeah, well you do know better." With a toss of his fair hair, Falon stepped back and scowled at me. "Tomorrow night. Midnight. That's when the spirit realm will be most active. Don't put it off. Otherwise it may kill you."

"Right, my pathetic mortal self can't take it. I know the drill." Shaky and feeling faint, I leaned back against the headstone, knocking the empty glass atop it into the grass.

Falon pinned Arys with a stern look. "Don't fuck this up. You have to make sure this happens. Do whatever you can to be ready for Shya when he gets there."

"Will you be there?"

Arys's question went unanswered. Falon had vanished without another word.

"Good pep talk," I muttered.

We stood there in silence for a moment, each of us lost in our own thoughts. I was going to die tomorrow night. It didn't feel real. I kept waiting for the earth shattering terror to strike. Other than the initial fear, I just felt…relieved. Soon the agony of the wait would be over.

"Arys? Are you all right?"

He stood stiffly, staring at the rows of headstones. I didn't think he was really seeing them though. I laid a hand on his arm, and he turned suddenly, sweeping me into his embrace. For a long time he just held me. His confusion and pain wrapped around me like a blanket. It echoed inside me as if it were my own. Perhaps it was.

"I can't believe it's happening," he whispered. "I'd started to think it wouldn't."

"Me too. Wishful thinking. Once it's over, we won't have it hanging over our heads anymore. It could be a good thing." My words were true, though my tone lacked conviction. I wanted to believe it.

"Everything will change." There was such tension in Arys, as if he might burst at any moment.

I threw my arms around his neck and stroked a hand through his hair. "Not everything. This won't change. Me and you, like this."

"You don't know that."

I forced him to meet my gaze. He was the strong one in the face of insanity, and I needed him to remember that. "I do. And so do you. You said it yourself. We are for always. Nothing can change that."

After a few minutes of consideration, Arys kissed my forehead and said, "You're right. It won't change us, but it will change you. I just wish it didn't have to be that way."

Though we didn't discuss it often, I knew that Arys carried a lot of guilt. He had blood bonded me almost a year ago, guaranteeing that I would rise as a vampire upon my mortal death. He'd known that it would tip the balance between light and dark that we shared.

"It doesn't matter. We will still have the light when we need it most. Tomorrow night when we destroy Shya's chance at greater power. It will be worth it."

Staying strong was what mattered now. Of course I might not be quite so confident when the liquor wore off.

"So what now? Do we tell Shaz?"

"No. We don't tell anyone. Not tonight." I turned to find the glass that had fallen, and the world seemed to turn with me. Somehow I righted myself without doing a head dive. "We go back to the party and have a good time. No, better than that. We have a fucking kick ass time. If it's my last mortal night on earth, then I want to enjoy it."

Chapter Twenty-Four

The party was raging when we returned to the yard.
Abandoned clothing littered the ground, a sure sign that there were
wolves roaming the night. I was tempted to join them, but I knew that
if I did I might never come back. So I stayed with Arys who stuck to
my side like glue.

Shaz and Coby were having a loud, drunken discussion about
cars. Apparently Shaz was trading his in and trying to decide if he
wanted a truck or SUV. Kylarai and Jez had gone to run with the
others, and Kale had left as he'd come, stealthy and unseen.

Those who remained were doing a great job of polishing off
what was left of the booze. I exchanged my glass for a bottle instead.
My last night with my favorite human vice called for it.

It was incredibly difficult to keep my thoughts from turning
dark and negative. Only when I'd filled my blood with whiskey did the
thoughts finally become too muddled to make sense.

We joined Shaz and Coby at the picnic table on the patio,
successfully avoiding their questions about Falon by redirecting the
conversation. I kicked off my heels, glad to be rid of the torturous
things. I groaned and rubbed a foot, vowing to never wear such torture
devices again. Too bad. They sure were pretty.

Shaz grasped my foot and began to massage the sore arch. He
flashed me a sly grin, and his touch became unbearably sensual. Oh
yeah, if I was going to die, I was going to do my damndest to die
happy.

Leaning against Arys, I stretched out on the bench between them. Naughty desires formed as Shaz ran a hand up my calf. With a brow raised flirtatiously and a teasing smile, I encouraged him. My gaze fell to the pulse beating steadily in this throat. I wanted much more than that though.

"The new Jeep Cherokee is supposed to be pretty bad ass," Coby was saying. His eyes were bloodshot, and the scent of beer clung to him. He was joyful though, and I savored it, knowing I could face the following night when those I loved were happy and safe.

"I like the new Dodge Ram, but I'm not sure I need a truck that big," Shaz replied, playing with the amulet tied around my ankle.

"Of course you do."

Arys had little to contribute to the conversation. Being stone cold sober had him trapped in reality. I had to put a stop to that.

I ran a hand along the inside of his thigh, pausing when I felt him tense up. With a gentle push of power, I touched him metaphysically, drawing his gaze to me. I gave him my best innocent expression, knowing I failed miserably when he grinned.

I giggled when Shaz tickled the bottom of my foot. Clapping a hand over my mouth to stop the girlish sound, I protested when he didn't stop.

"I suppose I'd better find my wife. We have a flight to catch in six hours," Coby announced, standing up and knocking over his beer bottle in the process. Beer soaked the table, running in a steady stream until it spilled over the side in a bubbly waterfall.

"Maybe you better let her find you," I suggested, finding it hilarious when he had a hard time stepping over the attached bench.

"Holy crap," Coby muttered, rubbing a hand over the stubble lining his jaw. "I can't believe I'm married. It feels surreal."

Mumbling to himself, he wandered over to one of the lounge chairs on the other side of the patio and passed out face down. I erupted into more annoying drunk-girl giggles and searched for a phone so I could take a picture.

Forgetting that I'd left my phone in the house, I settled for swiping Shaz's. After taking several out of focus photos, I accepted defeat. The noise had started to die down as people either became wolf or passed out.

"Shall we take this party upstairs?" Shaz asked, a hunger in his eyes that I knew I might never see again.

What if he didn't want me after it was all said and done?

Arys looked to me for a response. It had been quite some time since the three of us had shared a bed. The past few months had been filled with drama, pain, and poor choices. Looking at them both, I was enticed by the prospect of being nestled between them again as we fed our illicit hungers.

"Yeah," I said, clutching the whiskey bottle as if it were my lifeline. After one last swig from the bottle, I thunked it down on the table. "Let's go upstairs."

I was far too drunk to be nervous. Had I been sober, I would still have eagerly taken them both to my bed. I was a dead wolf walking. I needed to feel alive while I still could.

Arys was quiet, lost in thought. He hung back, ensuring nobody took a drunken fall down the stairs. When he stepped into the bedroom and closed the door, I clasped his hand in mine, sighing at the familiar spark that leaped between us.

'No worries. No thoughts. Just here and now.' I pushed the thought to him, willing him to be in this moment with me rather than already living in tomorrow.

I didn't give him a chance to stay lost in the future. Slowly I began to unlace my dress. His midnight-blue gaze was locked on me as I disrobed. Satisfaction thrilled through me when his desire ignited.

Shaz approached from behind, slipping his arms around my waist. His mouth was hot against the back of my neck. I reached to touch the side of his face, but my eyes were on Arys. With the other hand, I beckoned him to me.

I let the dress fall to my feet where it created a big pink puddle of soft material. Standing there in my underwear, I let the succubus force inside me spill forth to capture both men in my spell.

Arys shrugged out of his jacket and tossed it on top of my dresser beside the TV. For a moment he stood stiff, as if reluctant to touch me. Then he came to me and captured my lips in a kiss that conveyed everything he was feeling.

The force of his emotion washed over me. Fear, worry, relief, love. All of these things and more crashed through him, in turn crashing through me. My gasp was the only sound. The intensity of

Arys's emotions promised that he would burn hot in every way. And I couldn't wait.

The sensation of Shaz's lips and tongue on the back of my shoulder was rivaled only by Arys's tender kiss. My vampire kissed a path down the side of my neck while my wolf's warm hands slid along my spine, causing me to tremble.

Shaz hooked a few fingers in my skimpy black underwear and dragged them down my legs. I stepped out of the pile of clothing and climbed onto the bed.

"Your turn," I instructed them both with a mischievous wink.

The amount of liquor racing through Shaz's veins was evident when he was first to disrobe entirely. Arys hung back, taking his sweet time, watching Shaz crawl atop me on the bed and adorn my body with kisses. His platinum hair was feather soft in my hands. I hoped that I would never forget the way it felt. The touch of his tongue on my midriff got my pulse pounding. The atmosphere grew thick with arousal. It sated one hunger as it encouraged more.

"Arys." I said his name as if it were a plea and a curse, because it often was.

For a moment I suspected that perhaps he was afraid he would hurt me. But he peeled off his clothing one item at a time, allowing me a great view of his hard, naked body. He approached the bed, and I reached for him, trailing my fingers over his firm stomach. Down lower, I wrapped my hand around the smooth length of him. His eyes closed, and he groaned.

Shaz rolled over to the inside of the bed, giving Arys the outside. They put me between them, where I so desperately wanted to be. There was nothing better than being pressed between the gorgeous men on either side of me. I sought to take in all they were giving.

There was a desperation in Arys's touch that made my heart bleed for him. He held me like I might disappear if he dared to let go.

We fell all over each other. Shaz sought out the warmth between my legs and stroked me into a frenzy. Teasing, bringing me ever closer to the edge, he took command of my pleasure. Two fingers slipped inside me, forcing me to cry out. I needed so much more than that.

My cries were muffled by Arys's needy kiss. The sting of his fang was sharp against my tongue. Sucking on the tiny bead of blood that welled up, he sighed, a ragged sound that echoed in my ears.

The rush of power was intoxicating. How could I have forgotten how amazing we were as a trio? Together we created a delicious circuit of energy, all giving and taking in succession, growing the power to head-swimming heights.

I feasted on Shaz, drawing on his lust and shedding his blood. He offered me his neck, the way I had offered myself so many times to Arys. It empowered me, making me the one in command. There was danger in that kind of dominance.

The tangy taste of him stirred my guilt. I might never be able to do this again. It could be far too dangerous once I was a vampire. For a split second I considered blurting everything out. But Arys's hand on the curve of my hip kept the words from coming.

Rather than risk breaking the spell that held us, I threw myself headlong into it, seeking to lose myself completely. Closing my eyes, I focused hard on the many sensations: the salty taste of blood in my mouth, the insistent pressure of Arys's hands on my body, and the musky scent of wolf.

Together we worked as one, setting a pace that came naturally. As Arys claimed my body, thrusting slow and deep, I stroked Shaz with a hand while running my tongue over the bite mark marring his skin.

As the hours passed, we were satisfied several times over. They each claimed me, making me theirs as only those two men could. When at last I lay exhausted between them, it was almost sunrise.

It felt safe there in my bed with Arys and Shaz. Safe enough that I fell into a fitful slumber. My system had worked out most of the whiskey, though what remained held me in a state of dreamless sleep. For a while.

I came awake a few hours later, my mouth open in a silent scream. The only thing I remembered was red reptilian eyes. A wave of nausea racked me. I couldn't tell if it was a hangover or the thing Falon had given me sitting like a lead weight in my core.

A glance at my lovers revealed Shaz to be passed out beside me, snoring softly. Arys was rolled away, his face buried in the pillow.

I moved carefully, trying not to disturb either of them as I left the bed and fetched my robe.

Coffee did nothing to make me feel any better. However, it too would soon be taken from me. So I made a cup, snickered at the snoring leopard sprawled across the couch, and returned to my room where I stood near the window, watching the day through a tiny slit in the blinds.

I'd been overly sensitive to sunlight since Arys and I united as twin flames. Soon, it would be a deadly foe. I stared out at the golden light, refusing to look away even when it made my eyes tear up.

"Can't sleep?" Arys spoke softly, drawing my attention.

"Bad dreams, I think." I blinked a few times as my eyes readjusted to the darkened interior of the bedroom. "You?"

"I don't sleep much these days."

The silence fell, heavy and oppressive, launching us each into tortured thoughts of what was to come. I was torn between fleeing into the wilderness with my tail tucked between my legs and bravely striding onto the FPA property, ready to face the sword that dangled over my head.

"You can do this, right?" I asked, tentative and cautious, not wanting to appear as if I was doubting him.

Arys rubbed a hand through his mess of short, black hair. There was a storm brewing in his eyes. "Yes. I've had a lot of time to accept it was coming."

"That doesn't mean you're ready."

"I will never be ready." He was thoughtful for a moment before saying, "I know you've seen inside me. I know you've seen the way I hunger for your final moments. Please don't hate me for that."

I was tempted to go to him, to throw myself in his arms and hope to find comfort. There would be no comfort now, not from anyone. If I were to go to him, I would crumble. And I needed to be strong.

"Arys, I could never hate you."

"Lilah hates Salem. And I wouldn't doubt that it goes both ways. That's what it does, a bond like ours. It destroys."

"Lilah is weak." Bitterness laced my tone. "Salem too. Instead of learning to exist together, they have done nothing but imprison themselves. We're better than that."

"Are we?"

Arys's question hung suspended without an answer. Our time together had indeed been a rollercoaster of ups and downs. The conflict had brought us to some very dark places. It had hurt those linked to us. Shaz and Harley were prime examples of that. But we were still willing to fulfill the purpose of a greater good. If we gave up now, then all of that suffering would have been for nothing.

"We are," I declared. "Tonight we prove it."

I sipped the hot coffee, savoring every drop. If my stomach hadn't felt so queasy, I would have devoted the rest of the day to my favorite foods and drinks.

I noticed that Shaz's snoring had come to a stop. When had that happened? Cracking open his eyes he sat up and frowned.

"Is there something you two want to tell me?"

* * * *

Several hours later we sat in the kitchen with Jez and Jenner. The sun had just set. It hadn't been easy to say goodbye to the light. I'd drank up as much of it as I could though every second of warmth was plagued by the sense of great loss. The clock was ticking away the time I had left, and I couldn't help but be painfully aware of every second.

"It's going to be fine, Lex," Jez assured me though her green eyes sparkled with worry. No amount of prodding could convince her to stay behind. She insisted on accompanying me to the creepy old hospital. "You have to call Kale. He needs to know."

I frowned, wishing she wouldn't bring up uncomfortable forbidden lover drama in front of everyone.

Much to my surprise, Arys agreed. "Do it," he said. "Sinclair belongs to you. He has to be there. If we need to fight back against Shya and Gabriel, then we'll need all of the power we can get."

It was one of the hardest phone calls I'd ever had to make. I stepped out onto the back patio to speak in private. When it rang on the other end, I said a silent prayer that he wouldn't answer.

"Let me guess. You missed out on your chance to dance with me last night and you're calling to beg for a do over." Kale's chuckle was low and smooth, stirring the part of me that was his.

I couldn't bear the thought of him being in danger, but Jez was right. He needed to know. "Kale, I have the scroll. It was made with twin flame power, and it can be destroyed that way. I die tonight." Blurting it out hadn't been my intent, but what other way could I say it?

He took a moment to process what I'd said. "Tell me everything."

As I recounted Falon's visit for him, he listened patiently. With each word that left my mouth, the harsh reality of it all began to take hold. Nerves had me quivering though I was unafraid. Fear had no place here.

"You know I'll be there," he said after I'd finished. His voice was strained as if he fought to keep his emotions from coming through.

I wanted to tell him not to come, to stay safe in the arms of one of the many blood whores at The Wicked Kiss. That would be an insult so I said only, "Thank you."

After ending the call, I sent my sister a message. I was too chicken to call her and risk hearing her voice. It just might break the careful wall I'd constructed to cage the inner turmoil I ignored. It was a simple, straight forward message: *Midnight tonight Shya will be on FPA property. Do not come out to confront him. Any who do will die. I've got this one. Trust me. I love you.*

After some careful thought, I opted to ignore Falon's advice to involve Brogan. She was a highly skilled witch, but she was also human. The death of her mother weighed heavily on my conscience. I would not risk her life.

I also chose not to heed Shaz's suggestion that I ask Dayne to back me up. It was too soon in our alliance to involve his pack in something so volatile. I needed them to help establish my authority in the city, something they could not do if they were killed by Shya.

I stood outside, peering into the messy backyard. It was a relief to know that Coby and Kylarai were far from here on their honeymoon. From the wood grains on the patio railing to the scent of coyotes on the faint breeze, I lost myself in it all. I would be different when I stood here next.

Becoming a vampire was something I'd come to dread. Standing there, hours from my own death, I waited for the emotional meltdown. Tears, hysterical laughter, anything. It never came.

My resolve was strong. Hatred for Shya burned hot within me. Perhaps demons cannot be killed. However, they can be dealt with many other ways. Ruining Shya's shot at Lilah's throne was just the beginning. I would make that demon sorry he had ever uttered my name.

Chapter Twenty-Five

At half past eleven the first pang of fear clawed at the cage I'd locked it away in. We were at The Wicked Kiss where I joined Willow for one last shot of tequila. My companions waited, each of them as determined as I was. All of them with their own unspoken fears and worries.

Shaz and Jez hung out at the bar with us while both Kale and Arys chose to keep to themselves. Arys was outside with Jenner, waiting in the parking lot. Kale lingered near the door.

"To those who walk willingly into the dark because they know it's the only way for the light to shine." Willow held his shot glass up in a toast. His choice of words were nice, giving me a sense of reassurance that I was doing the right thing.

After the booze fest the previous night, tequila was the last thing I needed. But once I couldn't share a drink with my friend anymore, I would miss it. And so I downed the nasty shot in one gulp.

I put up a hand in polite refusal when he offered me the lime tray. "Nah, I'd rather let it burn. It is my last drink after all."

"I'm honored that you chose to share it with me." Willow smiled, but it was forced. Concern graced his lovely gold-flecked green eyes. "I'll be by your side through it all. Have faith that it will all play out as it should."

Anxiously I played with the black amulet around my neck. It lay beside Kale's cross. I had started to take the cross off back at home, then changed my mind. Something about it gave me strength. And I could use all the strength I could get my hands on now.

On impulse I threw my arms around Willow and hugged him tight. "Thank you for everything you've done for me. I know I'll never be able to repay you, but if there's ever anything you need from me, don't hesitate to say so."

"Ready to go?" Jez asked, looking positively miserable. She wasn't the type to hide her feelings, something I'd always admired about her.

"Not at all. But I guess I don't really have a choice."

I was dressed for a fight. In comfy yoga pants that hugged my body and a lightweight tank top, I was able to move without being hindered by clothing. The Dragon Claw hung in its sheath around my waist.

"If you get the chance to kill Gabriel, take it," I said. "But be careful. Don't try it if you don't have a clear shot."

She nodded, double-checking the dagger tucked into her boot and the smaller one strapped to the inside of her wrist. "I'm going to ride with Kale. He looks positively constipated, which means he needs to vent." She pulled me into a hug, squeezing so tight it hurt. "I can't believe this is happening. I love you, Lex."

"I love you, too. Are you sure you're up for this?"

"Don't worry about me. Seriously."

I glanced across the room at Kale. His expression was a perfect neutral mask. He wasn't going to let me see whatever he might be feeling. "Take care of him, Jez. Don't let him do anything stupid. Give Arys and me a few minutes to get into place before you join us. Be careful. Shya will be unpredictable."

I considered trying for a moment alone with Kale, then decided against it. We both needed to be tough right now. Poking at our vulnerabilities would only compromise our ability to think without emotion clouding our judgment.

Passing through the doors of The Wicked Kiss into the parking lot brought a smile to my face. Many times I had dreaded walking into the building. This time I dreaded having to leave.

Handing my keys to Shaz, I got in on the passenger side of the Charger and sucked in a deep breath. I could do this. I had to. If I didn't, I would become more of a slave to Shya than I already was.

"Fuck that," I muttered to myself. The more I thought about Shya, the angrier I became. As long as I was pissed off, there was no room for fear. Feeding the growing rage, I let myself recall the many things he had done.

There wasn't a lot of talk as we drove through the city. The radio filled the silence. Jenner and Arys were relatively calm in the back seat. At least, that's how they made it appear. Shaz, however, was unable to rein in his emotions. The harsh sensation of bitterness and loathing danced over me, leaving invisible pinpricks behind.

It wouldn't have surprised me if Shaz was churning with anger. He had been carrying a lot of hard feelings about Arys and me for a while now. It had changed him, and I wasn't sure it was entirely for the better.

"I went back to Doghead," he said suddenly, pulling my startled gaze his way. "The other night, after Dayne came by the club. He and I talked. I'm considering joining the pack."

"Oh," I said softly, trying to conceal my relief. "That's great. I think they've managed to do a good job of being organized. They seem to have an order that works. That tattoo will be crazy sexy on you."

I flashed him a flirtatious grin and received a slight blush in response. Damn I loved him. I would always wish that it was enough.

"I just wanted to let you know. I'm not ticked off about it. I know you care." He navigated through traffic, keeping his attention on the road so I wouldn't see the wolf in his eyes.

I felt it too. My wolf longed for his. If I could be anywhere in the world, it would be curled up with Shaz on the forest floor.

This was his way of apologizing for our argument. I knew it was only because he was afraid of what would happen tonight. Without saying anything to make a hard situation harder, I simply reached across and touched his leg.

He caught my hand in his and brought it to his lips, brushing a soft kiss across my knuckles. For the first time that night, I felt like crying. It had nothing to do with Shya or death. It had everything to do with my white wolf and the way things would change between us after this night.

We pulled up down the street from the scary-ass, old hospital, and my heart began to pound. It loomed large in the darkness. Already

I could feel the restless spirits taking note of our arrival. They likely were not the only ones.

A basic chain-link fence surrounded the property. It was broken in several places, creating the illusion that nobody maintained it. The windows were blacked out, revealing nothing of what was inside.

"Holy shit. This place is phenomenal." Jenner stared up at the hospital in awe. "I've never felt anything quite like it."

"Be careful, Jenner," Arys warned. "This place has a way of getting inside your head."

"You're telling me," Shaz scoffed. "If either of you vamp out on me, I won't hesitate to beat your ass."

The night Arys had turned on Shaz and me in this place would live forever in my memory. In fact, I didn't think I'd ever forget a second I spent inside the horrible building.

Kale's car pulled up behind us. Inside I was a quivering mess, but when I reached for the door, my hand was steady. Five minutes and counting.

I stared up at the hospital, seeking any sign of FPA activity. They were a covert op for a reason. If I hadn't seen it for myself, I wouldn't have believed any living being was inside that decrepit old structure.

"What does it feel like?" Jez joined me, scanning the perimeter closely.

"The key to Lilah's throne? It mostly just feels heavy, and dark." *Just like what's inside of you,* I thought but didn't dare speak the words. I meant to tell Jez what I'd felt nestled within her, but this wasn't the right time.

Willow appeared with a ripple of air and the sound of wings though his were not visible. The last time the three of us had been here together we'd been looking for Kale. It hadn't gone well.

"There's a demon on the other side of the building," Willow informed me. "I'm going to intercept him right before you enter the grounds. There's no way of knowing how much time you have before Shya shows."

"Great." I nodded, looking at each of my companions in turn. "I hope you all know how grateful I am to have you back me up. I won't ever forget it. That being said, I guess it's pretty much go time."

Without so much as a word, Kale came forward, took my face in his hands, and laid a passionate kiss on me. It left me breathless and a little giddy. Then he stepped back and turned away before I could react.

It shocked me to find Shaz holding Arys back. My dark vampire was seething and straining in Kale's direction. Suppressing his emotions with the strong, silent act was working against him, causing him to unravel. Shaz didn't look too thrilled either, but he was clearly more focused on the task at hand.

My love life was a fucking mess, but this was no time to dwell on that. Duty called.

I grabbed Arys's hand and pulled him along beside me. Following the fence to the first broken point, I stepped onto the hospital grounds and immediately collapsed on my knees. An overwhelming ill sensation rocked me, and I thought I might vomit. Each breath made the bad feeling grow. Arys pulled me up while throwing a bunch of questions at me. I could only shake my head. The abysmal force sitting like a foreign intruder within me recognized this place. I knew where to go.

I broke into a run as a sense of urgency gripped me. I ran the length of the building until I reached the end and turned to come up on the north side of it where two rows of trees lined an unseen path. With Arys hot on my heels, I ran down that path, certain I was drawing ever closer to where I needed to be.

Excitement flooded me with a rush of adrenaline. I ran like I'd never run before, my feet barely touching the ground. The closer I got to the invisible marker, the greater the force inside me seemed to swell. I was sure that I was going to make it. That we could do this after all without the interference I feared.

I was wrong.

Shya appeared directly in front of me. With the stench of sulfur clouding him and his black wings spread wide, he hit me, a solid body check that flung me backwards.

I hit the ground hard, feeling the impact reverberate up my spine. My teeth smacked together, rattling my jaw. I clawed desperately at the hard earth, scrambling to my feet. Arys put himself between Shya and me, but the demon tossed him aside with ease.

"Did you think it would be that easy to deceive me, bitch?" Shya hissed. His eyes flashed with a deep-rooted hatred that chilled me to the bone. Grabbing hold of me, he shook me hard enough to blur my vision. "How did you get it? Tell me how you got it."

His shouts hurt my ears. I struggled to get away, but he held tight with a strength so far beyond human it couldn't be measured. Though his angry shouts were worrisome, it assured me that Falon hadn't lied. This was no set up. Not for me anyway.

Shya smacked me hard across the face before throwing me down on the ground. He stood over me with a supernatural breeze ruffling his short blue-black hair. In a fit of temper, he kicked me, hitting my side, and I yelped. The wolf inside wanted to shift, to flee or fight. This weak human body was holding me back.

"Fuck you," I managed to say before lashing out at him with my own power. Arys's proximity boosted my strength, and the attack actually threw Shya back several feet. It wasn't much, but it gave me time to get on my feet again.

I sought to take in my surroundings, finding that Shya wasn't alone. Brook was doing a good job keeping Jenner and Arys busy while Shya targeted me. I couldn't see the others, but I hoped they were waiting for the right time to make a move. Rushing in too soon would get them killed.

Rather than engaging with Shya, I tried to keep moving. It wasn't far now. The place where I needed to be lay just ahead, between the two trees at the end. I could feel it.

I threw a shield up around me a second before Shya's blast of demon magic hit. It burned like someone had poured liquid sunlight over me, but my shield allowed me to keep running.

Until he rushed me with a sweeping kick that took my legs out from under me.

No sooner had I hit the ground than Shya was on top of me. He straddled me, fighting to get a hold of my arms. He couldn't take Lilah's orb with me putting up such a struggle. I knew it would require some effort and concentration on his part. I couldn't allow him that.

"Tell me who gave it to you," Shya shouted in my face. His usual calm and collected demeanor had been shattered by his irrational need for more power.

"Who do you think?" I gasped out, fighting to get him off me. "It was Lilah's. And because she's a twin flame, now it's mine."

"Like hell it is." He slammed my head against the ground, trying to knock me unconscious. I couldn't let that happen. "It's mine by right. I deserve it."

If I hadn't been fighting to stay conscious, I would have marveled at the demon's psychotic belief. Power was a deadly thing. Was there ever enough, or would it always make one crave more? Was this kind of insane pursuit of more in my future?

Desperation drove me to try anything. So I drove a long, sharp claw into his eye. The resulting shriek was ear piercing. He reacted like most would, reaching for the assaulted eye. I brought a knee up between his legs as hard as I could. Then I used a shot of power to toss him off me.

I didn't hang around to see how fast he recovered. The injuries he'd inflicted on me were numb. Adrenaline surged through me, keeping me moving.

I caught a glimpse of Jez's golden ponytail as she made an appearance. Silver dagger held high, she plunged it into Brook's back. Being the only metal I knew of that harmed demons, it had him flailing around in an attempt to dislodge it.

Jenner and Arys let him have it then, throwing everything they could at him before he could recover. A flash of white revealed Shaz, in wolf form, circling the feuding trio with fangs bared.

Willow was up ahead, near the unseen door to Lilah's kingdom. He was engaged in combat with another demon, one I recognized from Shya's evil party.

Lungs heaving, I threw myself forward, refusing to let anything stop me. When I reached the place where Lilah's key had been forged the demon orb inside me pressed against its mortal cage, seeking a way out.

I threw a circle up around me, hoping it was strong enough to buy me a few precious seconds.

It wasn't.

Shya was suddenly there on the other side. Blood stained the side of his face though his mangled eye had already healed. With no effort at all, he dissolved my circle. Panicked, I drew the Dragon Claw and instead of going for a wimpy wrist cut, I pressed the tip of the blade to my sternum.

"Bit of a one hit wonder, aren't you, Alexa?" Shya sneered. "You've already played the suicide card."

"Whatever works."

It was a desperate move, one I never got the chance to follow through on. With a snap of his fingers Shya ripped the dagger out of my grasp. It skittered across the ground, landing in a thick chunk of yellowed grass.

"Don't make me begin killing your companions. I'll start with Kale."

His threat made me glance around frantically for Kale. He was watching Jez's back as she brazenly continued her attack on Brook. The demon was weakening with every silver blow she dealt him.

Arys and Jenner joined me, one of them on each side as we faced off against Shya. The asshole grinned, and his characteristic amusement was back.

"You can't take me, Alexa. Even as one of the great and rare Hounds, you're no match for me. Not with all of that vampire power in your system. It comes from demons, you know." He seemed quite satisfied with himself, certain he had me now. "Give up now and save those you love. Otherwise, I'll kill every last one of you."

"You'll kill us anyway," I declared, my wolf shining in my eyes. The beast saw him for the evil he was, and she'd had enough of his shit. "There's no way I'm going to let you take over Lilah's kingdom. She was right. You're not worthy."

Pissing him off further wasn't my intent, not really. However, I was pretty pissed myself. The demon had been playing puppet master for far too long.

Shya's expression didn't change, but the atmosphere around him did. It grew hotter, tight, like something was about to snap.

"You know I think I will keep you alive after all," he mused. "Just you. It's been a while since I've had a vampire slave. You'll make a good one. I'll let my demons have their way with you, and you will spend the rest of your days begging for mercy."

It was a sick thing to say, but I wouldn't have expected less from Shya. Although it most definitely encouraged my need to end his reign of horror.

"Like hell you will," Arys snapped, slamming Shya with a blast so strong I felt it in my core.

Much to my surprise the hit seemed to have an effect. Shya's body jerked and smoke rose from his middle. He peered down at the point of impact and chuckled.

"You are a tough one, aren't you? I knew I was right to choose you to sire Gabriel." Before I saw it coming, Shya retaliated with a writhing mass of black energy that brought Arys to his knees. "Too bad you're so damn headstrong. You'd have made a great servant in my kingdom."

He took down Jenner next while I stood helplessly by. I braced for the blow that I knew was coming. Before it could hit, Willow threw himself in front of me and took the impact.

Willow and Shya struggled, engaged in a combat so violent thunder rumbled overhead. Willow drove him away from us, trying to give us some much needed space. But they were not evenly matched and soon my dear guardian friend began to get his ass kicked.

"That motherfucker needs to go down," Arys swore as he got to his feet.

"You have to do it now, Arys. You have to kill me."

Commotion was all around us. Jez and Kale had driven Brook off. He'd disappeared to the other side, or wherever it was that demons went to lick their wounds. The demon Willow had fought had vanished as well. Shaz lingered nearby, watching the perimeter for anything amiss.

Arys stared at me as if I'd spoken the words from his nightmares. I probably had.

Shaking his head, he stepped back. "I can't do this."

"You have to," I cried, my gaze darting fearfully to where the fallen angel and demon slammed one another against the building. "We don't have much time."

Jenner grabbed Arys and gave him a shake. "Get your shit together, man. You knew this was coming. If you don't do it, I will."

That was not what Arys wanted to hear. He backhanded Jenner with a metaphysical hit to go along with it. I gave a small shriek as Jenner slammed into one of the trees that lined us on either side. He hit the ground and lay there stunned.

"Arys! How could you do that? We need him."

"There has to be another way," Arys muttered, continuing to back away from me as if he couldn't trust himself to be so close. He wanted it, yet he was fighting the urge.

"There isn't, and you damn well know it." I advanced on him, determined to force him to do what needed to be done.

"Alexa, stay back," he warned, a hand raised, crackling with power.

I was saddened and distraught to see our bond being put to the test like this and failing. If I'd had to bet on one of us to fuck this moment up, I'd have said it would be me. There was no satisfaction in being wrong about that.

"Stop this shit right now. You're going to blow everything." I was ready for it when he threw the power he held. In a smooth motion, I absorbed the blast. His power was mine too. He could try to turn it on me, but he would fail. We had done this dance before.

For a guy who was usually so smooth and charismatic, a century of waiting had done more damage than I'd realized. Arys was visibly frazzled. I had to do something. In a reckless attempt to snap him out of the strange spell he was under, I ran to where Jenner swayed on his feet with a hand pressed to his forehead. He blinked cold blue eyes at me in confusion.

"Do it," I demanded, grabbing him with claw tipped hands. "Just make it fast."

Jenner glanced warily over my shoulder to where Arys stood lost in the chaos. "He'll kill me."

"Better him than me." My claws left deep scratches in his tattooed flesh. I was frantic, feeling our chance slip away.

Before I could bully Jenner further, there was a loud bang, and the earth shook beneath my feet. I turned to find Willow on his back, his face bloodied and his clothing torn. Shya stood over him with a cloud of black smoke swirling about him like a tornado.

He faded into the mist. It took me a moment to realize he was changing form, shifting into something other than the human façade he wore. Whatever it was, it was massive. The smoky mist began to take the shape of a dragon. Standing almost as high as the second story of the building with enormous ebony feathered wings, Shya swung his large tail.

It swept Willow off the ground and hurled him through the air. He crashed through the treetops before plummeting to the earth in a heap.

The dragon turned on us, blinking big red eyes that gleamed with murderous intent. Then he opened his mouth full of vicious, pointed teeth and breathed out a stream of fire.

Chapter Twenty-Six

Everyone fled in a different direction. Jenner grabbed my hand, and we ran for a patch of trees near the perimeter fence. It wouldn't do a whole hell of a lot if Shya wanted to scorch us to death, but at this point, he still needed me alive.

"If we survive this, you fucking owe me," Jenner said. He was pressed against a tree trunk as if it would hide him. "And I will call in that favor."

I would have shot him a glare, but I didn't dare take my gaze off Shya's bone-chilling new form. So I settled for a middle finger. "You do that."

Shya settled himself in right over the unseen door. Scanning the vicinity for us, he began to preen his wings.

"Come now, Alexa," his voice boomed through the night. "You're only prolonging the inevitable. Why must you make everything so difficult? Let's talk. Perhaps we can strike a deal."

Making deals with a demon dragon was not on my to-do list for the evening. Searching the dark for my companions, I was relieved to find Shaz and Arys together several yards away. Kale and Jez were nowhere in view, and I suspected they might have rounded the corner of the building.

With my gaze on Willow's prone form, I called out, "I have nothing to say to you, Shya."

I owed Shya some serious payback for the hell he'd put Willow through by killing his lady love. Dragon or not, that wouldn't change.

He stomped a foot in temper, and the ground rumbled beneath me. Never in my worst imaginings had I dreamed up a scenario like this.

Several shouts announced the arrival of the FPA swat team. What the hell were they thinking? They swarmed from around the building, aiming several types of weaponry at the black dragon. It seemed that they were packing silver tipped crossbow bolts and guns that more than likely held silver bullets.

I shook my head and watched their vain attempt at policing the darkness. Much to my relief Juliet was not among the small squad of people willing to die in order to satisfy Briggs's curiosity. Of course the self-righteous Fed was safely inside, probably watching from an upstairs window.

There was nothing I could do. Not without putting myself in harm's way. The agents swarmed Shya, shooting him full of bullets and bolts. It was pathetic, like watching children play superhero.

Smoke rose from the wounds in his thick hide, but otherwise Shya was unfazed. With a great roar he unleashed a stream of fire, engulfing the entire team of agents in one breath. The heat was unbearable, scorching despite the distance. The stench of burnt flesh quickly filled the air. I coughed and choked, trying not to be sick.

Hopefully that would keep Briggs from sending more people out. Those deaths were all on him. All he'd succeeded in doing was driving Shya into a greater frenzy.

He roared again and shot a fireball at the tree we huddled under. The top burst into flames, and I screamed. Jenner and I leaped out of the way before several burning branches came plummeting down.

"I will burn this entire place to the ground," Shya boomed. "You will watch your sister burn before you die, Alexa."

I groaned. Why did it always have to come back to Juliet? It was just too easy for her to be used against me. I was torn. If I gave in to Shya's demands he would win by exploiting one of my most obvious weaknesses. However, if I resisted, he would do as he said. I knew that.

"Don't do it," Jenner whispered. "Don't go to him."

We were getting nowhere. I couldn't keep hiding under trees until Shya roasted them all.

"I have an idea," I said, laying a hand on Jenner's arm. "If this works, then I'm sorry."

"What the hell does that mean?"

I didn't bother to answer. I was about to try something that might work or it might just make my head explode. Either way, it was all I had left to throw at the demon. I had to try.

Striding away from the pitiful coverage of the remaining trees, I tapped into the power I shared with Arys. It spilled over me like a dam breaking under the pressure of a flood. This would be the last time I would do this as a mortal. I wouldn't survive it this time.

Shya was right in that our vampire power was rooted in darkness. But I wasn't a vampire. I was a Hound of God, a creature of light with a natural ability to channel and manipulate energy. Any energy. Even dark energy.

The dark and light had existed together inside me for some time now. They had often been at war, battling for supremacy. Now I was going to make them work together for my purpose. Or die trying.

I reached for Arys, a metaphysical summons that he couldn't help but answer. The power rose hard and fast, causing my nose to bleed before I'd even done anything. Talk about going out with a bang.

"You want me, Shya. Then come and get me." My fingers crackled and sparked with swirls of gold and blue. I stopped short of walking right up to him. I wasn't that brave or that stupid.

Arys came to stand next to me. His eyes were wild, full on wolf eyes. My eyes. I was certain mine reflected him as well.

With him so close, the force surging through us both was amplified, and I struggled to stay on my feet. My intent was to draw on the mass of dark power I had access to through Arys and Jenner while using the light within me to bend it to my will. If it worked the way I hoped, I would essentially be fighting Shya's evil with my own dark power guided by the light.

"You won't survive such a foolish attempt," Shya said though he didn't seem convinced.

"Probably not. But hey, I came here to die. Why prolong it?"

Without a word of warning, I reached out to every vampire connected to me, drawing on their power and harnessing it as my own. In my mind I could feel them. From Jenner and Kale so close to me to

Sloane in Europe where she lounged in bed with a young human man. Even Hurst deep in the bowels of his hidden Las Vegas home.

Gabriel too was affected. Part of our bloodline, he was now a link in the circuit. And I could feel that he was close. The power of several vampires slammed through me, and I released it in a well-focused attack on the smirking dragon.

It smashed Shya into the side of the hospital before throwing him to the ground. Rather than individual shots I projected a steady stream of power. Even in his outrageous form, it held him down, giving me a chance to reclaim the place in the grass where Lilah's door lay.

Arys helped me to maintain the load. The pressure inside my head grew steadily, but it was manageable. I squinted through the throbbing in my skull and saw only the demon I needed to beat down.

Laughter filled the night. Shya found it funny that I was pouring so much into an attack. He couldn't be killed, but he could be weakened and driven back to the other side.

I tasted honey and smelled perfume. The vampires I channeled were very much in my head. So when Gabriel stepped into view, I was ready for the black magic he threw.

It hit me like a splash of hot wax, quickly cooling and flaking away. The cross pendant around my neck felt cold in contrast. Judging by the surprise on Gabriel's ashen face, he'd been expecting a different outcome.

Uttering something Latin, he tried a different tactic. The little heathen was disrupting my concentration enough that Shya was advancing on me.

Shaz was a blur of white as he leaped on Gabriel, taking the newbie vampire down. It was all I could do to keep my attention on Shya, even when I heard Shaz yelp.

I drew harder on my link to the vampires while grabbing hold of the spark of light that made me twin to Arys's dark. It was all I had to fight with.

Blood didn't just drip from my nose. It ran. Maintaining the flow of so much power was quickly taking its toll. Never before had I tried something so immense. It was breaking me fast.

Arys grabbed my hand and kept me on my feet. Together we channeled more power than any being should ever know. It kept Shya at bay though it didn't appear to do much harm.

All we needed was a window of opportunity. Just enough time for Arys to bleed me. I would beat him into it if I had to. There would be no backing out. We had to see this through.

Shya's laughter had stopped. The black mist clouded him once again, and I watched eagerly, hopeful it was a sign that he was weakening. Because I sure as hell was.

When the mist cleared he stood there in his human form with wings spread for balance. He had underestimated what a Hound could do. His outrage was written all over his face.

A surge of hope and renewal convinced me that I had him. If I could just keep it up a little longer, just maybe he would be forced to vacate.

"I can hold out longer than you can," Shya called. "You'll kill your vampires as well as yourself before you beat me."

"Arys," I tried to say, but my voice failed me.

Still he heard me. He squeezed my hand, trying to strengthen me. But it was no longer enough. Too many times, too much power, my mortal body was unable to take anymore.

Blood filled my eyes before sliding down my cheeks. Struggling for breath, I coughed, producing more blood. I'd killed several vampires like this. A forced power overload that results in the bursting of the heart. I supposed it was fitting that I would die the same way.

"Alexa, stop," Arys pleaded. "You have to stop. Now."

I wiped the blood from my eyes and lips with the back of my hand, doing little more than smearing it around my face. "You have to finish this, Arys."

Shya was on his knees when I collapsed face first into the dirt and dry grass. So close. I'd come so close to driving him off. I had called more power than ever before, and it still wasn't enough.

My vision swam as I struggled to look around. Jenner had collapsed near the trees. I couldn't see Kale, but Jez's shouts at me to stop rang in my ears. The only one still standing was Gabriel who emanated an unholy power much darker than our bloodline alone.

He had left Shaz unconscious, a pile of white fur amidst the dark of night. Jez rushed to my fallen wolf with a silver dagger in each hand, ready to protect him from further damage.

My grip on the flow of power faltered, and I was forced to let go of my connection to the others. It was just as well. I didn't want to take them with me.

Gabriel put himself between me and Shya. In a desperate move, I reached out to grab hold of his energy. If I'd been able to bind him to me during Shya's party it would have been easy to manipulate him now.

"Give it up, Alexa," Gabriel said. "You've got nothing on me."

I screamed when, with a snap of his fingers, my body was racked with pain. It felt like I was slowly being torn apart. It was obvious that he was buying Shya time to recover. It wouldn't take long.

Arys seemed reluctant to leave my side, but at the sound of my shriek he launched himself at Gabriel. The two of them became a mass of fists and fury. Though the fledgling vampire thrummed with black magic, Arys had centuries of experience and power. They were evenly matched, throwing one another violently about.

There was no one left standing between me and Shya. His red eyes gleamed with delight. Using the very last of my strength, I pushed to my feet. In my peripheral vision, I saw Willow do the same.

"I enjoy you," Shya proclaimed. With a flap of wings, he was standing again. "Really, I do. No mortal has ever given me a fight this good. It feels…pretty damn great. What do you say, Alexa? Do you have one more round left in you?"

The fact that I was on my feet was nothing short of a miracle. Breathing was a feat in itself. There was no way I could go another round with the demon. I was done. It was over.

"Don't die on me now," he continued, each step bringing him closer. "Not until I have the scroll. How many times have I saved your pathetic life now? Soon the darkness will claim you, and then you will belong to me."

I staggered like a drunk but didn't fall. If only I would just die and rob him of his precious fucking scroll.

"Sorry to disappoint you." Willow was just suddenly there, feeding Shya a series of punches clearly fueled by pure hatred. "You took Christina from me, but you will never have Alexa. I am taking her darkness."

Surprise crossed Shya's sharp features. "You would sacrifice yourself for the Hound?"

"That's right." Projecting his voice toward the sky, Willow shouted. "Do you hear me? I willingly take Alexa's darkness."

Whoever he was speaking to, it wasn't Shya. There was a flash of bright, white light. It struck Willow in the chest, holding him frozen in place. It happened so fast.

An anguished cry tore from Willow. I watched in horror as the darkness meant for me filled him. One by one the feathers of his wings turned as black as sin.

"No," I screamed, reaching for Willow as if I could stop what had already begun.

My name was a whisper on his lips when he looked at me with gold-flecked red eyes. Before I could touch him, he was gone, leaving behind only the stench of sulfur.

Tears streamed down my face. I shook with sobs. Not Willow. Dear God, not him. He didn't deserve such a fate.

I didn't feel like I'd been saved. Instead I felt very much condemned. Willow had sacrificed himself for me, and I didn't even have the strength to finish what I'd come to do. I had failed him.

Shya reached for me, and I cringed. Anticipating his vile touch, I prayed it would all happen fast.

A sword burst through Shya's chest, having been shoved through from behind. Falon stood behind the demon, holding tight to the hilt. Smoke rose from the silver blade.

Shya's mouth dropped open, but no sound came out. He blinked several times as realization set in.

"Alexa, please," he pleaded. "We can negotiate. Give me the scroll, and I'll make you my queen. Anything you want, it's yours."

"Go to hell," I said.

Gaping down at the blade protruding from his middle, Shya pitched forward, nearly crashing into me as he went down on his face.

In a sudden fluid motion, Falon jerked the sword free and swung. The blade whistled through the air before slicing through Shya's neck, effectively severing his head. Before my very eyes,

Shya's body faded away, disappearing completely. I would never have believed it if I hadn't seen it myself.

Without so much as a word to me, Falon targeted Gabriel next. He slashed at the young vampire, driving him and Arys apart.

"Finish this now," Falon shouted at Arys. "Shya will regroup fast on the other side. You don't have much time."

Arys wore several cuts and gashes, but otherwise he was all right. He caught me as I fell forward.

"Do it," I said, my voice thin and shrill.

He shoved away from me, muttering something inaudible beneath his breath. Arys was battling with himself. It was a fight he would not win. "I don't want to."

In direct contrast to his words, he grabbed me again and shook me.

I fought him, hoping to slap some sanity back into him. My hand cracked across his face, and he bared fangs at me. Fear clawed its way up my throat, and I choked on it. This was really happening.

Arys froze, staring into me and seeing something that freed the hunger he had carried for over a century.

"You know you have to do it," I murmured. "It's ok. I'm ready."

Bloodlust burned in Arys. He jerked me closer, and with no hesitation, plunged fangs deep into my neck. Targeting my artery, he bit with the intent to kill. Blood gushed from the wound. Arys was ravenous, biting a second time.

The power of our bond soared between us, much like it had the night we had first slept together, when our twin flame union had united us. We were inside each other. Random thoughts and feelings flitted through my mind, all of them Arys's.

As he consumed my blood and the power within it, I very clearly saw how much he loved it. Finally, after waiting for so long, after craving my death for decades, it was his at last.

There wasn't a single piece of him that didn't find absolute pleasure in this moment. He held me close, lovingly stroking a hand through my hair as he stole my life. Arys exuded genuine emotion. He loved me. I felt it. However, that didn't change the elation he felt at making me his in every way.

Something buried deep within me began to writhe and squirm. Lilah's key responded to my fading life, resisting the pull as I took it with me.

My surroundings began to fade. No longer could I smell the acrid odor of burnt flesh. The sound of Jez's shouts were muffled and far away. There was a sharp pain in my abdomen, which echoed throughout my mind. The dark, twin-flame forged key shuddered and seized before shattering like a burst bubble. I felt cold and then, only numb.

The last thing I saw was Falon standing over Gabriel's prone form. He watched us with a disaffected stare. Then my vision grew dark, and I succumbed to death.

* * * *

Everything was so white. I found myself in a plain room with no door, no windows, only a table with two chairs. A man sat in one of the chairs. His back was to me, but I knew who it was.

"Veryl? What are you doing here?"

Feeling strange and loaded with questions, I rounded the table and slid into the chair opposite him. A long off-white robe clothed me. Veryl wore a suit and tie in the same color. The absence of sound and smell bothered me, but I paid it little attention once I sat across from the vampire I'd killed not so long ago.

He looked the same as I remembered. Middle aged but handsome with eyes that reflected an inner knowledge I could only imagine.

"You don't have much time," he said. "I'm here to see you before you go back."

"Back?"

"To the other side. To the living. You're in between now but not for long." Veryl sat back in his chair and pressed his fingers into a steeple. "I warned you about Shya, did I not?"

I felt ashamed, knowing without a doubt that I'd been wrong to murder this man. "I'm sorry I didn't trust you. There were just too many secrets."

"There were," he agreed with a slight head nod. "I too am sorry. I wish things had been different between us. It was my intention to protect you, not too harm you."

I surveyed the small, simple white room. It felt safe and warm despite there being no obvious way in or out. "I suppose none of that matters now."

"You've done well," he said with a smile, revealing straight white teeth. There were no fangs. "I couldn't be happier with how you've grown into your abilities."

"So where is everyone?" I asked, feeling very disembodied. "Don't I get some big welcome or something? Do I have to face everyone I've killed? Or just you?"

Veryl chuckled, and it was a sound of carefree happiness. "Just me. Everyone else is on the other side. You don't get to join them yet. You're going back, very soon. So let me make this brief. You must be prepared, Alexa. The evil you've faced, it's not over. It is never really over."

"What are you talking about?" There was a pang of disappointment that I wouldn't see Raoul. Or Lena. I missed them both.

Veryl reached across the table and captured my hand in his. It felt warm and soft. "You're not going to feel like yourself when you return. The turn will dominate you, making you a monster. But you must embrace your light. You're going to need it."

"You're scaring me." Though I said the words, I didn't feel afraid. I felt detached, as if this entire thing were a dream that I couldn't take too seriously.

"You're not finished, Alexa. Not even close. As a Hound of God, you have a duty to uphold, regardless of whether you're a vampire or not. The dark side will lure you into blood and mayhem while the light will guide you in love and honor." Veryl's expression grew grave. He leaned in close as if sharing a secret. "Possessing them both will be a great challenge. But if anyone can overcome it, it's you."

His warning left me feeling sad in a place that didn't seem to recognize such an emotion. Sadness just didn't belong here.

"What if I don't want to go back?" I challenged. "Can't I just stay here with you?"

Veryl patted my hand in a fatherly way and gave me a gentle smile. "I'm afraid not. You're needed among the living. There are things you must do yet. A role to play that is yours and yours alone."

Hadn't I done enough? Was the face off with Shya only the beginning? I wasn't sure I could take any more of that.

"And if I refuse?" It was a stubborn, childish remark. Feeling backed into a corner, I had an irrational urge to argue his words though he had given me no reason to.

"You won't. It isn't your way." Veryl rose and held his arms out to me expectantly.

I moved lightly, as if my feet never touched the ground. His embrace was strong but gentle, parental and encouraging. Veryl had cared for me as if I were his daughter. And I hadn't known that until now, when I could feel it without him ever having to say so.

"I'm sorry for the ways I've wronged you." The words were not enough, but I had nothing else to offer.

He patted my back and smoothed my hair back before peering deep into my eyes. "Don't be sorry. Just be who you're called to be, a protector of mankind."

I stared at him in wonder. Only Willow had spoken those words to me. Had Veryl always known?

There were so many questions I needed him to answer. Before I could utter a single one, I was pulled away, drawn by an unseen force. It felt as if I were being sucked through a shrinking tunnel, watching the white room grow smaller in the distance.

Veryl's final words reverberated through my thoughts, an echo that followed me back to where I belonged: protector of mankind.

Chapter Twenty-Seven

A hurricane of sensations welcomed me back. From the overbearing scent of cologne, wolf, and paint to the immaculate touch of satin sheets on my skin, it all hit me at once.

Voices carried to me. They belonged to Arys and Shaz, and though they spoke in low tones, I heard every word as if they shouted in my ears.

"It's almost sunrise," Arys was saying. "She probably won't rise tonight."

"I don't care. I'm not leaving. And neither should you." There was such vindication in Shaz's tone. "Do you think she'll still have the wolf?"

"She died with the amulet on. If Lena knew what she was doing when she made that thing, then yeah, Alexa should still have her wolf. Don't worry, pup. She'll still love you either way."

My eyes popped open, and I sat up slowly. A dim lamp lit the room. Harley's room. I was at The Wicked Kiss. In my current state, I couldn't make much of that. Aside from an inner sense of disappointment, it didn't mean much to me.

My vision was impeccable. The wolf had given me superior eyesight, but it paled compared to how I now saw. It was like stepping into the light for the first time after wandering around in the dark. There were no words for how detailed and pure everything was. From the cracks in the ceiling to the fibers of the carpet, it all was richer and more complex than I'd ever noticed before.

With a vague curiosity, I slid my tongue over the tiny but deadly fangs in my mouth. They were much smaller than I was used to.

No conscious thought commanded my mental state. In a state of strange observation, I merely took in my surroundings, thinking and feeling nothing.

I wore the same clothes I'd had on when Arys killed me. It felt like two days ago though I wasn't certain. The dragon on my forearm looked especially black against my alabaster skin. I studied it for a moment and shrugged.

"I still can't believe you did it." There was judgment in Shaz's voice from beyond the door. "You loved it. Didn't you?"

A sense of detached surprise drifted through me when I lightly tossed the blankets aside and they slapped against the wall as if I'd hurled them in violence. *Weird.*

"Do you really want an answer to that?" came Arys's mysterious reply.

There was silence for a minute. The door opened and the two of them entered. They stopped dead in the doorway at finding me sitting up in bed.

I stared at them, uncertain and suspicious. They were familiar to me somehow. I knew that. But in that moment, I could only think in terms of instinctive feelings. The new dark, undead entity dominated.

"Lex?" Shaz barely breathed my name. Wide-eyed and speechless, he stared in disbelief.

The sound of his mortal heartbeat reverberated in my ears. His blood smelled wild and earthy. It called to me, and nothing else mattered. I needed it.

I sprang off the bed and cleared the room in a bound. The speed with which I moved was impossibly inhuman. It was invigorating, bringing me a gleeful victory when I easily took Shaz down beneath me.

Kneeling on his chest, I pinned him down and went for his throat. With a low growl, he flung an arm up to block me. My attack was vicious as I retaliated, fighting to get to that fount of hot, pumping scarlet nectar.

Suddenly I was airborne. I flew into the hallway, head over feet before smacking the wall and rolling into the middle of the hall. Feeling no pain, I was up and ready to face my attacker.

Arys stood in the doorway to Harley's room. He shoved Shaz behind him and faced me with hands crackling with power. There was a melancholy element to him. It confused me in my predatory state.

Our eyes met and I froze. I knew him. Something deep inside me recognized him as mine, and yet all I could think about when I looked at him was death. He was the one. He was the one who killed me.

"Alexa?" He took a tentative step toward me. "I can help you through this, but you have to trust me."

A snarl bubbled up in my throat. Arys's memories echoed inside me. He had killed me, and he had loved it.

All at once the remnants of who I was swam to the surface. I was immediately overcome by a torrent of emotion. It was intensified, imbued with an abyss-like passion that outweighed any feelings I'd ever had before. I wanted to cry, scream, and dissolve into hysterical laughter all at the same time.

Arys took another step toward me, his hands held up in surrender. "It'll be ok. I promise you, my wolf. Let me help you."

"Help me?" I repeated, not recognizing my own voice. "You did this to me. You knew what would happen, and you did it anyway."

I backed away, unable to understand why I should trust him. It just didn't compute amid the sudden confusion and mental distress.

"There will be time to talk about that later. Right now we need to calm your bloodlust before you run amok and terrorize the city. You know me, Alexa. All of me. You know you can trust me." Holding a hand out toward me, Arys pleaded with his eyes for understanding.

The hallway hummed with the intriguing energy of vampires. Like an intricate, fascinating song, it played through me, a beautiful piece of music that resonated in every fiber of my being. It was no longer merely something I felt from outside of me, but something that lived within.

Arys didn't give me a choice. He continued toward me, and I reacted. The power went out from me with no real thought to guide it. My intent was to ward him off and that's what it did.

Stronger than ever before, I threw Arys backward; he flipped over the small bistro table in the bedroom before hitting the floor. It had taken no effort on my part, sapping none of my strength.

I didn't wait around for him to get up. Turning on a heel, I darted down the hallway toward freedom. The red glowing exit sign was suddenly before me as I cleared the entire length from one end to the other in seconds.

The door slammed open, and I was gone, shooting through the parking lot like a bullet from a gun. Right away I felt the coming sunrise. It was less than an hour off. Instinct warned me to be careful. There was no taunting the sun and living to tell the tale.

I ran down the street, darting across in front of traffic, ignoring the sound of horns blaring and drivers telling me off. Running north, I followed the erratic urge to flee, paying no mind to where I was actually headed. My legs moved like the wind carried me. There was no gasping for breath. It felt like a dream.

Then something did bring me to a halt. As I passed the university a few blocks from The Wicked Kiss, the scent of humans and the sound of voices drew me to the dorm parking lot.

Despite the early hour there were people just getting out of a vehicle. I didn't pause to reconsider. There was no moment of tortured decision making. The bloodlust was in charge, and I was its slave.

They barely had time to scream. Two men and a woman, I was on them before they could react. The men went down fast and easy. Their blood sprayed, and I greedily consumed all that I could. The rush of their fear was perhaps the best part. Bittersweet and mesmerizing, it quenched a thirst I hadn't known I had.

The woman ran. She made it to the next row of vehicles before I caught her. With wide eyes and an expression of pure horror, she begged for her life. Not a single word penetrated the blood-crazed force commanding me.

Jerking her close, I breathed deeply of her scent. So human and so tantalizing. My fangs slid into her vein with perfect precision. It was leaps and bounds better than using wolf fangs. I could get used to this.

Only when she lay dead at my feet did I come back to myself. Slowly, like surfacing from a deep sleep, I became aware of where I was. I stared at her bloody throat, wide eyes, and mouth frozen open in a silent scream. At first I felt nothing but confusion. Then the fog lifted from my brain, and what I'd just done sunk in.

"Oh my God." I clapped a hand over my bloodstained mouth. This couldn't be real. It just couldn't be.

I backed away from the corpse, bumping into a nearby car, which set off the alarm. The lights began to flash, and the horn honked repeatedly. There was no time to linger. It would draw attention soon enough. I fled, continuing for several blocks. As I ran I asked myself if this was reality because if it was a horrible nightmare I really needed to wake up now.

When I reached Saint Joachim Catholic Cemetery I let myself stop. Amongst the headstones I felt a sense of safety. Everyone there was already dead; I couldn't harm them.

I walked along the paths that wound between the trees. Fallen leaves crunched beneath my feet, the only sound to accompany my descent into madness. It was impossible to wrap my mind around it all, what had happened and what I was now. It just couldn't be real.

But it was. Knowing that I'd been trapped inside myself while the bloodlust commanded my actions was terrifying. I could not be a prisoner inside my own body.

Slumping against a headstone, I lay down in the leaves and waited for sunrise. It was the only way out of this. What I had known of the bloodlust thus far had been nothing, a bare shred of what it really was. I couldn't control a force like this.

I dissolved into hysterical tears. With clawed fingertips I held tight to the headstone, praying that death would be fast. The stone gave beneath the pressure of my grip. With such little effort, it crumbled. Perhaps the claws should have been comforting, a sign of the wolf that dwelled within. In that moment I could only focus on the taste of blood and the memory of how damn good it felt to spill it.

"I can't do this," I whispered to nobody. "I can't do this."

Dawn crept ever closer with each passing minute. It wasn't suicide if you were already dead. Right?

The taste of honey in my mouth was sudden and sickly sweet. The overpowering scent of genuine leather accompanied it. *Kale.* His name drifted up into my thoughts, and I was sure it was a hallucination. Until he spoke.

"Aww, Alexa. How could Arys let this happen to you?" He knelt beside me and gently tried to pry my hands off the headstone. "Come on. We have to get you out of here before sunrise."

"No." I clung harder to the headstone, causing crumbs to flake off beneath my fingers. "Just let me die."

"It's hard at first. Actually, it's always hard. But if anyone can handle it, it's you." Kale touched the side of my face, drawing my gaze to him. There was such sorrow in those beautiful brown and blue eyes.

I shook my head and bit my lip as I fought back another wave of tears. "I can't be like this."

His touch was tender as he stroked a hand down my face. "You already are. Taking the easy way out just isn't your style. If you want to stay here to die, then I'm staying with you."

Alarm sang through me. "No! Just get out of here, Kale. This is my choice."

"Yeah, well, it's mine too."

I groaned and rolled away, turning my back to him. Maybe he would just go away. But as dawn drew closer, Kale stayed.

"Are you really going to make me watch you die?" he asked. "I think you're better than this. In fact, I know you are. The Alexa I know and love would never give in so easily."

I said nothing, choosing to stare at the 1973 etched into the headstone in front of me. Everything in me demanded that I flee the sun before it could roast me. I'd seen a vampire die that way, and it had been ugly. We were quickly running out of time. Doubt crept in. Fear was not far behind.

"All right," he announced. "You're forcing me to do this. As appealing as dying together is, I'd much rather exist another night with you instead. I hope you'll thank me later."

Without giving me a chance to protest, Kale lifted me in his arms. My claws slid across the stone, unable to get a grip. I was confused and afraid, an emotional wreck. Rather than fight him, I settled in to his embrace, resting my head against his shoulder.

As he carried me from the graveyard, back to the land of the living, I clung to him as if he were the only life preserver in an ocean of pain. I felt safe. In Kale I found the solace that my soul so desperately needed.

Epilogue

Arys

The soft scratch of my pencil against the paper usually brought me satisfaction. As I watched the image come to life on the page before me, I remembered why I'd given up this form of self-expression.

A dragon sneered up at me, a mocking gleam in its reptilian eyes. Every feather on its wings was drawn with precision and detail. It was one of my best. I hated it.

Three nights since Alexa rose. Five since I had killed her.

"Come on, Arys. You can't just sit here feeling sorry for yourself. Let's go out." Jenner wandered about my living room, bored and impatient. Though I had wronged him greatly in the past, the fact that he was still here spoke volumes as to his ability to forgive.

"Go without me. Shaz will go with you." I volunteered the wolf pup who sat on my couch frowning at his cell phone. "Oh, and I am not feeling sorry for myself. I'm choosing to lay low and reflect rather than act out by doing something rash."

Shaz and Jenner shared a look. I ignored it, knowing what they were thinking. I also knew that they were wrong.

"If you don't hunt soon you're going to snap," Jenner warned with a knowing look. He had seen me at my worst, something I didn't need to be reminded of.

"What you need to do," Shaz interjected, "is go bring Alexa home. Or I will."

"No you won't." I didn't look up from my sketchpad. "You will leave Alexa right where she is. If you force her to do anything before she's ready, you're just going to drive her further away."

Tossing his phone down on the coffee table, Shaz shot me a dark glare that I didn't have to see in order to feel. It was one of many such looks he'd given me over the last few nights.

"I don't know how you can sit on your ass and do nothing while she's with him. That's not where she belongs." The angry vibe emanating from Shaz was raw and predatory. If he knew how much it tempted me, he might have toned it down a little.

"No, it isn't. But it's where she wants to be right now. This is a difficult time for her, pup. Try to be understanding." It was a conversation we'd had repeatedly since the night Alexa awoke and ran out of The Wicked Kiss as if the devil himself chased her.

That's how she'd looked at me too. Like I was the greatest evil she'd ever laid eyes on. I wanted only to help her, and she saw only the monster who had delighted in every blissful second of her death. And I had.

Hurting Alexa was never something I enjoyed. That wasn't what it was about. It was about the moment with a victim when we are one. When everything they are becomes a part of everything I am. It's the brief but poignant moment where there is no way of knowing where they end and I begin. That is what I always desired when it came to Alexa. The need to consume her so fully, in a way that no other ever could. Being her twin flame should have been enough. But for me, a vampire, it wasn't. I had to have it all.

Then I did. And it was spectacular. She was mine in every way, and it drove her straight into Kale Sinclair's arms. Now she was his.

"Be understanding?" Shaz repeated, aghast. He clenched a fist as if he wanted to take a swing at me. "After everything that happened, you just let him have her? There's no way in hell I'll ever understand that. It's dangerous for the two of you to be apart, especially now."

"The wolf is right," Jenner said. He came over to where I sat on the recliner armchair and scrutinized my drawing. "You said yourself being apart takes its toll on you both. What do you think it's doing to her as a new vampire?"

I frowned and met his gaze, finding it held unspoken judgment. "Don't you have a plane to catch, Jenner? Vegas must be imploding without you."

"Trust me, brother. If I thought it was safe to leave you, I would have been gone by now."

My frown deepened into a glower. "I'm not a child. I don't need you to watch over me."

Jenner crossed his arms and studied me pensively. "A pointless argument. How many nights do you plan to while away sitting in this house starving yourself?"

"I haven't decided yet." Angrily I tore the page from my sketchpad and tore it in two. Then I tore it again, crumpled the pieces, and threw them on the floor.

Nobody had seen nor heard from Shya since the night Alexa died and took with her his only chance at overthrowing Lilah's empire. The demon was down but not out. Only a fool would think otherwise. It was only a matter of time until he finished licking his wounds and resurfaced.

Falon believed that Willow's descent to full demon might be keeping Shya at bay. As angels Willow far outranked Shya, and as demons it would be the same. Now that Willow was no longer in between, Shya had great reason to fear him.

Unfortunately, we might all have reason to fear Willow now. He too had yet to show his face. Though I know he loved Alexa dearly and cherished his guardianship of her, he was not that person anymore. The darkness reigned in him.

"I can't take this anymore," Shaz said. He grabbed his phone and stuffed it into a pocket as he stood up. "I need to see her."

"She'll try to kill you, pup. She doesn't have the self-control it takes to be around blood as potent as yours." Feeling exasperated, I set my things aside and rose. The headstrong wolf was going to force me to knock him out if he kept this up.

"Well, if you won't go, then you leave me no choice. Kale is taking advantage of the situation. He is the last person she should be with right now." There was such vigor in his declaration. He really believed it.

"As much as I wish I could agree with you, I'm afraid I don't." I braced, expecting his fury and accepting it. "Believe me, I'm not any happier about it than you are. But Sinclair loves her. She is safe with him."

Shaz glared at me with enchanting wolf eyes. In recent months he'd shown himself to be as much monster as he was man. Ready to fight as needed with a growing stubborn streak, he was really coming into his own as a werewolf. It was admirable. It was also likely to write him some checks his ass couldn't cash.

"Bullshit," he spat. "They've been killing together. It's going to get the FPA on their asses and then what?"

He threw his hands up as if he couldn't be bothered to waste another word on me and marched for the door. I was faster, blocking his path to the front porch.

"Get the hell out of my way, Arys." Fangs bared, Shaz clenched and unclenched his fist.

"Do you want to hit me, pup? Come on then. Let me have it."

Jenner's laughter followed us as he ambled into the kitchen where we stood staring one another down.

"You two really have to learn how to be a team," he observed. "It's the only way you'll get your girl back."

I could explain my reasoning to Shaz until he was old and grey, but he would refuse to accept it. In his mind Alexa was his mate, and he couldn't understand why he could not simply ride to her rescue.

What I tried to make him see was that she was in no need of rescue. Alexa had been with Sinclair for a few days now. If she wanted to leave, she would have. Her power was far greater than Sinclair's. She was no hostage.

Sinclair offered her something that I could not. Comfort. It was temporary though. Two vampires as mentally unstable as they both were right now would only feed that instability. They could never fix each other. Still, I knew I had to let her see that for herself.

"You think you have it all figured out, don't you?" Shaz demanded, getting much too close. He was in my face, trying to provoke me. "You're abandoning her when she needs you the most."

"She needs space, Shaz," I nearly shouted. With great difficulty I stopped myself from shoving him back a few steps. "She will come to us when she is ready. I can feel her, you know. In my dreams, I enter her thoughts, and I know that she is not ready to face either of us. Have some patience and back the fuck off."

With a growl, the stubborn wolf hauled off and punched me. It was a nice hit, square on the side of my jaw. It snapped my head to the side, and I swore.

Rubbing my jaw, I smiled. "Feel better?"

He scowled, seemingly disappointed at my lack of retaliation. "If anything happens to her because you sat back and allowed it, I will fucking kill you."

Brave words from a ballsy werewolf. He meant every one. I knew that.

I held my hands up in surrender. Engaging with him in a brawl would feel great. It would allow us to work out our pent up frustrations. But it ultimately wouldn't do us a damn bit of good.

Refusing to acknowledge his threat, I stepped aside so he could leave. "Go with Jenner to The Wicked Kiss. While he does his business there, see if you can find out anything new on Willow. Give Jez a call while you're at it. Find out if Alexa has been in touch with her."

"I still think you should come with us," Jenner insisted. "I know you need it. Just give in already and get it all out of your system."

"Tomorrow perhaps."

Shaz slammed out of the house spewing obscenities. I grinned and waved as he descended the front step.

Jenner turned to follow him, pausing at the door. "Arys, don't torture yourself. It was meant to happen. You had to do it. You've known that for a long time."

"Yes," I said with a nod. "But I didn't know that she would hate me for it."

"She doesn't hate you. She just needs time to adjust."

"Right. Try to keep the pup out of trouble, will you? He's got a short fuse these days."

I watched them go, pulling away with a squeal of tires. Shaz had every right to feel the way he did. It had to be confusing and hard for him to process as well.

Alexa could run, but she could never escape what we are. Being apart would soon start to weigh on us both. It just wasn't meant to be that way. Together we were one. Apart we were fragments of a whole, only a piece of what we should be.

Though I didn't say so to Shaz, it killed me to think of her with Sinclair. Her weakness for that vampire made me burn with rage. If I didn't love her so damn much, I would have killed him months ago.

Returning to the living room, I sat back down and grabbed the sketchpad. I flipped to a fresh page and began to draw. It was the only way I could stay calm.

Alexa would return to me. It simply wasn't possible for us to stay apart. The power that connected us would always draw us back to each other. I knew this, and she knew it too. She just had to stop fighting it.

Sinclair could have her for now. Because I would have her forever.

Thank you so much to everyone who has supported and enjoyed the series. You all make my job a joy and I'm grateful to be able to do this.

Check out TrinaMLee.com for information and excerpts from Smashed, Alexa O'Brien Huntress Book 8.5, an Arys Knight novella.

About the Author

Trina M. Lee was born in Edmonton, Alberta Canada. Writing fiction since childhood, a fascination with the supernatural developed in her early teen years and an immersion in paranormal fiction began. Trina enjoys hearing from readers and has an active social media presence.

Website: TrinaMLee.com
Facebook: Facebook.com/AuthorTrinaMLee
Twitter: Twitter.com/TrinaMLee

Printed in Great Britain
by Amazon